AGE OF VAMPIRES

# ETERNAL
# REIGN

## CAROLINE PECKHAM
## SUSANNE VALENTI

REALM G

THE
BLOOD BANK

REALM F

THE WASTES

REALM E

REALM H

REA

United States

Realm G

The Blood Bar

ALM A

NEW YORK
(BELVEDERE CASTLE)

REALM B

REALM C

New York

Belvedere Castle

Eternal Reign
Age of Vampires #1
Copyright © 2019 Caroline Peckham & Susanne Valenti

Interior Formatting & Design by Wild Elegance Formatting

Eternal Reign/Caroline Peckham & Susanne Valenti – Hardback ed.
ISBN-13 - 978-1-914425-89-9

*This book is dedicated to all those who believe their dreams will never come true. To reach the top of the mountain, you must start at the bottom, placing one foot in front of the other. Every journey is different and some turn back when it gets too steep, but the key is to keep shuffling on, stumbling, striding, leaping, limping. Whatever it takes to keep moving an inch forward on your path, do that. Then do it again.*

*This series was where mine and Susanne's journey together began. Welcome to the bottom of our mountain...*

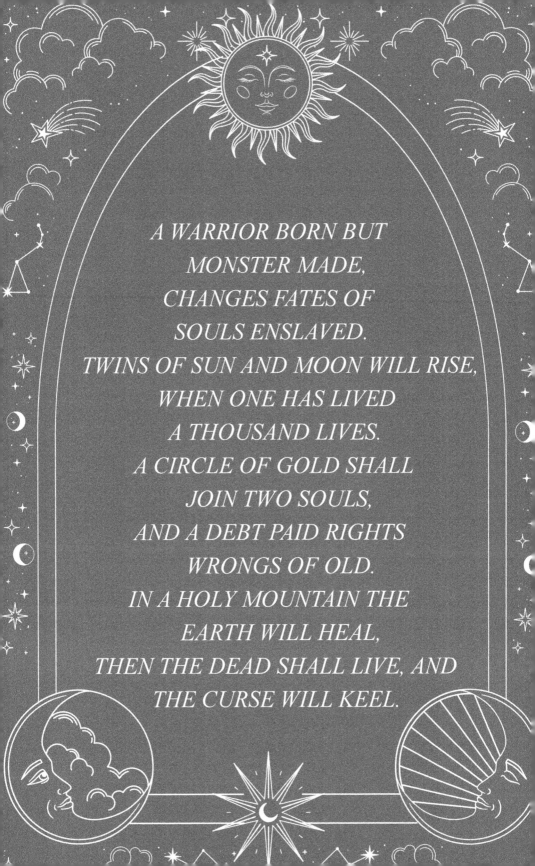

*A WARRIOR BORN BUT
MONSTER MADE,
CHANGES FATES OF
SOULS ENSLAVED.
TWINS OF SUN AND MOON WILL RISE,
WHEN ONE HAS LIVED
A THOUSAND LIVES.
A CIRCLE OF GOLD SHALL
JOIN TWO SOULS,
AND A DEBT PAID RIGHTS
WRONGS OF OLD.
IN A HOLY MOUNTAIN THE
EARTH WILL HEAL,
THEN THE DEAD SHALL LIVE, AND
THE CURSE WILL KEEL.*

# CALLIE

## CHAPTER ONE

The primal need to survive made even the weakest of mice fight with all the fury of a god. When your back was against the wall, you found out what your soul was made of, and I'd learned long ago that mine had been forged in fire and ferocity.

An icy drip splashed onto the back of my neck and raced down my spine, making goosebumps rush across my body. I fought the urge to shudder with all my might, knowing the consequences if I fucked this up. Any movement could give me away, and I couldn't risk getting caught. Not if I wanted my family to survive the winter.

Everything depended on this. On me.

Rain fell steadily, pinging off the broken metal rooftop above my hiding place in the derelict building, the scent of rot sweeping around me in the air. Freezing raindrops made their way through holes in the rusted roof, and I tried my best to ignore them, but a second drip rolled beneath my collar, stealing what little warmth my body held onto. I didn't adjust my posture though, there was too much riding on this.

The derelict building was half destroyed below me, little more than the steel beams left standing, a few crumbling bricks clinging to them for dear life. The wooden floors had taken life without walls the hardest, rotting so badly that holes pockmarked them, the remains soft and sagging. The wet weather which we enjoyed so frequently in what had once been Washington state only aided in the deterioration of what remained.

I was uncomfortable as shit, but I'd been waiting in the rafters for a reason, and I wasn't about to give my location away because of the cold. There were far worse things I'd faced in this life, and the bite of winter was something I'd learned to endure a long time ago.

I squinted down at the courtyard beyond the crumbling building I'd chosen for my hiding place, taking in the cracked flagstones four floors below me. The remains of a decorative fountain were decaying in the centre of the open space, but everything was so wet due to the downpour that it hardly stood out.

It was hard to picture anybody ever having lived in this place when it was whole, the streets not full of cracks, the buildings not full of holes. Only the rodents lived here now, and not even many of them dared linger too close to what had taken residence nearby.

It was a wasteland directly on the border of what remained in its wake. The only view I'd ever seen beyond my tiny piece of the world and everything about it was void of life, void of humanity, void of whatever it was I yearned for when I lay awake in the dead of night.

Everything in my world was grey, colourless. Except for blood. Somehow, the deep red colour of that always stood out so damn starkly in this place. Maybe because of the value it held, which amounted to my value too. Yeah, blood was the only thing that gave my existence meaning. At least, that was how *they* saw it. I was a commodity, just like my family were, and every other unfortunate human in the Blood Realms.

I scanned the surrounding area, crumbling buildings spreading out in all directions, the only bright thing in the landscape was the gleaming silver fence which blocked our exit from the Realm. It stood beyond the far side of the courtyard below me, and it ringed our entire world, penning us in and marking the line which we could never cross. The gleaming silver was sharp with razor wire and charged with enough electricity to barbeque any unwitting idiot fool enough to venture close to it. It caught in the meagre light, taunting me with its simplicity, with the fact that I could see right through it to the buildings beyond while never allowing me to pass through to them. Beyond it, the ruins continued, but there were more than a few buildings which seemed mostly intact, their windows keeping out the rain, their doors closed against the world.

I'd braided my blonde hair tightly to keep it out of my eyes, but I missed the warmth of it around my ears as the cold wind blew mercilessly through my hiding place. My hair was a dead giveaway, the golden hue of it eye-catching, and that was the last thing I wanted to be right now as I waited like a cat outside a mousehole, ready to pounce.

At last, Thomas stepped into the courtyard and moved towards the fountain, his movements jittery and anxious. He was a big fucker, mean too, though about as bright as a box of rocks. His dark hair hung limp around his neck, plastered to his skull by the rain, the patchy beard which covered his jaw peeking out from the top of the scarf he'd wrapped around his face. I wasn't sure why he'd bothered – if he was caught out here, he wouldn't escape. There was no chance of that, so trying to hide his identity seemed utterly pointless to me.

Thomas paused, pulling his collar higher, and taking a moment to brush the raindrops from his muddy brown hair while he scowled at his surroundings, checking for followers, or any sign of something out of place.

Satisfaction coiled through me like a living thing as he failed to spot me, and I allowed myself a triumphant smirk. He might have been dumb as shit when it came to most things, but Thomas did have one skill; he could track and hunt like a beast. I should know, I'd been mimicking him for a long time after all, learning what I needed, then demanding more of myself, surpassing him in that skill and many others besides. My family depended on my ability to do so, and I refused to fail.

I drew in a long breath, willing my heart to stop racing, for calm to fall over me and for my mind to remain sharp. If I was right about this, then everything might be about to change for our family.

Anything Thomas could do, I could do better.

The rain bounced off his shoulders as he hesitated there by the fountain, glancing about nervously as it slicked his hair to his forehead and obscured his pale grey eyes. I understood his need for secrecy. If anyone figured out what he was doing, they'd either follow him like I planned to, or worse; they'd turn him over to the creatures who were the very reason for our continued existence.

The vampires.

Monsters who fed from the lifeforce in our veins, bottled and corked for their pleasure. My upper lip curled back as my mind turned to them, the beasts who owned my body and soul, who kept us here in this pig pen. The only home I'd ever known and would ever know.

Most people in this place liked to keep their heads down, forget what we were, that the vampires treated us worse than cattle, let us remain hungry, cold, living a half-life that never sated any of our core needs. But my father hadn't let my sister and I forget that. He'd taught us the truth, and in doing so, he'd instilled a burning fire of hatred in us for the vampires, a fire that would never go out.

*They're demons given flesh.*

My dad's words made my jaw tighten as those acidic flames of hatred licked their way along the inside of my bones, the injustice of our reality eating at me as it always did, but now wasn't the time for anger at the lot I'd been handed. Now was a time for survival.

Another drip slid down my spine, and its freezing touch slipped into my veins. I longed for the end of winter already and it had barely even begun. With food scarcer than ever, it was shaping up to be a pretty horrendous season. Unless I could pull this off.

Finally trusting in the fact that he was alone, Thomas tentatively moved across the courtyard, his feet keeping to the crumbling flagstones, not so much as brushing against the weeds sprouting between the cracks. He was taking no chances, leaving no trail. This was as far as I'd been able to track him until now. I knew he came to this courtyard regularly, but for the life of me I had no idea where he went from here.

My twin sister's warning sounded in the back of my head. *"He could be getting it from a vampire. For all we know, he gets it by selling the rest of us out."* But my gut told me that wasn't it. A worm he might be, but I didn't peg Thomas for a rat. No. Somehow, he was getting in and out of the Realm. Undetected. Until now anyway.

I smiled to myself as he stepped over the partially shattered wall of the fountain and waded through the deeper water beyond it. Ripples spread out around him as he went, though he kept each movement slow as if he feared causing a single splash. A splash that might be caught by the ear of a monster.

He glanced over his shoulder one last time before climbing the higher wall on the far side of the fountain and dropping down beyond it. I could just make out the top of his head as he stooped low, and a dull sound reached my ears like something heavy being dragged over concrete.

My pulse ticked a little faster as I waited, craning my neck a little to try and catch sight of him again.

The noise stopped and Thomas stood upright again, surveying the area. I held steady in my concealed position in the rafters despite the cramp growing in my muscles. The shadows held me tightly in their fists. I knew he couldn't see me, but my heart leapt as his gaze swept across my hiding place.

The air stalled in my lungs, my heart thundering, fingers curling painfully tight around the edge of the metal strut I leaned against, but he didn't even give my location a second glance, turning back to look at whatever was by his feet, then dropping out of sight once more.

I cursed low and soft as I leaned forward an inch, squinting to try and see where he'd gone while the wind drove the pounding rain into my face. The noise it was making was like a roar of its own, good for a girl who wanted to hide her footfalls, not so good if something else happened to be stalking the dim morning light out here too.

I waited for a count of sixty, but it was no use. Thomas didn't reappear, and I had the sinking feeling he wasn't going to.

Indecision froze me in place. If this was another attempt to flush out anyone following him, then moving now would give me away. If he caught me spying on him, he'd never make the mistake of letting me do it again. This was my only shot. But if I didn't move soon then I was going to lose him. Heads or tails. Doomed or fucked. Not great odds, but then again, when were the odds ever great for us?

"Fuck it," I muttered as I gripped the edge of the thick beam I was perched on and swung myself out of my hiding place.

I hung suspended from the steel for a few seconds and used my toes to feel for the edge of the half collapsed wall beneath me. My gut lurched with fear as I struggled to find it, and my arms began to tremble with the effort of holding on to the slick metal. If I died here, falling from some shitty steel beam on the edge of nowhere, then I would never forgive myself for being such a fucking idiot. I'd spend the afterlife cursing my own name until the end of time, roaring at the wind for my stupidity and letting it blow my own anger right back in my face.

My right foot connected with the crumbling masonry, my pulse spiking, and I swung myself towards it until both of my boots found it. I tried to ignore the scattered bits of brick and mortar which tumbled to the ground far below, dislodged by my boots. If the wall had stood here this long, then I had to hope the weight of one skinny girl wouldn't be enough to topple it.

Once I had my balance, I released my hold on the beam and dropped into a crouch atop the wall, relief surging through me. That was the hard part.

A flash of movement caught my eye, and I looked up, a high-pitched squeak warning me half a second before a black bat almost collided with my face, its leathery wings flapping so close to my skin that I felt one of them brush against my cheek.

I managed to contain my shriek of surprise as I lurched backwards, nearly losing my balance. My stomach swooped and my right arm cartwheeled wildly before I lurched to the side and grasped the brickwork again, the pads of my fingers grazing against it painfully as I clung on for dear life.

The little creature spun away from me, zipping across the sky in a blur of motion as I tried to calm my nerves, adrenaline rioting in my veins. The sun was rising out there beyond the thick rain clouds, dawn under way, my time limited.

I'd left to come here as early as I dared, the sky only a shade lighter than the full darkness of night. It had been a risk to walk the streets so close to the time the vampires loved best, but I'd been careful, and I'd guessed that with the sun rising soon, their kind would be gone anyway. I'd been right in that assumption at least.

I glanced down at the courtyard I'd nearly been plastered all over and released a shaky breath.

*Nice work, Callie; why not throw yourself to your death because a creature the size of your palm made you jump?*

I forced my mind away from mentally berating myself and looked back towards the crumbling building I needed to get out of instead.

I scrambled down the inside of the wall where half of the second floor was still intact, landing on the floorboards with a soft thump that made fear rise up in the back of my throat.

The wooden floor was springy beneath my feet. Not exactly reassuring, especially when accompanied by the scent of decay which lingered everywhere.

Ignoring my concerns over the less-than-trustworthy floor and focusing on my goal, I jogged towards the stairwell, keeping my footfalls as quiet as I could manage and hoping to hell I could still catch up with Thomas.

Four of the wooden stairs hung suspended in the air, and the rest lay in a shattered heap below. The grimy remains of a carpet coated what was left of the first floor, and two decades of rain blowing in hadn't done it any favours.

The hole which used to be a staircase extended all the way to the ground, and the rope I'd used to scale the building hours ago still hung in place from the edge of it. I wrenched my makeshift grappling hook out of the soft floorboards and searched for something else to secure my rope.

There wasn't really any choice apart from the thick banister which marked the top of the decayed staircase, so I kicked it, trying to gauge its stability. It shifted slightly, which was less than ideal. It was that or lose my hook though, and the rusty piece of metal was practically priceless to me. Certainly irreplaceable.

I threw the hook into the small bag I wore on my back and tied the rope around the banister, placing my life in that moldy wood's hands and hoping for the best.

*Here goes nothing.*

I dropped over the edge and started shimmying down as quickly as I could.

A shudder trembled through the rope and a heavy creaking sounded above me that might as well have been the baying of hellhounds come to collect my soul.

"Shit," I hissed. My heartbeat thundered in my ears as the groaning intensified, warning me that the banister was seconds from giving out and sending me straight to hell.

My palms went slick as panic seized me in its grasp. I gave up on shimmying and let myself slide, my stomach staying somewhere far above me as I descended at speed. The rope burned my palms and pain lanced through them, making me spit a curse as I refused to let go.

I made it past the second floor and was level with the first before the sound of splintering wood rumbled above me and the rope went slack.

A scream built in my chest as I fell through the air, only remaining trapped there through years of instinct, knowing that screams only ever summoned monsters.

I slammed into the floor hard on my back, the air violently whooshing from my lungs and pain exploding through my body.

I blinked through the agony and found the remains of the banister hurtling towards me, the fucking thing insisting I die today. But I was not going out of this world crushed by a mouldy heap of wood.

I lurched aside, throwing my arms over my head before the lump of oak could flatten me, and the floor vibrated as it crashed down next to me instead of caving in my skull.

I peeked out from beneath my arms at the devastation I'd created, a heavy breath fluttering past my lips. There was no chance this would go unnoticed. The fucking bloodsuckers knew everything. *Nearly* everything anyway.

But there were no rules about staying out of the ruins, even this close to the edge of the Realm. There weren't even any rules about not destroying things out here. Who'd care anyway? So a useless banister fell down in a useless building. It didn't matter. What did matter was them thinking I was up to something out here, something they might just drain me dry for.

They didn't tolerate rebels; anyone who so much as raised their head above the parapet risked it being cut off. People disappeared from their beds all the time. It was why my dad rarely slept, and when he did, he'd place his back to the door of the room I shared with my sister and stay there on guard, ready to fight if one of the vampires came to take us. But despite the reassurance that had given me as a kid, I knew better now. My dad may have been a powerful, savage man when he wanted to be, but he was also just a man. And in this world, men sat firmly below vampires on the food chain. Not even ten of us could take on one of them, and in all my years in this Realm, I'd never seen a single human place a mark on a bloodsucker, let alone defeat one in a fight.

I pushed myself to my feet, ignoring the pain in my back and shoulders. I was pretty sure I'd have some impressive bruises by tomorrow, but nothing was broken. More importantly, nothing was bleeding. I'd have to be careful to cover the marks up around Dad to save him from losing his shit. Although, if this panned out, then I was sure he'd agree it was worth the risk. Maybe.

I just had to hope Thomas hadn't heard me. Or gotten too far away. I *had* to locate him again.

I ran out of the half-destroyed building into the rain, wishing my coat had a hood as the water washed over me. It had a hole in the right pocket and a fraying hem along the back of the blood-red material. Despite that, it was considered a pretty good coat by most people's standards, and I'd had to fight off more than one asshole who had thought to take it from me over the years.

But I saw what the vampires wore. Winter coats should be thick and warm and have hoods. The worst thing about it was that *they* didn't need to stay warm. They were as cold-blooded as snakes, but they wouldn't let us have proper clothes like theirs, and they damn well knew we could feel every icy kiss of the season.

Every winter, people froze to death. Some even volunteered for the blood bank rather than face the slow inevitability of that fate. Poor assholes. I'd rather die a thousand deaths than ever go there.

I made myself pause and look back a couple of times, hunting the shadows for anyone or anything that might be stalking my footsteps, but no sound came, no chill of being watched found me. I just had to hope that my instincts were as sharp as I believed.

I splashed across the courtyard and clambered into the fountain just as Thomas had. The freezing water washed straight over the tops of my boots, soaking my feet, and making me wince. *Perfect.*

Climbing over the back wall took two attempts, seeing as it was level with my chin and slick with rainwater, but I was hardly going to let a wall stop me now. I cursed it, heaved myself up the rough brickwork and swung my leg over the top before dropping down beyond it.

On the far side, I hit the fucking jackpot. Thomas had lifted a drain cover revealing a dark hole which led...well, wherever he had gone. A wild thought entered my mind as I considered whether this old drain might actually lead out of the Realm, and a thrill danced under my skin.

It was quickly replaced by something closer to terror as I imagined what might happen if the vampires caught me leaving the Realm. It wasn't worth me trying to run; the vampires could hunt us out there, and there was no human alive on this earth who could outrun them with their heightened strength and senses.

But there could be supplies in the old buildings that might keep me, my dad, and my twin alive through another winter. The sorts of things I'd noticed Thomas having more and more of recently. Clothing...*food*. My stomach growled like a beast at the mere thought of it.

I glanced about nervously. There was no sign of anyone amongst the ruins nearby, and all was still apart from the ever-falling rain. If the vampires were close, they'd be upon me already. Unless they were stalking me out there like lions lurking in the long grass, waiting for their moment to strike.

*No time for chicken-shit thoughts.*

I bit my lip and dropped into the drain, darkness swallowing me up before I landed in a crouch at the base of a rusty ladder. I squinted as my eyes adjusted to the gloom, my heart rate ratcheting up another notch as I took in the tunnel unfolding before me.

All of the old drains had been caved in along the edges of the Realm to stop this exact thing from happening when the fences went up. We'd been told in no uncertain terms that what I was looking at was impossible and yet, I could see light up ahead.

Cautiously, I started moving towards it. There were no sounds in the passage, so I guessed that meant Thomas was gone. It didn't matter anyway. If this got me out, then I could do what I needed and get back without him ever knowing I'd learned his secret. Unless he was as observant as me.

I'd noticed him having more to trade recently even though he'd taken care to spread himself between many vendors. I'd also noticed the healthy flush his family had on their cheeks and the subtle upgrade in their clothing. He was being smart about it. But there wasn't much that got past me. Especially when I was pretty sure that another harsh winter could kill my family. There was no way I would let that happen.

Sure enough, as I closed in on the light, I came across the caved-in part of the tunnel, the scent of rot and old sewage freshened by a breeze that rolled in from above.

Some of the rubble had been moved, lumps of rocks and masonry scattered along the walkway, making me step over them as I approached.

A breath of laughter, relief, and outright terror passed through my lips as I took in the hole which had been cleared at the top of the pile of shattered rocks, just big enough to allow a large man to crawl through. Which meant it was more than big enough for me.

I climbed up to the hole and hesitated. If I went beyond this point, I was officially breaking the law. Leaving the Realm could land me in the blood bank. If I was caught and they sent me there, it would tear my family apart. Dad and Montana were all that I cared about in this world, and the idea of being taken from them froze my limbs in place. Not to mention the horror I felt over ending up in the blood bank. I didn't know exactly what went on within those walls, but no one ever returned from there, and the rumours that swept through the Realm about ceiling hooks and feeding tubes were enough to keep me awake at night.

But if I didn't do this, then I wasn't sure we would make it through the harsh season. I'd been skipping breakfast for weeks, allowing the two of them to have a little extra without them realising it. I left the apartment first in the mornings, and I was gone before they woke. All

I had to do was leave a bowl drying on the rack to make it look like I'd eaten my portion of the oatmeal before I left. And even with that sacrifice, I could tell they weren't getting enough.

The rations we were given daily were slowly decreasing. Bit by bit we were receiving less food as the weeks wore on. My ribs already showed too clearly through my skin, and my hips jutted out in a way that spoke of the meals I'd missed. We needed more food. It was life or death, and if I had to risk the blood bank to make sure we survived, then so be it.

I took a steadying breath and crawled through the hole.

*No turning back now.* I'd just crossed a line I couldn't return from. I'd broken the law and left the Realm. I simply had to pray it would be worth it.

On the other side of the rubble, I found the rest of the drain awaiting me, the scent of old sewage stronger here, a dark puddle festering below the walkway to my right.

I lifted my head and spotted the source of the light above me, dim sunlight filtering down through another open manhole. A rusted ladder led the way up and I scrambled up onto it, testing my weight on the rungs before scaling it quickly, rust flaking off against my palms, the iron tang to the air making me think of blood. Always blood. Something that should matter so little and yet, somehow, mattered more than all else.

When I made it to the top, I peeked above the rim of the open manhole cover and stilled. There wasn't much that stood out about this place, ruined streets and old, weathered buildings stretching out around, but maybe the air tasted a little different. Or maybe I'd just been a prisoner so long, I was imagining that the air was slightly sweeter here beyond the electric fences that bordered the Realm. Either way, I took in a deep lungful of it and let myself indulge in the thrill of doing this, a tiny rebellion of my own creation against the vile beasts who owned me.

The street was much like the one I'd been standing on minutes ago, but it was alien in ways too. I knew every corner of the Realm, every street, alleyway, building, and ruin, memorized down to the last detail, but this place was new. I'd never been this far from home.

My whole life had been conducted and contained within that fence. The remnants of a long-dead town turned into a farm for my kind. That was it, always. Twenty-one years lived within clear boundaries. *Until now*.

This was an unexplored territory that made me itch to know more of it. I hadn't realised how much I'd craved this, but there was a deep need awakening in me now that grew so rapidly it almost hurt. I wanted to venture as far as I could beyond the Realm and see all the things I never thought I'd see. I wanted to look at the vast expanse of the ocean Dad had told us about and dip my toes in the frothy waves as they hit the land. I wanted to know what a forest truly was, and a desert, a lake, anything, everything, every last piece of it.

I tiptoed back towards the Realm, peeking out from behind one of the buildings and eyeing the fence for a long moment, the silver links so familiar and yet entirely new from this angle. I'd never thought I'd stand on this side of them. Never dreamed this reality might come to pass. Freedom called my name, urging me to run, run and never look back, despite how hopeless I knew that would be. It was so near, so tantalisingly close, and yet the truth of it was clear. If I ran, they'd chase, and despite how much I wished it wasn't so, I knew who would come out victorious in that hunt, my future painted in bloody clarity beneath the fangs of a bloodsucker.

No, I couldn't run. At least not now. But I sure as shit could explore for a while.

A thrill of anticipation burst through me, and I grinned as I turned from the fence and started down the street, anticipation gripping my heart.

There was no sign of Thomas in the surrounding streets, and I hoped it stayed that way. I knew his secret, but I'd prefer it if I could keep that information to myself. No need for him to know I knew. I'd rather he wasn't able to rat me out to the vampires if they got suspicious. If they caught him, they'd make him talk, and there was no way he'd die to protect my ass.

The closest apartment blocks had been ripped apart by whatever bomb had destroyed the ruins I'd been hiding in on the other side of the fence, so I skipped them, searching for somewhere more likely to house supplies. Nothing good would have survived in a building missing walls.

I jogged the length of the block and swung east, finding an intact apartment block at last. It was just as grey as everything else but the addition of doors and windows, and the promise of some shelter from the relentless rain, made it look utterly inviting.

I made a path for the entrance, and the rotating door groaned in un-oiled protest as I forced it to allow my entry, making my pulse race once more as I looked back to the street, fearing eyes on my skin but thankfully finding none.

I gazed around at the old stores, the glass windows holding faded signs meant for people who'd once been able to walk through this place, free, with money in their pockets, ready to buy whatever they could afford.

Dad had told us so many stories about the way it had been, and as unbelievable as it had all sounded, I could feel the truth of those words here. For a second, it felt like I was one of those people from the past, getting a taste of the freedom which they'd taken for granted so foolishly as excitement bubbled through my veins. I didn't know where to begin, but any doubts I'd had over this plan were falling to ruin quickly.

A corridor led away from me to my left, so I made a snap decision and took it, tiptoeing to the first door I came to which was ajar. I pushed it wide, holding my breath as the door's movement sent dust swirling ahead of me. The apartment looked untouched, and I doubted anyone had entered it since *before.*

Life without vampires had always sounded like a fairy tale to me. Montana and I had the bad luck to have been born the year they took over, so anything pre-*them* was nothing I would ever know. Yet here it was, the past lingering right outside the fences which held us, whispering the truth of all we'd lost.

Apparently, the whole human world had been at war, blasting each other with giant bombs that flattened entire cities, but once our population had dwindled just enough, the vampires had crept out of hiding and slaughtered the last of our armies, while the civilian masses were captured and placed in the Realms.

My dad hadn't been a soldier, but he'd told me the stories of how he'd fought for survival alongside my pregnant mother, spending weeks moving from one town to the next, trying to find refuge from the plague of vampires spreading across the land. But eventually, their luck had run out and they'd ended up here, never to taste free air again.

I headed further into the apartment and found a bedroom where the closet whispered sweet promises to me. When I slid the door wide, my mouth fell the fuck open. I felt like a dumbstruck bitch, but there it was. I stood there with my lips parted as I stared at the kinds of clothes I'd only ever dreamed about. Thick winter coats with actual, motherfucking *hoods.* I reached out hungrily, tearing a white coat from the hanger and swapping mine for it as quickly as I could manage.

It was better than I ever could have imagined, like being wrapped in a cloud which caressed every part of me. I pulled the furry hood over my head and hugged it close to my face, making a noise that was damn near sexual.

My eyes fell on a floor-length mirror and my puffy coat dream popped before it had even really begun. There was no way I could bring this back. No way I could ever explain it. It was too noticeable, the quality too perfect, and even as I thought about muddying it up and trying to make it look more worn, I knew it was no good.

My heart sank like a stone, drifting to the pit of my belly and shrivelling away as it accepted its fate. *Fuck my life.*

I stayed wrapped in the warmth of the coat for five more seconds before slipping it back off. I stared longingly at the perfect item as I carefully hung it back where it came from and retrieved my threadbare coat from the floor with a pout.

It was impossible to ignore the chill from the damp material as disappointment curled in my gut. But I couldn't be foolish now that I'd found this trove; it was no good bringing anything back to the Realm that would put a target on our heads. Subtlety was key.

I sighed as I hunted through the rest of the clothes hanging in the closet and at the back, I found something I could take. Sets of thick, thermal underwear were folded neatly on a slim shelf, so I grabbed two women's sets for me and my sister, and a men's set for Dad. New socks followed swiftly after.

I carefully folded them into my pack and turned my back on the coats which could have made such a difference to us. My gaze landed on the thick duvet covering the bed and I had to force myself not to cry. All of this was here, so close and yet completely out of reach. Everything the human population of our Realm could ever have wanted. What difference did it make to the vampires to keep this from us? They clearly didn't want it and leaving it to rot here, just a stone's throw from the boundary of our Realm, was beyond cruel.

I wondered if they laughed at us as we shivered, if finding people frozen to death in their beds was amusing to them. Hatred coursed through me more readily than usual as I thought on it. *What I'd give to watch one of them shiver and starve.*

My fingernails dug into my palms almost hard enough to draw blood and I hissed in pain as I made myself flex my fingers and release the rising tension in my body. I harboured so much rage in my heart over our lot in life that sometimes I ran out to the edges of the Realm and screamed until my throat ripped raw. The hatred I felt for the creatures who owned us was a poison which stained my soul, my hunger for vengeance and justice a wicked thing that writhed beneath my skin, left to fester there with no hope of an outlet for it.

I forced a heavy breath from my lungs, reminding myself that this was a win, even if I couldn't claim all I wished to from this treasure trove. There was no point in worrying about the things I couldn't take. I needed to focus on those I *could*.

A low scraping sound had me falling utterly still, the hairs along the back of my neck rising as I spun towards the door, the knife I wasn't supposed to carry a heavy weight in my pocket. I would be punished if I was caught with a weapon, but I couldn't stomach the thought of not carrying one. If they ever came for me, I wanted a way to strike at them, a chance, or maybe just a way to end my life on my own terms. Whichever it was, the blade seemed to call to me in that moment, something telling me that I wasn't as alone here as I thought.

The sound didn't repeat, the silence growing so thick that I began to question whether or not I'd imagined it entirely.

I was wasting time. The light beyond the dirty windows was growing, and I couldn't afford to stay out here much longer.

I shook off the fear that had paralysed me and hurried into the small kitchen, opening cupboards one after another, searching for the thing we needed more than any other. I'd already been here longer than I should have, and I needed to get back.

A soft groan of longing escaped me as I found several tins of food, my stomach growling desperately in recognition of the meal I longed for. I rammed the tins into my pack, not wasting time trying to decipher the scribbles on the labels which no doubt told me what was inside them. The pictures gave me a good idea and though I wouldn't have said I *couldn't* read, I couldn't exactly claim to be able to either.

It wasn't like I'd ever needed to anyway. Dad had tried to teach us, but I'd never had the patience for it like Montana had. Besides, I didn't see how reading would ever be of much use to me in this life.

The last cupboard I checked held stacks of plates and bowls, but peeking out from behind them, I spied a brown wrapper.

I pulled out the slab of plastic-wrapped food and frowned at it. I had no idea what I was looking at, but the kids pictured on the wrapper were smiling while eating it. Curiosity got the better of me and I ripped the corner of the packet open. After foregoing my breakfast rations and suffering through the increasingly small lunch and dinner supplies, my stomach was pathetically empty, and it rumbled in needy anticipation as I licked my lips.

The food inside was brown, and I wrinkled my nose, figuring it had gone bad, but a delicious smell reached me before I could toss it aside. I lifted it closer to my nose and sniffed again. It smelled *good*. Really fucking good.

I tentatively broke off a square and placed it into my mouth.

The most delicious thing I'd ever tasted started to melt on my tongue, and I let out a groan of pure pleasure. I'd never had anything like it before and I wasn't sure if I'd ever be able to get enough. Sugar burst across my tastebuds, the energy I so desperately craved waking up at the call of it and I closed my eyes to savour the taste as it slowly dissolved on my tongue, sparks of decedent sweetness igniting through my mouth. I *had* to show this to Montana.

Carefully folding the wrapper back down, I tucked the delicious food into my now bulging bag before closing it and throwing it over my shoulder. That was it. I couldn't take any more and get it back without drawing attention. It was more than we'd had in a long time. We'd have a decent meal tonight and something to keep us warm while we slept. That was more than I'd hoped for when I'd decided to follow Thomas.

I smiled at that thought as I headed for the exit. Things were going to be so much better now that I held this secret.

I slipped back through the door and instantly stilled, a chill tumbling through my limbs as I spotted a figure through the filthy windows which looked back out to the street.

Thomas. It had to be Thomas. Those words tumbled through my skull over and over again as the rain poured down onto the too small figure, whoever it was at least a foot shorter than the asshole I'd followed here. I remained entirely still as I stared at them through the filthy glass, hoping by some miracle they hadn't seen me even as the thing I was staring at turned oh so fucking slowly my way.

It had to be him. Had to be.

But it wasn't.

My hand trembled as I remained frozen in place, the figure lifting its head, the dim light catching on hollow cheeks and sharp teeth as she turned her gaze from the street and slowly moved her focus to the building I was currently hiding in.

I didn't dare move, didn't dare so much as breathe as I took in the ragged clothes, the haunted, feral look in her eyes and remembered the words I'd once overheard from some of the vampires who guarded our Realm.

*"There are rotters on the western border. We'll have to send a hunt out to deal with them."*

*One of them caught my curious gaze at the words and laughed, grabbing the front of my shirt and yanking me close so that he could speak in my ear, the frosty touch of his lips brushing against my skin and making me shudder.*

*"You think we're bad, little blood bag? You should meet the ones of us who are really hungry – out there beyond that shiny fence which keeps you all so safe and sound, the rotters hunt the shadows, desperate for a taste of a pretty little thing like you. You think feeling the sting of my fangs would be bad? They'd rip the skin from your bones and listen to you scream while they feasted until there was nothing but a husk left in place of all you'd ever been."*

I blinked the memory aside, the story I'd long ago dismissed as more of their lies designed to keep us compliant, laughing at me from the past.

It had been no lie. And now the truth had come to feast on me just like he'd promised.

The rotter's feral gaze met mine with a clang that echoed through every fibre of my being and as it shrieked in utter delight and broke into a run, I found myself doing the one thing I had long ago learned never to do in front of a bloodsucker.

I screamed.

# MONTANA

## CHAPTER TWO

*Even the blackest of nights hold a glimmer of starlight.*

My father always said that to us just before bed, trying to chase out the demons that often followed us into sleep. But something about those words kept catching in my mind while I waited in line to collect our daily rations. Maybe it was just the change in the air, fall giving way to the cruel bite of winter and promising even harder times to come. Would we find the starlight this time…or would the darkness devour us whole?

I pulled my collar closer to my neck as the cold fought to get in. It was faux fur. Well, sort of. The material was itchy, and half of the mottled fluff had fallen out over the years, but it helped to keep the icy rain at bay.

My gaze kept snagging on anyone with blonde hair who passed by, though none was as bright gold as my sister's. I knew she'd gone after Thomas even though she'd sworn she wouldn't, and anxiety raked against my chest as the time ticked by. She would have to come this way to get home, so there was no chance I'd miss her, but shouldn't she have been back by now?

My mind slid into a dark recess where I saw my sister strung up in the blood bank, her lifeforce siphoned away to be savoured by the vampires who ruled us. If she was caught breaking any rules, they would show her no mercy, and there was no fate more terrifying to me than losing her or my dad. We were a team, bound by love and the need to survive for each other, even more so than for ourselves. Our little family was already shadowed by the loss of Mom, and her death had woven threads of pain through all of us, crystalising us as one.

Without Callie, Dad and I would shatter. *So get your ass back here or I'll come get it myself.*

The mud was deep beneath my feet where people had been queuing all morning, the heavy sludge making a squelching sound every time someone moved. The road in this part of the Realm had worn away long ago and several harsh storms this fall had left the ground waterlogged. The vampires could have moved the rations station, but did they? Fuck no. They never did anything that made our lives easier.

I glanced over my shoulder at the apartment blocks in the distance, just a few hulking grey shapes as bleak as the lifeless sky. Dad had headed to the market – if you could call some ramshackle buildings where a few people traded questionable wares a market – but he would likely be home by now with the candles he'd taken the trip for. We only had power at certain times of day in the apartment blocks, and it wasn't even guaranteed.

I'd gotten here later than usual, having stayed up in the small hours while I tried to talk Callie out of following Thomas to who knew where. People didn't go out of the Realm, that was a simple fact, but Callie refused to believe me. She was adamant that he was getting in and out somehow and had left our room at the butt crack of dawn to try and hunt him down like she'd said she would.

But despite her certainty, I knew she had to be mistaken; no one got out of this hellhole. The fence was ten feet high, ran three feet underground, and was electrified for good measure.

It was a shiny 'fuck you' that spoke of the technology the vampires were capable of if only they deemed us worthy to share it with. But of course, we weren't worthy. We were crops waiting to be harvested, and it didn't matter to them if we were half dead when they took what they wanted from us. Blood was blood. As long as we were alive, we would always have veins full of it, so they did the bare minimum to keep us breathing. And I guessed those of us who dropped dead from exposure, hunger, or disease were just margins they were willing to allow.

My hands curled into fists and rage simmered in my chest, always lurking beneath the surface like a crocodile lying in wait of a kill. But that was a fool's burden, because I wasn't a predator in this world, even if long ago my kind had been the rulers of all.

The vampires were the true hunters, born to prey on humans, and everything about them, from their fangs to their strength, was made for capturing us. Fighting back equalled bloody punishments, I'd seen it too many times. I just wished the playing field was a little fairer so I could throw a few vicious punches of my own.

It was why, even though I feared for Callie's safety, I understood what was driving her actions today. She wanted to find something, *anything,* to give us an edge in this hellish life, and I simply couldn't fault her for it. It wasn't like I was happy to resign myself to this miserable way of living, but my twin was risking everything for the sake of following a man who might have found nothing but a few tins of beans. It simply wasn't worth being apprehended for, and I couldn't bear to see her caught and shackled by the guards. Whipped and chained, made an example of before they dragged her away to the blood bank. No. I'd do anything to protect her from that fate.

I shivered as I shuffled up behind Bert and Martha in front of me, forcing those thoughts away and willing Callie to be alright. She was strong, and she'd know when to turn back. I had to have faith in her.

Bert's hair had been reduced to a few grey tufts above his ears and Martha kept her thinning locks tucked under a threadbare hat. As usual, we greeted each other with curt nods and polite conversation, nothing more.

"Weather's bad today," Bert muttered.

"It'll probably rain for the whole month, like last year," Martha grumbled, bloodshot eyes darting left and right.

It was the unsaid things that haunted me. The weather was a safe topic, one that most people stuck to. But their hollow eyes told of sleepless nights, the fear of growing one year older. Bert and Martha were nearly sixty, and the older members of our society sometimes just...disappeared. No one would even mention it. One day they'd be here, the next gone. And everyone would act as if they never knew them.

It was a fate worse than death, to be so quickly forgotten, your names never spoken again like you never even existed, and the idea of that one day happening to my dad was more frightening than I could put words to.

The reality was that anyone, neighbour or otherwise, could be gone tomorrow, and that was why polite conversation was the furthest any of our interactions went. To care about someone was the simplest way to be sure you'd feel the pain of losing them. We kept to our families and focused on the few we couldn't live without; the rest of the community did the same. It may not have been what we wanted, but it was what it took to survive this place. We couldn't afford friends, and we couldn't afford pity. Every human here looked out for themselves and their families, and that was it. No exceptions.

But the problem was, my heart didn't submit to that idea so easily. Sometimes, when people who were a constant in my world went missing, it kept me up at night. It made my thoughts crack and shatter into fragments I couldn't keep together, until eventually, I found myself whispering my gratitude into the unforgiving air. Because it wasn't *us*. We were still here somehow, and in the end, that was all that mattered.

The couple turned back to face the front of the line and I shuffled up behind them, frustrated with how slow it was moving towards the rations station.

The emporium was the single building which had any kind of regular maintenance in the Realm. White walls stood out starkly against the rain and a slanted roof carried the water over the edges in torrents.

I ducked my head to see around Bert, trying to get a look at *them*. The vampires who were so unnatural in all their perfection. I despised them right through to my bones, but there was something about them which always set my pulse racing to a dark and wild tune. It was more than fear, it was curiosity in its most perilous form, an intrigue I would never voice out loud. From their pearly skin to their inviting eyes, their beauty was a wicked spell that was designed to draw the gaze of their prey, and sometimes they drew mine.

They provided the only hint available of a world beyond this one. Their clothes were well made. New. Which spoke of a place outside of the Realm that we had no idea about. A town? A city?

All I knew was that the vampires didn't live in squalor like we did, but I could barely picture what that place might be like. Most of the books from *before* had been burned a long time ago. We still had a few tucked beneath our beds back home, but the main source of information I had about a life beyond this place was from Dad, painted in my mind by him like artist strokes.

Dad told stories of beautiful cities, sprawling meadows, and a sparkling blue sea. What my mind had conjured in response was probably all wrong, but it kept me going all the same. Something to dream about when the days grew dark and the scent of blood carried on the wind.

And hell, did I dream. I dreamed so much, my mind was elsewhere more than it was ever here. Even now as I stood in the rain, under a gunmetal sky, I was lost to a fantasy of sunshine and birds singing merrily high up in trees as tall as the drab buildings casting me in their shadow.

In my head, I could fly up and away with those birds, spreading my wings and floating on an updraft through the wind. I didn't know what the world looked like out there, but I tried to picture it, creating a place inside my head that was full of rainbows instead of rain, the blazing kiss of sunlight instead of the soul-sucking monotony of clouds.

I tucked my long, dark hair behind my ears and shifted forward in the mud as my turn finally drew close. Callie and I were non-identical twins. I'd inherited Dad's ebony hair and equally dark eyes, whereas Callie was fair like Mom with her green eyes, golden locks and sun-kissed complexion. I often grieved her through my childhood memories and through the memories Dad shared of his past with her, never letting myself forget who she was or how much she had loved us. There was a hole in my chest where she belonged, and nothing would ever fill it.

"Next," a vampire barked up ahead.

There was a counter in the front of the Emporium, and as Bert and Martha took their small linen bag of rations, I moved under the shelter of the porch, approaching the vampire. His hair was black as raven feathers and his skin dewy in the gloomy light, like there was something radiant within him I could never possess.

"Name," he demanded, his pale eyes moving from my rain-soaked hair to my neck and the pulse he could no doubt sense pounding there. My shoulders tightened and hatred crawled over my skin, trying to draw my lips into a sneer. But I was well versed at playing the good little human, even if there was a caged rebel living inside me.

"Montana," I said. "Of the Ford family."

"Ford," he growled my surname, eyeing a list before him which was typed, not written. He struck out the name as he found it, his perfectly manicured nails biting into the pen in his grip.

I couldn't read particularly well, but Dad had told me about the technology from *before*. The only time I'd ever witnessed it was here at the Emporium, and it always seemed like something *other*, almost magical in its capabilities. Beyond the vampire was a series of screens which showed live footage from around the Realm, a feed from the marketplace and outside the housing apartments playing in real time right before my eyes.

The public places were closely monitored with CCTV, but that still didn't explain how the vampires always knew *everything*. It was like their eyes could see beyond what was right in front of them, and Callie and I had come up with all kinds of wild theories of how they did it. Once, we'd come up with the idea that the vampires stood outside our apartment block, their ears extending like slugs, then sticking to the wall and climbing up to slither in our window. We'd screamed and laughed, then checked that the window was locked tight before slipping back into our wild imaginings. Callie always came back to reality first, while I tried to linger in my delusions, wanting to be anywhere other than here.

The vampire slammed a linen bag down before me, and my nose wrinkled. It was small. Smaller than usual. I pulled it open, taking a glance inside as my heart beat out a furious tune.

"Only one piece of bread? We're a family of three," I blurted, my sharp tone barely held in check. Reducing our rations qualified as a threat to my family, and I'd be damned if I would walk away from here without our full supplies.

The vampire gazed down his nose at me with obvious disdain. "Cutbacks," he announced, then glanced over my shoulder with a cold disinterest. "Next."

I remained rooted to the spot, my fingers shaking in fury as I clutched the bag.

"We're barely getting by as it is," I pressed, trying to keep my tone level.

Raising your voice to a vampire was a punishable offence. We were supposed to bow our heads to their every whim, but even *they* must have known starving us to death was fucking themselves over too. They needed the single thing we provided. The sole value of our existence. Blood. How many deaths could they really allow when we were their most prized resource?

"Be thankful for what you're given, human," the vampire snarled at me, a warning flashing like lightning in his eyes.

Anger bubbled in my chest, and I bit down on my tongue, trying to contain the hungry wolf in me. Because I really was hungry, starving actually, and the people I loved were too. We were expected to shut our mouths and be grateful for whatever we were offered, but we were already struggling to get by in this harsh winter, and this could be the end of us if they continued to cut our rations.

As the vampire dropped his gaze to the list and someone tried to approach the counter, I slammed my hand down under his nose.

"We need more than this," I demanded.

My pulse thundered in my ears as I stared at this monster before me who could tear my head clean from my shoulders if he wanted to. But these rations were a death in themselves. My soul was always doused in gasoline these days, and one spark could send me up in flames.

My hot head had gotten me in trouble in the past and keeping it in check made sure I was safe. But if my family became too weak to function, we'd all be sent to the blood bank, and I simply couldn't let that happen.

The vampire's upper lip curled back, his features twisting into a deadly warning. "Step away, human."

Someone tried to get past me again, but I wouldn't budge, digging my heels into the mud and fixing the vampire in my sights. I forced myself to take a breath as Dad had taught me, pushing down the wild animal in me who was so desperate to break free, and changing tactics before I lost our rations altogether.

"Please," I lowered my tone, sickened by the plea in my own voice.

The people waiting in line began to mutter, my name passing from one mouth to another.

*"Montana Ford. Whatever is she doing? Did she just make a demand of the vampires? She'll be whipped for sure."*

At my insufferable begging, the vampire's lips dragged up into a smirk and he revealed a shiny watch on his wrist.

"Do you know what this is?" he purred, and my heart beat harder at his velvety tone, sure there was some threat in it I wasn't perceiving.

"A watch?" I'd seen them before, and we were allowed the dignity of clocks in our homes, though he was looking at me as if I had two brain cells and I didn't know what to do with either of them.

"Yes. And this watch is the difference between you and I. It holds value. Like I do. Like all of my kind do. But you..." He leaned closer and the scent of fresh linen filled my nose. A smell I only knew because of *them*. "You are *food*. Roaming cattle. When crops don't flourish, the animals have to go hungry. And the crops aren't flourishing, human." He ushered me away and my pulse rose so high, I could feel myself reaching breaking point, the pressure in my chest like a volcano about to blow.

Someone touched my arm and I turned, finding my neighbour Lilian there. She was a year older than me and so thin, I knew she was going hungry to feed her three kids. I felt a tug in my chest over that fact and worked to smother it away. Caring for someone was too slippery a slope to fall down, but some days were harder than others when it came to shutting people out, especially when I saw Lilian trying to support her children.

We were encouraged to *breed*, but one of the few things I still had control over in my life was my body, and the last thing I would ever do in this bitter world was bring children into it. They would just be more blood bags for the vampires to suck dry, and this wasn't a life I would inflict on anybody.

"Leave it, Montana. Go home," Lilian urged.

In her watery eyes, I found my resolve. We were doing better than her family. Though it looked like our dinner was going to revolve around beets for the whole week. It would be enough for us, though. It would have to be. But, fuck, I hated beets. Dad always said 'eat your beets to beat your eats'. It made me laugh, and the beets went down a little easier with amusement sweetening my mouth. It wasn't like I was going to refuse to eat them either way.

I nodded to Lilian, then threw a scowl over my shoulder at the vampire and headed away across the muddy terrain, the rain twisting through the air.

I made it three feet before something jammed into my back and what felt like a thousand volts of electricity burst through me. I hit the wet ground with a scream, my vision stamped with white stars as I jerked and writhed against the pain.

*Hold on, just hold on a second longer. No pain lasts forever.*

I was on the verge of throwing up my pathetic excuse for a breakfast when the torture stopped, the agony in my body darting away like a thousand terrified butterflies.

My eyes unclouded and I found myself gazing up at the vampire from the Emporium, my breaths falling heavily from my chest as the world came back into focus, a cattle prod hanging loosely from his fist while feral amusement danced in his cold eyes.

Visceral hatred clawed at my gut, tearing at my insides, begging for an outlet. I ground my teeth together, forcing myself not to say another word despite the stream of curses I longed to hurl at him, but a threat sparkled in his gaze, and it wouldn't be pretty if I pushed him to deliver on it.

His face twisted into a sneer. "You'd do well to keep that mouth of yours strapped shut. One more toe out of line and I'll have you strung up and drained for the whole Realm to see."

I shuddered beneath him, my veins turning to ice as the puddle surrounding me soaked through my clothes, the chill of the day biting into my very bones.

It was an empty threat. People were rarely killed outright by the vampires. Our blood was too precious. But there were plenty of ways they could hurt me without ending my life.

I gritted my teeth, swallowing my pride and nodding at him, forcing my eyes to drop from his in submission.

He stalked away, splashing more mud over me as he went, and I rolled to my knees, finding the ration bag sinking into the mud, half the contents emptied on the ground.

My heart lurched and I bit back the curses sitting on my tongue as I gathered up the spoiled food, knowing I'd only made my family's situation a whole lot worse.

*Why can't you ever keep quiet and accept what you're given?*

*Because if I do that, I'll die inside. I'll become like the others who've lost the light in their eyes.*

If there was one thing Dad did for us daily, it was stoke the flames of our hearts so we'd never give up, no matter how hopeless things became. But on days like this, that only felt harder, more of a burden than something to cling to. We were trapped in this Realm, this life, and no amount of hope nor love for each other would ever change that.

As I ran through the monotonous rows of apartment blocks, I spotted my dad hurrying up the cracked pavement toward me with worry in his eyes. His coat was too big - but too big was always better than too small.

His eyes darted left and right as he jogged the final steps between us, his dark hair spilling down his forehead as he looked me over, frowning at the mud and shame which clung to me.

"What happened?" He eyed my filthy clothes and haywire hair, glancing beyond me to look for trouble, which thankfully hadn't followed me.

"Nothing. I fell," I lied, not wanting to put the burden on him of my stupid mini uprising at the Emporium.

I knew better than to behave like that. My heart weighed with guilt and my veins burned with all the lasting heat of my ire. We'd go to bed with growling bellies all week because of these pathetic rations, and there was nothing I could do about it.

"Where's Callie?" he demanded.

"She's not back yet?" I gasped, then heat struck my cheeks as I gave away that I knew exactly where she was.

"Back from where?" Dad snarled, his tone angry but his eyes betraying fear.

He knew as well as I did that Callie and trouble were a mix which went together far too often. She was impulsive and, worst of all, fearless. And in the world we lived in, fear wasn't something we could afford to go without.

"She went to the scrapyard," I lied quickly.

It was mostly a graveyard of unwanted electrical items from the *before*, alongside any trash that came out of people's apartments. There was rarely much to be salvaged there, but sometimes there were bits and bobs that could be used to fix things at home.

Dad seemed to relax, though I could tell he wouldn't feel entirely relieved until he saw my sister with his own eyes. My shoulders slumped too, but I couldn't help but wonder what the hell Callie was up to and why it was taking this long. She was tough and resilient, but those ingredients didn't always equal smart, especially when she took one of her supposedly calculated risks.

"They've cut our rations," I said, opening the bag and revealing the muddy contents, my skin prickling with the reality of our situation, remorse burning the base of my throat as I looked at the mud-soaked bread.

Dad's brow creased with worry, but he covered it quickly, knocking his fist under my chin and raising my gaze to meet his. "We'll be fine, little moon. I have some saved from yesterday."

He winked like we were sharing a secret, but his pretty lies didn't fool either of us. I couldn't help but fear what would come of our family if the rations continued like this for much longer. I'd thought they couldn't get any worse, but this...

He dropped his arm over my shoulders, squeezing me tight and pressing a kiss to my forehead before steering me back down the street the way he'd come.

I released a long breath, leaning my head against his shoulder and savouring this moment stolen in the rain, the heat of his body calling to mine and helping chase off some of the chill from my saturated clothes. With Dad, everything always seemed alright. He was the wall that kept the demons at bay, and there wasn't a single crack in his bricks.

We passed through grey streets and passed by even greyer looking faces as the deep and depressing colour of the storm clouds seemed to sap everything and everyone of all lustre and life.

"I thought of a new one," I said, and Dad looked to me with an arched brow, knowing exactly what I meant. It was our little game, one that always worked to brighten our moods. I liked to call it *A Thousand Ways to Kill a Vampire*.

"Oh yeah? Me too, actually. You first," he encouraged.

"So, imagine a vampire is strolling through the Realm, whistling happily to his little psycho self," I started, and Dad nodded, a grin already crinkling the corners of his mouth. He had so much stubble, I was pretty sure he was intending to grow another beard again for winter. The scissors he used to keep it short were blunt as hell anyway and too close to the point of breaking to try and sharpen them. "He's having the time of his life, twirling his cattle prod in his hand, the electricity crackling on the end of it as he looks for a hungry human to jab with it and cook up for his dinner."

"Morbid. Go on," Dad chuckled.

"But - oh no," I mock gasped. "He's tripped over a rogue aardquark-"

"Aardvark," he corrected with a snort.

"Right yeah, that thing. And he flips fang over ass through the air, his fancy shoes flying from his feet only to slap him in the face before he lands in the mud with a *splat*. He's scrambling to get up as the aardshark-"

"Vark."

"Right, yep. So the aard*vark* bites him on the ass in fury, tearing his pants clean off. But then he realises his cattle prod is missing, and as he looks up, he finds it falling from the sky only to land right between his ass cheeks, so a thousand bolts of hellfire blast him in the butthole and fry his insides to shit." I turned to Dad with a triumphant grin, and he burst out laughing.

"Alright, that was half decent," he said, reining in his amusement. "But mine's better."

I narrowed my eyes at him as I continued to smile. "Go on then, but you can't easily beat a cattle prod up the ass."

"No, only my daughter could be quite so creative, but you get your imagination from the king of delusions." He jabbed his thumb against his chest. "So, imagine a vampire is straining away on the toilet, preparing to take the shit of a lifetime."

"Is this going to start the dump debate again? Because I still don't believe they take shits," I said stubbornly, and he sniggered.

"Well, there ain't aardvarks in this country either, so if we're getting pedantic, I'll be docking points from you too," he said.

"Alright, I'll suspend disbelief." I nudged my elbow against his side, encouraging him to go on.

"Good. So, he's a big fella, straining away for his daily dump, but what he doesn't realise is there's a whole host of piranhas who've come swimming up the drainpipe into the toilet."

"They're those monster fish, right?" I asked keenly.

"Yeah, they've got sharp teeth and a taste for flesh." He gnashed his teeth at me, and I ducked back to avoid the fake bite, mirth skittering through me. "So, while Count Dumpsula is heaving and groaning, trying to get that human head he ate for breakfast out from between his shiny ass cheeks, the piranhas creep up on him then – splash!"

"He did a shit?"

"No! The piranhas dragged him under ass-first, didn't they? Then they shredded through him so fast it's like a blender in there-"

"A blender?"

"Like for making smoothies."

"Smoothies?" I frowned.

"It's when you chop up loads of fruit into a mush that you can drink. There was a machine you could buy for the kitchen that would do it," he explained, and I added that to my stockpile of knowledge for the *before*.

"Nice," I said with a laugh at the image he'd painted, but Dad's mood seemed a little sullied.

"I wish I could show you everything from the old world, Montana," he said heavily. He'd said it before, and I ached when he said it because I could see this other life in his eyes which was full of everything we could have had if only things had been different. If only, if only, if only.

We finally made it back to the apartment block we called home, the rectangular building looking just like every other in the Realm; tall, unassuming, and basic.

Dad wrenched open the wooden door which had swollen in the rain, making sure it got stuck every time someone used it. Stepping into the icy stairwell, we headed up the dank stone stairs towards the first level. I walked this path every day, always the same, endlessly eternal, my life one rotating wheel of repetitive, predictable nothing. We didn't live here, we simply survived in this space, and with the rain battering the windows and the wind howling through the forlorn streets, I couldn't help but wonder just how much longer that survival could continue.

I unlocked the rickety door to our home, jiggling it to get it moving, and revealing our meagre living quarters beyond as it swung wide.

"Did you get the candles?" I asked.

"Sure did," Dad said. "Old Bob gave me a good price. I only had to trade two cigarettes for ten."

I smiled as I stepped over the threshold into our apartment, thankful I'd at least contributed on that part, though the reason we had those cigarettes at all was because Dean Parker had gone missing last week. The moment anyone vanished, their apartment became a carcass waiting to be picked clean. I'd made it in there among the first of the vultures and scored us the rare pack of cigarettes along with a trove of toilet paper. It was like a morbid free-for-all, but hey, that was life in the Realm, and I knew if the three of us ever went missing, this place would be descended on just as fast, our belongings rifled through and anything with value stolen away by the masses.

A bell rang loudly across the whole of the Realm, harsh and piercing like the tolling chime of the Devil's arrival, and I froze, terror shooting down my spine, rocking me to my core. That sound meant one thing and one thing only.

Once a year – though we never knew when – a group of Elite vampires would come to the Realm and test people's blood. They'd go door to door seemingly at random, then take away whoever they deemed to pass their 'test' once the results came back a day later. No one knew where they went, and no one wanted to find out. The only thing we knew for sure was that those who were taken never returned.

So far, Callie and I hadn't been tested, but every time that bell rang, it sounded ominous, like an oncoming storm, the whisper of a god promising an unwelcome future, something even more horrendous than the one we faced in this place.

"Get inside," Dad murmured, his throat bobbing as he looked out into the empty corridor beyond our front door, and I hurried to obey. "They're not here for you. Don't you worry, baby girl."

"We'll be fine," I agreed. "We always are." It felt like a lie, the words leaving a sour flavour in my mouth, like a taste of the future that was headed our way.

Our home seemed smaller today somehow. The wallpaper had its usual damp patches, faded brown flowers staring back at me from all sides, playing pretend at happy and hopeful while only achieving drab and disheartening. I knew every petal and leaf like the back of my hand, and I wasn't sure if I loved or hated them now. Those flowers were the backdrop to my life, every memory I cherished with my family had been created before that patchy wallpaper, the dingy blooms watching each moment as they passed us by.

I placed the linen bag down on the single wooden work-top in the kitchenette, the room making up half of our living space beyond the two tiny bedrooms. There were white tiles on the counter which had yellowed with age and a stainless-steel sink which shone brighter than anything else we owned.

On the other side of the room sat a brown couch which was barely wide enough for two people, a table with three wonky legs, and a single, battered armchair which had always been Dad's. That was it. Home. One brown flowered wall to the next. Entirely ours, and yet so temporary in how easily it could all be snatched from us.

My spine tingled with nerves as the bell continued to ring, on and on.

The tolls seemed to whisper threats to my family, the promises they made filling the air and making me shiver with something far worse than the cold. But my fear wasn't for me, it was for the girl I loved with all the ferocity of my heart, my other half who was out there somewhere when the worst of the vampires were about to come marching into our Realm.

*Callie, get your skinny ass back here.*

# CALLIE

## CHAPTER THREE

**M**y boots pounded the carpeted floors of the apartment block outside the Realm as I ran for my fucking life, the desperate snarls of the rotter chasing me into the depths of the building.

I took turns at random, avoiding the doors to the apartments themselves for fear of ending up trapped inside one, the darkness thicker here now that I was away from the dusty windows. My heart lifted as I spotted the sign for a stairway in the dim light, and I ripped open the door, racing through it with a burst of speed.

My pulse was thundering in my ears, adrenaline drenching my body and making me run faster than I ever had in my life. I was fast, but that thing was faster. My only advantage was the small measure of time it had taken for the vampire to get into the building while I ran. But she was gaining on me now.

I hesitated as I met with the stairs, my eyes tracking from the set leading up to those leading down.

A loud bang in the corridor at my back made me flinch into action; instinct, insanity, or just random luck propelling me towards the stairs which could only lead to a basement.

I thundered down them, my boots echoing loudly in the open space, hoping that the vampire chasing me might not be able to tell whether I headed up or down and could guess wrong.

I stumbled as I reached level ground again, the light almost non-existent now that I was in the bowels of the building, my inner voice cursing me for picking down. *What the fuck had I been thinking?* If there were no doors or windows down here, then I really would be trapped.

I moved forward blindly, reaching out, my hands brushing over a stone wall and three doors.

I yanked one open at random, almost falling as I found another staircase dropping away to a further sub level.

That seemed like a terrible idea, so I spun away, grabbing another door and yanking that wide instead.

The heavy slap of bare feet echoed down to me as the rotter closed in, her grunting, desperate noises making her seem like nothing more than a beast as she hunted me. There were no words, no laughter or mocking like I would have expected from the vampires in the Realm. This thing was so far beyond humanity that I doubted it even remembered how to speak, how to do anything at all aside from *feed*.

Terror clutched my heart, but I refused to give in to it, hurrying into the darkness of the room and barely managing to contain a scream as a light suddenly flickered into being above my head.

The low hum of a generator kicking in accompanied it, and I had to assume my presence had activated it somehow.

I twisted around, eyeing the machines lining the walls, their round doors open, some baskets filled with clothes laying on top of them.

There was a laundry house in the Realm where we took our clothes to be cleaned which reminded me of this place. As I took in the shelves of cleaning products and further clothes hanging from rails to the far end of the room, my heart sank.

There were no windows, no doors, nothing at all but pale walls and that single, flickering bulb.

The rotter snarled loudly from somewhere far too close by, and I sprinted toward the back of the room, snatching an iron from a shelf as I went, looping the cord loosely around my wrist.

I dove into the meagre cover offered by a sheet hanging from a rail on the ceiling and slapped my hand over my mouth to hide my breath at the sound of the door slamming open.

The light flickered overhead, then went out.

Silence followed, my hand shaking where I pressed it to my mouth, my lungs burning with the desire to suck down a huge breath of air.

The rotter growled again, the slap of her feet marking her movement through the dark space.

My limbs shook as I remained where I was, praying to all things on this earth and beyond that by some miracle she might not find me.

My mind filled with thoughts of Montana and Dad, the knowledge that they would never figure out what had happened to me. Or worse. Perhaps my remains would be found by the vampires who ran our Realm. Perhaps they'd recognise whatever was left of me and realise I'd made it beyond the fence. And I simply *knew* they'd punish my family for it. They'd take them to the blood bank and force them to face a fate far worse than what awaited me in this room. All because I came out here, all because I refused to pay enough attention to the risks.

I couldn't allow it. I wouldn't.

The sound of the rotter's footsteps grew closer, her desperate snarls boxing me in as I tightened my hold on the iron and waited, raising it as I prepared to strike.

The light flickered on once more, a silhouette outlined through the thin fabric of the sheet.

I roared my defiance as I threw myself forward, swinging the iron with all of my strength.

The heavy metal slammed into the rotter's skull, the crack of bone and splatter of blood across the white sheet filling me with disgust.

But I didn't stop, my momentum propelling us across the room, the sheet tangling around her as she screamed in furious desperation, and we collided with the wall.

I shoved away from her, throwing the iron at her as hard as I could and sprinting for the door.

I had seconds. Less than that. The open doorway loomed before me, the promise of escape so close and yet too fucking far.

I screamed as the rotter grabbed my ankle, ripping my leg out from under me and sending me crashing to the ground so hard that I cried out in pain. Blazing heat scorched along the inside of my right arm then faded, leaving nothing but adrenaline in its wake.

I rolled over, kicking and thrashing, spitting, and hissing like a cornered alley cat while the half-starved monster writhed against the sheet which had tangled itself around her body, only her arm free of it, her nails biting into my skin through the fabric of my leggings. She was strong, stronger than me, but if a rotter felt nothing but unending hunger, then it stood to reason that they were at their weakest in this state, and that meant I had a chance.

I kicked and kicked, the lights going out once more just as my boot connected with her wrist hard enough to force her off of me.

I didn't hesitate, shoving to my feet and blindly sprinting for the door once again, a cry parting my lips as I fell through it, my hand closing around the handle despite the dark.

I slammed it shut at my back so hard that the sound echoed through the stairwell, my hand moving to the lock and twisting sharply.

The rotter collided with the far side of it, and I cried out as I leapt back, the hinges rattling from the force of her attack, but the door didn't give.

Again and again, she slammed into it, the door continuing to hold as I backed up then turned and fled, the sound of her trying to break through chasing me all the way back up the stairs and leaving my pulse rioting.

I threw the next door shut too, racing across the hall to the closest apartment and dragging a heavy desk back out to barricade it, wedging it between the door and the wall so there was no way she could move it.

I collapsed over the desk the moment it was done, panting and laughing, the weight of my bag on my back a welcome friend as a few relieved tears sprung free of my eyes and my laughter grew towards manic.

I had no idea how the fuck I'd managed to survive that, but I didn't care. I was still breathing, that thing would be left down there to starve, and my family would have warm clothes for the winter.

"Shit," I breathed, pushing myself upright and swiping a hand over my face as I tried to shake off the lingering adrenaline which was making my heart thunder in my chest.

I'd done it. The smile on my face was staying put all the way until tomorrow at the earliest.

*We'll eat well tonight.*

That wasn't something I'd been sure of in months. The thought alone stopped my stomach from growling for the first time in a long time.

I took off down the dim corridor, running back towards the exit and stepping into the rain, the freezing droplets pouring down on me once more, but I couldn't have cared less.

I checked my surroundings carefully, aware that rotter might not be the only one lurking on the outskirts of the Realm, but I found nothing hiding between the buildings or stalking my steps as I circled back to the drain which had led me here. There was still no sign of Thomas, so it looked like his secret was my secret, and he was none the wiser.

I dropped down into the darkness of the drain, my mind fully occupied with thoughts of the meal we'd be consuming tonight as I scrambled through the hole in the rubble and passed beneath the fence back into the Realm.

The smell down here was pungent, somehow worse on my return, the scent of freedom still lingering on my skin as I made it to the ladder and quickly clambered up it. I wanted to sprint all the way home and show Dad and Montana what I'd found – I probably wouldn't mention the bit about the rotter though or they'd never let me head out here again.

Montana was going to freak out. I'd *told* her what Thomas was up to, and she hadn't believed me. She could eat her words alongside her meal.

I released a laugh of pure smug satisfaction just as I made it to the top of the ladder and climbed out into the rain.

"Bitch!" I barely recognised Thomas before his fist made contact with my jaw.

I was thrown backwards by the blow, landing heavily on my side and slamming my elbow into the concrete.

I reeled from the sudden attack, blinking through the muddle of my thoughts and the raindrops slamming down on my face as my mind caught up to what was happening.

I rolled over, rising onto my hands and knees but his foot connected with my stomach before I could gain my feet. I yelled out in pain as I fell back to the concrete and rolled away before he could kick me again.

My heavy backpack jammed into my shoulder, one of the tin cans catching my ribs painfully.

"Wait," I gasped, raising a hand to stave him off but there was nothing beyond utter violence in his eyes as he sneered at me where I lay in the dirty puddles before him.

Thomas advanced on me again, rage glittering in his gaze, his fury too potent a thing to be held off by mere words. I'd always pegged him for a mean son of a bitch, but I was beginning to think I'd underestimated him. He was more than just mean; that look made me think he might just kill me if he thought he could get away with it, and I knew he wasn't going to stop until he had me bleeding at his feet.

I scrambled back, keeping myself out of his reach as he advanced, the shock of his attack wearing off and my survival instincts kicking in. I wasn't going to let him beat the shit out of me for this, though I wasn't entirely sure how I was going to stop him yet either. The only weapon I had was my knife, but if I stabbed him, someone would find out I had it, meaning a one-way trip to the blood bank for me. *Fuck that.*

Thomas was half as tall as me again and twice as heavy, though the meagre rations had lightened his muscle mass some. If he wanted to kill me, I was dead, but I sure as shit wouldn't be making it easy for him. *Why the fuck did I let him catch me?*

I'd be berating myself for not checking my surroundings more carefully if I survived this, but right now the only thing I could focus on was the murderous-looking bastard who was stalking towards me.

I spat a wad of blood from my mouth and managed to get to my feet, backing away further.

"I won't tell anyone else," I swore, holding a hand out defensively. I was pleased that it wasn't shaking despite the fear licking its way down my spine.

"You won't be able to when I'm through with you," Thomas growled. "How did you even find out?"

Okay, so reasoning with him wasn't going to work, perhaps taunting him would do the trick.

"You're not as clever as you think you are." I shrugged, slipping my bag from my back as he closed in on me and I kept retreating, like this was a dance and we were simply following the steps. The space behind the fountain wasn't all that big though and I could only retreat a little further before my back would be up against a wall.

"I'm the one who made that tunnel," he hissed. "It's *mine*, you little thief."

"Perhaps you should have been a bit less obvious about it then," I said, my pack slipping down my arms until I was gripping the strap tight in one fist. "It was easy to figure out what you were doing as soon as I started paying attention. You were like a lumbering ogre stumbling around out here. I've seen you here a hundred times, but you never saw me once. No wonder I figured out your poorly kept secret – you might as well have screamed it from the crumbling rooftops."

Thomas's lip curled back in a feral snarl as he lunged for me, but this time I was ready. I ducked aside and used my momentum to swing my pack as hard as I could, aiming for his thick head and that dripping mop of hair that topped it.

The pack connected with a solid thunk. Eleven cans of food slammed into the side of Thomas's skull and dropped him like a sack of shit.

My lips popped open as I stared at his prone body in shock, the roaring silence in my skull punctured by the plink of raindrops hitting cement. Thomas lay in a growing pool of blood which seeped into the murky puddles surrounding him. I released my pack and it fell beside me, splashing water over my boots.

My heart thrummed in my chest.

*I've killed him. Holy shit, I've fucking killed him.*

I started to back away then stopped. If I really had killed him, I'd have to confess to it. If the vampires found him... they hated dead bodies, wasted blood. Maybe I could come up with an excuse or some reason for them to let me off. Tell them he'd attacked me or... *Pull yourself together Callie. Check his fucking pulse.*

I battled against my fear and moved closer to Thomas's fallen body. I leaned down slowly, edging the toe of my boot away from the blood gathering beside his head. My fingers trembled slightly as I extended them towards his neck, half expecting him to lunge upright and attack me again at any moment, my free hand curling around the knife in my pocket just in case.

His skin was warm beneath my cold fingers. I couldn't feel anything at first, but then the faint beating of his pulse came alive beneath my touch. I sagged in relief. He was an asshole and I'd have to tread very carefully around him from now on, but better a living asshole than a dead one. And now he knew I could defend myself if he forced me to.

Thomas groaned and shifted beneath me, making me stumble away. I backed up quickly and half tripped over my pack on the ground but managed to stay on my feet.

Thomas opened his eyes at the noise, and I stared at him as he met my gaze, a curse accompanying the hand which moved to the wound on his head.

"I know your secret, and now it's mine too," I said more bravely than I felt, but fuck him and fuck this shitty lot we'd been dealt in life. I wasn't going to let him keep me from this opportunity, I wasn't going to let him scare me away when all of those supplies lay waiting just there beyond the fence, more than my family needed to survive this winter. "So just keep your mouth shut, and so will I. They'll never know."

They. The vampires. The one thing he had to fear no matter what he thought of me. Truth was, he couldn't kill me even if he wanted to. None of us could risk that kind of attention and letting me use his precious tunnel was far better than trying to get away with murdering their livestock.

His face contorted angrily, but I didn't give him the chance to reply. I'd told him how it was and shown him how I reacted to his threats. It was done.

I grabbed my pack from the puddle beside me and turned to heave myself over the back wall of the decorative fountain. I landed heavily on the far side, sloshed through the water, clambered over the lower wall beyond it, then broke into a sprint designed to get me as far away from that asshole as possible.

The cans rattled as they bumped into each other, and despite the blood I could taste from my split lip, the two feral beasts who had made an attempt on my life, and the fact that I was soaked to my goddamn core, I couldn't help but feel lighter than I had in months.

I kept running towards the occupied part of the Realm, weaving around the broken chunks of masonry and over crumbling streets that zigzagged between the dilapidated buildings. There were no rules against exploring the ruins, but hardly anyone bothered. There wasn't anything left out here worth taking, and most people didn't see the point in wasting their energy.

I liked it in the ruins though. It was the only place that I could go where it was truly quiet, where my thoughts didn't feel locked in a cage and where I could get a glimpse of the world beyond the fences.

I ran on, but suddenly, the pounding of the rain wasn't the only sound I could hear. A high-pitched ringing was coming from the town centre, repeated over and over again, sending trepidation spiralling through my soul. I knew that sound. And it meant that I had to get home *right now.*

I increased my pace and started sprinting. The pack on my back suddenly seemed so much more conspicuous than it had a moment ago. I didn't know if I should try to hide it before I got back or if I was better off concealing it in the safety of our home. There was no explanation I could give for the contents of it, nothing I could say which would hide the truth if it was found.

The ringing grew louder as I made it to the outskirts of the inhabited part of the Realm. The roads were deserted. Everyone had already headed back to their homes, following the rules we all knew so well. There was no time for me to try and hide my treasured pack. I'd just have to get it back to our apartment and stash it there. Assuming I made it back in time at all.

Fuck, *fuck.*

Of all the days for this to happen, why did it have to be the one when I needed more time, when I had a secret painted all over my skin?

I raced down abandoned street after abandoned street, the emptiness making my skin crawl. I was late. I didn't know what that would mean if they came knocking on our door before I made it back, but it couldn't be good. There was no tolerance for breaking the rules, and I knew the bloodsuckers wouldn't give a shit what my excuse was. The bell rang, you got your ass home. Everyone knew it, and I was just the dumb bitch who had been so far out into the ruins that I hadn't heard it chime.

I finally made it to the junction of our street and turned onto it, keeping my head low and my direction firmly in mind as the windows on the buildings which surrounded me seemed to peer closer. How many of our neighbours were watching me now? How many had noted the full pack on my back or the mud which hadn't fully washed from my clothes in the rain? Worse, what about the blood that still stained my bottom lip?

I pulled up short, my boots skidding in the mud as I spotted a group of vampires heading straight for the doors to our apartment block, my breath stalling in my lungs, my luck turning on me like a scorned lover.

*Shit.*

I didn't move, just stood there like a fucking statue staring at them, somehow going unnoticed as I shivered in the rain and watched. I'd never seen them wandering the Realm like that. Not in a group. Sometimes the guards stalked the streets when they were feeling vindictive, hunting out small rule breaks and harshly punishing those they caught, but they were always alone. It was a taunt in itself. Flaunting the fact that a single one of them was easily a match for so many of us.

But now, there was a group, five of them in total; four stood in an arrowhead formation around the one in the centre who was clearly far more important than any of the bloodsuckers who regularly patrolled our Realm. They all moved with cat-like grace, their motions fluid in a way that defied nature and set the hairs along the back of my neck standing up. It wasn't natural. Nothing about them seemed remotely human to me beyond the vague shape of their bodies. They were monstrous in their perfection, unholy in their existence and utterly terrifying in their strength.

The four guards wore thick red cloaks lined with golden thread, the hems trailing in the mud, clearly some kind of uniform. They had long swords strapped across their backs, but they looked more decorative than practical, the metal gleaming as the rain struck their sheaths. It wasn't like they needed weapons to overpower us anyway.

Their skin was radiant in the faint sunlight which made it through the rain clouds. I knew it wasn't enough to hurt them on a day like this, but if the clouds just broke then *poof.* Or maybe not poof, maybe it would be more of a slow burn, a smoulder that would turn to flicker, then a full flame, barbequing them for all to see.

I wasn't sure exactly how it would kill them, but I suspected it would, and Dad said that was what the old stories used to say about them. One step out into the sun and they were done for. Perhaps we'd be granted a miracle and the clouds would break for that very purpose. I glanced up at the thick rain clouds almost hopefully, but if the ominous grey of them was anything to go by, then there was no chance of that. And to be honest, no one knew for certain if the sun would kill them. The one thing I could be sure of was that they couldn't face direct sunlight for one reason or another; if the sun was shining, we never saw them. Not that there was much hope of that during this storm.

As if he'd felt my attention on him, the vampire in the centre of the group stilled and turned towards me. His movements were so unnatural. When he froze, he literally stopped moving. I didn't even think he was breathing. *Do they even need to breathe?*

His icy blue gaze locked with mine and his too-perfect mouth curved into a mockery of a smile. He was stunning, his hair a sleek silver, smoothed back without a single strand out of place, his face all perfect angles and high cheekbones, constructed from a dream set to seduce and ensnare, but I had never once looked on one of them with any kind of lust or feelings of attraction. Their appearance was simply another weapon, a way to lure us in before they sank their teeth into us, and it didn't fool me.

I knew he was one of the Elite without having to be told. I hadn't seen many of them in my lifetime, but even amongst the other vampires, they stood out as something…more.

Their beauty was beyond eye-catching; it nearly stole your breath, making the other vampires fade to near insignificance in their presence despite their own chiselled looks and ingrained allure. Everything about the Elite drew you closer, making people spill secrets and lose their minds to desire, but a feeling in the pit of my stomach always warned me away too. It was like I could *feel* how dangerous they were. Like some ingrained, primal part of my makeup recognised the predator that lay beneath their stunning exterior.

His clothes were like something from one of our Dad's old fairy tales. He was wearing a cloak. An emerald cloak and britches with gold buckled boots. *What the fuck?* It would almost have been funny if I couldn't see my death glittering in his eyes.

The vampires guarding him stepped forward, and he turned away from me as they guided him inside. His attention turning from me like I was nothing and no one, as insignificant as a speck of dirt, and I certainly hoped I was to him and his kind.

As if a spell had been broken, I reclaimed the use of my limbs, a breath shuddering through my lungs as I shook off the feeling of bugs crawling all over me and turned back the way I'd come. No way was I following them inside, but I could make it in through the back and be to our apartment long before they got close to our floor.

The dumpsters behind the apartment building were overflowing as usual, and I leapt up onto the closest one. The fire escape ladder hung a few feet above my head, and I jumped up, catching hold of it. My shoulders throbbed with pain, reminding me of the many injuries I'd sustained today, but I had no time to listen to the protests of my body, my one and only focus on getting back inside before my time ran out.

I heaved myself up onto the ladder and started climbing, the weight of my pack dragging at me and reminding me of all the glorious food I'd gathered for our family.

I made it to the top of the rusted rungs and slipped onto the metal walkway that marked the first floor. I tiptoed across it quickly, cringing at the way the metal creaked beneath my weight before climbing off the other side of it and gripping a thin lip of concrete that lined the brickwork. I refused to look down as I shimmied towards our window, my time exploring the ruins making the task simple enough, though the prospect of a fall was never one I enjoyed.

I tapped on the glass urgently as I reached it, and Montana's worried face appeared through the window a moment later, her chestnut eyes wide with concern, her dark hair still damp from the rain and clinging to her cheeks.

She shoved the window up and I threw my leg over the sill, then half fell inside.

"Callie, what happened, are you-" she began but I shushed her as I turned to secure the window again, all too aware of the vampires prowling through our building.

"Look," I whispered excitedly as I pulled the bag from my back and opened it to reveal the contents.

Montana's eyes lit up as she spotted the haul of food and clothes. "You were right?" she breathed, her surprise clear, and I smirked at her.

"Never doubt me," I teased. "You should have seen it, Monty, there's all kinds of things just left to rot out there; food, clothes, blankets, it's insane. I wanted to take so much more than this, but we're going to have to be careful."

She opened her mouth to ask something more, but before she could, a sharp knock came at the front door.

We both froze, looking towards our bedroom door in horror.

"A group of vampires entered our building right before I got back," I breathed. "There was an Elite with them."

"You think we're on their list?" Montana hissed in alarm, the fear on her face echoing what was coursing through my veins.

The door to our room opened suddenly, and I about shit my pants before my gaze met Dad's. His alarm slipped to relief as he spotted me, sodden and dripping in the small space between mine and Montana's beds.

"Just a moment," he called for the benefit of the monsters beyond our front door, waving a hand at me, ushering me to hurry the fuck up.

We'd never been tested before. Why would they come for us now?

My heart pounded wildly as I began to consider the alternative, that this was about me slipping out of the Realm and not the testing at all. But then, they wouldn't simply knock if they'd come here to haul me away. The pretence of politeness only ever accompanied their official bullshit, and this reeked of the pomp and secrecy that surrounded the testing.

Dad swung the bedroom door shut to buy us a few more moments, and Montana snatched the bag from me, tossing it beneath her bed before pulling the worn blanket down to cover it. I grabbed the knife from my pocket and shoved it into the slit I'd cut in the edge of my mattress next, knowing that nothing good could come from me being caught with it.

"What the hell happened to your face?" Montana whispered urgently and I raised my fingers to my split lip guiltily, the taste of blood still lingering, and that really wasn't a good thing when I was about to come face to face with a pack of bloodsuckers.

"I'll explain later. How bad does it look?" I hissed.

She shrugged and bit her lip, letting me know it was pretty awful, but there wasn't a lot we could do about it now. I quickly shed my jacket and kicked off my mud-caked boots as I heard Dad heading for the front door, his footsteps as slow as he could get away with, but the seconds were ticking by.

Montana grabbed a clean shirt from my closet and tossed it at me as I threw my saturated one to the floor. We repeated the process with clean pants, and I kicked my sodden clothes into a corner before grabbing another fresh shirt and trying to scrub the worst of the dirt from my face and hands. Montana gave me a reassuring look, but I was going to guess I still mostly looked like shit. I had to assume we all looked like shit to those monsters though, and it wasn't like I was hoping to impress them. I was just hoping to survive this encounter, and I tried to ignore the blood from my split lip as the iron tang washed over my tongue once more.

*They drink blood by the bottle, one little cut won't interest them.*
*Sure, keep telling yourself that.*
*Fuck.*

I moved to stand beside my twin sister at our rickety bedroom door. It was the final barrier between us and whatever fate those creatures had set in our way, and I wanted nothing more than to stay right here on the other side of it with her. We shared a look that hummed with our bond, and I was reminded of countless nights dreaming up new realities in this room together, painting pretty pictures in each other's minds as we tried to block out the truth which lay beyond these walls. But of course it had come for us again. It always did.

The sound of Dad sliding the deadbolt out of place rattled through the silence, filling my mind with images of the vampires who were waiting beyond it. The icy blue gaze of the Elite had burned its imprint onto my retinas, and I didn't relish the prospect of facing him again.

With a deep breath, I moved closer to Montana and we inched toward the door, preparing to face our fate together. I simply hoped we'd survive it together too.

# MONTANA

## CHAPTER FOUR

"The Ford daughters are to be tested today. Bring them to me immediately," the demanding voice filled our house, sending a tremor through my heart.

I gazed at Callie, curling a hand around her wrist as we pressed our ears to the bedroom door. Though neither of us voiced our fears, I knew we were both putting off going out there to face the testing. This room had always been a sanctuary, a place no vampire had ever stepped a foot inside, but beyond this door, the demons were always waiting. And now they had come to feast upon our souls.

I had hope though, even if it was a fragile creature with broken wings. But the fact was, the majority of people failed the testing, and the Elite went on their merry way, humming their favourite little vampire tunes as they headed back to whatever creepy hole in the ground they called home. This would be the same. It had to be.

"Of course," Dad answered in a flat tone. "Please make yourselves at home. I'm afraid we've only got a few chairs, but I'm sure some of your fine asses will be quite comfortable on them. Oh, but do be sure to wipe the seats first, we don't want our human taint to get on your elegant gowns."

His sarcasm was clear through the simpering voice he was putting on, and it brought a rebellious smile to my lips. He was just subtle enough that they probably thought he was ass-kissing them to save his neck though.

"These are cloaks," the same growling voice reached us again, and Callie's burning green gaze met mine as danger fogged the air.

"Forgive me," Dad said. "My mind is too small to appreciate the intricate differences between gowns and cloaks. They are very fancy all the same. You wouldn't want to sully them here in our humble pig pen."

My smile widened, but my grip tightened on my sister's wrist too. Fear and amusement were swirling together inside me, creating a dark concoction, but I knew which of them would win out. Dad's casual confidence always kept the threat of reality at bay, acting as if he was immortal so we'd never falter in his footsteps. But growing up meant seeing the truth as it was, and my smile finally slipped as that truth took hold of me by the throat and forced me to face it.

"Your daughters, Mr Ford," the cold voice insisted. "I will not ask again."

Dad's footsteps thumped in our direction, and Callie arched a brow in question, a single moment of tense defiance ringing between us. It was like an ethereal force was urging us to fight, pressing a hand to each of our backs and gilding our hearts in steel.

Then I blinked, and she did too, the moment dissolving as quickly as it had come, because to resist was a death sentence, pure and simple. Though why it had felt so plausible for a second, I didn't know. Maybe it was the madness this situation was invoking, the very small, yet very possible chance that we could pass the testing looming on the horizon. Then the vampires would take us from Dad, from the Realm, and who knew where we'd end up? Somewhere even more horrifying than this, I was sure.

But that fate hadn't even been handed to us, so there was no point acting as if it had.

"We won't pass," Callie whispered.

I nodded firmly, opening the door before Dad reached it, and we moved into the main living space of our small home, ready to face the testing side by side.

My gaze met with Dad's, his mouth stretched into a painfully thin line, the worry he always worked so hard to hide shining in his dark eyes as he looked between us.

"I've got you," he vowed, his voice low and just for us as he towered above us with all the ferocity of a warrior. "There's no world in which I'd let them take y-" He didn't finish that sentence as the Elite vampire's voice cut the air to ribbons again.

"Here. Now."

We moved past Dad, rounding into the kitchenette as he walked at our backs like a sentinel ready to protect us at any sign of trouble.

My heart stumbled at the sight of the three vampires before us, everything about them polished and dazzling. The front door was wide, revealing two more standing on either side of the entrance like they were guarding the door, but against what I had no idea. No one in the Realm would be dumb enough to take on one vampire, but five? Suicide didn't even cover it.

I swallowed a lump in my throat as I forced myself to look between the monstrous beings who had stepped into our tiny bubble of solitude and burst it with such vulgar finality that I had to wonder if the brown flowers on the wallpaper might wilt beneath the weight of their presence.

I'd never seen so many of them together like this, never felt the weight of their utter dominion over us quite as keenly as I did with them invading our private space, the quality of their clothes and radiance of their skin only accentuating how very little we had in comparison.

The obvious leader was dressed in an emerald cloak with a spotless white shirt and what looked like freaking britches beneath it. He had a dangerous glint in his eyes as they swung between Callie and I, his focus landing on her mouth, hitching on the split to her lip and the wet blood which stained it, though she refused to flinch beneath his gaze. His silver hair was neatly cut and slicked back, unlike all the human men I knew who shore their hair off with kitchen scissors at best, or simply left it long, and his sharp jaw was perfectly clean-shaven.

He was stunning, utterly captivating and impossible to look away from in an unearthly, menacing kind of way. A beautiful, deadly bastard.

There was no doubt he was an Elite. Even the glamour of the vampires who accompanied him paled to insignificance with him here. But his beauty was arsenic hidden in honey, and one bite would see you dead.

None of them had taken up Dad's offer of a seat – not surprising considering they looked as though they wanted to be in our home about as much as they wanted to ram a handful of rusty nails up their asses. But the tiny table had been pulled up before the small couch, evidently waiting for Callie and I.

"Sit," the leader ordered, and we dropped onto the couch side by side, our hands clasping instinctively. "Out," he spat at Dad, and I forced myself not to look at him as he hesitated, but we all knew this could only go one way – *their* way.

"I would prefer to stay," Dad said, a very subtle yet very sharp edge lacing his tone.

"And I commanded you to get out," the Elite vampire flashed fangs at Dad, and I turned to him anxiously, giving him a look that begged him to go.

Dad's jaw ticked, but as he met my gaze, his shoulders dropped a little and he gave in, turning and heading into his bedroom, though I noticed he left the door ajar.

I felt the loss of his presence keenly as we were left alone with this pack of heathens, but I had Callie. And the two of us together had always been a tenacious unit.

The Elite's eyes slid between us, surveying, calculating, pausing on Callie's bleeding lip once more.

"I am General Wolfe of the New York Elite. Do you know what that means?"

I shrugged and Callie shook her head, neither of us inclined to speak unless we absolutely had to.

"It means I own you. Every damn hair on your head and every single blood cell in your veins – even those which seem to be finding their way out of your body." He eyed Callie again and I shifted in my seat, wanting to shield her from view, but she squeezed my hand in warning. "I will not tolerate disobedience during the testing, understand?"

"Yes," Callie bit out, and I gritted my jaw as I nodded.

This vampire wasn't like the guards who patrolled the fences. He emanated power. And when he said he owned us, I had no doubt he was telling the truth, no matter my feelings on the subject. This creature was the master of our fates. He could pounce on us right here and now, his fangs piercing flesh, sucking every drop from our bodies, and no one could do a damn thing about it. We were at his mercy, and if the cruelty I felt festering in his gaze was anything to go by, that didn't bode well.

Wolfe gazed at Callie with narrowed eyes. "What happened to your face?"

Callie touched her swollen lip and my nails bit into her hand, my pulse thundering in my ears.

*Lie well, Callie.*

"I fell," she said easily.

"Hm," Wolfe grunted, evidently satisfied, likely not even caring for the truth, his nature simply drawing his focus to the blood.

The tension ran out of my shoulders as his attention moved on from her.

Turning, he gestured to the robed vampires beside him, and one of them produced a syringe with a slim needle on the end.

They moved toward Callie first, her gaze moving to the far wall as the vampire rolled back her sleeve and tightened a torniquet around her bicep. She didn't even flinch as the guard drew a large vial of blood from the crook of her elbow, acting as if it wasn't happening at all, like no violation was taking place here.

I supposed after years of enduring regular 'donations' to the blood farmers, one vial was nothing, but somehow this felt different. They weren't taking our blood to simply feed themselves. This held a purpose they were keeping from us, one which was decorated with bad omens.

When the guard moved to my side with a clean syringe, a drop of revulsion cascaded down my spine like cold water. I folded my own sleeve back, offering the pale skin of my arm to him, wanting to claim some small measure of control over this process even if I wished I could turn and run from it altogether.

A sharp pinch followed a too familiar dragging feeling in my vein, and my eyes remained on the needle the entire time, tracking the blood as it spilled into the vial. I'd always hated the donations, hated the feeling of them stealing the very thing which granted me life and taking it to sustain their own.

They claimed this was for our benefit. That the Realm protected us from far worse things beyond our borders and that harvesting our blood this way saved lives from being lost to bloodlust if the vampires were to simply bite their prey. It was all very fucking civilised, apparently. An empire built on organised cruelty. And I dreamed of tearing that empire down, brick by merciless brick, to watch them all fall.

My gaze kept moving to Wolfe, his name fitting for the predator he was, and something about his movements solidified that. All his refinery felt like it was disguising something violent and callous, and it lurked there just beneath the surface, waiting for an opportunity to present itself and unleash terror on anyone who fell in his shadow.

Finally, they wrapped up the vials of our blood in a sheath of leather and Wolfe tucked it inside his cloak, proving its importance.

"You will be notified of your results in twenty-four hours," Wolfe said, moving toward the exit, his attention shifting from us to the next family on his list.

I had no idea what qualified any one of us for testing, but the fact that both Callie and I had been selected sent trepidation tumbling through me.

I rose from my seat, my heart pounding frantically as my chair screeched backwards across the floor.

"What happens if we pass the test?" The words left my lips before I had time to rethink them, the need to understand this threat to us overriding the common sense which demanded I stay silent and let Wolfe's attention move on.

The general glanced over his shoulder with a menacing glare. "You will only find that out if you pass."

"What if we fail?" Callie demanded, standing too, and tension spilled through the air.

Wolfe grew eerily still, his icy blue gaze flicking between us and then landing on the cut to Callie's lip once more.

He stalked back into the room, each of his steps measured, the heavy thump of his boots making the air itself vibrate in warning.

Callie raised her chin as he closed in on her, his eyes never leaving that small wound, the darkness in him rising up from wherever he kept it.

"Questions are for beings with rights," he hissed, taking the last step between us so suddenly that I flinched.

His hand snapped out, his grip tight on Callie's jaw as he tipped her chin up and inspected the wound, his thumb brushing over it roughly, making a drop of blood bloom.

Every vampire was staring at her now, at that tiny drop of what they all craved so desperately. Wolfe slowly licked his lips, watching as the blood rolled down her chin before tumbling to the floor, and I swear the sound of it hitting the worn floorboards was audible in the silence that pressed in on us.

My fingers itched with the need to shove him away from my twin, and I forced them into fists before I acted on the urge, knowing that path would only lead to a punishment for us both.

"But unfortunately for you, the law does not recognise humans as such," Wolfe said, his fangs flashing with the words, the threat there clear.

Our lives were his, he could do whatever he pleased with us; he could snap my sister's neck in the blink of an eye or pounce on her and drain her dry. Maybe he'd start a feeding frenzy, all five of them devouring my family right here in the tiny room where the faded wallpaper watched everything, our demise its final point of witness.

Wolfe shoved Callie hard enough to make her stumble back into the table, turning for the door once more, his emerald cloak billowing out around him.

Anger flared in my veins hot and fast, as potent as hellfire. It burned, blazed, roared, and it was so consuming that I was lost to it in a flash.

I took a step forward with wild abandon, but a hand slammed down on my shoulder from behind, halting me in my tracks. A quick glance over my shoulder informed me that Dad had returned, the fear in his eyes enough to still the reckless vengeance that had possessed me.

"Thank you, General," Dad spoke loud and clear, forcing the

conversation to end.

Wolfe shot a look back at him with disdain before exiting our home and leaving the door wide open as he strode away with his guards in tow. None of us dared move as we listened to their footsteps carving a path down the hallway and into the stairwell, all five of them heading deeper into the building in search of whoever else was on their dreaded list.

Dad exhaled at last, stepping around us and pushing the front door shut before pressing his back to it.

"Take a breath, little moon," he urged me, and I did, drawing in a slow, calming lungful of air which helped to ease the mist of rage still clouding my thoughts.

"Fucking asshole," Callie muttered, rubbing her ass cheek which had slammed into the table.

"You good, Callie?" Dad frowned and she nodded, her eyes hardening with a flush of resilience. I felt that same resilience flowing between us all, binding the three of us as one again, a team never to be broken.

Dad's jaw ticked as he folded his arms, stress evident in his rigid posture. "You're going to pass...I just know it."

He pressed his fingers into his eyes, and chaos reigned in my chest, his words so full of certainty that they terrified me. Dad never lied to us, never tried to paint false pretences of the world so we could live in ignorant bliss. He prepared us for it, and I loved him for that, how he'd always seen us as capable and helped mould us into survivors. So those words from his lips didn't even sound like a hopeless worry to me, they sounded like a fact. And there was nothing that could have prepared me for the crushing horror they caused.

"How can you know that?" Callie demanded. "We don't even know what they're checking for. There's no reason to think we'll be selected. They'll be testing a hundred people from the Realm and last year only twelve were taken. The odds are-"

"The odds are stacked a certain way, I just know it," Dad growled. "We must be prepared."

"What happens if we pass?" I asked, wanting to know our options so

72

we could find a choice, a sliver of light between two chasms of hellish dark. Though I wasn't sure what I was expecting him to say. How could he know anything about it?

"You'll be taken away," Dad bit out.

"Where to?" Callie whispered, her green eyes flaring with the same fear I felt rattling my heart.

"Somewhere you won't come back from," Dad murmured, a deep crease forming between his eyes.

Despite the strength he always exuded, in times like this, when hope drifted a little out of reach, I saw the broken man in him. The one who had fought to keep us from this world and failed, who had lost his wife and who had never truly recovered since. He was so desperate to save us that everything was to the detriment of himself, and I wished for once I could save him instead. To hold him and promise everything would be alright, but I didn't want to lie to him, just as he had never lied to me. And I couldn't vow that everything would be okay when maybe it really wouldn't be this time.

"There's something you aren't saying," I said, seeing a secret rising in his eyes.

He sighed, moving to sit in his armchair and motioning us both toward the couch. Secrets never lasted long between any of us, and something told me I wasn't going to like the reveal of this one.

We did as he'd asked and sat, Callie's jaw gritted against all the words she was biting back. Dad was the only person she ever held her tongue for like that.

"I don't know for certain, but those of us who have been around since the beginning have noticed some…similarities about the candidates who are selected whenever the testing is done," he started, his frown only deepening.

"Such as?" I prompted.

"They only pick people over the age of twenty-one and never the elderly. It's usually more women than men; all fit, strong, healthy-"

"What's your point?" Callie pushed, and Dad sighed.

"I don't know. Some people mutter about them…upping their numbers-"

"You mean turning us?" I said in horror while Callie shoved right out of her seat, a snarl ripping from her lips as she pointed at the door.

"If that motherfucker or any other of his kind tries to turn me into a monster like them, I'll kill them," she hissed.

"How?" I bit back, not meaning it to sound as harsh as it did, but she knew as well as we all did that there was no killing them.

"If not them, then me," she said darkly, accepting the truth of my accusation. "I'd sooner death than that."

I gaped at her, unsure what to even say, the idea so horrifying it didn't bear thinking about, but the alternative...did I feel any differently? Wouldn't I sooner pierce my own heart with a blade than face that fate?

"There are laws," I protested, shoving that abhorrent thought from my head. "They don't turn humans. Never. Their numbers-"

"All we really know about them is what *they* tell us," Dad growled. "So how can we trust a single word they say?"

"Then what are we supposed to do?" I demanded, standing again too, and Dad followed me to his feet, taking hold of us and pulling us into his arms like we were two little girls in need of their daddy. But this world hadn't ever really allowed us to be that; we'd learned early on that survival was the only thing that mattered, and our upbringing had simply been an exercise in making sure we did.

Dad started muttering to himself, his thoughts clearly moving too fast for him to verbalise them all at once. The longer I stood there in his arms with his scent of musk surrounding me, the more fear crept into my bones. If Dad was afraid, I knew we should be too. I just didn't know how to avoid this fate if it had already been decided for us.

"We might not pass," Callie offered, and Dad nodded, though he didn't seem convinced.

"Hopefully not, little sun. I just need to think a while." He let us go, and I could feel him dismissing us as he moved to brace his hands on the kitchen counter and frown into the empty sink.

Callie and I moved back to our bedroom in tense silence, shutting ourselves away, knowing Dad always thought best in solitude.

Our two single beds were practically touching in the small space, just a small path between them which led up to the lonely window.

Perched on the one bedside table in the room was a half-burnt candle and a stagnant glass of water.

Last night, Callie and I had kept the candle alight longer than usual, telling each other stories and imagining a life beyond the Realm. Fantasy was my favourite way to escape this world, but life always dragged me back kicking and screaming. The reality was, we were trapped here, and our conjured dreams of safety had just been thoroughly stamped out.

No pretty delusions came to me now, my imagination trickling into darker realms, where fangs grew in my mouth and a hunger for blood awoke in my belly. I shuddered at the vivid image my mind painted for me, and as I looked to Callie, I couldn't help but picture her like one of them too, her beauty heightened to the point of abnormal. The idea of her being turned into one of them was somehow more awful than being turned myself.

I dropped onto my bed and Callie sat on hers, our knees nearly touching. The room seemed more monotone than usual, even my sister's golden hair appeared dimmer, her green eyes glazed as her thoughts ran away with her.

"Where did you get the food?" I whispered, wanting to speak about anything else but our encounter with Wolfe.

"There's a way out. I told you Thomas was getting supplies from beyond the fence." Her eyes lit up with mischief as she reached under my bed, extracting the bag and pouring the contents onto the mattress. Eleven tins of food and three pairs of thermal underwear made up the haul, and I sucked in a breath, my stomach growling desperately and an impossible wave of joy cresting in my chest. I couldn't remember the last time I'd felt full, but there was enough food here to fill our bellies for an entire week.

"Oh shit," I breathed as realisation stabbed at me, bursting the happiness which had blossomed at the sight of the haul and tainting it with concern. "If they find out, Callie, they'll-"

"They won't find out," she insisted. "Thomas has been sneaking in and out for months. If that giant dipshit can do it, then I certainly can."

"It won't go unnoticed forever," I said, feeling like we were on track for destruction at this rate. The testing, Wolfe, and now this. We were in serious trouble one way or the other, and the look in Callie's green eyes said there would be no talking her out of this madness even if I could summon the energy to try. But as I looked at the food again, I knew I wouldn't. It was selfish and reckless, but a continued food supply would keep us alive through the winter…assuming we were still here to eat it.

"You're crazy and I love you. But just be careful, and let me help next time, okay?" I said, frowning at her split lip. "What really happened to you?"

"Thomas punched me in the fucking face. Kicked me while I was down too." She scowled, her fingers knotting in her bed sheets like she wished it was his neck, and anger sparked inside me.

"Shit, Callie, how did you even escape him? That asshole is huge-"

"I maybe cracked his head open with a bag full of tinned food." She tried to look innocent, but she wasn't fooling me with that smug as shit gleam in her eyes.

"Oh hell. Is he-"

"I left him licking his wounds and warned him to keep out of my damn way. It's all good, Monty," she swore, but that didn't sound good to me. It sounded like she'd made an enemy who would be aching for another opportunity to get back at her. But, of course, she didn't see it that way. Callie was basically a magnet for trouble, and there was no chance of keeping her from it.

"And maybe there was a teeny tiny little rotter out there which I had to run from," she added before I could release a stream of abuse against Thomas, my mind jarred from that new information.

"A rotter?" I gasped, fear splintering through me, the fact that those things were even real scoring through my mind.

She fell into the story, telling me everything, my imagination running rampant over all she'd been through. I was scared for her life at points, even though she was right here in front of me to prove she'd made it out alive, but the excitement in her voice spilled into me too. It was a whole new world out there, one that was full of peril, but so much freedom too, and she'd stolen a moment in it.

"Maybe we won't be here forever." Callie's mouth pulled up into a grin, and I knew she wasn't talking about the testing.

"What do you mean?" I asked.

"We could leave. Take Dad and get out of here. You heard what he said; he thinks we'll be selected. I won't become one of those monsters. And I don't want to die either. What if this is all just fate coming together, me finding a way out of the Realm, the testing being today-"

"We wouldn't get two hundred feet before they caught us. And then they'd throw us all into the blood bank." My hands shook with the mere idea of it. All our lives, we'd looked out for each other. The three of us. Now our safety seemed like an illusion. But leaving was just another way of getting ourselves strung up and drained.

Callie knotted her fingers together, thinking on it. "Maybe there's a better world beyond the fences, Monty."

I cringed at the nickname she knew I hated, but she continued on, ignoring my expression.

"We've always dreamed about it. What if there are still places out there like the ones in Dad's stories? And even if there's not, do you really want to spend your whole life in the Realm? Or worse, face whatever the results of that fucking test might bring our way?"

My gut prickled. I didn't want that. No one wanted that. Regular blood-givings may have made us valuable to the vampires now, but we all knew what happened when we grew old, useless, weak.

An ache grew in my chest.

"Of course I don't," I sighed. "Shit, Callie, I want freedom more than anything. But if we try to escape and get caught, it's over for us."

"I know," she said earnestly, reaching out to rest a hand on my knee. "But Dad's convinced we're going to pass the testing, and when has he ever been wrong?"

I swallowed the sharp lump rising in my throat.

"Never," I whispered, and I looked to the window, my gaze trailing over the bleak sky and latching onto a faraway bird soaring through the clouds. My mind fixed on it, and I let my thoughts sail through those clouds too, summoning the false tingle of water droplets against my skin, but Callie squeezed my leg to get my attention again.

"Don't check out, Monty. I need you," she urged, and I blinked hard as I looked to her, my fantasy tossing me back into reality without grace.

But I knew what I wanted now. I was tired of chasing freedom in the false illusions in my mind, and if this was a choice between being taken away from Dad and forced into a dreaded fate, or risking everything for true freedom, then I knew the path I wanted to take.

A knock came at the door and Dad entered, a grim expression pinching his features. He was probably more of a rebel than us at times and the dark glint in his eyes told me he had come to a conclusion, but Callie spoke before he could.

"We're leaving," she said, and he released a breath of amusement.

"You stole the words right from the root of my tongue, baby girl," he said, resting his shoulder against the doorway. "I can get some shovels from the market, maybe we can dig at night and-"

"No need," Callie interjected. "I know a way out." She lifted her chin and gestured to the haul on the bed, making his eyebrows arch in shock.

"Holy shit, are the fates really aligning for us?" he muttered, his thumb tracking over the delicate gold wedding ring he wore on a silver chain around his neck. It was mom's, of course. And he never took it off.

"The patrols will be extra tight while that Elite bastard is still here," I said thoughtfully, adrenaline washing into my blood. "The guards always try to impress them with how vigilant they are, so getting past them is going to be a bitch of a problem."

"Yeah, the vampires will be on their best behaviour today, and we can't risk it at night, so we wait until tomorrow morning-" Callie said.

"And hope the sun's shining," Dad finished for her, solidifying our decision.

"Shit, we're really doing this," I whispered.

"We're really doing this," Callie said with a laugh, and the room seemed to brighten again as rays of sunlight streamed through my chest.

If we could pull this off, we might actually reach the freedom we'd craved our whole lives. Maybe we'd find somewhere the sun shone all day, where the bloodsuckers could never find us. I could almost see it now, somewhere green and beautiful and entirely ours. Somewhere we never again had to flinch from sparking cattle prods or cringe at bells that tolled like the tome of death.

Callie looked between us with eager enthusiasm. "If this is kismet, then I've never known such a clear sign – the stars are practically screaming at us to change our destiny. Short of one of them tearing down to earth and making a deal with us in person, I don't think they could send us a better signal to do this," she said, her confidence unwavering, and damn, I loved her for that.

"Then you'd better show us the way out, little sun," Dad said, and I noticed he had a kitchen knife in his hand, his fingers spinning it with a vicious skill. "Because I'm not letting those sons of bitches take my daughters anywhere."

# CALLIE

## CHAPTER FIVE

I didn't sleep that night. There was no way I could switch off the swirling thoughts which chased their way through my brain. We were leaving the Realm. I didn't know if it would be the most exciting thing I'd ever done or the most terrifying. Both, I guessed.

The biggest question I kept turning over was where we would go once we got out. Dad remembered the world before the vampires, but the places he'd known had been mostly destroyed in the Final War. Even if he could figure out somewhere for us to go, there was no way of knowing if it was safe. Or even if it still existed.

South had been his suggestion, our current location on the upper west coast leant itself to rain and overcast weather, meaning the vampires thrived here. The further south we got, the brighter the sun shone and the longer it shone for. More sun equalled less vampires. Probably. Hopefully. At least during the day.

We'd be heading towards a hope and a dream, an imagined paradise where humans roamed free like the animals Dad had told us about in so many stories. A made-up sanctuary which likely didn't exist at all. Which really wasn't very reassuring. *Stop being so fucking negative, Callie. Better to aim for freedom than to pass their test and face whatever consequences go alongside that.*

I rolled over for the hundredth time and considered voicing my concerns to Montana. We'd talked ourselves hoarse when we'd finally turned in for the night and eventually drifted into silence, but I was sure she was still awake too.

Somehow, breaking the illusion of sleep didn't appeal to me though. We'd promised Dad that we would try and get some rest before our journey, and starting up another conversation felt like breaking my word.

It wasn't like there was anything she or I could say anyway. We were heading into the unknown. Plans wouldn't matter one bit once we made it past the fence. We knew nothing of the world beyond the Realm aside from the stories Dad had taught us. I didn't even know if those were all true. He'd told us just as many myths and legends as he had memories of the way the world used to be.

I could very well have gotten some of them muddled up in my mind. Maybe there really were trolls hiding under bridges and it was the giant redwood trees he'd visited with Mom that didn't exist. The more I thought about it, the more my brain ached.

At least I'd gone to bed with a full stomach. We hadn't held back on demolishing the supplies I'd found. Dad had reasoned that we'd need our strength for tomorrow, and I wasn't going to argue against a decent meal. We planned on collecting more supplies of food and clothing from the apartment block I'd raided when we got that far anyway.

I'd had to admit to Dad about my run-in with the rotter, and although he'd about lost his mind, he'd agreed it was better for us to know the risks those things being out there might pose. We were going to need weapons in case we ran into any more of them on our journey, and I was just hoping to hell that we wouldn't.

*Is there really any way we can survive this?*

The negative voice in the back of my skull wouldn't be silenced by the promise of a warm coat and tins of supplies. I sighed loudly and pressed my thin pillow over my face, resisting the urge to scream into it.

*Maybe we shouldn't risk running.* There was a good chance we wouldn't pass their test despite Dad's fears, then we could just carry on living here. I'd have to get up and follow my normal pattern of hiding in the ruins and avoiding interactions with the people who lived near us. Keeping to myself so that I didn't have to risk feeling the pain of loss when someone went missing. Slowly watching my family starve to death while the vampires breathed down our necks, just waiting for an excuse to take us and bleed us dry...

The thought alone was enough to make my heart sink. Although the idea of escape was terrifying, it was also the realisation of a dream I'd never dared to believe in before.

Life in the Realm was no life at all. The only time I ever felt free was when I escaped into the false reality of one of Dad's stories, and I always had to come crashing back to the misery of our lives when it ended. This could be our one shot at true freedom. And no matter how fleeting it might end up being, we *had* to take it. Maybe even one day of freedom would be worth whatever punishment they gave us for it if they caught us. Especially if the alternatives were as bad as we feared.

My mind drifted to the blood bank, and I wondered if that was really the case. The stories about what happened to the people who got sent there were so horrendous that I struggled to believe they were true. But sometimes at night when the wind was blowing in the right direction, we could hear the screams coming from that place.

It wasn't even in our Realm. The huge building was at the top of a large hill miles to the south, beyond the ruined city and a band of woodland. But we'd had the direction pointed out to us on multiple occasions, the threats of what went on there hanging in the air at all times; whispers, rumours, warnings. The vampires got an ugly gleam in their eyes whenever they spoke of that place, the darkness of their nature showing in the excitement they clearly felt over sending any one of us there.

On the occasional bright day, black smoke poured from what was rumoured to be a giant chimney which dominated one end of the building, rising up to taint the clouds above. And though it was too far away for us to really smell it, sometimes I woke with the taste of ash on my tongue. Like a warning about what would happen to me if I ended up there. That was where we went if we didn't follow their laws. That was what happened to anyone who disobeyed them. No one who was sent there ever came back, but the vampires sometimes liked to taunt the people of our Realm about the horrors within. Their fear mongering was spread far and wide, whispers passed from one human to another until they were added to or changed, twisted into something wholly new. I didn't know what was true, but I damn well knew to fear that place regardless.

A shiver ran down my spine and the doubts crept in again. *Is it worth the risk?* It had to be. My soul yearned to be free, and I had to embrace the chance to get out of here.

My heart fluttered like a butterfly trapped in a jar, aching for the lid to be lifted. Freedom. It was like a whisper in the dark that had always called to me, and I hungered for it. I'd never wanted anything the way I yearned for that sweet promise. No one to answer to, no one to take my blood from me for their own sustenance. To be more than just a food source for a bunch of parasites. A life of my own.

A smile tugged at my lips, and the fear slid back like a retreating tide.

Our battered blind was pretty useless at actually covering our window, so I watched as the space beyond it slowly brightened into a new day.

I gave up on any pretence of sleep and got to my feet to look out properly. Between my worrying through the night, I'd desperately wished for a sunny day to aid in our escape, but luck wasn't on our side. There was no sign of the sun beyond the thick grey clouds which blocked out the sky. At least it wasn't raining. But I'd have given anything for a blue sky and blazing sunshine to give us more time to run without them being able to follow.

"Do you really think this will work?" Montana asked from her bed beside me.

I looked around and found her wide chestnut eyes gazing up at me from beneath her blanket. I didn't blame her for staying put; the temperature had dropped below freezing in the night and my toes were already beginning to feel numb despite my thick socks.

"It has to," I replied more bravely than I felt.

She didn't voice any more doubts, even though I could see them written across her features. I was sure a hundred of my own were painted on my face for her to see too. No matter how much of a front we put up, we'd never been able to lie to each other. We were bound even more deeply than simple blood. Twins couldn't keep secrets from each other, even if we tried.

I caught her fingers between mine and held on tightly.

"We're going to be *free*, Monty," I whispered, smiling at her. She didn't even protest at the nickname she hated as a smile gripped her features too.

"Free," she breathed in agreement, and I could hear the same wonder in her voice that I felt. If we just clung to that hope, then the fear could hold nothing to it.

We'd both been born prisoners here; the concept of freedom wasn't something either of us could fully understand. And yet it called our names in the silence of the cold nights. Whispered to us over the growling of our empty stomachs. It was the voice we'd never dared to listen to before, but now that we were, it was screaming our names.

I wrapped my arms around her and gave her a tight squeeze before heading for the bathroom.

As I entered the small space, the light bulb flickered above the cracked basin, and I shivered, hurrying to brush my teeth in the ice-cold water.

When I was finished, I observed myself in the small mirror, hoping to banish some of the fear that glowed in my green eyes before I had to head outside. The mirror was tarnished and had a jagged crack running through the centre of it, so I'd never really seen a good reflection of my face.

I wondered how I looked to other people. Would they see the fear I was trying to hide? Worse than that, would they see the truth? If anyone guessed that we were going to run, then they might tell the vampires. Turning in traitors got you extra rations, new clothes. I couldn't expect any loyalty from the rest of the humans in the Realm. They had their own families to worry about, and they wouldn't think twice about handing us in.

News would have spread by now about our tests.

I started brushing my blonde hair, teasing out the tangles caused by my restless night. It hung to my waist in loosely twisting curls. I knew it would be more practical to cut it short, but I couldn't bring myself to do it. It was the one thing I'd gotten from our mom. Whenever I thought of her, I had trouble remembering much about her features apart from her long golden hair and bright green eyes. It was soothing somehow to carry that little reminder of her wherever I went, even if it was hard work to look after.

Once I'd removed the knots, I expertly braided my hair down my back to keep it under control. I rarely left it loose during the day despite how much I loved it. It attracted too much attention, and I preferred to go unnoticed.

One complication I didn't need in this life was the attention of men. At least not anything serious. I'd spent time seeing several men over the past two years. My type was mostly focused on hot guys who were assholes so that I could use them for sex without needing to worry about falling for them – while being extra damn careful not to fall pregnant. Any time one of them asked to make it into something more or if ever I felt the stirring of actual fondness for them beyond orgasms, I'd cut it off.

Relationships just gave you someone else to love and lose. It was hard enough worrying about Montana and Dad all the time without adding anyone else to the mix. Losing Mom had nearly killed Dad, and I could still see the pain of her loss hiding beneath the surface when he thought we weren't looking, even after all these years. So a man wasn't a distraction I wanted or needed, meaning I didn't have one to say goodbye to.

Once I was done, I headed into the kitchen and started on a big batch of pancakes. Seeing as I'd been skipping the first meal of the day a lot recently to preserve our rations, I didn't see the harm in indulging now. We wouldn't be coming back here anyway, and there was no point in leaving it behind. Besides, a big meal was just what we needed to set us up for the day ahead.

Dad appeared at the scent of the food, and I dished out the first plate.

His hair was black like Montana's, but a few grey strands ran through it now. He smiled enthusiastically at the meal as I pushed it towards him, but it didn't reach his eyes, his concern over our plans clearly weighing on him.

"Are you ready?" he asked seriously.

"No," I replied honestly. "But how could I ever be ready to run away from everything I've ever known? I'm excited though, if that's not insane."

"It's not. Do you know how long I've waited to get a chance to show you the real world? To show you all the things I told you about? I know this is danger incarnate, but I'm excited too, baby girl."

I smiled, relieved at seeing that same fire in him. I may not have inherited his looks, but we had the same spirit. Montana had always been more fascinated by the romance and magic in his stories, but I'd always loved them for the adventure. Though I'd never thought I'd be able to see what the world held beyond our Realm, I'd dreamed about it every night for as long as I could remember. I wanted to be Jason leading the Argonauts to find the Golden Fleece or Hercules fighting the Hydra. In a terrifying way, all of my wishes were coming true, a quest of its own presenting itself, the prize a far greater treasure than any of the stories spoke of if only we could get far enough to claim it.

"I've dreamed of getting you girls out of this fucking place since the moment they herded us in here, and it's finally happening." His eyes glimmered with enough hope at the possibility that I put my fears firmly aside. I needed to focus on this plan. There was no point in wasting energy on the idea of it not working.

Montana came out of the bathroom with her dark hair brushed and her cheeks flushed from washing her face in the cold water. She accepted a plate of pancakes, and I took my own over to the small table to join my family in devouring them.

"Did you sleep okay?" I asked her, already knowing the answer from the shadows under her eyes.

"Like a pig with a prickly pear shoved up its ass, you?" Montana replied and I snorted a laugh that was echoed by Dad.

"About the same," I agreed. "But with a pokey potato jammed

against its back too."

"And a horny nit's nest on its head," she added.

"A what?" I winkled my nose in thought, unable to place that.

"Hornet's nest," Dad corrected with a smirk, and Montana blew out a breath of amusement at her own mistake.

The three of us managed to find more laughs between bites of food, and as was always the case when we were together, the darkness of the world lifted just a little. Enough to see a glimpse of the sun beyond, though unfortunately the weather clearly had no plans of mirroring the little rays of sunshine we'd summoned indoors.

"Just you wait until you see the ocean," Dad said, and my heart rate picked up.

"Tell us about it again," I urged.

"It's like a slice of a summer sky placed right at the edge of the world," he said, always having such a way with words, artfully painting the beauty of his past into our minds. "The sand runs right up to the edge of it, as golden as your hair Callie."

I hooked the tail of my braid around my finger, and Montana rested her chin on the heel of her hand as she waited for Dad to go on, always so hungry to escape into her imagination.

"The sun loves the ocean, it dances over your skin and sparkles on all the waves, beckoning you into the water," he continued, a wistful ache in his eyes. I hated to think of how much he must miss it. At least Montana and I had never known anything different than this hollow life, but once upon a time, Dad's life had been rich, full of daily miracles I couldn't even fathom.

"It's waiting for you two out there," he promised, emotion blazing across his dark eyes, but his features were hard, his jaw tightening with a fiery determination to see us get there.

"It's waiting for all three of us," I said.

"Four," Montana said, reaching out to touch Mom's wedding band on Dad's little finger. "She feels closer today somehow. Is it crazy to think she might be here now, ready to come with us?"

Dad cleared his throat, his fingers curling around Montana's and squeezing as a lump raised in my throat. "Yeah, baby girl. She's here.

And we're gonna get her out of here too and find her a damn good place for her spirit to rest."

Tears pricked my eyes, and I blinked them back with a fierce resolve. I needed to be strong today so I could lead my family to the ruins and into the great unknown beyond the fence.

"Freedom's calling," I said, and the pain in the air gave way to something pure and sweet and good that chased away the dark again.

We all smiled at each other eagerly as the reality of what we were about to do settled over us. Yeah, it would be dangerous, but if it all worked out then we would really be free. For the first time in mine and Montana's lives, we would be able to choose our own destinies.

I fell on my pancakes ravenously, pushing aside the twist of guilt I always felt when I ate well. For once, we weren't being frugal, and I was confident that we could scavenge more than enough food outside the Realm in the abandoned buildings.

As we finished our breakfast, I pulled the brown packet I'd found yesterday from my pocket and held it up to show them.

"Just wait until you try this," I said keenly as I broke the brown food into three equal pieces.

"What is that? It kinda looks like a solidified turd," Montana said as she reached for it unenthusiastically.

"Trust me, it tastes better than a turd," I promised. "And you'll know, because you ate that rat turd last week."

"I thought someone had spilled some raisins," Montana said in horror at the memory. "And I didn't eat any, I just, maybe, touched one."

"I bet you had a little nibble," I teased, and Montana swiped at me, the two of us grinning as we shoved each other.

"You're the one who's shown up here with a turd bar," Montana tossed back.

Dad picked up his slab of the food, not even attempting to break up our fight as he turned it over in his fingers. "Well goddamn, I haven't seen chocolate in a long time. Your mom loved the stuff. I used to pick up a bar every Friday night on my way home from work and we'd share it while watching trashy TV."

"The picture box thing?" I asked as Montana and I called a truce. Dad had explained about the kinds of technology they'd had before the Final War and the vampires seizing control, but hardly any of it was allowed in the Realm anymore. The only TV I'd ever seen was the CCTV monitors at the Emporium, and I couldn't really imagine myself wanting to spend hours watching that.

"Yeah," he laughed at the look of confusion on my face.

"Well, if it was Mom's favourite..." Montana took a tentative bite, looking as though she'd already decided she wouldn't like it, but as the chocolate hit her tastebuds, her face transformed. "Oh shit."

I grinned at her and quickly followed her lead, taking a bite of my own chocolate and closing my eyes for a moment as I lost myself in the taste of it. I wasn't surprised it had been Mom's favourite. I couldn't imagine anyone eating it and not wanting more.

As we finished eating, Dad took our plates and placed them on the counter beside the sink. He didn't wash them though and gave me a knowing smile as he walked away from the mess. We wouldn't be needing them again anyway.

I headed back to our room and grabbed my pack. We couldn't take much with us or it would arouse suspicion, but each of us could carry a small bag without being noticed. It wasn't like I had much worth bringing anyway.

I tossed in a small sketch our mom had drawn of a soaring eagle. The corners of the page were wrinkled and marked from years of me holding it, but I'd always loved looking at the way she'd captured the bird's movement. Dad had other pieces she'd drawn, but it had been hard to come by the supplies she'd needed for her art, so there weren't as many as there should have been. The vampires even took that from her.

Aside from that, there was nothing personal I wanted to bring, so I added a change of clothes and my toothbrush to the bag and then zipped it shut.

I dressed in the thermal underwear I'd found yesterday and topped it with a pair of faded denim jeans and a long-sleeved shirt which had probably been a much brighter shade of green when it was new. I threw on my boots, a black sweater, and my dark red coat to finish it off and headed for the door again.

Montana opened it before I got there and gave me a tight smile as she collected her own bag from her bed. She was dressed in her best clothes too, though they weren't anything special; dark jeans, boots, and her own well-worn coat. I hoped we'd be able to upgrade our over-used outfits quickly once we were out of the Realm.

I glanced at the pair of beds, realising this would be the last I ever saw of them. We'd spent every night of our lives in this room, and the idea of leaving it behind was scary, but it was liberating too.

"Is it strange that I won't miss this place?" I asked as we gave the bedroom one final look.

"This might be the only place we've ever lived, but it was never our home," she replied, an iciness coating her words that was aimed entirely at the vampires.

"Then it's about time we went and found somewhere to call home for real," Dad said loudly behind us, and I flinched a little at the unexpected sound of his voice, finding him standing there like a menace with a kitchen knife in his hand. I'd never seen him hurt a fly, but he had this aura about him that spoke of the brutality he would fall to for all of us. That was Dad, a beast who had been caged for far too long, who would see his captors dead, given the chance.

"Let's get going," he said, stowing the knife beneath his tan coat, and we all headed out of the bedroom together in silence.

I didn't look back. I didn't care about leaving it behind, and I hoped I'd never see it again.

# MONTANA

## CHAPTER SIX

There were enough people wandering the streets that we milled among them for the first few miles, not walking too fast or too slow, just making a casual path across the Realm and drawing little to no attention. Everyone's business was their own here, and it was rare for anyone to ask questions. The most common interaction we had with people was the odd, awkward eye contact that was quickly dropped and forgotten. It was entirely normal, and it felt far too easy.

Slowly, the buildings around us became more derelict until we reached a point in the road which no one usually ventured beyond. The ruins awaited us down that cracked and broken concrete, where tall weeds had sprouted and reclaimed the man-made streets. The persistent rain made sure the worn roofs were turning green, moss and ivy climbing into every space, competing for dominance in a land that had once been stolen from them. Maybe all life found a way to thrive against the odds, and given enough time, we could thrive again like this too, reclaim what had been stolen from us just as the plants had here.

"Where now, Callie?" Dad murmured, tossing a subtle glance over his shoulder as we slowed our pace. I didn't look but eyed his expression closely until he gave us a little nod to assure us there was no one on our trail.

"This way," my sister whispered, quickening her pace down a side alley where the shadows were deeper.

The air became even cooler as Dad and I followed her into the passage, the tall walls either side of us looking one strong wind away from tumbling down. Callie's golden hair was like a beacon ahead of us, lighting the way on and brightening the shade.

We moved in tense silence, our footsteps sounding too loud as our boots hit the damp concrete. But there was nothing here except the wind and the whisper of a lost world that had once belonged to our kind. Now, it was little more than a ghost of a violent past, a reminder of who had really won the Final War.

I kept glancing over my shoulder as I walked, paranoia gripping me as I half expected to find vampires racing down the bramble-strewn path at my back, but all was still, silent, nothing here but the lumps of brick which had fallen from the wrecked walls long, long ago.

I'd always wondered why they'd included so much of the ruined earth and so many of the destroyed buildings in the piece of land they had selected for our cage, the remnants of the damage left in the wake of the Final War mocking us from the edges of the Realm. Was it to remind us of what lay beyond the wire fences? To make us think twice about running because they wanted us to believe there was nothing left beyond them? Yeah, that sounded about right.

We rounded onto a brighter street, and static crackled in my ears before I even saw the electric fence that slashed through the land, giving a view of a barren world beyond. More ruins for as far as the eye could see and nothing but a few ravens perched on the rooftops to witness our escape. Or perhaps our fall.

Grass grew up high and tickled the metal wire that parted us from the outside world, dancing with the current that ran through the metal, a promise of death at a single touch.

"There's the motherfucker in all her glory," Dad said, resting his hands on his hips in the most typical Dad pose I'd ever seen. "She's a deadly bitch if ever I saw one."

Callie picked up a rock, tossing it at the fence, and a flash of electricity ricocheted out from it in a wave of blue sparks.

"Why is it that whenever I mention danger, one of my daughters has to go dancing with it?" Dad said sternly, and Callie tossed a mischievous smile back at him.

"Because even chickens in a coop like to wave their feathery asses at a fox sometimes," I said.

Callie jogged on, leading the way further into the ruins, and the wind sent a shiver through to my bones as I kept a steady pace behind her at Dad's side.

Dad dropped an arm over my shoulders, tugging me hard against him and speaking in a low voice. "You ever get cornered by a fox, then you fight with all the feathery, beaky madness of a hen who's got nothing to lose, you hear me?"

"But you're always telling me to keep my head, to swallow my anger and breathe," I reminded him, and he shot me an intense look.

"Those rules won't apply beyond that fence, little moon," he said, and trepidation echoed through me at the underlying fear in his voice.

I found myself nodding, but I'd spent so long crushing down that rage inside me, I didn't even know how to unleash it fully.

Callie turned down another overgrown road and a crunch made me gasp. I cursed as I spotted the broken glass beneath my boot, and Dad and Callie braced in fear before realising the source.

We shared a little nervous laughter and walked on towards a shattered house, just a hulk of stone under the grey sky.

Dad said bombs had rained down on the world during the Final War, people dying in their millions in every country on the planet. The war where humans on both sides had fought so hard to win while ultimately causing nothing but loss for us all.

I felt exposed as we worked our way through the labyrinth of broken stone and fallen mortar. Why Callie liked coming to this place was a mystery to me. It was a constant reminder of the war that had landed us in this hellhole, and there was nothing here but broken dreams and desolation.

"This is it," Callie announced keenly as we arrived in a wide courtyard where a damaged old fountain awaited us. She leapt up onto the wall at the edge of it, turning to us and gesturing for us to follow.

I threw a surreptitious glance at the buildings around us, darkened doorways and broken windows creating perfect hiding places for the vampires. But why would they skulk in the shadows when they could descend on us with a fist of fury and power? They had no need to sneak around after humans when they were so perfectly designed to hunt us in plain sight.

My pulse ticked faster as I followed Callie over the wall, wading after her through the green water that had collected there. By some miracle, my boots didn't leak, and I made it to the high wall on the other side before hoisting myself up and clambering over it in her wake.

Dad was close behind me, his movements making far more noise than mine, and my heart thrashed in my chest, urging me to move quicker in case a monster's ears decided to turn this way.

I landed on a patch of concrete beyond the fountain, the fence frighteningly close here and a wall hiding this spot almost entirely from view.

Callie pointed to a metal drain cover on the ground, and we shared a look mixed with glee and terror. Moss covered it, but the edges were clear, proving it had recently been moved, and anticipation burrowed into me as I found myself staring at the escape I had never dreamed would be truly possible.

Dad moved forward, bending low to open it, and when it didn't immediately budge, Callie and I dropped down to help him. I clawed my fingers into the groove at the edge of the metal cover, and the moment we managed to tug it free from the sticky sludge keeping it in place, Dad dragged it aside, the sound of it grinding against the concrete filling me with terror.

We all fell deathly quiet, listening for any response to that sound in the distance. The rush of fast footsteps, the ringing of an alarm bell. But all remained still, silent.

A dark hole gazed back at me from the drain, and the scent of mildew and old sewage reached my nose, making me hold my hand to my mouth.

"It's dark and wet and so gross, but it's not far to the other side,"

Callie said, moving onto a ladder to one side of it.

She descended into the abyss, and I hung my legs over the edge, placing my feet on the first metal rung of the ladder. Carefully, I eased myself lower, counting my breaths as I went down, down, down, glancing up at my dad as he watched me go, his raven hair falling forward around his face.

He moved onto the ladder last, pausing to drag the manhole cover back into place above us so I could no longer see the Realm, and the reality of what we were doing closed in all around me alongside the dark.

I made it to the bottom just as a scratching noise followed a hiss and a match illuminated before my eyes in Callie's hand.

"Hey, Monty," she whispered.

"*Callie*," I complained half-heartedly. I hated that damn nickname, but it was hard to care so much when we were in an old drain with freedom calling our names on the other end of it. "Where next?"

"Not far now," she promised. "You're gonna lose your shit when you see the supplies out there. There was this coat-" she moaned almost sexually. "I need the coat, Monty. I *need* it." She grabbed my arm and squeezed, and I released a laugh.

"You can have the damn coat, and as many turd bars as you like too, just get us to them," I said, and she looked to Dad as he stepped off the ladder.

"Come on then," she urged, a giddiness about her as she held the match higher to light our way forward. The old tunnel was nothing but rubble and dirt, and ahead, a glimpse of daylight shone like a guiding star.

I followed my twin through the tunnel, having to traverse lumps of brick and rock before making it to a huge heap of rubble where the drain had been caved in to secure the Realm. Callie grinned through the light of another match, pointing to a crawl space near the roof before flicking the match aside and scrambling away up the pile of broken bricks.

I followed her through the shadows, the dim light ahead almost entirely blocked as she scrambled through the crawl space, but eventually the passage opened up again and a ladder came into view, illuminated by a circular shaft of light.

My throat thickened and I didn't know if I was terrified, thrilled, or a concoction of both, but I knew one thing. I needed to get out of here and taste free air, I needed to run and run and run away from this place with my family and find any other life but the one we'd been trapped in forever.

We hurried up to the ladder and Dad strode past both of us, giving us hard looks.

"I'll go first, wait until I tell you to follow. If I don't, then you both need to run back to the Realm and get home. Don't waste a second, don't look back, do *not* come for me."

"Dad-" I started my refusal, but he shook his head to silence me.

"Do as I say," he commanded in his most authoritative tone.

"We're not going to leave you," Callie said, and I nodded my agreement of that.

"We're in this together," I said. "We're a team. You always said that."

"Not today," he growled. "Today, I'm your father, and I am in charge. You will run if I demand it."

I clenched my teeth stubbornly and Callie pursed her lips, but there was clearly no point arguing. It didn't mean either of us were going to abandon him though.

His face softened and he moved forward, kissing Callie on the forehead, then tugging me close to do the same. We leaned into him, embracing, holding onto this moment which felt safe yet so fleeting, it was already turning to ash and fluttering away on the wind.

"I love you both," he breathed. "You are the most beautiful creations of my life, and I would not have chosen to spend my days anywhere but here at your sides."

"Stop," I gritted out as my heart thumped furiously against my ribs. "You're saying goodbye."

"I don't do goodbyes, baby girl," he said, releasing us and cocking his head to one side with that roguish confidence of his as he looked between us with all the admiration of an artist before his finest painting. "But I'll be damned if I don't say I love yous on the cusp of oblivion."

He turned, scaling the ladder before we could say a word in response to that, but I instinctually moved closer to Callie, our arms brushing and our bond sharpening for a moment in the dark.

Dad heaved himself out of the drain, and I craned my neck to try and catch sight of him, but all I could see was the sombre sky.

Callie moved forward, placing her hand on the first rung of the ladder. "If he thinks we're just gonna stay down here and run away like little frightened lambs if he tells us to, then-"

"All clear," his voice carried to us, and I sighed my relief.

"Well then," Callie muttered as she stepped on the ladder. "This little lamb is going to get her coat."

"Can the little lamb lead me to some new underwear? I accidentally put on the wedgie panties today," I said, feeling those no-good bastards climbing between my cheeks.

"Oh no, not the wedgie panties," she sympathised.

They blended right in beside my other panties, so I never knew when the wedgie panties were gonna make an appearance. And by the time they started their expedition up my ass, I was always out of the house. Today of all days, I did not need them cursing my ass cheeks. But here we were.

"I'll save your buttcrack, Monty, there's bound to be heaps of new panties out in the free world. Panties designed for premium ass comfort."

I smiled at the thought as she climbed out the top of the drain, and as I followed her up, Dad thrust his hand down to help me to my feet.

My head breached the hole and air rushed into my lungs that tasted like endless possibilities and a future that was starting to feel real enough to touch.

The shadow of a bird sailed over us, and Dad straightened, his hand sliding into his coat to produce the kitchen knife he'd stowed there. "Let's keep moving. We're too close to the fence, we could be easily spotted."

Callie nodded seriously and tension spread between us again as she took off at a fast pace towards an apartment block ahead. I jogged at her side and Dad kept at our backs, like a guardian angel ready to wrap his wings around us and fly us to safety if danger came our way. But sadly, he was capable of no such thing.

Callie pushed through a door, and we followed her into a dingy atrium, gently shutting the door at our backs. It wasn't exactly safety, but we were out of view here, and from the look on Callie's face, I sensed she had a plan.

"I'll go grab some clothes from the apartment I visited last time. There's an old food store across the street that way." She pointed to an exit on the other side of the atrium. "You two head out, grab whatever food you can, and I'll meet you there. Ten minutes max, then we can run into the sunset and all that shit," she said.

"I think we should stay together." Dad frowned.

"It'll be quicker this way," Callie promised. "I'll be fast."

"I just wanna get the hell away from here," I said, glancing over my shoulder, feeling the closeness of the Realm.

"There's no guarantee of supplies beyond this point," Dad said worriedly. "We need to get what we can while it's available to us."

"Then let's stop wasting time." Callie turned and took a door to our right, and I watched her go with concern.

*She'll be fine. She's a badass, and we'll be together again in ten minutes.*

"Let's just hurry up," I said, jogging to the door across the atrium and pushing my way through it, dislodging some dust so it showered over my shoulders.

The street beyond held the promised food store, a sign above it having worn right away, but the glass front of it was miraculously still intact. Dad and I hurried across the street, and he forced the door open with a hard ram of his shoulder, revealing the space beyond.

"Fuck a duck," he exhaled as I followed him inside and my jaw went slack.

"Fuck a whole flock of ducks," I said, taking in the trove we'd just uncovered.

Food.

Tins, packets, bottles, you name it, it was here. Not endless amounts, but enough. Untouched and so freaking close to the Realm that it was an absolute travesty at how hungry we'd gone with all of this so close.

Ripe for the picking.

"You've got to be kidding me," I snarled. "Those assholes. This was here all this time? All this fucking time?" I rounded on Dad, breathless and full of fury.

I could see that same rage in him as he stalked forward and snatched a tin from one of the shelves, squeezing it so hard that the metal buckled in his fist.

I wanted to scream – no, I wanted to fight. I wanted to see those vampires go hungry, I wanted them to feel the pain of starvation, I wanted them to hurt and bleed and-

"Breathe, baby girl," Dad encouraged, placing the tin in his pack and moving forward to cup my cheek. I looked into his chestnut eyes which were a mirror of mine, feeling the burning acidic taste of injustice rising in my throat. "Stay with me. You've got this."

I took a breath, then another, settling down the vicious animal which had awoken inside me, and finding my way back to a calmer, more detached place.

"It's not fair," I whispered, knowing how pointless those words were, how rarely any of us ever bothered to voice them. Because of course it wasn't fair. It wasn't meant to be fair.

Dad dropped his hand from my cheek and gestured to the tins. "Let's go find something fairer then. Grab what you can carry."

My heart lightened at the reminder of how close we were to salvation, and I quickly stowed as much food as I could get into my pack while Dad did the same.

I shouldered the bag, the weight of it a vow of several good meals to come as we exited the store.

The moment my feet hit the cracked tarmac outside, I knew something was wrong. It was a change in the atmosphere, the way the wind seemed to whisper our ruin into the sky. And as the rush of bare footfalls came this way, there was one word that seemed to stand out among the chaos, chiming through my head like my own voice screaming at the top of my lungs.

*Vampire!*

The rotter rounded the apartment block ahead of us, shrieking inhumanly, eyes wide, fangs bared and a look of starved mania about her. My instincts told me to run, but there was no way I was leaving Callie behind, and as Dad took the kitchen knife from his jacket, I knew he had the same inclination.

"Run, Montana," he barked, then he raced forward with the roar of a madman leaving him, swinging the kitchen knife in preparation of the collision.

"No!" I cried in horror, dropping my pack and taking out one of the tin cans with frantic fingers.

I hurled it at the rotter before she made it to my dad and the tin smashed against her face, sending her staggering sideways.

Dad kept running towards her, throwing his full weight at her while she was dazed and sending her flying back into the ground floor window of the apartment block Callie was in. The glass was already half broken, and it shattered further as she went sailing through it with a scream, hands reaching frantically for my dad and her teeth snapping together. Then she was gone, and a faraway thud reached my ears as Dad leaned through the window to look.

"Get back from there," I called in fright, rushing over to him.

"It's alright," he said with a shaky laugh. "The floor's rotted through. She's fallen right into the basement."

"Holy shit." I leaned through the broken window to see, finding the vampire glaring up at us from the gloom below, jumping up at the wall and clawing at it for purchase. But she found none.

"That aim of yours, Monty." Dad turned to me, lifting me up into the air and spinning me around, making me squeak in surprise. He planted me down and scruffed my hair, a wide grin on his face bringing a smile to mine. "That was out of this goddamn world."

I laughed, shoving him back as my heart rate slowed down again. "Well, what about you? You went running in to fight a vampire bare-handed like a freaking wild man."

"I had a knife," he pointed out, but his chest had puffed up and he looked smug as shit.

I frowned, thinking about how badly this could have gone. "We should really get moving. There could be more of them."

"Yeah, Callie will be back any…" He trailed off, his shoulders stiffening and his head snapping around. "D'you hear that?" he hissed at me, and I strained my ears, my pulse working hard to be the only thing I could hear in the quiet street. But then I heard it.

The thundering of heavy footfalls, several sets. Boots.

"Oh fuck," I exhaled in terror, looking up at Dad as that same fear sparked like a livewire in his eyes.

They were moving too fast. Too fast for us to hide, because they were already here. Eight vampires in total with General Wolfe among them, his emerald cloak billowing around him as they ran out onto the street before us.

"Seize them!" General Wolfe ordered, falling to an unnatural halt as the other seven vampires in red cloaks raced past him. His piercing blue eyes drove into me as his lips peeled back in a snarl that spoke of the carnage he wanted to reap here.

Fear snared my heart, and I knew there was no running from this. I wasn't going to die with my tail between my legs, I'd die fighting if I had to die at all.

Dad's gaze met mine for the briefest of moments, grief and regret tarnishing all the hope I'd found there before, and he shook his head the barest fraction in a silent apology before tearing away from me into the fray. His knife was raised, his bellow echoing from wall to broken wall, and I ran after him with a battle cry of my own, no weapon in hand.

A vitriolic hatred gilded my heart, built from years of torment, from the anguish of all that had been stolen from us. They had taken the blood from our veins time and again, and if there was no hope for me now, then at least let me see their blood spill in kind.

# CALLIE

## CHAPTER SEVEN

I dropped the pack of supplies I'd been gathering as I spotted my family through the grimy window of the apartment block. My mouth fell open in horror as I stared at my Dad racing towards eight vampires while wielding an old kitchen knife.

Montana bent down as she ran, grabbing a rock from the rubble at her feet and hurling it at the female vampire who was now racing for her. The monster ducked it, her speed increasing as she charged straight for my sister.

I broke into a sprint, the years of grime which coated the windows all along the ground floor of this building blocking my sight of my family as they fought for the freedom they'd barely even gotten a taste of.

"Dad!" I called desperately, knowing they couldn't hear me but needing them to feel me coming, to know I hadn't abandoned them. "Montana!"

The first door I found rattled violently as I tried to force it open, the locks holding firm despite my desperate need to get to the people I loved more than anything in this world.

My heart throbbed with the agony of my need for them, terror burrowing beneath my skin and taking root in every piece of me as tears sprung from my eyes.

"Not like this," I begged, turning from the door and running for the next, the seconds ticking by, my family fighting for their lives without me there to help them.

"Please," I prayed to no one and nothing, the empty words falling on deaf ears as they always had, any god who had ever watched over my kind having abandoned us to the hands of monsters long ago.

I collided with the door at last, the metal protesting as it flew open, banging into the wall of the alleyway it had dumped me in, then groaning as it swung closed at my back, like it was crying too, like it knew I was already too late and all I was running towards was my own death.

But if that was the case, then so be it. I'd take death at their sides over life without them in it. They were all I had, all I'd ever had and all I ever wanted.

I clambered over a heap of rubble, rocks tumbling aside beneath my feet, my hand slicing open on a piece of metal which jutted out from the pile. I cursed then grabbed it, my bloody fingers slipping on the cold lump of metal which I would use to fight for my fucking life and more importantly, for the lives of those I loved.

I slipped as I crested the heap of rubble, bricks tumbling out beneath my feet and sending me crashing to the ground. I rolled over, my fingernails biting into the cold bricks of the wall to my right as I heaved myself to my feet, my sister's screams echoing out from the patch of light that illuminated the end of the alley.

"I'm coming, Monty," I gasped, my boots pounding the concrete as I broke into a sprint once more, tearing along the narrow alleyway where I caught glimpses of the fight taking place beyond.

Montana raced past the end of the alleyway, her dark hair whipping out behind her as she ran from a vampire with long copper hair, her boots slamming into the concrete and sounding like a war drum in my ears.

I tightened the grip on the lump of metal I'd claimed for a weapon, the slickness of my blood coating it.

"Montana, watch out!" I yelled, urging her into action as the vampire sprinted towards her. She threw herself aside at the last second, ducking low and grabbing a lump of brick right before the vampire collided with her, sending them both crashing to the ground.

I was almost at the end of the alleyway, my sister fighting for her life beneath a monster from legends which should never have come back to life, the weapon in my hand primed to find its rotten heart and banish it from this world.

A door flew open in front of me, and I screamed as a huge figure slammed into me from the darkness within.

The man grabbed my arm and propelled me into the darkness of the building as I yelled out in alarm.

He threw the door closed behind us, leaving only the dim light which made it through the filthy window to see his hulking form as he swung me around towards the wall.

My back collided with it hard enough to shatter the breath in my lungs, and I swung the jagged piece of metal at him as adrenaline rocketed through my veins, my brain whirling to catch up to what was happening.

His forearm smashed against mine just as the tip of my makeshift weapon made contact with his side, his blood spilling, but not nearly enough.

He caught my wrist as I swung at him again, his other forearm smacking against my chest as he shoved me back against the wall, pinning me in place with brute force.

The motherfucker smacked my wrist into the wall so hard that I almost lost my grip on my weapon, a cry catching in my throat at the pain of the blow before he repeated it, twice, three times, until the pain finally forced my grip to release, and the jagged bit of metal clattered to the floor beneath us.

I thrashed against his hold on me, aiming my knee between his legs before he flattened his enormous body to mine, pinning my legs too as I fought to kick and stomp on his feet.

I opened my mouth to scream but his hand slapped down across my lips, silencing me once and for all.

I kept struggling, furious tears burning the backs of my eyes as I thought of my family out there, needing me, waiting for me while I was trapped so close and unable to help.

I started punching him in the side with my free arm, striking him in the kidney over and over, but it was like the blows I landed didn't even register with him as he turned his attention to the barely visible view through the murky window.

I sank my teeth into his hand as his attention wavered, and he yanked it back with a grunt of irritation, but before I could scream, he gripped my throat instead, squeezing hard enough to stop any sound from making it to my lips.

Panic dove into me as his fingers dug into my skin, leaving an imprint which I knew would never wash off as I found myself utterly helpless to what was playing out beyond the filthy glass.

Tears spilled from my eyes as I forced myself to look, my heart thrashing so wildly that I was certain he could feel it where his body was pressed so tightly to mine.

I could only watch in horror as Montana struggled beneath the copper-haired vampire on the ground, her arm flailing beside her as she hunted for a weapon. Her fingers closed around a broken hunk of concrete, and she screamed her rage as she slammed it into the vampire's temple. Hope poured into me as blood spilled freely from the wound, but the vampire barely reacted, grinning down at Montana as my fearless sister swung her arm back for another blow.

Dad roared his defiance as he swiped the kitchen knife at three vampires while they toyed with him, circling him like a pack of wolves, the hunger in their eyes a dreadful thing.

My attention paused on General Wolfe who stood just beyond the group, utterly still, not even blinking as his emerald cloak fluttered in the wind and he watched my family fight for their lives with the desperation only a human could understand. Our mortality might have made us weaker than them, but it made our lives so much brighter too, the inevitability of our deaths making the moments we shared with the people we loved so pure and real.

Montana screamed, bringing my focus back to her as she swung the brick at the vampire again. But this time, the monster caught her wrist, slamming it onto the ground and ripping the weapon from her hand before flipping Montana over and forcing her arms up behind her back, locking them there with metal cuffs.

My eyes burned with the tears that flooded from them, my breaths shallow, insignificant things as the beast who held me controlled my sobs through the tightness of his grip on my throat.

I tried to struggle, punching him over and over, but nothing I did made the slightest bit of difference.

With a nod from Wolfe, the vampires who had been toying with our dad all lunged for him at once, his furious cries met with the swinging of his blade, but despite the stabs he managed to land, nothing could stop them as they took hold of him, forcing him down on the concrete.

"Which way did she go?" General Wolfe's cold voice dripped over the silence that fell, the sound of it carrying through the filthy glass as I was forced to watch this sick show play out.

Montana's head was wrenched back, forcing her to look up at the general as he approached, his pristine boots stepping over the blood and grime which marked the shattered road beneath them with careful consideration.

My sister glared at him with such potent hatred that I could feel it colouring the air, the hairs on the back of my neck standing on end at the desire for violence and vengeance which burned in her chestnut eyes.

Her upper lip curled back as she sneered at him.

"Fuck you," she snarled, and I knew no matter what he said or did to her, she would never offer me up to them, the love between us so pure that even death couldn't force us to betray it.

A sob rocked my chest as my tears splashed onto the hand of the bastard who had captured me, and hatred unlike anything I had ever known before built inside me for him and what he was forcing me to endure, to witness, to allow.

Wolfe's boot collided with the side of Montana's head and a strangled noise of horror broke from my lips as she collapsed to the ground, unconscious or dead, I didn't know, and the terror that incited in me was all-encompassing.

"It's too late for them," the motherfucker who held me breathed in my ear, the scent of leather and oak surrounding me as he continued to hold me at his mercy, his grip unrelenting.

With a lurch of shock, I realised the beast who had captured me wasn't a vampire. That this wasn't just a part of their game but something else, something I couldn't understand, the heat radiating from his body where it was pressed against mine proving that he was just as human as me.

But then why do this to me? What difference did it make to him to hold me back while my family needed me?

Tears ran freely down my cheeks while I watched in despair as the vampires took my loved ones from me. A soft whimper escaped my throat as my whole world fell apart, and I felt my captor's tension increase at the sound now that silence had fallen among the vampires.

The bitch who had been restraining Montana stepped away from her and started looking around at the surrounding buildings. I held my breath, fear coursing through me as her gaze passed over the filthy window where we were hidden. We were deep within the shadows, but her eyes seemed to see more than what was in front of her, and I couldn't help the chill that sank into my core.

Her gaze swept on though, and my lungs forced a shallow breath past the hold on my throat.

"I take it she's still alive?" Wolfe sneered, using the toe of his boot to roll Montana onto her back.

One of the guards moved to check her pulse, the nod he gave allowing my heart to beat once more as relief fell through me like a rushing river. Alive. If she was alive, then she could still be saved. There had to be something I could do, some way to bring her back to me.

"Yes, sir," the guard said, lifting her unconscious body into his arms like it weighed nothing.

General Wolfe directed him back towards the Realm and he carried her away, the pain in my chest tightening like a vice with every step he took, my eyes riveted to his back while I kept trying to fight my way free of my captor.

I tried to cry out, a muffled sound barely making it past the hand which crushed my windpipe. His grip tightened painfully, his fingers digging into my flesh so hard that I could feel it bruising, my breath cut off entirely as my chest felt like it might cave in from grief alone.

My pitiful attempt at a sound was drowned out by my father's pleas as he begged the vampires not to take his child from him. The man who had always been so stoic and strong, reduced to pleading at the feet of those monsters for one of the only things he had to love in this world.

"She was only following me!" he cried. "I asked her to help me search for food out here - take me instead!"

"Don't worry," the general replied, a cruel smile twisting his beautiful features. "We haven't forgotten about you. Your daughters have a price on their heads. Where is the other one?"

"Back in the Realm," my dad lied for me, and my heart shattered into a thousand pieces as Wolfe struck him. The blow looked almost casual, but it sent my father flying to the ground. A gash opened up across his cheek, spilling blood to the sidewalk, more tears spilling down my face as I was forced to watch. Dad had always seemed so unshakeably strong, but beneath Wolfe's might, he was as brittle as paper.

"Don't lie to me, *human,*" General Wolfe warned. "You will tell us everything we want to know eventually anyway."

"I'd sooner die than betray my children," Dad hissed as he struggled to regain his feet.

Wolfe shoved him back and my dad fell to the ground as if he'd been struck with a baseball bat. He skidded backwards on the concrete, his tan jacket tearing at the impact.

The monster with the face of an angel advanced, reaching out to brush his fingers along the bleeding wound on my dad's cheek. Wolfe lifted his hand to his mouth and licked the blood from it, closing his eyes as he savoured the taste.

Shock stilled my attempts to escape as I stared at the act taking place before me. Never once had I witnessed one of their kind drinking our blood. We knew they did. We were forced to donate it as regularly as we could without dying, and yet they always maintained this pretence of civility about it. Like we were the beasts and they were the more advanced creatures.

Acid burned my throat as revulsion raced through me while General Wolfe groaned in appreciation, sucking his fingers clean with languid slowness.

The lesser vampires all shifted like cornstalks in a breeze as they watched the interaction. I could practically feel their hunger. The truth of what they were was clearer than ever before as they eyed my father like a freshly prepared meal. A shiver passed across my skin as their excitement grew, my fear increasing as my gaze remained riveted to my dad, watching as he kept his chin high, facing his fate like the man he had always been. Fearless and brave and strong.

"I always did prefer my meals... *fresh*," the general hissed as he opened his eyes.

The bland look had been banished from them and a dangerous gleam glowed desperately behind his pupils. He seemed to take a moment to try and restrain himself but gave up with a snarl worthy of the greatest hunter known to time. He pounced, fangs bared and muscles flexed, crushing my father to the ground beneath him so fast that the movement sent a judder of shock right through me.

Dad bellowed in rage and agony as the demon sank his fangs into his neck, but Wolfe caught his arms, holding him in place as easily as if he were a child instead of a full-grown man, straddling him while he feasted straight from the vein.

I thrashed even harder against my captor's grip, not caring that I couldn't breathe, that it was pointless and would almost certainly end with those fangs in my throat too. But I couldn't lay witness to this and do nothing. It was breaking me, ripping all that I was to pieces and scattering what remained to the wind. Without my family, I was nothing, and I would far sooner die at their sides than be forced to watch this horror unfold before me and live with it until the end of my days.

The man growled with frustration as he pressed himself against me more firmly, stopping me from running to my father's aid, black spots appearing before my eyes as I continued to struggle for breath.

Finally, the general released his hold on my dad and sat up, blood running down his chin, all pretence of etiquette lost. The monster in him was revealed for all to see as he turned his head to the dim sky and sighed in contentment, his burning blue eyes alight with satisfaction. My father raised trembling fingers to the wound on his neck as the vampire climbed off of him and returned to stand before him like nothing had happened.

"Where is your other daughter?" Wolfe asked again, tipping his head to the side in a gesture that looked anything but human.

Dad pushed himself to his feet before he answered, and more tears pooled in my eyes as he staggered with the effort of doing so.

"Go to hell." He reared back and spat straight in the general's face, pride and terror spilling through me in equal measure as the lack of oxygen started to take hold of me, my limbs growing weaker, my attempts to escape faltering.

Wolfe flinched, blinking as he wiped the wad of spittle from his cheek, the darkness in his eyes deepening at the insult, and fear consumed me as he spoke once more.

"It would be rude of me not to share my meal," Wolfe said icily.

The six lesser vampires understood more quickly than I did, and they all leapt at my dad excitedly, knocking him back to the ground, his cry of terror echoing the screams which were resounding through my skull as the beasts fought over him like a bloody hunk of meat, fangs sinking into flesh, fists flying, bones breaking.

He roared in pain as six sets of teeth sank into his veins, and I screamed around my captor's fingers as my father's limbs flailed wildly beneath the attack.

"Don't kill him," General Wolfe added lazily while my heart broke apart and my world was ripped out from under me. The blackness pressed in on me, death whispering my name while my lungs burned with need. "He still needs to tell us where his other daughter went."

The man holding me seemed to realise that I was on the point of unconsciousness, and I sucked in a violent breath as he released his hold on my throat, his hand moving to my mouth once more and my nostrils flaring as I fought to get enough air into my lungs.

The lesser vampires reluctantly stopped their feasting at a barked command from the general and they moved away from my father's body. He wasn't moving. I could see rings of tooth marks bleeding on both of his arms, as well as one on his leg, where the vampires had shredded his pants in their efforts to devour him alive.

My stomach clenched and flipped over at the sight, bile filling my mouth as I fought back the urge to vomit.

General Wolfe sighed impatiently as he realised my dad had lost consciousness. "I suppose we will have to finish this conversation later. Bring him." He snapped his fingers at the vampire standing closest to him. "He will answer my questions when he wakes. The rest of you, search this place for the other Ford girl. She can't have gone far, but do not forget that the Royals want her. She is not to be bitten."

The five remaining vampires turned and headed into the streets surrounding the buildings like dogs hunting a scent, though through some miracle, none of them headed towards us.

I watched with a sinking heart as Wolfe and the vampire carrying my father headed out of sight, the crumbling street abandoned once again, only the bloodstains on the shattered concrete proving that the entire thing hadn't been some fucked up nightmare.

"We have to move," the man holding me hissed in my ear, his voice a low growl that set my skin prickling.

He shifted back a few inches, and I glared at him over his hand which was still pressed firmly to my mouth, the scent of his skin enveloping me, twisting itself up with this moment and burning its way through my veins.

I didn't know why the fuck he was expecting me to go anywhere with him, and he was deluded if he really thought I would.

The motherfucker huffed out a breath like I was pissing him off with my glare alone, and I tried to bite him again. I didn't care about the vampires who were hunting me. All that mattered were the seconds slipping by as Montana and Dad were taken further and further away. I needed to follow them, to find a weapon or come up with a plan, whatever it took to get them back, no matter how hopeless the thought of that was. I just needed to stop them from taking my family away.

The asshole seemed to realise I didn't plan on going anywhere with him, his grip on my arm shifting as his gaze roamed over me in the dark, studying what he could see of my face, thoughts churning in his shadowed expression. My eyes had begun to adjust to the darkness of the room, and now that my attention was fixed on him, I could take in more of his appearance.

He was absolutely huge; likely closer to seven feet tall than six, his body stacked with muscle, broad shoulders tense where he held me. Men in the Realm didn't look like him. They were all half-starved creatures like me, the wrong side of slim with hollow cheeks and haunted expressions. His expression wasn't empty in the way theirs was, it was full of ire and wrath, whereas everyone I'd grown up around was filled with self-pity and despair. He had long, dark brown hair, partially braided on the right side of his skull, the rest hanging loose and wild around his shoulders, and the strong cut of his jaw was shadowed with a rough beard.

His eyes were the most striking thing about him, my skin burning wherever his gaze fell. They were golden in colour, bright and unyielding despite the darkened room we were hiding in.

He kept his hand pressed firmly over my mouth and glared right back at me, his contempt rising up to meet with my own.

"We can't stay here," he growled, his voice so rough it scratched against my soul. "There are too many of them right now. But if you come with me, I'll help you get your father back. I know where they're going."

He studied me for several seconds like I was some kind of cornered animal, unpredictable and untrustworthy. I just glared at him the entire time, not a single one of my thoughts flickering across my expression.

Slowly, he removed his hand from my mouth, though he continued pinning me to the fucking wall with his immense body.

"Where are they taking them?" I demanded, wanting the answer to the only part of what he'd said which had even registered with me.

"What would you do with that information if I handed it to you?" he asked.

"You know full well what I would do with it," I spat back, and he grunted in amusement, making my hackles rise.

"You think this is funny?" I snarled. "Who even are you? What are you doing skulking around out here? You aren't from the Realm, and you aren't a bloodsucker, so who the fuck-"

"I saved your life," he said gruffly, his shadow engulfing me as he kept me pinned at his mercy. "What else do you need to know?"

With a furious snarl, I shoved him back, and at last he let me, releasing me from his hold and taking a single step away, the heat of his body swiftly replaced by the chilly winter air.

I wanted to push straight past him, rip open that door, and race after the vampires who had stolen away the people I loved most in this world. But as I glanced at the door, I found myself hesitating, my attention flicking back to the stranger who was watching me with waning interest. If he was telling the truth, then he might be the best chance I had of getting back to them. He could be the *only* chance I had of retrieving them, in fact.

I wasn't a fool. I knew running blindly after them would only end with me facing their fate alongside them, and though that was far preferable to trying to escape alone, it would also only end in death for all of us.

"How do you know where they're taking my family?" I demanded angrily.

I didn't like the idea of blindly following some stranger and trusting in his promises of help, but my options were thin at best and non-existent at worst. At the very least, he might prove to be a good distraction for the bloodsuckers, drawing their attention from me and buying me some small measure of time to help my family.

"I've seen it," he replied simply, his patience clearly wearing thin as he moved to the door. "So either come or remain here to die. It makes little difference to me."

I wanted to refuse, to tell him to go fuck himself and run after my family before the vampires could get too far away, but a small, defeated part of me knew I couldn't help them. I'd only get myself caught. And that would only get them dead.

My eyes slid back towards the courtyard which was now empty. The only other option I had was to chase after them, but then what? It was suicide and I knew it. They'd capture me as easily as they had my family, and then we'd have no chance of escape. If this man really knew where they were being taken, then maybe I'd have a chance. Albeit a slim one...

With a surge of resolve that tore my heart in two, I nodded. "Fine. I'll follow you. But if you try to fuck me over or use me as bait for those bloodsuckers, or some other fucked up shit, I'll stab you again. And this time it will be a lot deeper."

The asshole glanced down at the bleeding wound on his side, a soft scoff escaping him, like he hadn't even noticed it. He clearly thought as little of my threat as he seemed to think of me as a whole. I had no idea why he'd even 'saved me' as he put it, because he certainly seemed more than a little put out by me now.

"Come," he instructed, like I was a dog to command.

I bristled with anger as I pushed my hand into my pocket and wrapped my fingers around the little knife I had hidden there.

He pulled the door wide, the dim daylight illuminating him better, and I frowned at the clothes he wore, the pants and jacket made from what looked like brown leather, well-worn and practical but not modern in any way, and his shirt was a rough linen with ties to secure it. In fact, he looked kind of like the warriors my dad had told us about in stories, the ones who fought dragons or defeated trolls. I dismissed the nonsensical thought and forced myself to take a steadying breath before scrubbing the tears from my cheeks. My heart was still consumed with terror for my family, but crying wasn't going to get them back, so I needed to push that fear aside and focus on all I could do for them now.

The asshole listened at the door for several seconds, then turned away and started walking, not even bothering to glance back and check if I was following.

I scowled at him as I studied the two heavy golden blades strapped across his back, their hilts covered in strange lettering, unlike any language I'd seen before. Not that I was particularly well studied in that kind of thing.

"Who are you?" I asked again, knowing without doubt that I'd never seen him before. No one in the Realm was anywhere near as big as him or as intimidating, and that opened up a whole plethora of further questions. Because if there were people out here, living free so close to

117

the Realm itself, then-

"Silence," he instructed fiercely, and I recoiled from him, then cursed myself for it. *Fuck him.* I hoped his side was hurting like a bitch.

I fell still, glancing back to the street where my family had been minutes before, and I wondered if I should just go after them myself instead. This asshole could be delusional for all I knew, and I didn't have time to waste chasing him about if he was full of shit.

He took three long strides towards me, boxing me in against the wall, and my grip tightened on the blade in my pocket. I forced myself to stand straight and tilted my chin to hold his eye as he loomed over me, my jaw set stubbornly, my hatred for him unhidden. Regardless of what he claimed to be offering, or what he might know about the place my family had been taken, he'd forced me to watch as they were attacked, and nothing he said now would ever change the ire I felt burning through me as I looked into his golden eyes and dared him to test me.

"If you don't follow, they will hunt you down and kill you, or worse. Perhaps they'll make you their blood whore, or just pass you from fang to fang until you beg for death. I am going to free the humans they have taken. Come with me or don't. It's your choice."

"Not much of a choice," I muttered angrily.

He smirked at me, and the desire to punch him square in the face rose up in me so potently that it was a test of will not to do it. He turned away without looking back to see if I was following again, and I ground my teeth as I fought off the impulse to just let him leave, knowing that he was the only possibility I had of getting my family back. If this asshole really did know their destination, I just might have a shot at rescuing them.

No one would expect another human to be outside the Realm, and even though they knew I'd escaped, they'd never expect me to come after them. They'd expect me to head south and keep running until the burning sun stopped them from following. But I wasn't going anywhere without my family.

The general had said the Royals wanted me and Montana for something, which I guessed meant that we'd passed their damn test.

Whatever they wanted us for, it couldn't be good. I hadn't even known the vampires *had* Royals, but it didn't really matter. They could stick a crown on their undead heads or stick one up their asses, it didn't make a difference to me. I wouldn't bow down to their wishes, they'd be no monarchs of mine, and I'd do whatever it took to get my family away from them. Even make a deal with the Devil himself.

Maybe they'd decided that our blood was particularly delicious and wanted to serve us up like the main course at a feast. Perhaps in the east where the Elite were rumoured to live, they liked to drink their blood fresh; biting straight through flesh as Wolfe had done to my father. The thought of their razor-sharp fangs piercing my skin sent a wave of fear rolling over me. The agony present in my father's screams when they'd bitten him told me all I ever wanted to know about the pain their bite caused. He was no coward and no stranger to pain, yet the sound that had escaped his lips had been filled with an agony so potent that I couldn't stop it from repeating inside my skull over and over.

I hesitated just a few more seconds, then cursed as I hurried to catch up to my new pal. As much as I didn't want to admit it, he seemed like my best chance of survival for now. At the very least he would make a more appetising meal for the bloodsuckers if they found us. A big motherfucker like him had to have far more blood in his veins than I did. And while they were dealing with him, I'd have a chance to escape. Just hopefully not before he followed through on his promise and helped me retrieve my family.

He led us away from the building where we'd taken refuge, taking turns between the ruins so rapidly that he must have been familiar with the route. He didn't look back to check that I was following him even once, but I knew he was aware of my presence.

The further we went, the less damage we found to the buildings that surrounded us. There were rusted cars and creeping vegetation staining unkempt streets, but most of the buildings still had four walls, doors and windows, and less rubble blocking our path between them.

It was so quiet out here that every step I took felt like a clap of thunder announcing my location with reckless certainty. But as I struggled to keep up with the motherfucker's long stride and fast pace,

I had little chance of keeping my footsteps silent.

"Stop," he said suddenly, putting a hand up to enunciate his point and damn near smacking me in the face. "One of them has found us."

"What?" I hissed, looking over my shoulder, studying the tightly pressed walls of the alleyway we were halfway through and finding nothing behind or before us.

"Wait here." He didn't so much as look at me as he strode on, casually grasping the hilts of the two blades over his shoulders and pulling them free of their sheathes. They glinted like actual sunlight, the metal purest gold and impossibly beautiful.

"I'm not just waiting down some dark alley in hopes of staying hidden," I hissed, hurrying after him with irritation burning a path straight though me, but I staggered to a halt as I spotted the vampire standing in the road less than fifty feet away.

It was like she'd sprouted from the ground itself, suddenly there without so much as a whisper to announce her arrival. Silent, deadly, the ultimate hunter.

She turned towards us with a triumphant smile, her scarlet hair twisting around her devastatingly beautiful face in a breeze I couldn't feel from within the confines of the alleyway.

"There you are, sweet girl," she purred, her gaze fixed on me, her prize in sight, the asshole apparently not even catching her attention even though he was practically blocking me from sight with his bulk.

My fist tightened around the pathetic little blade, and I drew it from my pocket, refusing to go down without a fight.

She bit down on her bottom lip, her fangs taking up all of my attention as she studied me hungrily, and I wondered how she could ignore the man-mountain prowling towards her with a pair of swords in favour of me.

"If you want her, you'll have to come through me," he rumbled as he closed in on her.

The vampire finally switched her attention to him, and her eyes narrowed as she pulled her own sword from her back.

"Slayer," she growled in shock. "We'd begun to think you were all dead."

"You thought wrong." He twisted towards her so suddenly that I almost missed the motion. His sword swept low, aiming for her stomach, but somehow, she leapt above it, parrying his second blade with her own.

The clash of colliding metal set my heart galloping in my chest and several birds took off from a nearby rooftop with squawks of protests carrying across the sky.

They danced back and forth, matching each other blow for blow in movements so graceful they almost seemed choreographed. The man-mountain moved far faster than I would have believed possible for someone of his size. Each time the vampire leapt at him, he was ready for her and drove her back onto the defence.

My heart galloped in my chest, my gaze scoring over the surrounding area, the feeling of eyes on me making me half expect an attack to spring from the shadows at any moment.

The vampire swung her sword with a furious cry, and I stumbled back as the movement turned the two of them, putting her closer to me, her eyes snapping my way, the thirst in them sending a chill right down to my core.

I turned and ran.

Nothing but pure instinct and the desperate desire for survival drove my actions as I broke into a sprint and tore back the way we'd come.

My boots thundered against the broken concrete, the man's roar of challenge chasing after me as I felt the vampire closing in. Vampires had strength far beyond anything I possessed, her powerful strides eating the distance between us despite my desperate flight.

My foot caught against something heavy, almost tripping me, and I glanced down to find a broken brick rolling aside from the force of its collision with my boot.

I bent down and grabbed it just as the vampire slammed into me. She hurled me against a crumbling wall, lumps of masonry spilling over us as my cheek scraped along the rough brickwork.

Her hand fisted in my hair, nails scraping against my scalp as she shoved me down beneath her, and for a moment, I couldn't help but feel like I'd been in that position for my entire life, forced beneath the heels of these beasts, shoved down into the dirt at their feet and used for whatever they wanted, no matter the cost to myself or my kind.

The fury that awoke in me was so potent that I felt it gilding every part of me, a roar building in my throat which was followed by a flare of resolve as I threw my weight forward and unbalanced the bitch who was holding me.

I swung around, the brick biting into my fingers as I hefted it at her, slamming it into her side with a force brutal enough to shatter bone.

The vampire shrieked as I knocked her off balance, my second blow forcing her to release me altogether just as the man caught up to us again.

I stumbled to keep my feet as their blades collided once more, the heavy ring of steel echoing through my skull as I shoved myself upright, panting and cursing while the fight grew more furious between them.

I shifted back a step, wondering if I should run, but I was unable to tear my gaze from the battle before me.

Again and again, the crash of steel colliding echoed between the buildings, the noise carrying over the deserted city, my skin prickling as I wondered where the other vampires were. I'd never seen a man fight a vampire like that, clearly able to meet her strength, and I couldn't help the awe I felt at witnessing it.

The vampire hissed as she retreated, the cockiness falling from her bit by bit as he swung his swords faster, making her fight for every block and parry, never once giving her the chance to take a swing at him, instead backing her up, closing in with every movement.

My hatred for that bitch and her kind overwhelmed me and I hefted my arm back, trying to take aim despite the speed of their movements, the brick in my hand aching for a taste of her blood.

The vampire noticed my movement, her head twisting towards me as her eyes flared.

He took her momentary distraction as a gift and swung forward viciously, and his blade sliced straight through her slender neck like it was nothing but paper, her eyes widening with shock in the moment of her death before her head fell from her body with a wet thump.

I sucked in a breath, able to do nothing but stare at the impossibility of what I'd just seen as her body crashed to the floor too.

Her head rolled towards me, spilling blood across the concrete and sticking in her hair. My mouth fell open in some mixture of horror and delight as my gaze became riveted to it.

Heavy footsteps made me look up from her face which was frozen in a moment of confused realisation, her death only seeming to have occurred to her at the exact second it came for her.

Dead.

A vampire lay dead in the dirt before me, her body broken, eyes unseeing. It was the most impossibly beautiful thing I had ever witnessed, and my racing heart was struggling to comprehend the reality of it.

"What's this?" he asked, pointing at the brick which I now held so tightly it was cutting my palm.

I dropped it in embarrassment, wondering what the fuck I'd even been thinking in grabbing it when presented with the sheer brutality that was him. It clattered loudly as it hit the ground, and I slipped my tiny blade back into my pocket, shame staining my cheeks as I wondered how easily that creature would have overpowered me if she'd found me here alone.

"You killed one," I breathed.

No other words seemed relevant. No other facts mattered at all. I'd dreamed of killing one of those things every day of my life, wondering if it had ever been done, if they would even bleed or whether they might scatter to ash on the wind, or burst into flames like the vampires from Dad's old stories. I'd imagined up a million different scenarios in which one of those beasts might meet their end, but I'd never believed it was actually possible.

He glanced at the decapitated body as though he'd almost forgotten it was there, like the sight of it was nothing special to him, nothing new. My pulse picked up at the thought. Had he done that before? Could he do it again?

"Not quite," he said roughly, turning one of his blades in his palm as he strode back to her corpse, kicking it so that the decapitated body flopped onto its back. Standing over it, he drove his golden blade straight through the vampire's heart with a savage, precise blow.

A sound like falling raindrops filled the air, and I watched in twisted fascination as her body disintegrated into thousands of tiny pieces like grains of sand, her head following suit, even the drops of blood which stained the ground, every piece of her becoming nothing until only a heap of charred ash remained.

Some of the dust which had once been part of the vampire caught in the breeze and swirled towards me.

I held my breath and took a step back, recoiling from it as I buried my mouth and nose in the crook of my elbow, not wanting to breathe in a single speck of her rotten soul.

"You've never seen one killed?" he asked with a frown, studying me with almost as much fascination as I felt toward him.

I shook my head feebly, even my hatred of this beastly man tempered by the awe over what he'd just done.

"I'd begun to wonder if it was even possible," I admitted.

His frown deepened, and he looked about at our surroundings as though he were seeing them for the first time, his golden gaze tracking from apartment blocks to the rusted shells of cars, studying the concrete jungle and the plants which fought to return some of the old civilisation to their domain.

"What year is this?" he asked slowly, the question bringing me up short, the absurdity of it seeming so out of place with what he'd just survived.

But as I looked into his golden eyes, the contempt and anger I felt towards him shifted, the pure need I found haunting his expression stalling my tongue. He needed my answer. And though I could have withheld it from him, he had just saved my life. A simple truth seemed like a low payment for such an impossible act.

"It's twenty-one thirty-three,' I supplied, watching his reaction spill from confusion to denial to pure horror. He looked from me to the ruins surrounding us, seeming to truly look at it all as he sought to confirm my claim somehow. "Why?"

His gaze darkened with a pain so sharp that I felt the stab of it biting into me too as he turned away from me to gaze up at the grey sky.

"Forgive me, brother," he muttered, raw agony lacing his voice as his grip on his swords slackened and the world seemed to dim with his words. "I slept too long."

# MONTANA

## CHAPTER EIGHT

Something was tearing apart inside me, a blade forged of terror carving up the centre of my being. It was a living nightmare born of all my worst fears, but the cold, steel box I was trapped in could only be real.

I was chained to a hard metal bench, sitting on it with my hands and feet clad in cuffs while the box juddered and rumbled with unceasing movement.

I thought of Callie with a tug in my chest, praying she'd made it to safety. But even if she had escaped, did that really make her safe? The vampires would hunt her tirelessly, and her only hope now was to run and run as far as she could to the safety of the sun. She needed to lose herself in the ravaged world beyond the Realm and never, ever be found.

My mind turned to Dad, and a groan of pain shuddered through my chest as I thought of where he surely was. Where they took all those who defied them. They'd send him to the blood bank and keep him alive as they harvested his blood. If we were free-range blood bags in the Realm, then the blood bank was the vampires' version of intensive farming. Though the reality of being kept as an unconscious source of food attached to tubes didn't explain the screams we sometimes heard on the wind from that place. The rumours of what sport the vampires practiced in the shadows of that building were too terrifying to give thought to.

*Not there. Anywhere but there. Please be okay, Dad.*

I was jostled from side to side in the large metal box, wondering if I would see him soon at least. My fate was as certain as his, and all I could hold onto was that I might get one last chance to see him, to say goodbye.

I bowed my head, a sense of surrender creeping up in my chest, and a heavy sigh rattled through my lungs. My mind slipped towards somewhere far from here, somewhere that didn't even exist except for in the corners of my mind. There was light there, an offering of sweet numb bliss. But then the memory of General Wolfe's triumph came crashing through my skull, and a snarl peeled back my lips in defiance. A roaring filled my head that was suddenly pouring from my lips in a furious scream. I would *not* give up.

I thrashed and kicked the metal floor, fighting with all the fury of a tempest to try and free myself from this cold dark cage, but I was well-chained to the hard bench beneath me. I let my body bruise, let it hurt and call out for the freedom it had so long been denied, but no answer came to it. My plight did nothing but offer an outlet for some of the anxious energy flowing through my veins, and it was an outlet I clung to, refusing to let my mind slip away because then the door of this cruel fate might close on me for good. I fought for me, but most of all, I fought for my family, wishing I could bust through these walls and find my way back to them.

A rumbling noise vibrated through me, and I was shunted to one side on the bench as the box stopped moving.

"State line, let me see your papers," a voice cut through the air beyond the metal walls, and I held my breath to listen as another male voice sounded from the front of the vehicle. "I've got one in the back from Realm G. She's bound for NYC."

"You're heading to the airfield?" the first voice asked, and I started slamming my feet against the floor again, making a cacophony of noise as I fought to break free.

"Let me out you assholes!" I yelled as the word 'airfield' circled in my head. I tried to place it, searching through all the things Dad had taught me but coming up short.

"Open up, let's get a look at her."

My heart stumbled as footsteps moved across hard ground outside of my metal prison, and I cursed myself for drawing their attention to me. A pair of doors were wrenched open and daylight fell over me, though it wasn't much more than a vague glow between the dark clouds. The empty space surrounding me was revealed, nothing more than a box which must have been suspended at a height because the two figures who peered in at me didn't have to stoop to allow their gawking. I'd never seen anything like this in the Realm, but Dad had told me of the mechanical things humans had created to ride around in, but the name of them escaped me now.

A fine drizzle hung in the air around the two vampires standing there, the rain never far off in this miserable slice of the world.

Both were alluring in that way which sent my gut churning, my pulse picking up as I studied them in reply to their curious gazes on me. A pair of predators eyeing a meal. But I was no wounded doe awaiting my death.

I fell silent as I scowled at them, and the one wearing a smart black uniform inhaled deeply through his nose.

"Delicious," he sighed, and my skin prickled.

Despite knowing I was a food source for these creeps, I'd never been looked at like I was a steaming hot meal ready and waiting to be devoured. The vampires in the Realm had been aloof, meticulous, cold…but perhaps they'd just been fed well before coming to interact with us. The hunger in this creature's eyes suggested he had skipped a few meals.

My eyes slid to a paved road behind them surrounded by a thick forest so green and bright, I was sure I'd never seen anything so vivid in nature before. I drew in a breath of my own, the familiar streets and apartment blocks nowhere to be seen, the smells and sounds of the Realm absent, leaving only the distant call of birds to toy in the breeze which rolled through the trees. Though even the birds were falling quiet now, the kiss of death which followed these monsters warning all living things to beware.

"Where are you taking me?" I demanded, my tone level while I fought to hide my rising panic.

"She hasn't figured it out yet," murmured the one who I assumed was my driver.

The other one chuckled. "They keep 'em stupid in the Realms for a reason."

"Wait-" I cried as the driver strode forward, slamming the doors in my face and drowning out any more protests I might have been able to conjure. Fighting this was useless. They didn't see me as an equal; I was their inferior. They weren't going to let me go, no matter how much I begged. So I only had one option left: escape.

With my hands and feet bound, that wasn't a possibility right now, but they had to unshackle me eventually. Didn't they?

The time crawled by, and I soon grew tired of fighting with the uncaring, unyielding metal walls. And as I sat there with dark thoughts descending on me, the constant rocking motion of the box and the utter exhaustion creeping into my bones sent me into a kind of trance. One that was filled with those green, green trees and my family waiting beyond them.

I was only half-aware when the box stopped moving again and the doors cracked open. Though I bolted upright the moment the chill wind touched my skin, adrenaline scoring though my chest as I stared out at my latest surroundings.

My pulse ticked loudly in my ears as I eyed the faint glimmer of sunlight beyond the clouds, sitting fat and low in the sky. There could only be a few hours of daylight left, and Dad had drilled into me how important it was to stay inside after dusk. The vampires were in their element at night, and that was when people went missing.

The driver climbed into the box with me, all hint of his features shadowed, leaving me utterly uncertain of his intentions as I shuffled back on the bench as well as I could manage.

My heart hammered as I tried to get a good look at him, needing to at least see my fate coming for me if this was it. The vampire hissed as I moved, and I finally got a look at his face as he turned his head and his features were brightened by daylight. No bared fangs, no feral look in his eyes. If anything, he simply seemed irritated, bored, the truth of that a welcome relief - though it didn't fully sate my fears.

He freed the chain that secured me to the bench, but my hands and feet remained bound together as he drew me toward the doors. With inhuman strength, he lifted me into his arms and threw me over his shoulder, not so much as a word spoken to explain himself or to tell me where he was taking me.

"Where are we going?" I growled, his silence the only answer I got. "Where is my father?"

Rage spewed through me as the vampire continued to act as if I hadn't spoken at all and I slammed my shackled hands into his back over and over, struggling to fight my way free of his hold, but his only response was a musical laugh.

He kept walking, my view little more than the shirt on his back and the concrete passing beneath his boots until he finally planted me down on my feet, the sudden shift in position almost seeing me on my ass.

I found myself facing an enormous, winged *thing*, constructed entirely of metal and standing on a wide expanse of concrete. A short flight of stairs led up to a door where I could see fearful faces staring out at me from little round windows. Human faces. The thing was like a giant, ugly bird, lit up from the inside out, my fate mocking me from within it.

Another vampire approached, dressed in a dark red uniform with an emblem on his breast pocket which I blinked at, reading the words beneath the symbol of a skull gripped in the fist of a god.

My eyes lifted to his smiling face, my breath catching at the beauty of his symmetrical features, his dark eyes seeming to see all the way to my soul as he studied me with bland interest. They were deadly in so many ways, but their beauty had always seemed like the worst of it to me, this deadly trap set to trick our kind, to lure us in despite how easily they could defeat us without needing to play such games.

"She's the last one." The guard took my arm, drawing me away from the driver and tossing him a bottle which glinted red in the moonlight. Blood. My price apparently was little more than a single drink, my worth measured in that and nothing else.

My heartbeat grew frantic as the new vampire tugged me toward the giant bird thing, my heels digging into the hard concrete as I fought to resist him, and he didn't even seem to notice.

"What is that?" I asked in trepidation as we approached a female vampire in the same uniform. She was waiting at the bottom of the metal staircase that led up into the bird, her dark hair pulled back into a neat bun. Her bright eyes landed on me and she cooed, her face melting into a smile.

"Aww, she's so cute." She patted her knees like I was a stray dog, and my nose wrinkled with distaste.

"You're such a soft touch, Maria," the male holding me spoke, his voice silken.

"I don't know why we can't keep them as pets." Maria pouted, gesturing for the man to take me up the stairs.

"Because we're not animals," I spat at her.

Maria's eyebrows went skyward. "Oh, gwumpy little human," she chuckled, turning to my escort again. "I love when they're gwumpy. Do you think they'll miss one?"

"Yes," he clipped, and I glared at her as he tugged me up the steps.

"What is this thing?" I asked him again, and he eyed me curiously for a moment, seeming to actually see me for the first time.

"An aer-o-plane," he spoke slowly like I was a complete dumbass, and I frowned as that word sparked memories of the time my father had told me about the flying vehicles. And suddenly I didn't want to take another step forward.

"No," I gasped, throwing my shoulder back against my escort to try and break his grip on me. "I can't fly. I can't *leave*. I have to find my family."

My escort barely reacted, his grip firming as he pushed me along with ease, even as I turned and pushed my full weight against him.

He flipped me off my feet as I struggled like a hellcat, and he rounded into an aisle, passing through rows of people as they stared at me. In every single seat, a human was bound in place. Men and women in a similar state to me with ragged clothes and hollow cheekbones.

The only feature that unified us was our youth, just as Dad had said. At a guess, I'd say no one among them was more than thirty-five. The youngest my age. A few I recognised from my Realm, but most of them I didn't. Callie and I had guessed there were other Realms, though the vampires had never confirmed it. But I knew everyone in my Realm, if not by name, then at least by sight. Most of these people were strangers, and that hinted at the scale of the vampires' oppression that went far beyond the small piece of reality I knew.

I was tossed onto an empty seat and my escort shoved a hand roughly against my chest to pin me there before I could try and get up. He shackled me in place next to a man with a ragged mop of dark hair and a thick beard on his face. He smelled of sweat and mud, but I probably did too, so I wasn't about to complain. I'd take the grit of my kind any day over the too-clean, too-perfect state of the vampires.

My escort stood up with a triumphant look, pushing a lock of hair back into place and leaving me there to struggle fruitlessly against my bindings.

My eyes travelled to the empty seat on my other side, and my heart jolted as I put two and two together. It must have been meant for Callie. But she wasn't here. They hadn't caught her, and I drank in that truth like liquid relief.

*Keep running, don't ever let them catch you, Callie.*

My escort gazed at everyone, seeming to count us, and with a stiff nod, he banged on a door behind him and called, "All set for take-off!"

The female vampire closed the door, locking it tight with a large red lever, then looking at us humans with undisguised glee, even tossing out a wave here and there and tickling one woman under the chin.

I sucked in a sharp breath as the roar of an engine rumbled through the seat beneath me, the sound only getting louder as the aeroplane slowly began to move.

Fear rolled through me as the plane picked up momentum, my eyes locked on the dark space beyond the small window until we were hurtling along at a pace so fierce it was all I could do to bite back my screams. The window only allowed a glimpse of faraway trees as we whipped past them at high speed, but that was more than enough to set my heart galloping and terror speeding through me at the thought of what was to come.

My stomach clenched. My pulse rose.

I glanced at the man beside me who seemed to be muttering prayers under his breath while someone behind me started sobbing loudly and others screamed at the top of their lungs.

I was pushed back into my seat as we took flight, and fear devoured me as we climbed ever higher, defying the laws of nature and hurtling into the sky. My nails bit into my palms and my throat constricted so tight I could barely draw in a breath.

The terror of what was happening didn't even come close to the fear of leaving Callie and Dad far, far behind. I didn't know if I'd ever see them again. And the thought of that was so devastating that it felt like it cut right through me, bleeding me out for all to see, every moment that passed taking me further from them and all I had ever known.

When the plane finally levelled out, the male guard pushed a trolley down the aisle, handing us each a small plastic cup filled with a syrupy orange liquid. My throat burned for moisture, but I hesitated to drink it, sniffing its saccharine sweet scent and trying to work out what it was.

"Drink up!" the guard demanded when everyone had a cup in hand.

The man beside me brought the cup to his lips with trembling fingers and swallowed the contents.

"Better we drink it by choice, huh?" he whispered to me with a fearful gleam in his eyes.

I bit down on my tongue, gazing at the syrup, certain he was right even as every part of me rebelled against the idea of simply following the commands I was given, my free will stolen entirely.

"Is this really a choice?" I murmured, and he reached over, resting a hand on my arm.

Despite not knowing this man, the gesture was surprisingly reassuring, the kindness in his eyes real.

"No, but it helps to pretend." He gave me a ghost of a smile, and I tentatively returned it. "I'm Hank." He blinked heavily as I pulled my gaze from his and looked down at my cup.

For a second, I considered not responding, the code we had all lived by for so long making me wary of offering out my affection to anyone, even in some small measure, knowing they may soon be gone. But no one here knew my name, and I didn't want to be just another number in the masses.

"Montana," I whispered, seeing my eyes reflected in the gloop. I knew this wasn't a choice, but submitting had never been in my nature, and an icy rebellion glazed my heart as I lifted the cup, tilting in preparation of tipping it all on the floor.

My hand was caught in a flash, and I found my escort looking down at me once again, his hard grip forcing the cup to my lips. "Drink."

His other hand gripped my jaw, forcing my lips to part, and I struggled uselessly as he poured it into my mouth, then clamped his large palm over my lips and nose.

It was the sweetest thing I'd ever tasted, the sugar no doubt hiding something wicked in its depths. I had to swallow, and almost as soon as I did, wooziness washed through me, and my eyelids felt weighted with lead. Death wasn't the aim here, or I could have found it a hundred times at the hands of these monsters in far easier ways than this.

The vampire released me, and I drew in a shaky breath as the drug took hold of me. I found Hank's hand reaching for me, like he'd had some intention of helping me, even though it had been futile.

He slumped forward in his seat as the effects pulled him under too, but with the last dregs of my consciousness, I caught his fingers in mine, holding on to them as tightly as I could manage while the world fell away around us, clinging to another human in the dark.

As the drug needled its way deeper and dragged me down into a dreamless sleep, I felt Hank's shoulder press against mine, and the smallest measure of comfort found me at the fact.

*If I'm headed toward a terrible fate, at least I'm not alone.*

# CALLIE

## CHAPTER NINE

I couldn't help but stare at the open landscape around me as we made our way through it. Our Realm had small patches of grass growing among the mud, but nothing like this. My mind scoured Dad's stories until I found the word I was hunting for. *Meadow*. I'd never seen anything so green. I wondered how it would look in the summer when the flowers were blooming.

My silent companion continued to lead the way. He hadn't spoken since I'd told him what year it was, and I wasn't foolish enough to breach the silence he'd built between us.

We'd left the ruins behind hours ago, and though I couldn't help but look over my shoulder repeatedly, I was beginning to believe we'd actually managed to escape the vampires who'd been hunting me.

I wasn't sure if I should thank my companion or not. He'd certainly saved my life from the red-haired vampire, but I still felt a burning rage when I remembered the way he'd pinned me in place while my family needed help.

I was beginning to wonder if I'd been wrong to follow him. I didn't know the first thing about him, and the longer this silence stretched between us, the more uneasy I felt about my decision. What if he was wrong about where the vampires had taken my family? Or perhaps he'd simply been lying. What if he was just some crazy asshole living alone out here who wanted my company in his crazy asshole shack?

*That one might be a bit of a stretch, Callie…*

My mind went back to how easily he'd killed that vampire, and my worries eased a little. Anyone who could do that would surely be able to free my family too. But I didn't even know his name, and I certainly didn't feel the desire to ask. Whatever his intentions were, he was a means to an end. Our paths aligned for no longer than the time it would take for him to lead me to my family. I didn't need to trust him beyond that.

I shook my head to banish the worrying thoughts and focused on my surroundings instead. I'd never been outside the Realm, and the world was a whole lot bigger than I'd ever dreamed.

Everything was new to me, from the soft earth beneath my boots to the sound of the wind twisting through the bare branches of the trees. Even the smell was different here. Away from the press of human bodies, everything was so crisp and clean. I'd never really smelled the rich odour coming from the pine trees which lined the meadow we were crossing. Or the clean fragrance of air that hadn't passed through corridors of concrete. There was a whole world out here beyond the fences, and a hungry, aching part of me longed to see every piece of it.

The sun was dipping low towards the horizon, and I bit my lip as I thought about what that meant. Night was when the vampires were at their strongest. It was *their* time. No human could stand a chance against them beneath the light of the stars.

I pulled my new coat tighter around my neck. Though we hadn't spoken in the time that had passed since he'd killed that vampire, we *had* looted an apartment. While he'd stocked up on food, I'd taken the opportunity to get myself some warmer clothes. It wasn't the white coat I'd wanted, but I'd begun to think that was a good thing; white wasn't exactly a great colour for staying out of sight. The thick coat I now sported was deep green and it still had the fur-lined hood I'd dreamed of.

Winter was well underway, and as the sun dipped, the temperature plummeted. I'd never owned something like this coat before, and the fact that I wasn't shivering my ass off proved its effectiveness. The man-mountain had pulled on a thick grey cloak lined with fur, which only added to his gladiator-like appearance.

My mind was beginning to teem with unasked questions, but the bruises on my neck and my general contempt for him were holding my tongue in check. I was afraid to open my mouth - both for fear of his reaction and for fear of the words I might be tempted to hurl at him, but it was getting to the point where my curiosity was going to overrule those concerns.

We'd been walking for what seemed like an eternity, and I only had the promise he'd made hours ago to make me think we were heading after my family at all. I needed to know how he knew where they'd be, as well as the destination itself, plus how he expected to get them out.

Somehow, I couldn't voice my concerns. The sadness that had seemed to fill him when he learned of the year was so constant that I almost felt it myself. If I hadn't had enough of my own worries to last me a lifetime, then I would have asked him about it already, but that was breaking one of my own rules. Never ask personal questions. Don't form unnecessary bonds. Not that I was likely to feel anything but ire for the son of a bitch who had made me watch as my family were captured and tortured, but I had my rules for a reason.

I'd been fucking a guy for the best part of the summer, the two of us barely exchanging words beyond the first few when we'd met, heated looks and subtle instructions on where to meet were about as far as conversations had gotten between us. It had seemed so perfect. A physical release with a man who understood the confines of what we were and what we never would be. Or so I'd thought. Then one afternoon, with his cock buried inside me, he'd gone and blurted some declaration. I couldn't even recall most of the words, but he'd said something about feelings and having me stuck in his head all the time, wanting me to meet his family – honestly after the fifth or sixth word I'd been more concerned with shoving him off of me and finding my discarded clothes than I had with listening to him. I hadn't so much as acknowledged him since that day, the worst of it being the small part of me which had been flattered by his interest, that weak slip of humanity which yearned for something more than I could ever allow myself to risk offering.

But I'd snuffed it out just as certainly as I had always sworn I would, and I hadn't made the mistake of asking personal questions of anyone since. This asshole would be no different. He was a means to an end, a convenient distraction if the bloodsuckers happened to find us, and most of all, dispensable.

My silent companion veered from our path and turned aside, making his way between the trees which lined the meadow, each of his footsteps so carefully placed that I never heard a single one of them. I followed carefully, breathing in the fresh green scent of the pines, my lungs expanding as I drank it down.

I had everything I'd ever dreamed of and my worst nightmare all at once. As amazing as all of this was, it didn't mean anything without having my family here to share it.

We walked through the trees for a short while, the pine needles crunching softly beneath my boots. I couldn't help but look about in wonder, and I even caught sight of an owl hopping between the trees, watching our progress. I paused to look up at the bird, a smile tugging at my lips. It seemed so carefree. I wondered why it found us so interesting and lifted my hand in a kind of greeting to it.

A flash of movement caught my eye and a small blade swept through the air, knocking the owl from the tree to fall dead on the forest floor. I let out a shriek of horror and ran towards the beautiful creature which lay utterly still on the ground.

"What did you do?" I demanded angrily as the motherfucker responsible stalked towards me, his gaze locked on the owl, either not noticing or not caring about my reaction to his violence.

He bent down to retrieve his knife, not even offering me the courtesy of looking at me, let alone answering my rage. Before he could turn away, I grabbed his wrist and forced his gaze to meet mine. His golden eyes seemed dimmer than they had before, like something in them had broken, and maybe I hoped it had. He was a cold, heartless beast of a man, everything he had done since the moment I met him proved that to me. Yet our fates were entwined all the same, leaving me trapped in his presence for now.

"Why did you do that?" I spat, grief for the dead bird stoking my anger and lending me extra bravery.

"That was a familiar," he replied, his voice even and patronising. "I saved your life again."

"A what?"

He looked down to the point where I grasped his wrist, and I released him just as swiftly as I'd grabbed him, remembering all too well how that hand had felt around my throat, how easily he'd overpowered me and left me at his mercy.

He didn't seem inclined to strike me for my anger though, his chin jerking towards the dead bird, forcing my attention back to it.

"A beast whose soul is tethered to a vampire. Its purpose is to be their eyes and ears. A living, breathing spy. There is nothing of the creature they were left inside them once the bloodsuckers' corruption delves into their veins." He continued his original task of retrieving the knife, and as he pulled it from the owl's chest, the bird dissolved into dust just like the vampire had that morning.

I recoiled in disgust, and realisation swamped me, a thousand petty secrets revealed, all the distrust within the Realm, the people blaming each other for their punishments, thinking humans were ratting each other out when really little eyes had been everywhere, reporting back.

"That's how they always knew what was happening in the Realm, wasn't it?" I said, almost to myself, the realisation making bile rise in my throat. The humans mistrusted each other to the point of isolation. Families kept to their own, children hardly dared play with one another for fear of who might snitch on every little misstep. But it hadn't even been our kind who were spying on us. "They had eyes on us all the time."

I couldn't believe we'd never realised it. There were more than enough rats in the Realm for them to be watching every one of us. If I added birds and other animals to the mix, then it was no wonder no one had ever been able to keep anything from the vampires for long. It was a wonder Thomas had made it in and out of the Realm as often as he had without being caught.

His eyes roamed over me for several seconds, the darkness between the trees and the rough beard which covered his jaw making it near impossible to determine his expression, but the frown on his brow made me wonder what was running through his mind.

Instead of voicing any of those thoughts, he only nodded at me before replacing the knife in a sheath at his hip and continuing with our journey through the trees.

*I guess we're back to not talking then.*

I followed him again but before I could question him on our destination, he led me out through a final group of pines and pointed me into a cave which was formed in the hollow of a large rock face.

I stepped after him cautiously, glancing back at the darkening sky as I tried to decide if the idea of heading into the unknown depths of that cave was preferable to being out in the open beneath the trees. On the one hand, it would be harder for anything to creep up on us in the dark if we were hidden within the cave. On the other, we would be trapped if the vampires made it to the entrance, leaving us with no choice but to face them. Then again, I imagined my chances of actually outrunning a vampire once they got close enough to see me were slim to none, so I supposed the shelter of the cave would be preferable.

I gave my companion a head start, letting him move into the cave and allowing him all the time he needed to check for bears or whatever else might be hiding in a nice dry spot like this. I wasn't an idiot, and my dad had told me enough stories of wild animals to know that I was better off letting the helpful stranger risk his neck. I'd be no good to him or Monty if I was eaten by a bear after all.

"Come," the man-mountain barked, his tone full of grit and making my spine straighten in defiance of his bossiness. Who the hell did he even think he was?

I resisted his order, standing there in the waning dusk while knowing how stupid it was to remain outside once darkness fell. I had to assume there were no bears in the cave, so I simply answered his summons with a scowl and followed him into the shelter.

Once I'd stepped inside, he moved to the threshold, dropping to one knee and taking the dagger from his hip before using it to score strange symbols into the dirt outside. My skin prickled as I watched him, a faint hum seeming to build with each mark of his blade in the dirt. Goosebumps rose along my skin, the feeling of eyes watching me making me lift my head to the trees beyond our shelter and frown into the darkness.

As he finished, a wave of warm air passed over me and a shiver raced down my spine. It wasn't unpleasant, but it sure as hell didn't feel natural either.

"What the fuck was that?" I whispered, taking a step away from the entrance and further into the cave. My hand fell into my pocket, fingers curling around the blade of knife as I hunted for an explanation to the strange sensation.

"I've placed a ward on the entrance to this place. No evil being shall find us or be able to pass over it," he said, like that wasn't fucking insane.

"Sure. And I'm just about to shit a solid lump of gold which we can use to buy pastries at the squirrel bakery over there by that tree," I deadpanned.

"That sounds painful," he replied stoically, not a flicker of amusement in his eyes as he strode out of the cave, leaving me staring after him without an answer to his bullshit.

"So you're just sticking with your magic runes story?" I called after him, folding my arms as I leaned against the cave wall, watching as he gathered a stack of wood into his arms.

"You asked a question, and I gave you the answer," he replied, his back to me now as he moved further from the cave mouth, leaving me with that bullshit reply and the creeping concern that he might be batshit.

I frowned down at the symbols he'd drawn in the dirt, my skin prickling once more. I couldn't deny the strange pressure I'd felt in the air as he'd finished them, but that was more likely to have been an errant breeze than some magical form of protection. I scoffed at the absurdity of it. Maybe the only way he could get any sleep at night was by convincing himself there was magic keeping him safe.

"What are you?" I asked suspiciously.

He sure as hell wasn't from the Realm, and it wasn't like he'd brought me to some secret camp or hideout full of others like him. He seemed utterly at home here in the wilderness and yet hopelessly lost all at once.

"Something the world forgot and time left behind." He moved further away on his mission to gather firewood, and I sighed, knowing I should help him instead of lingering in the cave like an asshole. His answer left a lot to be desired, but I could see he was set on giving me riddles instead of truths, so I wasn't going to waste my breath asking again.

I took a step towards him, but as I moved closer to the so-called ward, I had the strong urge to head back into the cave instead.

*Better to stay where it's safe and nothing can hurt you.*

Without really meaning to, I turned and stepped back inside, pressure seeming to nudge at my back until I was fully within the cave once more and the need to get to safety abandoned me.

I shook my head, wondering what I'd been going to do, then trying to figure out how I could have forgotten to help collect the firewood.

I turned back to the cave entrance, spotting my companion further down the slope which led back to the forest, his arms almost full with branches fit for the fire. His muscles bulged with the weight of them and my gaze cast over his powerful frame briefly before I yanked my eyes away.

As I approached the ward again, I half turned away from it, the desire to stay inside gripping me fiercely.

*Stay inside, it's safer.*

The thought flitted through my mind, but it was like hearing someone else speak, their wants not in line with my own, and as I focused on that, the strength of the words seemed to falter. I didn't want to stay inside, dammit.

I clenched my jaw and crossed the threshold despite the rising urge to stay in the cave. My steps felt like they were made through quicksand as I passed the ward and I glared at it, sure his bullshit claims had somehow planted themselves in my head and were making me go crazy too.

No doubt it was just the anxious thoughts filling my head, my fear for my family at the forefront, my awe and terror over escaping the Realm a close second. It was no wonder I was close to cracking. But I certainly wasn't going to start believing in magic scribbles in the dirt and thinking they held some kind of power over my mind.

I broke free of the desire to turn back and stay within the cave, shattering the thoughts with a grunt of frustration before stepping out onto the hillside where I started gathering firewood.

As I filled my arms, I noticed the man-mountain watching me, the intensity of his gaze too much to ignore and I stood upright to glare back at him.

"Yes?" I challenged when he didn't drop his gaze, those golden eyes assessing me like I was somehow far more interesting than he'd thought I was before.

The evening light illuminated the rich bronze colour of his skin and lit a fire in his golden eyes, making my throat bob as I stared at him. I hadn't ever met anybody like him before. It wasn't just his powerful frame or that blazing look in his unusual eyes, it was something deeper than that, something fiercer, and I realised with a jolt what it was. He was fearless. Utterly, entirely without fear. He didn't run scared from the vampires, didn't bow to their commands or fall to their orders. He was their equal, or perhaps even more than that because he refused to allow them to break that thing which had been broken so long ago in every human I'd ever known. Perhaps it had even been broken in me too.

I realised I was staring and blinked a few times to break the connection between us, the heat in my veins making me clear my throat as I made to turn away from him once more.

"Why didn't you stay in the cave where it's safe?" he asked slowly, and I stiffened as I realised the voice in my mind had felt like his somehow. Except that was insane and I didn't believe in his bullshit magic runes.

"Because I didn't want to. Besides, how different is it being here than there? It's ten paces away at best," I replied, raising my chin defiantly.

He may have been better prepared to fight off vampires than I was, but that didn't make me some meek damsel in need of his help with every mundane thing. I'd been surviving on my own cunning, strength, and instincts for my entire life, and I was still here thanks to that, which was more than could be said for a lot of the people who had once lived in the Realm.

"The runes should have kept you inside," he said, as if that made any sense.

"The scratches in the dirt? Yeah…sorry to break it to you, but I just stepped right over them as if they were, well, scratches in the dirt…"

He arched an eyebrow at me, and I arched one right back. Two could play the silent asshole game. I'd once gone a week without saying a single word simply because Montana had bet me I couldn't.

"And you felt no urge to stay inside?" he asked.

I clucked my tongue, not wanting to admit to having felt any such thing.

"Was that some kind of trick?" I asked, although the words sounded mad the moment they left my lips and I wished I could draw them back.

"I only wanted to keep you safe," he replied, eyeing me far too curiously once again. I think I'd preferred it when he'd been ignoring me. "The ward was just to encourage you to stay within the protection of our shelter where you would be less likely to get into any trouble. I'm surprised you were aware of its effect on you, and even more surprised that you were able to overcome it."

"You think I'm going to believe you're some kind of wizard or sorcerer?" I scoffed, images from my dad's stories filling my mind of children going to magic schools and wise old men who wandered the woods. He didn't look like either, and I was pretty sure none had ever really existed anyway. "Because I'm not in the mood for any of your bibbity-bobbity-bullshit, so-"

"Any such men died out before my time. Which is a long fucking time ago."

"Riiight." I took half a step back, wondering if I should just get out of here, leave the insane man to his cave in the woods and go after my family on my own. Only problem was, I had no idea where to even start looking for them, and he didn't seem inclined to share.

"I only use the power of the wards, and they have many limitations." He stepped forward and took the small stack of firewood from my arms without giving me time to question his nonsense further, adding it to his own much more impressive heap. Without another word, he turned away and carried it into the cave.

I opened my mouth to further protest his supposed power, but as I glanced about at the darkening woodland and wondered if any more animal spies were watching me, I hesitated. So vampires and familiars were a yes, but I was going to draw the line at magic runes? I blew out a frustrated breath, my own inner monologue betraying me as I wondered for a moment if he might not be entirely full of shit. After all, the world beyond the Realm was entirely unknown to me. He was the one who lived here. But seriously? Magic runes?

"For fuck's sake," I muttered to myself.

I hugged my arms tight around my body and jogged after him, deciding to suspend disbelief for at least as long as it took to get my family back. What did I care if he liked drawing scribbles in the dirt and believed they held power? If it did hold any truth to it, then that would be to my benefit and if not, it made no difference whatsoever.

As I crossed the wards again, I felt another wash of air passing over me, almost seeming to welcome me in. Fuck. Was anything I thought I knew about the world even true? If scribbles in the dirt could hold power and vampires could tame beasts to do their bidding, then what was to say there weren't boogie men in the woods and the moon wasn't made of cheese?

The cave wasn't too deep, but the back of it widened out, grey stone walls arching overhead, the floor littered with dry leaves and twigs, nothing too ominous about it.

I wondered what he expected me to do now that we were here. He seemed to be quite content to linger in silence, but despite my usual aversion to any kind of conversation with people outside of my family, I had questions. Most of which involved them and how to get to them, but I guessed an effort at manners wouldn't go amiss, no matter how painful the prospect seemed.

"I'm Callie," I said as I moved to take a seat opposite my companion who was starting to build the fire.

I had no real idea how to help him, so I just leaned back against the wall and watched while he stacked branches and gathered kindling.

The silence stretched uncomfortably, seconds ticking into minutes until I finally let out a huff of irritation.

"This is the part where you give me your name," I prompted, not really meaning to sound as pissed as I did, but whatever, my neck was still bruised from the grip of his fingers, so he deserved at least a little spite from me.

"A man's name holds a lot of power." He finished building the fire and began striking two flints together to light it.

Okay then. As I'd suspected, he was insane.

I scowled at him and started coming up with names for him in my head. If he didn't want to give me his name, then I'd give him one myself. Like Asshole or He-who-doesn't-talk or Arrogant-jerk or Fucking Shawn or Phillip....

The fire bloomed to life and he leaned back to watch it. "My name is Magnar Elioson, first of the Blessed Crusaders. It means warrior of the sun. I was my clan's Earl before I slept." He pushed a hand through his long hair and sighed like the weight of the world lay on his shoulders.

"What's that supposed to mean?" I asked in confusion, my gaze tracking the way the small flames sent light dancing across his skin.

"I'm a slayer, perhaps the last of my kind. It was our job to protect mortals from the wrath of the vampires. They should have been wiped from this world nine hundred years ago, but something went wrong. I was betrayed."

"You... betrayed? What do you mean nine hundred years ago?" Instead of his answer helping me understand the title which he claimed went with his name, it only seemed to present me with more questions. Questions which I really shouldn't have been asking, but shit, I wanted to know.

"That is a very long story." His gaze lingered on the growing flames, and I wondered if he planned on telling it to me or not. "A long, long time ago, the leader of the Clan of Prophecies foresaw the downfall of those monsters. She saw me leading the Slayers' Crusade against them and bringing down the Belvederes once and for all."

"Sorry, who?" I didn't like interrupting him, but he'd already lost me. I had no idea who the Belvederes were or what they had to do with the vampires, and he was talking about them like he assumed I held those answers already.

Magnar turned to look at me, and I could tell he was more than a little surprised by my ignorance, his golden eyes roaming over my features and making me fight the urge to squirm beneath his focus. For some reason, my brain chose that moment to remind me of the tightness of his grip when it was locked around my throat, the way my pulse had thundered as he held me at his mercy, how easily he could have ended my life while supposedly saving it. Heat burned through my veins as I took in the sight of his powerful body before it was doused with the reality of him having done all of that purely to stop me from running to my family's aid.

"That is the name the original vampires gave themselves when they crossed the sea to this land. They are the ones who started all of this over a thousand years ago. Do they go by another name now?" he asked.

"I've never heard of them, but I don't really know much about what goes on outside of the Realm. The vampires never bothered to tell us about the way things are run." I shrugged. "We are food, and as such, we don't possess the right to question the ways of our masters," I quoted bitterly.

Magnar growled like a beast awoken in the night, the sound sending a shiver right down to my core, making me wonder just how dangerous he really was as his fist curled tight around the hilt of his dagger for a moment before he forced himself to release it again.

"My dad always said the vampires keep us ignorant on purpose because the less we know about them, the less likely it would be for us to find a way to rise up against them. He said that humanity's greatest weakness is ignorance. But the cure to ignorance is knowledge, so if you know something I don't about them, then I want to hear it. All of it."

Magnar considered me for a moment, passing a hand over the beard which covered the lower half of his face before sighing, giving me a nod.

"I suppose they wouldn't want you to know how they came to power," Magnar said thoughtfully. "But my people have always known that bringing down the Belvederes would be the key to the downfall of the entire vile species. We hunted them to the ends of the earth, until they were forced to separate and hide from us like the worms they are. No matter how hard we searched, we couldn't locate any of them. But then the prophecy came to light."

"Prophecy?" I asked, figuring I needed to put aside my doubts and hear what he had to say, no matter how insane all of this sounded.

"They were going to be together, gathered in the same place for the first time in a century. I was supposed to lead the Slayers' Crusade against them with my brother, Julius, beside me. Our victory was written in the runes." He sighed, looking into the building flames instead of at me as he continued. "The only issue was that it wasn't going to happen for a hundred years, and there was only one way that I could be there to fulfil my destiny. While the rest of the clans prepared for the battle and raised the next generations ready to fight for the freedom the world deserved, I was to be shielded from the ravages of time so that I could lead them. My brother and I were put into a rune sleep for one hundred years so that we could wake ready to lead the crusade and bring the vampires to their knees."

"A rune sleep?" I wasn't sure if anything that he was saying made sense. It sounded like he was claiming to be a thousand years old, and though I knew the vampires were immortal, I had never heard of a human man sharing that gift.

"Yes. My mother was of the Clan of Dreams, whose people had power over sleep. Among their gifts was the ability to trap someone in their dreams, locking them in place with a rune much like those I carved outside this cave. Such runes lose their power over time, but my mother was powerful enough to be able to choose the exact moment when their effects would run out. If she chose to lock someone in a dream for an hour or a month or a year, then they would stay there with no way to free themselves unless she released them."

150

"And they wouldn't age during that time? Or die of thirst?" I asked with a frown. Even if I believed what he was saying, then it was hard to imagine how someone could survive in such a state.

"That part took a little help from a goddess."

I opened my mouth to deny the existence of any such being. My dad had told us all about the old religions, and I knew people in the Realm who still prayed to one god or another daily, but I'd never believed in anything like that. What kind of god would just sit by and watch all of the horrendous things that were happening to their followers?

I clearly hesitated long enough for Magnar to catch the gist of my thoughts because he released a breath of amusement.

"Cursing or denying the gods' existence in my presence won't offend me. I curse them daily. They do not offer mortals much beyond pain and suffering for their own amusement. But the goddess Idun has helped the slayers many times over the centuries because she shares our hatred of the vampires."

"Why?" I blurted, unable to help myself, deciding that I would simply listen to his story for what it was and not question any of the impossible things he was describing. In a world ruled by vampires, who could say where the line of reality had been drawn anyway?

"Because they are immortal, and that gift should never have been given to them. She is the goddess of eternal youth, and no one but her should have been able to bestow such a thing. It has left her rather bitter," he explained.

"So, if she didn't make them immortal, then who did? And can't she just undo it if she's so unhappy about it? What's the point of being the goddess of immortality if you can't take it away from those who don't deserve it?" I demanded.

"Feel free to ask her if she ever deigns to speak with you. The gods seem to be a lot better at making messes than they are at fixing them. Or perhaps it just amuses them to watch us as we struggle to deal with what they've set in motion. Who knows?"

The idea of gods and goddesses laughing at the destruction which had befallen the world set my blood boiling, and I ground my teeth angrily as I tried to turn my mind from the idea.

Dad had told me that people who believed in religion always did so blindly anyway. So Magnar's story about a goddess helping him could be nothing more than a fantasy he'd convinced himself of. Although, if that was the case, then I wasn't sure how to explain his time-hopping abilities, and something in my gut told me he wasn't lying about that. He really was a thousand years old. Or at least he believed himself to be so.

"What went wrong then? You said your mother knew exactly how to set the runes so that you could sleep for a hundred years. Did she fuck it up somehow?"

"She didn't fuck it up," he sneered. "She would never have made such a mistake. This must have been caused by someone else. Someone who betrayed us all," he growled darkly.

"And that's why the vampires are still around but the slayers aren't?" I asked, that part making sense at least.

If he was destined to lead the battle which would destroy them but never showed up to fulfil his role, it stood to reason that they would have won instead, changing fate, setting this whole situation in motion.

He nodded, a darkness in his gaze which made my skin prickle. "A thousand years has passed, and I have woken to a world ruled by the monsters I fucking despise and void of my kin." He shifted slightly, his attention never wavering from the building flames, and I felt his rage and sorrow like a physical force. He was alone in this world, everyone he'd known was dead, and the destiny he'd thought he was following hadn't even come to pass.

Despite all of the new questions his story presented, I knew in my gut that he was telling the truth. No matter how insane that might be.

I had no idea what to say in response to such pain. My family had been taken from me, but I still had hope. There was a chance, no matter how small, that I might be able to get them back.

I might have hated him, might have resented him and felt such anger towards him that it was twisting my insides into knots, but as I watched him across the flickering flames, a small piece of me tightened with sorrow for this beast of a man.

Magnar was completely alone.

# MONTANA

## CHAPTER TEN

My eyes flickered open, and I found clouds skimming through an unwelcoming grey sky, my gaze catching on a bird that danced in an updraft, mocking me as it drifted this way and that, then flew to wherever the wind was going.

*Take me with you.*

The sky was grey and oppressive, no sliver of true sunlight, not a crack, not a gleam. Iron bars curved overhead, telling me I was in a cage, and the bump and jostle of my body informed me I was in another one of those moving metal things.

*A vestibule…no, but it was definitely something beginning with ve… vectible? Vehicle!*

My little triumph was quickly lost to the reality of my situation, and as my thoughts sharpened, I realised I needed to try and get out of here. I lifted my head high enough to find others bundled in beside me like sardines, all of them laying in a wide, open area at the back of the vehicle. We weren't chained up, my hands and legs free to move, but with the cage holding us here, there was no chance of making a run for it.

I craned my neck to get a view beyond the cage and my heart

slammed into my throat at the sight unfolding around me.

We were crossing an enormous bridge over a gleaming river, its rusted metal struts rising high on either side of us with imposing steel towers standing at either end. Ahead was a city. It had to be. It was too large to be a town, and the buildings were frighteningly tall, all stacked in rows upon rows like an army of giants turned to stone.

In the distance, I could just make out what appeared to be the bombed ruins of the city's suburbs. A demolished bridge poked out of the water, the broken remnants of the structure twisted and bent. Whatever remained of this part of the city had clearly been incredibly lucky to survive at all.

The truck slowed to a halt, and I quickly dropped back down, pretending to be unconscious like the others still were. My heart strummed a frantic tune as I peeked through my eyelashes, spotting a couple of vampires with large swords investigating us.

I remained still as they gave the order for our driver to continue, and we sped off of the bridge, passing through an iron gate that thunked shut behind us with a finality that said it would be no easy feat to get back through it.

The gleaming glass of towering skyscrapers leered down at me, reaching so far toward the sky it made me dizzy.

This place was beautiful and untarnished, just like the vampires themselves. And the further we travelled, the more glitz and glamour shone down at me. Whoever lived behind these sparkling walls held the fates of humans in their palms, and one tight squeeze would crush us all.

We arrived at an enormous brick wall that stretched above me by at least twenty feet. It was painted white and looked newly built, at odds with the buildings surrounding it. I tried to lift my head to see more, but guards filed around the truck, checking it over.

I kept my eyes closed until we started moving again, then caught a glimpse of another iron gate as we headed through the opening in the wall. The scent of freshly cut grass and the rush of a thousand wind-blown leaves snatched my senses, like the promise of something pure and natural at the centre of all those towering buildings.

A fan of branches stretched above me as we passed along a smooth road, winding through a forest which was growing right through the heart of the concrete city. I could hardly believe the sprawling sight of coloured leaves, mixtures of brown and deep gold, preparing to fall with the next breeze. I'd seen the woodland on the edge of the Realm do it a hundred times. Their leaves dying and cascading to the ground before returning the next summer. The trees seemed to be taking more time here – wherever *here* was. But the trees near the Realm were long dead, their colour drained from the world.

I lifted my head, desperate to see more, but only trees and a mosaic of golden leaves on the ground stared back at me.

I lurched as the vehicle hit a bump and someone groaned beside me. Glancing down, I found a blonde-haired girl sleeping soundly at my side. As my eyes trailed across the others, I realised they were all female, and something told me that was no coincidence, but I couldn't for the life of me figure out why.

When the truck eventually stopped, I caught sight of a tower between the trees. A flag stood atop it with red and white stripes, and one corner held a blue rectangle speckled with white stars.

As uniformed vampires surrounded the truck once more, I returned to feigning sleep, not wanting to be drugged again or worse. And I wouldn't get two feet from all those assholes if I made a run for it right in front of them.

The shift of bodies spoke of vampires climbing into the truck, and I was soon hauled into strong arms, carried over a male's shoulder as he descended from the vehicle with light grace.

As he silently walked along, I dared to open my eyes once more, trying to get a look at where I was being taken.

Frustratingly, my hair veiled my view, and lifting a hand to move it would have alerted the vampire to my wakeful state.

A shadow fell over me as we entered a building and a moment later, I was dumped on a vaguely damp floor. Without warning, water cascaded over me in a torrent, and I yelled in surprise, wincing from the blast. I heard the other girls rousing and quickly sprang upright. My adrenaline spiked as I found myself in a white tiled room with drains at our feet, and I counted fourteen other girls standing beneath the shower that was raining down from the ceiling.

But it wasn't ice-cold like the showers I'd been privy to my whole life; it was warm and kissed my skin like heated raindrops. The tension in my body ebbed away as I tilted my face into the flow and stole a moment in the heat of it, realising how deep the cold winter air had bitten me.

Before us stood three vampires, all male and staring at us with impassive expressions as they clutched their red cloaks away from the water. One of them spoke, lifting his chin, his eyes two murky pools of green.

"Wash. Use the soap provided. Remove your clothes and place them in there." He pointed to a metal container on one side of the room which looked suspiciously like a trash can. The space was tiled and unnaturally clean, and I guessed it was some sort of bathroom.

The other girls started stripping and picking up the bars of soap left in a pile at the back of the shower. I pushed to my feet, looking between the vampires with tense wariness, but they simply stood there waiting for us to do as they'd ordered.

None of this was making sense, but with the cold thawing from my bones and the promise of being clean presented to me, it wasn't too difficult to follow this command. Besides, Dad once said 'when life gives you lemons, squeeze 'em, throw in some vodka, add some sugar and you'll have yourself a half decent ducktail'. Then he'd sighed and told us about all the different ducktails he used to drink with mom at fancy bars. Point being, life was giving me lemons right now, so I needed to make the most of it while it lasted.

I turned my back on the vampires, pulling off my sodden clothes. Being naked sent a ripple of vulnerability through me, but I tried not to let the pounding of my heart overwhelm me as I picked up a bar of soap and started scrubbing. The scent of honey filled my nose as the soap lathered, making my mouth water and my stomach growl in hopes of an unlikely meal.

The blonde from the truck stood beside me, her golden skin growing brighter as she washed the filth from her body.

"Hey," I whispered, but before she could answer, one of the guards barked, "No talking!" and the girl turned away from me.

I ground my teeth as I gathered up my clothes, moving to the container and dumping them in it.

One of the vampires approached me, and I didn't miss the way his eyes slid down my body. There was no lust in his gaze, just curiosity, like he was surprised to find I had tits or something. *Yeah, asshole, I've got tits galore, and I'll claw your eyes out if you come anywhere near them.*

Alright, so maybe I didn't have tits galore thanks to how many nights I'd gone hungry in the Realm, but still.

He stepped past me, close enough to brush against my arm, and I recoiled, baring my teeth like a feral creature. But he didn't turn my way as he picked up a bottle of something and tossed it to me. I caught it, frowning at the word conditioner on the bottle, not knowing its meaning.

"Scrub it into your mane, then wash it out," the vampire clipped. "Hurry up about it."

I turned the bottle over in my hands suspiciously, finding a beautiful woman on it with luscious long hair and a serene smile on her face. I guessed it was some kind of hair soap, and as I popped the lid open, a fruity scent reached me and I squeezed a measure into my hand, passing the bottle to the next girl. I rubbed it into my hair, then let the water wash it out, catching the blonde girl's eye as she did the same.

The moment the last woman was finished washing her hair, the water shut off and we stood there naked and waiting for direction. One of the vampires beckoned us forward and we padded along after him, turning a corner into a room with plain wooden benches and a rack full of white robes.

"Well don't just stand there dripping water all over the floor," he growled. "Put on a robe."

He tossed a few our way and I caught two, passing one to the blonde girl beside me.

"Thanks," she breathed, and I nodded, a pathetic excuse for a smile tugging at my lips as I pulled on my robe. "I'm Paige."

"Montana," I whispered, securing the robe in place. "Holy shit this is soft."

She breathed a small laugh.

"*Quiet*," the vampire snapped as he marched through the chamber and beckoned us to follow. "Keep moving." He pointed at the way ahead; a white corridor leading out of sight.

My gut prickled with nerves. What if we were being herded to the slaughter? Were they having us wash so our bodies were clean when it came to the butcher's axe?

*No, they won't kill us. Vampires don't kill, they drain.*

My stomach roiled and I fought for my courage as I hurried along with the other girls into the corridor. One glance over my shoulder told me the other two vampires were following, keeping us together in a tight group.

We were escorted into another room where racks of dresses sat across from a wall of mirrors, all lit by bright bulbs. I scoured the place, confused as a female vampire appeared beyond the dresses. She was clad in a white jumpsuit that showed off her toned arms and a set of shiny high heels peeked out beneath it, clicking across the tiled floor as she moved.

"Hello, my name's Felicia. I'm here to look after you," she said in a disarmingly soft tone that I refused to let fool me. "Take a seat in front of one of my beauticians and we'll get started."

She waved her hands at the male vampires behind us, and they left us to it, shutting the door as they retreated, a sharp click telling me they'd locked it too.

Rows of cushioned chairs sat before the mirrors and more vampires were waiting beside each one, all of them dressed in those weird white overalls, looking to us curiously.

My eyes skipped around, hunting for a window, a door I could slip out of when the monsters were looking elsewhere. But the door across the room was bolted shut and there were no windows to be seen.

Some of the girls floated toward the beauticians, but I remained in place, scowling at Felicia.

"What's this for?" I asked, and she gave me a too-sweet smile.

"You're going to see the royal family." She beamed as if that was a wonderful treat for all of us. *Well you can stuff your treat right up your ass and redigest it, Felicia.*

The Elites clearly thought so much of themselves that they actually had a *royal* family. It was a joke. What did they want with us anyway? Weren't we just a food source?

My gaze trailed to a rack of beautiful gowns hanging on a rail at the back of the room, but my eyes snapped onto the real threat in the room as Felicia laid a hand on my shoulder.

"You can be with me. What's your name?" She steered me towards the nearest seat, not seeming to notice me digging my heels in as her superior strength forced me to do as she willed.

With a push from her, my ass hit the seat and I found myself looking at myself in the mirror. My black hair was a wet mop that hung right down to my chest and my eyes looked almost as hollow as my cheeks. I could count on one hand the number of times I'd seen my full reflection. Mirrors were a luxury in the Realm, and the tiny cracked one my family owned had hardly shown anything of our bodies. And why would I care about looking at myself anyway?

Felicia gently pulled my hair back from my face and I tensed from her touch, expecting her nails to cut into my scalp, but no pain came.

"What do you want?" I snarled.

"Your name."

"Where's my father?" I demanded, my eyes locking with hers in the mirror as my heart thundered wildly.

"Back in your Realm, I imagine," she said disinterestedly, running a thumb along the line of my right cheekbone. "You are very beautiful. Most beautiful things have beautiful names. So what's yours?"

I clenched my jaw, refusing to give it to her, and she rolled her eyes at me as if I was being petulant. She picked up a strange metal device from the counter in front of the mirror and with a click of a button, it made a roaring noise. I tried to dive out of my seat away from it, but she grabbed my shoulder, tugging me back into the chair and casually pulling a leather strap over my chest, tightening it in place to hold me still. I cursed, jerking against it as she turned that strange device towards my head, and a whoosh of hot air blasted my hair. It took me another second to accept she wasn't trying to roast me alive with it and was instead using it to dry my hair. The other girls were watching me, and none fought to escape as the vampires attending them turned those same machines towards their heads.

Felicia combed her fingers through my hair and soon it was completely dry, floating down around my shoulders in feathery waves, looking sleeker than I'd ever seen it before.

"Your name?" she asked again as she grabbed a brush and combed out the tangles. I didn't answer as she picked up a new device that clamped down on my hair and then ran over it, straightening it out bit by bit.

"You'll feel better once your face is done," Felicia said brightly when I didn't answer. "Then maybe you will tell me your name."

"What do you mean? What are you going to do to my face?" I awkwardly reached up to the strap over my chest, trying to tug it free, but it was secured at the back of the seat.

Felicia thumbed through an array of dark and light powders next to some coloured sticks on the surface before the mirror.

"What is that stuff?" I asked, cringing away from it.

"Just hold still," Felicia encouraged, dabbing a brush in a pot of pale liquid. I stiffened as she brushed it against my cheeks, the sensation strangely affectionate as she continued to paint my face in gentle strokes.

She used powders next, then picked up a brush dipped in black liquid that she carefully pushed against my lashes. When she ran a red gloss over my lips, she smiled appreciatively at her work and stepped back so I could see myself in the mirror.

"What do you think?" she asked excitedly.

My breath caught in my throat as I took in the way my face had been painted to hide blemishes and enhance my features. The heat in my veins grew to a dangerous burn as I grew angry. Fucking furious.

"You look stunning," Felicia cooed. "I think a hairclip just here would suit you." She tugged a lock of hair back from the front of my face. "Yes, I'll go grab one." She headed off to some drawers across the room, and my gaze remained latched to this new me she'd created with her strange face paint.

My skin itched to remove the stuff plastered to it, so I brought up the sleeve of my robe and started rubbing. It didn't come off easily and left me with two streaks of the black stuff from my eyes bleeding down my cheeks.

My face was a mess, but I didn't give a shit as Felicia came rushing back over with the hairclip tumbling from her fingers.

"For the love of the gods!" she gasped. "What have you done?"

"What's this all for? Why are you dressing us up and trying to make us look like- like-" I struggled to find the end of that sentence, but then it hit me like a heart attack as I looked between the other girls with their carefully styled hair and painted faces, realising exactly what their intention was. "Like *you.*" *Like vampires with their glossy hair and perfect skin.*

Paige spoke up, her chin rising. "She's right, what's this about?" Her tone was strong, and it gave me hope that I wasn't the only human in this room willing to fight this fate.

More murmured questions sounded from the girls until Felicia slammed her hand down on the table to shut us up.

"Enough," she hissed. "You are to be presented to the Royals. They will not be pleased if you haven't made an appropriate amount of effort."

A knock came at the door and Felicia straightened.

"Two minutes," a male voice boomed from beyond it.

Felicia looked to my spoiled face in horror, but her shoulders dropped in defeat. "You've ruined your chances, human. You have no idea what you've done." She seemed a little emotional as she unstrapped me from the seat and I sprang out of it, backing away from her as she turned to the other women.

"Please pick out some underwear and a gown. You will need to look your absolute best, so be sure to choose something fitting for your complexion."

"What's a complexion?" one of the girls muttered, and Felicia pinched the bridge of her nose, pointing us over to the rack of dresses with a sigh.

Most of the girls headed to the rack, hesitantly picking out clothes, but I remained rooted to the spot. I didn't want to parade in front of some royal assholes dressed up like a doll. I'd never worn a dress in my life, and I had no intention of starting now.

The others started putting on the gowns, each of them long and flowing, like something from a fairy tale Dad had told us. I'd never seen anything like those clothes in the Realm. They didn't seem at all practical, and I didn't need some dangly frills tripping me up when I made a run for it. But then again, I wouldn't survive long outside in just a robe. If I got a chance to escape, I needed to be wearing more than this.

I reluctantly approached a stack of underwear, pulling on the simplest black pairing I could find amongst the lace and silk. One of which was just a sliver of material that looked like it wanted to climb my ass and make a home there. *Not today, ass goblin.*

When I was done, I wrapped my fluffy robe back around me, gazing at the girls in their glitzy dresses.

With a breath of decision, I turned to Felicia. "I'm not wearing one."

Her eyes practically popped out of her head. "Oh, human, you must!" She stepped forward and I backed up, expecting an attack as her eyes flashed. "If you go out there like this, I will be held accountable. I must present you as well as I can."

"No," I said through clenched teeth as she advanced on me, and a ripple of angry mutters passed between the beauticians.

"How will you please them like this?" she almost whimpered, looking to the other vampires who shook their heads mournfully.

Fear tempted me toward the dresses, but rebelliousness kept me rooted to the spot. These monsters had ripped me from my home, taken me from my family, and now they expected me to *please* them? Well I sure as hell wasn't going to play along.

A persistent drumming noise sounded beyond the room, and Felicia looked at me in alarm. "There's no more time. You'll have to go as you are."

"Fine by me," I muttered, falling into line behind the other girls as Felicia led the way through a door.

Another corridor. More white walls.

The drumming grew louder, and the sound of a crowd gathered in my ears. Nerves scraped at my veins as a door was thrust open and pale daylight spilled over us.

I was the last to step out, and Felicia snatched the robe from my shoulders as I passed her. My cheeks flamed as I turned to her, reaching for it as the cold air whipped around me, but her expression said no before she slammed the door in my face.

Hundreds of vampires stared down at me from a huge stand, rising high up above the stone courtyard we'd been ejected into, and my pulse rioted at the intensity of their stares.

The girls behind me gasped, and I turned, seeking what they'd seen, and my gaze fell on a podium opposite the crowd, high up above us. Four vampires sat there dressed in regal clothes; three male and one female, all sitting on chalk-white thrones.

The youthful-looking woman sat between the painfully handsome men; her head was crowned in ornate silver and diamonds, her skin glitteringly pale and her golden hair like sunlight given life. The perfect symmetry of her face stole the breath from my lungs, her beauty something only an artist could create. Her lips were two perfect rose petals, her eyes blazing blue and endlessly deep. Her dress was cream and flowing, the folds and swathes of silk pooling at her feet, but no gown could match the sheer perfection of her, no garments could ever be worthy of such a woman. She was a goddess walking the earth, her face hard to look upon without some deep reaction taking root in your soul. She was more than Elite, far more. The most powerful vampires I'd ever seen paled to nothing beside her, and the only beings on this earth capable of matching her allure were the three creatures sitting at her side.

The magnetic pull of those three males was so intense that I simply found myself staring, drinking in the sight of them with eternal curiosity. All were dressed in deep navy suits with heavy cloaks hanging from their shoulders the colour of the night sky. Swords were hitched to their waists and medals glinted on their chests, while the female's sword caught my eye where it leaned casually against the side of her chair.

Despite the males' unified clothes, they were all so different, equally beautiful, but in their own unique way. Upon their heads were crowns, just simple rings of black metal, whereas the female's crown was a thing of beauty, wrought iron twisted into sharp points around glittering diamonds.

The male vampire on the far left had fair hair which was pushed back in an almost careless way, the warmth of his skin a contrast with the pale colour of those sleek locks. His eyes were two bright pools of a summer sky which drew me in and made my pulse quicken without warning. His jaw was square, and his lips tilted naturally towards a smile, making it look as though he was on the verge of laughter or enjoying a private joke. His hand rested lightly on the arm of his throne, fingers tapping against it, nonchalance clinging to him in a way that spoke of how utterly privileged he was.

I forced my gaze to move on, looking beside him to a vampire with a mane of rich brown hair pulled into a tight ponytail at the base of his neck. His powerful body seemed tight with tension, contempt rolling from him so thickly that it caught in the back of my throat as his icy gaze roamed over the assembled crowd. His bone structure was sharp, ruthless, entirely captivating like the first male, but far harsher too. His cheeks were hollowed out and his nose was a chiselled rectangle. Brutality clung to him like a cloak which I doubted he ever took off. His eyes were two dark pits of rust but were inviting in comparison to the final vampire whose eyes were iron itself.

He sat on the far right of the line-up, his constricted jaw looking as powerful as a weapon. His suit hugged his muscular frame, his posture speaking of constraint, discipline, and dominance. His hair was as black as coal, shaved in harshly at the sides then pushed back on top with perfect care. His features were all angular lines which carved his punishingly attractive face, and his eyes were deep set, the colour of ash, like some great fire had once burned in his gaze, only to flicker, fade and turn to dust. But between the beauty and hostility clinging to every inch of him, it was his tortured expression that captured me most, his mouth pulled down in grim tedium, his brows drawn low as if he was already long tired of this day and perhaps the rest of them to come. And some part of me wanted to know what could possibly cause such apathy in a creature who clearly held the world in his fist.

The four royals finally gave us their attention, tension rolling down my spine as anticipation set the air humming.

A door opened on the opposite side of the courtyard and men stepped out to join us. Humans, all clean-shaven with close-cut hair that was rarely seen in the Realms. Their clothes were the biggest joke of all. Suits, the kind I'd seen the vampires wearing at times, practising their importance.

With a spark of recognition, I spotted Hank amongst them, his long mane now cropped short, and as his gaze locked with mine, his brows tugged together. He gave me a small nod of acknowledgement which I returned, before his gaze turned to a question at my lack of clothes. I followed his line of sight to the silken black underwear I wore, my meagre bust barely filling out the cups of the bra.

Felicia appeared on the podium several steps away from the so-called royals, lifting her chin to speak. "Princess Clarice of the New Empire, and Princes Miles, Fabian, and Erik, I present to you this year's finest human stock of the Realms." Each of the princes nodded to their name, marking them in the order they stood from left to right. Visually, they appeared to be in their mid-twenties, but I knew about their unageing faces. They could be hundreds of years old or more.

Applause broke out from the crowd behind us, and I refused to turn, refused to cower like some of the women did, or even bow low like one girl who was in a dress of rose-gold.

I stared up at the Royals, glowering and embracing the semi-nakedness of my body. I wouldn't let them see me cringe from their scouring gazes or bend my back in any semblance of submission.

Princess Clarice lifted a single finger, winding it through the air with a playful smile pulling at her lips. "Spin for us."

I scowled as some of the men and women complied, turning on their heels in a slow circle. The rest followed. Even Hank did a kind of half-pivot. But not me. I pressed my bare feet to the icy stone, and when the entire royal family turned their gazes on me, I fought the flash of fear that struck my heart.

"Turn," Clarice asked me, softer this time, her voice a siren's song luring me to my death.

I considered obeying, I really did. But as I drank in their opulence, I thought of the cutbacks on our rations. I thought of the vampire jamming a cattle prod into my back. I thought of Callie and Dad and the worn eyes of the people in the Realm. So instead of doing what this *princess* said, I spat on the stone floor before me and sneered at them all, letting them see what I thought of them. I'd been taken from the people I loved most in this world, and I'd spent too many years biting my tongue and bowing my head to these monsters. I had nothing left to lose, and fury was my only friend as it wound its way through my chest and cheered on my defiance.

Silence stretched so far and wide that it rang out like a gong, echoing into eternity and beyond. My heartbeat ticked like a timer in my head, counting down to the inevitable backlash I was surely about to receive. Punishment? Death? Perhaps the first followed by the next. I'd be made an example of so the rest of the humans would be reminded who was in charge, who was *always* fucking in charge.

Erik, the bored looking prince with the penetrating eyes lifted his head, a glint of dark amusement flickering through his gaze.

"This is what you call the finest in the Realms, Felicia?" he taunted.

My eyes whipped to Felicia, her composure draining from her head to her spine as she sagged in apology.

Fabian tutted at Erik, then turned to the fair-haired prince at his side. "Make your choice, Miles," he instructed.

The line of girls shifted uneasily as Prince Miles' bright blue eyes trailed across us. Some of them dipped their heads or clasped hands with those beside them, and I ground my jaw, willing away my fear as I tried to work out what being picked might mean. Surely nothing good.

"What's your name?" Miles called down to the group, pointing at a raven-haired girl with ebony skin and large eyes.

She stepped forward, lifting her chin, and I noted the defiance in her stance. "Brianna," she replied, smoothing down her mauve dress.

"Nice to meet you, Brianna," Miles said with a sideways grin, and he turned to Felicia with a nod, but Brianna spoke up again.

"What's this about?" she asked, and low chatter sounded from the crowd behind us.

I threw a glance over my shoulder, taking in the stands filled with vampires. They didn't look anything like those who patrolled the Realm, all dressed up in gowns and fine suits. They were smiling, leaning in close to one another, seeming enthralled by this whole event.

"We'll explain everything soon," Miles replied, his eyes shining with warmth. But I wasn't fooled. There was something terrifying hiding behind his amiable expression. A monster behind the mask. There always was.

"I choose Brianna," Miles called to Felicia, and my heart thundered as a guard stepped forward from the edge of the courtyard, taking her arm and guiding her toward a door. As she stepped through it, she glanced back at us with a flash of fear in her eyes.

"Princess, are you ready?" Felicia asked Clarice.

The golden-haired vampire beamed as her eyes dragged over the group of men in the courtyard.

"Those two," Clarice pointed at a tall man with fierce eyes and another with broad shoulders and a shaved head. "Oh, and throw in that one." She pointed to Hank and my heart squeezed. The small moment of unity we'd shared on the aeroplane still seemed important to me, and seeing him chosen made my bones turn to ice. Perhaps they were picking which of us they wanted a drink from, like we were some kind delicacies now that we were clean and dressed in pretty clothes. But it all came to the same thing if they were simply going to stick a needle in our arms and take the blood they desired. Surely they wouldn't make such a parade of it if that was their intention. Then again, I was far beyond guessing the whims of psychotic beasts who had placed crowns upon their heads.

Two guards escorted the men away, taking them through the same door as Brianna, and goosebumps peppered my bare skin as the cold wind blew around me.

Was being chosen better than not being chosen? I had no idea, but the way my spine prickled with unease told me I didn't want to be selected.

"Prince Fabian, have you decided?" Felicia asked him and the royal vampire with the long hair stepped forward, his rust brown eyes whipping across us with intense scrutiny. As his gaze fell on me, a fire sparked in my chest and my shoulders trembled with anger. I hoped he didn't mistake it as a sign of weakness, because I was wrath embodied right now, and the will to fight was the only thing left to me.

A small smile tugged at the corner of Fabian's mouth, twisting his unnaturally stunning face into something purely wicked. It wasn't kindly like the one Miles had offered up; Fabian made no attempt to hide what he was with that smile, fangs flashing, the beast revealed.

My gut squirmed and I looked toward the other girls, my eyes falling on Paige. She was biting her lip, gazing back at me with concern like she expected to see death fall upon me at any second.

Fabian followed my gaze to her, and his brows arched with intrigue. "Name?" he asked, pointing at her.

Paige's cheeks paled as she stepped forward, and sickness gripped my stomach as I realised I'd drawn attention to her.

She cleared her throat and the sound echoed off of the stone walls. "Paige West."

Fabian tilted his head, giving her a hungry grin before turning his eyes to Felicia. "I've made my choice."

At his words, a guard strode to Paige's side, taking hold of her arm. She released a squeak of fright as he led her away, and I took a step in her direction, my heart drawing me after her.

"Don't hurt her," I commanded, like I held any sway in this world at all.

"Quiet!" a guard snapped at me, and I fought the urge to bite back at him.

Felicia wrung her hands as her eyes wheeled to Erik. "Um, Prince Erik, will you be making a selection this year?"

Erik looked up from a device in his hand, having been completely ignoring the world around him in favour of it. "Hm?"

Fabian bared his fangs at him. "She said, are you going to choose this year, or will you play your usual games, brother?" he growled, and Erik straightened, his cold eyes flaring with a challenge.

"I rarely play games, Fabian," Erik said with a dangerous glower, his voice a deep tenor that made a pit hollow out in my stomach. "But when I do, I always win."

Tension snared the air between them, their rivalry obvious.

Slowly, Erik's gaze dropped to the line-up of girls and slid briefly over us. When his eyes landed on me, I ground my teeth, glaring calmly back at him. He regarded me and my wild appearance with a ruthless inspection that had me feeling as though those ash grey eyes were peeling my flesh apart and sifting through the essence of who I was. He was measuring it all with a cold detachment that made me feel so inhuman that it summoned a wave of scalding hatred in my chest that crashed roughly against my heart.

Erik looked away from me and shrugged as if I'd made no impact on him whatsoever, and a flicker of relief darted through me.

Fabian looked to Felicia with a polite smile. "I think we're done here-"

"That one," Erik announced loudly, and it took me several long seconds to realise he was pointing at me, his finger like an arrow piercing through my chest and serving me an unquestionable fate.

My pulse thundered in my ears as his gaze locked with mine and his mouth hooked up into a cruel smirk.

"Name?" he demanded without any farce of sweetness.

I didn't want to give him my name. Doing so felt like offering him a piece of myself. But there was one thing I could give him and that was a reason not to choose me. Because anything had to be better than being picked by this formidable creature.

"I'm the girl who will make your life a living hell if you choose her," I said, enunciating every word to make sure he didn't miss a single one of them.

Erik's eyes glittered with malice and he sat up straighter in his seat, a predator with his appetite stirring. He was suddenly terrifyingly alert, no longer disinterested now that something had captured his attention, and of all the things in all the world, why did it have to be me?

He looked to Felicia with a nod and terror strummed a painful tune in my heart, playing a song that was heavy with dark fortunes.

"She is clearly disobedient," Fabian said quickly, seeming irritated.

"Choose appropriately, Erik, or do not choose at all."

My breaths quickened as I waited for my fate to be decided for me, my eyes seeking an escape from this den of wolves, but it seemed only one destiny was available to me.

"I've made my choice." Erik gave a half-shrug. "This is the offering and I've chosen a girl from it. Do make up your mind, brother. One moment you demand I pick, the next you bitch about my choice."

If possible, the grey sky grew greyer and the air became too thick to breathe.

Clarice moved between the two supposed brothers who didn't look related at all, placing a hand on each of their chests to keep them apart. "She's lovely, she just needs a little TLC."

Erik smirked and Fabian snarled at him, baring sharp canines which made my stomach knot.

"Fine," Fabian snarled, throwing a nod to the guards. One of them approached me at a swift pace and I backed up, shaking my head as a wild fear took hold of me.

But what could I do? Run, fight, scream. All the options I had led to one thing and one thing only. Erik had chosen me. And I was going where the others had been taken. There was no way out.

I didn't like the way Erik's eyes followed me or the way he sneered in my general direction. And as the guard's hand curled around my wrist, I decided to fight despite how futile it was. I was too afraid of what would happen if I let him take me to consider what might happen if he didn't.

I scratched his steely skin, trying to claw his hand off of me and some of the crowd started booing like I was the villain in their show. But this wasn't some performance for their entertainment, it was my life.

Panic seized my bones and I dug my heels in as the guard hauled me across the courtyard and shoved me through the door without care. I stumbled into a bright room, finding the chosen ones waiting inside it, all clustered together like we'd be safer together, but that was a lie, and they all knew it.

Paige ran to me, sliding her arms around my shoulders with

overfamiliar ease, like she wasn't afraid to care for people the way I was. "Are you okay?"

I nodded as she let me go, but I wasn't. Not even slightly.

"What do they want with us?" Brianna hissed, but no one had an answer.

My eyes locked on Hank whose face was taut with despair and ravaged by hopelessness. "This is gonna be bad," he said.

"Don't say that," Paige whispered fearfully. "There's hope yet."

No one answered, the quiet concealing the rioting voices in everyone's minds as they imagined whatever horrors were about to happen. My own mind was on overdrive, painting bloody futures I didn't want to consider, but I couldn't shut them out.

As the sound of the crowd died down beyond the walls, the silence thickened, and the tension followed.

Eventually, a door opened on the other side of the room and a woodland became visible beyond the heads of two male guards.

"Follow us," one of them commanded, and Hank led the way as we filed out of the room.

I kept close to Paige and Brianna, moving after them onto a stone pathway that disappeared into the trees. We marched on in silence and I gazed around at the expansive garden, wondering if it was worth trying to run. But the vampires were always faster. I'd never outpace them with their unnatural strength and stamina. My only chance was awaiting an opportunity to slip out unseen, to escape while no beast's eyes were on me.

We continued walking for several painful minutes, our footsteps the only noise between us.

A large building built of grey stone with high walls came into view, several towers rising from it leading to pointed tiled roofs that looked sharp enough to pierce the sky. It was perched on a rocky hill that overlooked a dark lake, and as we wound up towards it, I could see where ancient stone met with newer rock in the brickworks, as if towers and wings had been added over the years to create this imposing beast on the hillside.

A series of steps led up to a large stone pavilion where two vampires stood on guard with menacing swords strapped to their backs.

They stepped aside, watching us closely as we passed between them, and I swear one of them breathed in deeply as if trying to taste our blood on the air, while the other hollered, "Welcome to Belvedere Castle."

We passed through the pavilion and along a walkway towards two open wooden doors that led into the castle. Inside, a beautiful marble hallway greeted us where arching pillars held up an ancient ceiling and a wide staircase swept away to another floor.

I hardly had time to absorb the sight before we were led up the staircase, my bare toes pressing into the soft red carpet that covered each step. More guards greeted us at the top of the stairs and a vampire with cold eyes gripped my arm, leading me away from the group as everyone was taken in different directions. My heart tripled its pace as Paige disappeared down a corridor to the left while my escort directed me to the right, and Hank and Brianna were guided up another flight of stairs with the other two men Clarice had chosen.

"Wait," I growled, but the vampire pulled me along, giving me no choice but to follow him.

My throat swelled with anxiety as I stumbled on, unsure what I could do.

*If I run, they'll catch me. If I fight, they'll hurt me.*

We soon arrived at a wooden door, and he pushed it open, nudging me inside. As I stepped into a lavish bedroom, the door swung shut behind me and a key turned in the lock.

"No!" I slammed my weight against it, hammering my fist on the door and twisting the handle to try and get free. But there was no chance of getting through.

With my heart in my throat, I turned to face my prison, taking in the most luxurious room I'd ever seen. It stretched away from me in a space at least twice the size of my family's entire apartment with fine red carpets, carved mahogany furniture, and ornate iron fixings that were polished to perfection. A door across from me stood open, revealing a small, windowless bathroom decorated in cream and gold tiles.

To the right of it, maroon sheets sprawled over a massive bed, meeting with a huge wooden headboard of black painted wood. Beside the bed was a dressing table with an oval mirror inlaid with sparkling green gemstones, reflecting a girl in the glass who was wide-eyed with black streaks down her cheeks and a shiver running through her near naked body. I blinked at myself, looking so out of place in a room built for opulence and grandeur that my brow winkled in confusion.

Dark shutters were clamped over the single large window on the far side of the room, keeping all daylight out, meaning the crystal chandelier overhead was the only form of illumination.

I headed to the closet and ripped the doors open, finding an array of ridiculous dresses inside. I rifled through them, hunting for something more practical, but the only thing I found was a white robe like the one I'd worn before, so I grabbed it, wrapping my bare body in its soft embrace. I hurried to the shutters covering the window, finding a heavy lock holding them shut and cursing as I fought to break through it.

It was no good, I was trapped.

My heart stuttered as I moved toward the bedside table, ripping open the drawer and hunting for a weapon, but it was empty. And with a sinking feeling, I knew even if they'd left a whole freaking sword in here, it wouldn't be enough to kill one of them.

I sank down onto the bed, balling my hands in my lap as I tried to work out a plan. But all my mind would fix onto were those terrifying royals and the power they wielded. I could still feel the temptation of them now, like one look at them had corrupted a piece of my heart and made it beat just for them.

I closed my eyes, trying to will away the fear creeping into my body, but all I saw were two ashy eyes staring back at me with furious intent. An intent I was still oblivious to.

Whatever Prince Erik wanted with me, it couldn't be anything good. And as I moved up the bed to press my back to the headboard and stare at the door with nothing but my racing pulse for company, my imagination stole me away into a vision of torture and misery.

# CALLIE

## CHAPTER ELEVEN

I woke as the sun broke through the trees and blinked around at my strange surroundings in confusion. For twenty-one years I'd woken in the same bed every morning. Looking up at the grey stone of the cave's roof was more than a little disconcerting and doing so while in the company of a strange man was even more so. But in the end, exhaustion had won out over caution, my need for rest overriding my fears, concentrating on the fact that I would need my strength to rescue my family.

I rolled onto my side and blinked the sleep from my eyes as I looked at the embers from our fire the night before. I missed the warmth it had offered and without it, the frosty bite of the stone beneath me had worked its way into my bones. I shivered and reached out hopefully towards the charred pieces of wood remaining in the ash, but no heat found me. I sighed in disappointment and tugged my hand back inside the sleeve of my coat instead, fighting the urge to let my teeth chatter.

I sat upright and a thick fur cloak slipped off of me to pool in my lap. I ran my fingers over the soft grey fur and frowned at it in surprise. I'd fallen asleep wrapped in my coat but remembered shivering in the night as the fire died down. Magnar must have placed it over me.

The gesture was so at odds with his stony attitude towards me and the bruises which had left their mark on my throat that I wasn't sure what to make of it. Was it a kindness or simply practicality? I supposed me dying from the cold wouldn't have been ideal for whatever purpose he had for me. Because that was one thing I'd come to realise in the night. No man, free or otherwise, had ever offered up the kind of help he was giving me for nothing. Which meant he wanted something.

I hunted for Magnar and spotted him sitting in the cave's mouth, gazing out at the woods beyond it. He was unnaturally still, lost to his own thoughts or perhaps just caught up in the view, and I took the opportunity to observe him unnoticed.

Now that I was looking for it, everything about his clothing spoke of another time. My clothes were made from cotton and polyester, but he wore a leather jerkin and pants secured with silver buckles. With his cloak cast aside and his linen shirt sleeves rolled back, I noticed tattoos on his muscular forearms, something about them awaking a yearning in me for a time long past. There were men and women in the realm who had tattoos too, all of them older than me, wearing relics of their freedom on their flesh, but I remembered asking a man about his once. He'd told me the symbol on his shoulder was Viking, haling back to the warrior race who had once conquered half the world and something about the marking on Magnar's flesh reminded me of that.

My gaze moved over the ink on Magnar's deep bronze skin, wondering if there could be any truth to that guess. He certainly had the look of a warrior come to conquer the world and if I really was going to believe that he'd been sleeping for a thousand years then it certainly could check out…

I shook my head at myself, wondering if I was insane to believe his tale, but the way he told it, the brutal pain in his eyes as he recounted what had happened had been near impossible to deny.

Magnar's face was sombre but dangerously alluring too, though much of it was hidden beneath the rough beard coating his strong jaw. There was darkness in him, the kind which drew secrets to it and twisted them into weapons. He was savage, yet despite the fact that I'd never seen him smile, something about the natural curve of his mouth made me think that it used to be something he'd done a lot.

I imagined his deep voice raised in laughter before everything had been stolen from him, and my own pain over losing my family stabbed sharply through my chest. I couldn't imagine waking up to realise that everyone you'd ever known had died a thousand years ago. How did you even begin to grieve a loss like that?

Everything in his posture reminded me of a wild beast, a mountain lion or wolf, positioned to strike and kill at a moment's notice even though he was just sitting there, staring out at the trees as though lost in thought. I seriously doubted he'd missed the sound of me waking up and realised that probably meant he could tell I was staring too.

I cleared my throat uncomfortably as blood rushed to my cheeks.

"Thank you," I said awkwardly as I folded the cloak and held it out to him. He didn't turn my way, so I placed it on the ground instead. "For the cloak," I explained as he continued to maintain the silence.

"You were cold." Magnar still didn't turn from his observation of the trees and my jaw ticked with irritation.

"Did you sleep well?" I asked, forging on with the one-way conversation in the hope that he might ease up on the growling a bit. He clearly had plans for me, and that meant I intended to make my own plans for him. If I had to manipulate him first then that was fine by me, I wouldn't be taken unawares when the time came for him to turn on me, and if that moment did indeed come, I planned on stabbing him in the back before he managed to slip his blade into mine. Of course, figuring out his plans and preparing my own would be a hell of a lot simpler if we were at least civil to one another.

"I rested a little. Sleep does not hold much appeal since I awoke from a thousand-year slumber," he muttered.

"I can imagine," I replied.

"No. You cannot."

*Back to being an ass today then.* I clucked my tongue, even more certain that his plans for me couldn't be anything good if my presence annoyed him so much. Why else would he stay with me?

"You said you'd help me get my family back," I began. "But how do you know where they've been taken? Montana passed some test the vampires forced her to take. They were planning something for the two of us, and I can't waste time-"

"Planning what?" he interrupted, and I pursed my lips against the urge to bite back at him.

"I don't know. But we were afraid enough to run from it. So I want you to tell me where my family is and how much longer it will be before we reach them."

Magnar sighed, giving me the impression that the fate of my family hadn't been on his mind in the least, his own troubles consuming his thoughts, but I didn't have time for him to waste on pain over people who had died a thousand years ago. I didn't care if that was harsh. There was no helping any of them, but my family still had a chance. I had to believe that, and I couldn't let them wait any longer than I had to, knowing what cruelty the vampires were capable of.

"When I awoke thirteen moons ago, I scoured the area for signs of my kin and found my enemy instead," Magnar rumbled, twisting his dagger between his fingertips as he leaned his forearms on his knees and continued to watch the woodland. "I observed them, and I saw what they did to the mortals under their care. I had hoped to track down my brethren before confronting them but with the news you delivered, I fear they are all gone. Without me, the Slayers' Crusade was doomed to fail, but they would have tried anyway. My people were not the kind to back down from a fight, no matter how likely they would have been to lose. While I slept, they were slaughtered by those fucking animals, I know it in my heart. And if the vampires won that battle, they would have swiftly hunted down every clan, every bastard born child, every single drop of our bloodline, and eradicated them. The task now falls to me alone." Magnar stood and turned to look down at me. He seemed even more intimidating from my position on the floor as he towered over me, his muscular form blocking most of the light from the cave entrance behind him.

"I'm sorry but you're losing me again. What task?" I asked with a frown.

"The sole purpose of the slayers is to hunt down and destroy the vile creatures who have enslaved your kind. Though that task will be harder alone, I will still take it on. And I'll start with destroying the place where they hold your family."

I'd already suspected it, but his words made me ask the question I'd been trying to avoid. I had to know what we were heading into even if it confirmed my worst fears.

"Do you mean... were they taken to the blood bank?" I asked, my voice barely cracking beyond a whisper. I wasn't sure why I'd even been hoping that it might have been somewhere else, somewhere that we might have stood a chance of rescuing them from, but my hope crumbled, the tiny spark I'd been clinging to falling to ash in my chest and leaving nothing but terror in its place.

"I don't know what they call it, but that name would seem to fit. It's where they take all of the humans they remove from the caged town. They torture them and drain them of their blood with the most vile of practices. I was hard pushed to stay my blade when I first discovered it, but that was when I still had hopes of finding my kind. I had thought to surround them on all sides, destroy not just that place but the fences which contained your people then take down every festering corpse who had claimed dominion over you. I see now that such plans are not to be. I will not hold back this time."

"Well, for what little it means, you're not alone." I stood, raising my chin and giving him a look which dared him to deny me.

I didn't try to hide the fact that we both knew I wasn't going to be much help, but I wanted him to see that I wasn't afraid, that I'd do whatever it took and gladly face the consequences of failure if this task turned out to be as impossible as it seemed.

Magnar surveyed me for a moment, still towering over me even now I was on my feet. I wasn't short, standing at five foot eight myself, but he dominated the space surrounding me without even trying, standing at least a foot taller than me.

He took a step closer, blocking more of the light as his gaze locked with mine, the masculine scent of his skin surrounding me as I found myself encased in his shadow, my back to the wall. My skin prickled with the closeness, my muscles tensing for an attack which didn't come as he hunted my eyes with that impossibly golden stare.

Magnar moved closer still, my back brushing against the wall as he pressed a hand to it above my head and leaned right in to me, still hunting my eyes, the intensity of his expression halting the breath in my lungs. His presence was larger than the physicality of him, he devoured all the air in the room and made the ground quake beneath his boots. If his word was to be believed then he was a legend returned to life, and I had the feeling the world itself had taken note of his awakening. I wasn't sure what he was looking for within me, but I found my jaw locking tight as the weight of his aura pressed down on my shoulders, urging me to blink, to flinch, something – but I just held my position and stared him down defiantly. In any other situation, maybe I would have buckled beneath that penetrating stare, but not now, not with my family on the line and their only slight hint of a chance resting fully on my shoulders.

Magnar exhaled roughly, the note of a growl lacing the sound and I could have sworn the faintest crack formed in the wall he had built behind his gaze. He nodded once, some kind of affirmation which he clearly wasn't going to explain any further, and he pulled a blade from the belt at his hip.

"Here. If you are to be a warrior, you shall need a blade." He offered it to me, holding it in the small space between us, the hilt almost brushing my chest, but I didn't reach for it.

"I have a blade," I replied, realising my fingers had made it into my pocket and curled themselves tightly around it.

Magnar's gaze fell from my face to my pocket, my fist locked tight inside it. He snorted softly, returning his own blade to his belt before shoving his hand into my pocket so swiftly that I sucked in a sharp breath at the contact.

I tried to jerk my hand away, but his fingers clamped around my wrist, digging into some pressure point which made me curse as I released my hold on the little blade.

Magar snatched it before I could so much as shove him, swinging the weapon straight at the wall beside my head and making a cry of fright fall from my lips before it struck the stone with enough force to snap the blade.

I tried to jerk away from him as the broken blade fell to the floor, but I only smacked into the arm he still had pressed to the wall on my other side, caging me in.

"A slayer's blade is no mere piece of flimsy metal," he said, the gruffness of his voice raking right down my spine as I met his blazing eyes once more. The surge of adrenaline and flash of fear made my breaths come uneasily, my chest rising and falling heavily between us. "This dagger will not fail you the way that just did."

"You're insane," I hissed, the cold wall pressed so firmly to my spine that I almost shivered from the contact with him. I hunted for space, wanting to retreat to somewhere I might escape the overwhelming presence of *him*.

"And you're unarmed." Magnar took his blade from his belt once more and offered it to me again.

I eyed it cautiously, wondering if I might manage to pierce his heart with it at this small distance. I just had to grab it from him and act swiftly enough. Though something told me I wouldn't stand a chance even at this close range. Magnar Elioson was not a man who would be felled as easily as that. Besides, I wasn't exactly the murdering kind, no matter how loudly common sense was screaming at me to take my chances against this dangerous creature while I had the chance to do so. But I needed him. My dad and Montana needed him. And as dangerous as he was to me, he was dangerous to the vampires too. I wouldn't stand a chance alone, but if our purposes truly were aligned for now, then I had to trust in this opportunity that fate had presented.

I tentatively reached out to accept the blade, hesitating just shy of actually touching it as I studied it. The metal was golden in colour, the hilt and blade both carved with a collection of runes which seemed to shift in the shadows.

The intensity of Magnar's focus burned into me, watching me with such heat in his gaze that it made me want to squirm before him, but I couldn't tear my eyes from the blade in his hand to tell him to back off.

I pressed a single finger to the hilt, and I swear the runes marking it purred at my touch, a vibration passing through my skin where it was pressed to the heated metal. I looked more closely at the beauty of the intricate designs they formed and drew in a breath, uncertain why this moment felt so much more important than me simply accepting a weapon.

I grasped the hilt and a powerful surge juddered through my body, resounding into the depths of my chest, my back striking the wall as I jerked at the feeling. I let out a small gasp as the strangest sensation flooded through me, like déjà vu, as if I'd been here before, done *this* before. Though there was nothing at all familiar to me about standing in a cave with a barbarian while accepting a dagger from his hand.

Something about the small weapon felt *right* against my skin. Like it was calling to the essence of my soul deep within me. The sensation seemed so familiar although there was no way it could be. Like the memory of a dream.

"Fury," I murmured, the name skipping through my mind like the whisper of an old friend.

"What did you say?" Magnar stepped towards me suddenly, boxing me in entirely, catching my wrist in his grip as he stared between the dagger and me. "How do you know that name?"

My heart leapt with surprise and more than a little fear as his burning gaze tore into my own. I recoiled from him, dropping the blade and trying to pull my hand out of his grasp. He ignored my attempt and twisted my hand in his own, roughly pushing the material of my coat up to reveal my forearm.

He brushed his fingers along the exposed skin of my inner arm as if he was trying to remove something from it. Goosebumps rose along my flesh at his rough touch, and I yanked my arm away more firmly, finally managing to break free from him and shifting towards the cave mouth in retreat.

"What the fuck are you doing?" I demanded as I kept backing up. I was more aware than ever of the differences between us, of his size and strength, the power he could use against me so very easily. If he attacked me, I'd have no chance of defending myself. He was even more formidable than the vampires; at least with them I knew my blood was too precious to spill.

Magnar glanced at the exit beyond me, a thousand thoughts spinning through his eyes which he banished with a blink that shuttered every one of them from view.

"By the gods." Magnar spread his hands slowly and took a step back, offering me more space and making me frown in confusion. "For a moment I thought..." He shook his head bitterly, dismissing whatever he'd been going to say before he continued. "I was trying to see something that couldn't possibly be there. I've lost so much, and I leapt to the wrong conclusion. I will not make such a foolish mistake again." He stooped to retrieve the blade I'd dropped and offered me the hilt again, seeming pissed about something, though I had no idea what.

I eyed the blade suspiciously, but something about the weapon had been comforting. I liked the way it had felt in my palm, the strength it had seemed to offer me.

"You grab me like that again and I'll stab you in the balls," I growled, my foot on the runes which he'd scored into the dirt at the mouth of the cave, freedom just a step away, but I wanted something more than freedom now. I needed vengeance and I needed his help.

"Feel free to try, but you are likely to end up in two pieces if you do," he said, his arrogance only making me want to attempt it. But I got the feeling he wasn't joking about the slicing me in two part.

I slowly reached out to take the dagger for the second time, that same sense of power and relief rushing into me as I held it again. I wrapped my fingers around the hilt more tightly, the metal oddly warm in my palm, like it was heated from within.

Magnar released it fully into my hold and a flutter of energy seemed to pass between the blade and some intrinsic part of me which I couldn't describe. I concentrated on the sensation, I heard its name in my mind once more. *Fury.* I wasn't sure how I knew it but that was what this blade had been named by its creator. I could almost feel the heat of the furnace, hear the sound of the hammer striking the metal.

As I focused on the sensation, other images flashed through my mind. I saw the blade wielded by many sets of hands, spilling blood and slicing through flesh. It had taken lives and saved them, passing from hand to hand as hundreds of years passed, each master wielding it for years on end before passing it on.

It had killed vampires before too. Images of them falling to dust as it was torn from their chests spun through my mind, the blade almost seeming amused by the memories, proud of them. And I knew it could do it again.

I looked up at Magnar in astonishment, words forming on my lips which stalled where they were. Nothing in his expression said he knew what the blade had shown me, and I hesitated to tell him of it after his reaction to me knowing its name. I didn't want him manhandling me again or demanding anything from me which might take time away from focusing on my family.

"Thank you," I breathed, unable to say anything else without revealing the power I felt from simply holding that weapon in my hand.

Magnar dipped his head to me and turned away. He retrieved his cloak from the floor and wrapped it around his shoulders, making sure that he could still reach his swords as he strapped them across his back. He stamped on the final embers of the fire then stepped out of the cave, striking his boot through the runes he had carved on the threshold.

I felt their power fizzling out of the air around me, a lump forming in my throat as the truth of his claims sank into me. I couldn't deny what he was, but I also couldn't let that distract from my plan.

He continued away from me, lost in his own thoughts again and I hurried to follow. He might have been all kinds of terrifying and a complete asshole, but the vampires would think so too. And while he was busy drawing them away from me, I'd break Montana and Dad out of that hellhole, and we'd run for the freedom we were owed once and for all.

# MONTANA

## CHAPTER TWELVE

An ice-cold hand gripped my calf, shaking it once. Then again. And again until I winced as the stranger's fingers squeezed almost hard enough to bruise me.

"I know you're awake," a dark voice poured over me like liquid fire, making my gut clench.

Somehow, I'd fallen asleep after hours of being left alone in the fine bedroom and now I wished I never had to wake up. But there was no point feigning sleep any longer, so I reluctantly opened my eyes to face the demon who lurked beyond my dreams.

My heart pounded wildly as I discovered Erik towering over me beside the bed, his navy cloak and suit jacket removed to reveal a black shirt as dark as his hair. I recoiled on instinct, my pulse elevating further as I took in the hell-born vampire. He was the most captivating monster I'd ever seen, and up close, the godly power he wielded was even more obvious. His face was a picture of masculine perfection, from the straight edge of his brow to the clear-cut diagonals of his cheekbones, and the silvery lacquer of his skin was punctuated by the fortress of iron in his gaze. Power emanated from him in a way that made me feel as brittle as a branch in a hurricane, because I knew he could tear my heart clean from my chest if he willed it. But there was no guessing what he willed, his eyes taking me in with raw judgement and nothing more.

At least I'd had the sense to wrap myself in a robe before I'd fallen asleep because I didn't want to be exposed so close to this formidable beast.

"Hey rebel, guess what?" he drawled, moving to sit on a dark-wood armchair and leaning back into its red velvet cushions, those intense eyes never leaving my face.

"What?" I bit out, fighting hard not to lose my nerve as I pushed myself upright. I'd never been in a room completely alone with a vampire before, and if I had, I wouldn't have expected to step out of it with any blood left in my veins.

"You're now my property. And if you have any notions of escape, of fighting back or even slashing open those pretty veins of yours to end it all, I urge you to forget about them. At least until this ritual is over anyway."

"What ritual?" I breathed, gathering myself to the edge of the bed and knotting my hands in my robe. My fingers were itching for a weapon, but I didn't know if there was an object sharp enough in this world to pierce that perfect sheen of skin.

Erik blew out a breath of irritation. "Don't ask me questions. You can think of yourself as a glorified pet if it helps. Whatever keeps you quiet and doing what I say."

"No," I snarled immediately.

Prince or not, royalty didn't mean anything to me. In fact, the only thing it meant was that these vampires were not only my enemies, but they were the ones who'd decided to shove humans into the Realms and strip us of our rights. They were responsible for everything my family had suffered, and if he thought I was going to obey his word, he'd soon find out I'd rather bleed.

I may not have been alive when humans were at the top of the food chain, but whatever driving force had gotten us there once still lived in my veins.

"No?" Erik echoed, seeming confused by my response.

One second, he was flattening out a crease in his fancy trousers, the next he was standing above me with a penetrating glare. A breath stumbled out of my lungs at that impossibly fast movement, and fear coiled up in my chest like a snake. I'd never seen a vampire move like that, not even the Elite, and it made me terrified of what else he was capable of.

"What kind of human says no to a Belvedere Royal?" he barked, and I fought the instinct to recoil, his voice cracking through the air like a whip.

I thrust up my chin. "A kidnapped one." *One taken from her family by force.* But I didn't air that thought. My family were locked away safe inside my chest, and I didn't want this asshole to have any leverage on me.

His heavenly, haven't-smiled-in-years face lifted into something resembling a grin, but it was a wicked thing indeed.

"Kidnapped?" he laughed cruelly. "You're *food.*" He shook his head in confusion then tapped my forehead with a cold finger. "This is a privilege, you realise? I think the other humans have grasped it, are you slow or something?"

My scowl grew and my rage followed, a gush of acid rising in my throat. "Why did you bring me here? What do you want from me?" I demanded, gaining my feet so I didn't feel so small on the bed. It was useless considering he had nearly a foot of height on me, and even if he hadn't, he was a damn vampire, so I had absolutely no chance of fighting him.

"Two reasons..." He stalked a little closer and the clean, enticing scent of him reached me, like cypress trees in the rain. "The first is none of your business. And the second is because you did not want to be chosen. So that intrigued me."

"Why?" I hissed, my spine straightening.

"Because as much as humans try to pretend they're above abandoning their precious morals, they rarely pass up a chance to gain privileges. You, however..." He released a derisive laugh that cut to the core of me. "Well you're either stupid or you have more of a backbone than most of the humans who walk into the royal palace."

"And what good does that do you?" I asked through my teeth.

"You'll find out soon enough." He shrugged one shoulder and took another step closer, that scent of him catching in my lungs. Something about it urged me to trust him, to let my guard down and offer up my secrets to him. It was the most intoxicating kind of temptation, to fall under his spell, but my hatred rose up to meet it, fighting off the effects of this heinous creature.

He reached out, taking a lock of my dark hair between his fingers and examining it like he had a right to touch me. Like I truly was his possession, and though I had always known my body wasn't my own when it came down to it, I had never felt that so deeply as now.

"Enlighten me..." he purred, his gaze moving up from my hair to stare directly into my eyes. Into my goddamn soul. "Why did you walk into that courtyard looking like a rebel today?"

"Maybe I am one," I whispered truthfully, letting him see the fight in my eyes, the dreams I'd had of killing his kind for all they had done to mine.

"Lucky me then, because a rebel is just what I need." He pinched my chin between his finger and thumb, his hold rough and terrifyingly strong. He inspected me and I refused to let him see how rattled I was at having a vampire's icy hands on my skin. But inside, my heart thrummed like the wings of a frantic bird as I fought to keep still, struggling not to show any fear on my face.

"My brothers have chosen pretty kittens to entertain them, to play their little game, but I'm entering a feral one into the competition to cause some chaos." He smiled darkly, releasing me at last and my hatred for him inched deeper into my chest. "Oh, don't look so sad, rebel, if you play along maybe I'll put you back in the pig pen with the rest of the bacon."

Fire coursed up my throat and spewed from my mouth, "My name is Montana! And I'm not a pig. I might be your food, but you'd be nothing without humans, so maybe you should show us a bit of respect, you arrogant asshole."

Dad had told me how humans once used to feed on animals, and being subjected to that lifestyle myself made me more than sympathetic with them. I could never eat the flesh and blood of another creature; that would make me like *them*. These soulless beasts.

I awaited a punishment from Erik, certain it was coming. I'd dreamed of shouting at one of the Elite like that, of seeing some acknowledgement of the wrongs they did. Some pity, or regret, or *something*.

Erik's eyes were shadowy and blank, not a hint of regret passing across his beautiful stony face. He didn't care how humans were treated. All he cared about was our blood somehow making its way to his stomach.

I seethed, I glared, I considered trying to scratch some emotion into his chiselled features, but it was all in vain.

He smirked, smoothly turning his back on me and moving to the exit, letting me get away with my rudeness for some unknown reason.

"Hey, rebel?" He glanced over his shoulder as his hand landed on the doorknob. "The next time you want to wound me, don't bother aiming for my heart. It's impenetrable to you or anyone else for that matter, and it is long beyond *feeling*." He gazed at me icily, showing the true monster beneath, his glassy eyes holding no emotion at all. "Just do as I say, and I might send you back to whatever Realm they scraped you out of. You don't have to behave for the others, but you will behave for me. And if you do not, you will see the truth of me, the monster you fear so deeply, the one your heart is pounding uncontrollably because of. If you think you can guess the evil my exterior hides, I assure you, you cannot even fathom the depths of villainy that lurks under this guise."

The door slammed between us and I threw myself at it, ramming my fist into the pristine wood. I snarled my anger as my fingers curled up and pain flared across my knuckles.

"I hope you choke on your next drink, you piece of shit!"

He didn't reply, but he must have heard me and that gave me some satisfaction at least.

I gazed down at my swollen hand, shaking it out as I started to pace the beautiful room with his threat lingering in my mind. I didn't want to admit I was shaken, but learning that he'd brought me here to play some twisted game of his was setting my anxiety on fire.

My feet carried me to the window, and I tried to prise open the shutters for several long minutes, fixing my mind on escape and nothing else. I couldn't get past the lock holding them in place, so I started to search the room for a key.

The drawers were filled with lingerie and more dresses, but I gasped in delight as I found one that held pants and shirts. I dragged on a pair of jeans which were snug around my legs, then tugged a fitted grey sweater on too.

At last, I was dressed in something I could run in if the opportunity presented itself, though Erik's threat continued to burrow into my skull.

My mind turned over the promise in his words too, that if I played along, I could go home. Back to Callie, back to Dad. Or at least close enough to try and find them. Here, miles away locked in a castle, I was no good to them at all. If I got back to the Realm, I could find out where they were, I could make a plan to reach them.

I headed to the dressing table across the room, examining my face which was still smeared with the black liquid from my eyelashes. Grabbing a pack of moist wipes from a drawer, I started rubbing it off, revealing clean skin beneath.

I pressed my lips together, thinking of my family, my eyes burning with love for them in the mirror, then slowly my expression hardened and resolution found me.

If Erik wanted a rebel, he was going to get one. But the worry that he might not really send me back to the Realm settled over my heart. I couldn't trust him, but I could go along with this for now, at least until I found a way to escape.

I'd let him claim me as his plaything, let him believe I was dumb and weak, and maybe he'd let his guard down, maybe he'd forget to lock the door. And perhaps I'd find myself free sooner than I could ever hope.

Worry ate into my chest like a hungry animal, and after being left for hours on end in the luxurious bedroom, I'd reverted to thinking about what these royals wanted.

It was a sad fact, but I knew what value I held in this world. Food.

Nothing more, nothing less. My mind had been burdened with that truth my entire existence, and now these vampires were throwing it into question.

To someone who hadn't been branded as a blood supply since their arrival in the world, the answer might have been more obvious. But this was shaking the foundation of everything I knew to be true.

Vampires drank human blood.

Humans were weaker and therefore unable to avoid said vampire-feasting.

Vampires didn't give two shits about human rights beyond the continuation of them breathing and producing their delicious blood cells.

So what the hell was this about?

Finally, someone opened the door, but that someone didn't fill me with any hope of getting answers, all it offered me was dread.

Erik strode into the room, leaving the door ajar as if to emphasise his ability to catch me if I considered trying to escape.

He gave my attire a sweeping glance, then snarled, "*No.*"

"What?" I gasped, taking a step back as fury flashed in his gaze, and I swear I caught a glimpse of his sharpened canines.

"You will be the belle of the ball tonight, Miss Rebel. A baggy sweater is not going to cut it."

He moved around me, and I eyed the open door.

I could run.

He would catch me.

But maybe I'd find a window to launch myself out of first.

Then I'd have to run like the fires of hell were up my ass and try to scale that big wall...

"Rebel?" Erik questioned in a bored tone. "Stop staring at the door like you're going to make a great escape. I promise you it will be a waste of your meagre human energy."

My legs moved and I fled, because why the fuck not? I was a damn prisoner, and I wasn't going to be a compliant one.

Erik's chest collided with my face. Or maybe it was the other way around. Either way, it hurt like hell and sent me crashing down onto my ass in a heap. I reeled from the speed he must have moved to get around me like that. It was superhuman, beyond anything other vampires were capable of.

His hand caught my wrist, and he yanked me back upright again with so much strength that I bashed against his chest once more.

"Stop manhandling me," I growled, my free hand coming up, curled into a fist like I really intended to hit him. But years of living under the vampires' rule stopped my hand in its tracks. I couldn't fight back; I knew that all too well. It would end in a severe punishment, and the likes of this royal monster would be capable of far more terrible things than even the Elite.

A trickle of fear rolled smoothly down my spine as Erik arched an eyebrow, his gaze sliding to that curled fist as I lowered it to my side. He knew. He had seen the desire in me to strike him, and my throat thickened as his gaze slid back up to meet mine and I awaited the consequences.

His hand around my wrist was like an iron shackle, unyielding and penetratingly cold.

"Go on then," I said in a voice barely above a whisper.

Erik lifted my wrist and forced me to twirl as he shoved me towards the bed, and my heart juddered in fright as his free hand fell to my hip and his body pressed flush to mine from behind.

But before I could consider the frantic, fear-bound ideas of what he was going to do to me, I spotted a blood-red gown on the mattress.

"Put this on," he growled by my ear, sending a shudder through to my core at the coolness of his breath. "Don't test me. I'll put it on you myself if I have to."

He stepped away and I released the breath that was jammed in my lungs, the feel of him still clinging to my body as I realised he wasn't going to punish me. I frowned at the dress as I crept toward it, wondering if some evil lay within it.

"Why?" I turned, finding Erik's head dipped toward me, his grey eyes shadowed and his mouth pulled down at the corners. He was darkness embodied, a walking bane who had sown seeds of torment into this land, and now he'd come to reap the rewards of his gruesome harvest.

"What did I tell you about obeying me?" he warned, and I swear I shrank before him, his deadly aura closing in around me and reminding me of how very fragile I was in his presence. "You do not wish to displease me, I assure you. So I will tell you only one more time, rebel. Put. It. On."

I blew out a breath, forced to give in or else face the wrath of this psycho, so I pulled off my sweater with fumbling fingers, tossing it aside. I immediately regretted it as Erik's penetrating gaze collided with my bare skin, and even though he'd already seen me standing in my underwear back in that courtyard, it felt far more intimidating now we were alone.

I swallowed around the tight lump forming in my throat, not giving him the satisfaction of seeing me falter as I dropped my jeans too and kicked them away from me so hard they hit the wall.

"Now the dress," Erik prompted, his gaze skipping up to meet mine.

I took it from the bed, my eyes remaining on his in a warning to keep back in case he decided he was going to put it on me. He folded his arms, impatience dripping from him as I stepped into the material and tugged it up my body, sliding the thin straps over my arms, feeling his attention on me the entire time. I reached around the back to do up the zipper, but no matter how much I twisted and stretched, I couldn't get the thing to go up.

Erik stepped towards me with purpose, and I backed away, my ass hitting the bedside table and making the lamp rattle precariously.

"I can do it," I insisted, bending my arms to their limits.

He cocked his head to one side, amusement brightening his gaze to liquid moonlight. "Stop it. You look like the worst contortionist in history."

"A what?" I snapped, giving up and dropping my hands.

He ignored me, catching hold of my waist and flipping me around with a speed that made my head spin. He took hold of the zipper and dragged it up my back so fast, I squeaked at how close it came to catching on my skin.

"There, that wasn't so hard, was it?" he said, his breath caressing my bare shoulder and making goosebumps flutter along my skin from how cold it was.

"You're freezing," I exhaled.

"Yes, rebel," he said, shifting my hair over one shoulder and letting his knuckles graze the back of my neck until I shivered. "And you are so very warm."

Hunger bathed in the depths of those words, the very reason for the heat of my skin stirring a desire in him that was entirely predatory, and it made fear drip through my chest.

His hand was suddenly on my waist, pinching me through the clingy material and I fought the instinct to lurch away. "Don't you eat in your Realm?"

I released a derisive laugh, figuring he was joking. And a cruel joke at that.

"I'll take that as a no," he muttered, turning me sharply to face him.

"Stop spinning me around like a ballserina," I growled.

"You mean a ballerina," he corrected with a smirk that was all taunt.

"That's what I said," I muttered stubbornly, but heat rose along my cheeks.

"Such a dumb little creature, it's almost endearing. If I had any inclination to be endeared, that is, but I do not." He flicked me under the chin, and I jerked my head away with my teeth bared. "Face. Hair," he demanded.

I shook my head in dismay, and he growled in frustration, making the back of my neck prickle in warning. I was too close to this beast, far too close.

"Fuck, what do the others do?" he murmured to himself then an idea lit up his ashen eyes. "Wait here."

"Where else would I go?" I deadpanned, but he'd left the room by the time I'd finished speaking, gone in a flash as if he was powered by lightning. It was creepy as shit.

I gazed down at the dazzling dress that fell to my ankles, scowling at my bare toes. What the hell was this about?

The door finally reopened, and Erik appeared pushing a flustered-looking vampire into the room. She was short with petite, pretty features and wore a black dress.

"Oh, um, Prince Erik, I'm not sure I'm the right choice for-"

"Nonsense," Erik cut over her, steering her toward me. "Your hair and makeup is always impeccable, and that's what I would like you to provide for this...train-wreck."

I wasn't quite sure the meaning of the insult, but I knew it was one, and I pursed my lips.

"She's very beautiful already," the vampire girl commented, tucking a luscious brown curl behind her ear.

Erik's lips pressed together as his gaze dripped over me like he was trying to decide if she was right. He grunted - which could have been an affirmation or a denial, I didn't really care which.

"She is not fit for tonight. Make her so. Everything you need is in the dressing table," Erik commanded, and the girl bowed low.

"Yes, sir," she said, and her eyes remained on the floor until he left.

The sharp click of the door seemed to echo on for an eternity, and I eyed the newcomer warily.

She glanced up, looking nervous as she floated toward the dressing table. "So...do you like your hair up or down?"

I glowered, not answering.

"Okay then, let's go with up." She searched around in the drawers, taking out some makeup – the same stuff Felicia had painted on me – and a hairbrush.

The girl patted a cushioned stool in front of the dressing table. "Sit."

I drifted closer, knowing I was going to have to face the wrath of Erik if I didn't comply, and despite the desire to refuse every order he gave me, I really didn't want to call his bluff and lure out the monster within.

"My name's Nancy, what's yours?" she asked as she picked up the golden brush and started running it through my dark locks.

I considered withholding it like I had from Felicia, but what did it really matter? They didn't care what we were called so long as they were getting regular blood from our veins.

"Montana," I said quietly.

She beamed, seeming to relax at hearing me speak and I regretted giving her the little happy boost. "Well, Montana, I think you're going to like it here."

"Ha," I spat, and she looked kind of hurt.

Nancy continued to brush my hair, then started braiding it with skilled fingers. "You're the first human Erik's ever chosen, you know?"

"Lucky me," I muttered.

She sighed, evidently frustrated with me. Well, she obviously didn't know what it was like to be kidnapped did she? That was real frustration, *Nancy*.

We fell into silence as she coiled my braid and pinned it into a bun. Next, she started painting my face and I begrudgingly let her. The gentleness of her cold hands didn't fool me. She was a vampire through and through, and those hands could break my bones as easily as fix my hair.

When my face was transformed into something more like a mirage than my true features, Nancy stood back to admire her work while I grimaced at it.

"You look perfect, if I do say so myself." She grinned and two dimples formed in her cheeks. I did not smile back.

Nancy moved to the closet, returning with a pair of shoes that had ridiculous heels on them.

"No," I refused, folding my arms. I wasn't going to put anything on my feet that I couldn't run in.

"Oh…" Nancy looked concerned, and I expected her to force the issue, but for some reason she didn't. Instead, she returned to the closet and produced a dainty pair of flat shoes.

They would have to do, so I took them from her and slipped them on, finding them perfectly sized for my feet. I wondered how it was possible that these vampires knew my measurements, and disgust gripped me as I realised they must have been taken at some point during my kidnap.

I glanced down at my fancy dress and the delicate shoes on my feet, my stomach hardening into a cold ball.

"What is all this for?" I asked Nancy, wondering if she was about to drop the nice act and show me her true colours. "Am I going to be served up as some sort of freaky sacrifice to the Royals?" My fingers shook a little at my own words and I curled them tight against my palms to make them stop.

"Oh, Montana, hasn't anyone told you?" Nancy said in surprise.

"When would they have told me? When I was being viciously torn away from my family? Or when I was shackled in the back of a vehicle? Or maybe they would have saved it for the part where they drugged me on an aeroplane. Is that when they should have told me, *Nancy*? Because I'll tell you something, *Nancy*-"

"Why do you keep saying my name like that?" she stammered, looking rattled by my behaviour, and I had to admit that it wasn't my usual style to goad my monstrous rulers. But I had the feeling Nancy wouldn't be doing anything to me without Erik's say-so. Of course, that didn't mean a severe punishment wouldn't be waiting for me later.

"No one told me anything," I finished, curbing my tone at the last second to try and save myself a date with a cattle prod.

Nancy's lips parted and her eyes widened to saucers. "Oh, um, well, you see, the thing is… You're here because-"

The door flew open and Erik stepped back into the room in a jet-black suit, white shirt, and black tie to match. His dominating form made a breath catch in my lungs as I witnessed the power of him all over again. My mind hadn't been capable of recapturing it in his absence, but now he'd returned, I was all-consumed by the dark energy rolling from him and the danger he presented. As finely dressed as he was, it was more as though a hungry wolf had just prowled into the room in search of its next meal.

"Done?" he clipped at Nancy before his eyes fell on me.

I hated the way he looked at me. It was like the sun staring at the earth. All-powerful and radiating importance. And I hated it even more as his gaze dragged across every inch of me, an assessment I wanted to pass and fail in equal measure.

"Is this what you had in mind, sire?" Nancy prompted when he said nothing.

He jerked his head in a barely apparent nod, then held out a hand to me. I gazed at it in confusion before he rolled his eyes, stalked forward and took my palm in his, crushing it tight in his arctic grip.

I suddenly missed Nancy's quiet demeanour as he hauled me to my feet, then out into the corridor, towing me behind him like a dog on a leash. Halfway down the hallway, he pulled up short, dropping my hand and taking a moment to straighten his fine suit jacket, thoughts crossing his eyes that he clearly had no intention of sharing with me.

I flexed my fingers, the pain of his grip enduring.

Erik smoothed his hair back even though it was already perfectly styled, then he offered me his arm.

My nose wrinkled in response, and he eyed my scrunched-up face with irritation. "That's an order, rebel."

"Montana," I corrected harshly, but took his arm all the same. I wasn't about to start a fist fight with a vampire, and in truth, I was already playing with fire with the way I spoke to him. I was shocked he let me get away with it at all.

"I truly don't care," he said.

"You cared enough to make up a nickname for me," I pointed out.

He released an amused breath through his nose. "A nickname? I was naming my new pet."

I bit down on my tongue to hold back the curses I wanted to hurl at him, reminding myself how bad an idea that would be.

As we walked, he reached out his other arm to unveil his wrist, exhibiting a glitzy silver watch that likely cost more than all the rations I was given in a year. Hatred curdled in my gut, and I took a slow breath as heat climbed the back of my throat.

*Keep it together, little moon.*

The words were Dad's, and tears pricked the backs of my eyes as I worked to keep myself in check for him. I was no good to him dead, but it felt like a betrayal to be walking here at a vampire's side even if I didn't have a choice in the matter.

"Do you have something you want to say, rebel?" Erik goaded, clearly aware of the battle I was fighting.

I didn't know if it was his heightened senses or if it was just that damn obvious, but either way I didn't lift my head to meet his eye. I simply kept walking, my teeth still digging into my tongue and my heart blasting out a violent tune beneath my ribs.

"You're very worked up," he continued, that edge of mocking to his voice only making my rage spark hotter, but I managed to stop myself from exploding.

At the top of a grand staircase, he tugged me to a halt again, his eyes moving to his watch once more as if he was overly conscious of the time. My gaze slid to the red carpet which ran down the centre of the stairs, curving into a large hallway of tan and white tiles.

I grew anxious as we stood there, unsure what the hell we were waiting for. The watch reminded me of the vampire back in the Realm who'd jabbed a cattle prod into my back, and the longer I looked at it, the more I despised these royals and every single one of their lavish possessions.

Erik's gaze slid up to my face. "Do you have a problem with my watch? Or perhaps your tiny brain cells are trying to work out what it is."

"I know what a watch is," I hissed. "And it's disgusting."

A cloud of confusion crossed his gaze. "That's an odd choice of word."

I tried to bite my tongue on my next outburst, but if he wanted to know then why keep it quiet? He obviously wasn't in any rush to cut me open and drain me of blood, so what did it matter?

"It's the principle," I growled, my spine straightening. "My dad told me about the value of stuff like that in the old world. And that watch could have fed a family of ten for a year."

"What?" he balked, evidently trying to work out a riddle in my words I was sure wasn't there. "Oh, you mean a *human* family." The penny dropped, but I didn't spot any regret over that fact in his expression. "You're all kept in luxury compared to what you deserve, I've seen it for myself. You should be damn grateful to us for the life you're given." His jaw snapped shut as if the case was closed, but it was far from closed.

"*Luxury?*" I snarled. "You think we should be kept in worse conditions than we already are?"

This asshole was a piece of work. How could he flaunt his wealth and not give a shit that the humans who kept him well-fed were half-starved?

"Yeah, know why?" He shoved up against my body, pinning me to the banister with impossibly hard muscles, making my heart leap into my throat. "Because the humans who end up with my brothers and sister are always snivelling and begging for better conditions. In my opinion, it's greed. You see what we have here, and you want more. Never happy. You wouldn't be satisfied even if I handed you my royal sceptre and let you rule the world."

The word sceptre threw me off balance, despite the stream of insults he'd just dished me.

"Sceptre?" I murmured, feeling foolish as I racked my brain for the meaning of that word.

His beautiful features skewed again as if he thought I was an idiot. "Been missing school lately, rebel?"

I had to laugh at that one: a hollow, angry laugh obviously. He was really toying with me now, making a freaking mockery of my life.

I reverted to sarcasm, trying to stave off the anger rising to a dangerous level in my body. "Oh yes, we're quite well-educated in the Realm. The vampires love to teach us a good lesson or two." *With their cattle prods and their constant threats and bared fangs.*

Erik's eyes were back on his watch. "Uh huh," he grunted, evidently done with this conversation and all the inhumanity that went with it. He didn't care. Of course he didn't. He was the reason the humans were caged and treated like dirt in the first place.

"Right, that's long enough." He yanked my arm and guided me down the staircase, turning me sharply as he shouldered through a set of double doors.

The scent of cooked food hit me so hard, my tongue wasn't ready for it. I salivated like a hungry animal at the sight of a banquet stretching across a large table at the heart of the room, unable to remember the last time I'd eaten.

Tapestries hung from the walls, a roaring fire danced in a hearth, but all I could focus on was the mouth-watering feast before me. More food than I had ever seen in one place before.

The humans who'd been chosen by the Royals sat around the table, the five of them still wearing the same dresses and suits from earlier.

My spine prickled and I sensed the danger in the room even before I saw them, all thoughts of food ebbing away in the face of the other royals.

The three of them stood at the back of the room in a rigid line as if they'd been waiting for us, the males in suits to match Erik while Clarice had changed into an electric blue gown that hugged her curves and made her look otherworldly.

"Late as always. You're getting on my last nerve, Erik," Fabian growled, his upper lip curling back to reveal glinting fangs, and I had to wonder if Erik had made us late on purpose.

"Come now, brother, we all know your last nerve died a long time ago." Erik steered me toward the table, planting me in the only remaining seat beside Paige.

"Have you been playing dress-up with the rogue human, Erik?" Miles asked, pushing a hand into his sleek blonde hair as he grinned.

"She cleans up well, don't you think?" I felt Erik move close behind me, his finger trailing up the back of my neck and capturing a loose lock of hair in his grip. I stiffened in my seat, my eyes locking with Paige's as Erik carefully tucked it into my bun and moved away, leaving my skin tingling insistently from the contact.

"Always the perfectionist, Erik," Clarice jibed, pushing a lock of golden hair over her shoulder. She was so beautiful it was almost painful to look at her, my eyes sliding over her full lips and delicate nose, before falling into the depths of her eyes.

Erik moved toward them, joining the line-up with a smirk dancing at the corner of his mouth.

"It is easy to create perfection out of a creature that is already so close to it," Erik said, and I twisted in my seat to look at him, finding him watching me with an intensity that was at odds with how he had been treating me before. Perfection? What the hell was he talking about?

His eyes slid to Fabian whose mouth twitched with annoyance, and I sensed whatever was going on here was less about me and more about them.

Paige caught my hand under the table, drawing my eyes away from the Royals as they spoke in low whispers.

"Are you okay?" she breathed, and I nodded firmly.

"Are you?"

"Yeah, just hungry." Her soft green eyes fell to the food, but my gaze remained on her light features, the golden hair and sun kissed skin, my thoughts wheeling to Callie. This girl's looks were sharper but everything about her colouring was the same. It made me ache for my twin in a way that cut right to my soul.

Brianna leaned around her to catch my eye. "Do you think they'll make us stare at this all night?" she said. "Maybe it's a goddamn punishment."

"Go ahead and eat," Clarice encouraged, clearly hearing Brianna.

I glanced over at our weird entourage who stood in a formal line, watching us like birds of prey hovering over fat mice.

The men and women tucked in, and the clink of fine porcelain was the only sound to taint the silent air.

"Music," Miles groaned. "It's so awkward without music." He glanced at a guard in a corner of the room, and I spotted more of them hiding in the shadows, as still as statues. No wonder I hadn't noticed them.

The guard Miles had addressed moved to a large wooden thing against one wall, lifting its lid and placing a black disc at the heart of it. Music filled the air; a soft instrumental piece that was completely alien to me. All I knew of music were the songs sung by the people in the Realm and the clash of instruments made from steel drums and kitchenware. This was…unreal, beautiful, the tune seeming to pluck the very chords of my heart.

I started filling my plate with potatoes and steaming veg, my stomach growling too much to even consider starting a hunger strike. Besides, why would the vampires care if I didn't eat? The only person I'd be fucking over was myself. I needed my strength for running, or fighting, or punching arrogant vampires in the face. Alright, the last one was particularly unlikely, but imagining it sure helped to brighten my mood.

I glanced across the table at Hank, and he gave me a small nod as he chewed on his food.

"You alright, wild one?" he asked when he'd swallowed. The other two men shifted in their chairs, glancing over at the Royals as if they were nervous to speak in their presence.

"Wild one?" I scoffed.

"You sure looked wild the last time I saw you," he said with a grin, and it lit up his handsome features.

"I thought they were gonna whip you for sure," the guy with a copper beard and thick muscles whispered.

"Whip me?" I frowned.

"That's what they did in my Realm whenever anyone was out of line," he breathed, and I glanced over at the monsters, finding them deep in their own whispered conversation, speaking so quietly I couldn't catch a single thing they said. But it was clear they were done paying any attention to us.

"I'm Joshua by the way," the guy added, and I gave him my name too.

"It was beatings for us," the other man said grimly. He had deep brown skin and broad shoulders, his eyes so dark they were like two pools of ink. "I'm Luke."

"We got the cattle prods," Paige said.

"Same," I said at the same time Brianna did, and we shared a slight smile at our fucked-up common ground.

Everyone tucked into their meals, and I followed suit, devouring a plateful of the delicious vegetables, my tastebuds alive with the well-seasoned food. I reluctantly ate one of the beets on my plate, wrinkling my nose as I chewed through it.

"How is everything, rebel?" Erik called across the room, making my heart lurch at his sudden attention. He shot over to me at such a speed that I shrank in my chair, picking up my fork and bringing it up in defence. The other humans flinched from his arrival, all of them dropping their eyes from his.

Erik laid a possessive hand on my shoulder, leaning down and letting the tip of my fork press to his throat.

"I dare you to try and stab me," he breathed just for me, his gaze flickering like he wanted me to do it. But I wasn't going to give him a reason to punish me in front of everyone.

I lowered the fork, fighting a tremble as his fingers dug harder into my shoulder.

"Everything is fine," I said tightly, answering his initial question.

"Then why did you look like you were about to choke on that beet?" he mused. "Our food not good enough for the little insurgent?"

*Because beets taste like salted asscakes.*

"It's wonderful," Paige cut in. "The best thing we've tasted, isn't it?" She looked to me imploringly.

"It's delicious, Montana was just saying so." Hank gave me a look that urged me to play along, and my heart squeezed, unused to strangers trying to protect me.

Erik caught my chin, drawing my gaze away from the man and onto him instead. "I wasn't asking the rabble. I was asking the rebel."

"Let them eat, Erik, you'll turn them off their meals," Clarice insisted.

"I think that's his intention," Fabian said with a wicked look. "But if that's the game, I can cause a little bloodshed instead. That will have them shaken, Erik, what do you say? Clarice has humans to spare."

Erik straightened, his hand remaining on my shoulder while a look of fear passed between us all, the three men Clarice had selected looking particularly tense.

"Stop being an asshole, Fabian." Clarice rolled her eyes like his threat of violence was perfectly common. "You will do nothing to my humans without my say so."

"Then perhaps I will play with your one, Erik," Fabian said, and my heart juddered. "You won't mind, will you? Mine is a little skittish, but I think yours would play well…"

Paige shot me a fearful look and terror clogged my lungs.

"Hm," Erik grunted, his hand falling from my shoulder. "I would prefer mine remains in one piece for now."

He returned to the others, and I took a steadying breath as Fabian and Erik shared a look that was a challenge wrapped in a threat. I didn't know quite what was going on between them, but I sure as shit didn't want to be in the middle of it.

We continued eating, though my appetite was a little shot after the interaction, but I knew better than to waste food. Who knew when the next meal would come?

"Be careful how you act around your prince, wild one," Hank whispered, leaning forward a little as he tried not to gain the vampires' attention.

I glanced over at the Royals who had returned to talking in voices that were so quiet I couldn't catch a single word. Their mouths barely moved as they whispered, so I couldn't even lip read the words passing between them.

"I will," I said.

"I'm glad I got the blonde. He seems five percent friendlier than the ones you two are stuck with. No offence," Brianna said to Paige and I.

"Fabian's unpredictable," Paige exhaled, fear flashing across her face. "I get the feeling he enjoys wielding the power he has."

"He didn't hurt you, did he?" I asked.

She shook her head. "Not yet."

"Clarice is deadly," Luke said, leaning in closer to tighten our circle. "She's hypnotising, with an allure that's impossible to resist. I even felt myself wanting to do as she bid. One word from her and it's like my will falters."

"We all felt it," Hank agreed darkly, and Joshua nodded, a shudder passing through him.

"They're like the Elite on crack," Brianna whispered ominously.

"What's crack? Like an asscrack?" I asked before I really thought that comment through, and Hank snorted as Brianna suppressed her own laugh.

"It's a drug, I think," Paige supplied with a hesitant smile, like she couldn't quite let herself feel amusement under these circumstances.

"Yeah, it's from the old times. My mamma told me about it," Brianna said, a glint of pain in her eyes telling me her mamma was no longer around. And hell, I shared that pain.

"Did any of your vampires shed light on why we're all here?" Hank asked, looking between us, but none of us had anything to offer.

"One of us should ask them," Joshua said, throwing a nervous glance at the Royals.

"We could play rock, paper, scissors to decide who asks," Paige suggested.

"I've already made myself a target, I'll do it." I rose from my seat before any of them could object, steeling my nerves. All eyes in the room snapped to me and my bravery dipped for a moment as Fabian's wild gaze found me followed by Erik's sharp one.

"Are we going to get an explanation for what this is all about?" I forced myself to say.

Paige and Brianna gave me a hopeful look that served me the strength to remain standing.

Erik threw a bored look at Clarice who promptly stepped forward, and Miles' bright smile faltered a little, his gaze moving into the shadows where the guards stood then back to the table.

"You're the luckiest humans in the Realms," Clarice announced with undisguised excitement, bobbing a little on her towering high heels. "Every year, a handful of you are tested for the quality of your blood. You've all passed with flying colours, which means you're very valuable to us."

"In what way?" Hank asked, taking my cue to rise from his seat in a show of solidarity. Erik's eyes skipped from him to me before he ran his tongue across his teeth.

"You are now taking part in a formal ritual, and by the end of it, all of the women will be officially paired with a prince, and the men will be paired with me." Clarice beamed, but the men shared anxious looks, and I eyed the girls who shifted nervously in their seats, sharing in their discomfort.

Clarice went on, "In the sake of fairness, we're giving you time to make your own choice. You don't have to choose the prince who picked you, girls, but I'm afraid the men are stuck with me. However, as I prefer to have a willing harem, I will offer the men another choice which will be discussed in private." She grinned mischievously, but none of them returned it.

"Why would we choose any of you? What does it even mean to be paired?" My hand tightened around a dinner knife I hadn't realised I'd been holding.

Erik's eyes honed in on me, but it was Clarice who answered. "Because the prince you choose to pair with will sire you."

Breaths were sucked in around the table, but I didn't know what that meant and clearly a few others didn't either.

"What does that mean?" Paige asked before I could.

Fabian's eyes clawed over her. "It means, we'll turn you into vampires and bestow upon you the greatest wealth in the New Empire."

Shock slammed into me, making my ears ring and horror ricochet through my chest.

"It's a very important decision because your Sire will be your guide in your new life as a vampire," Clarice added brightly.

"Great, isn't it?" Miles muttered like he couldn't be less enthused.

Silence.

My heart ticked painfully in my ears. The expression on Joshua's face said that possibility was a godsend to him, and it was entirely at odds with what I felt inside.

"You mean it?" Joshua asked hopefully, rising to his feet. "We can become like you?"

"Yes," Clarice said. "Immortal, wealthy, powerful. How does that sound?"

"It sounds like a fucking nightmare," Hank barked, banging his fist on the table.

Paige started crying, and I felt like I was trapped in a terrible dream, standing there as the world went on around me, chaos breaking out as Hank demanded another option, Brianna buried her face in her hands and Luke started muttering to himself like he couldn't quite decide if this decision was good or bad.

The idea of being *sired* made me sick to my stomach. So much so, my legs grew weak. Dad had been right; this was what the testing was for. Finding humans they deemed suitable to join their ranks.

"And if we don't choose?" I spoke at last, visions of becoming one of these monsters flaring all too brightly inside my mind.

A ghost of confusion gripped Clarice's features before she answered. "Well..."

"You'll be sent to the nearest blood bank," Erik said with a cold look that drove a sliver of ice into my heart.

Rage and terror collided inside me, sending me into a spiral. "I thought you said I could go back to the Realm!"

"I lied," Erik replied coolly, shattering all illusions of that possibility as simply as that.

He was a demon sent to torment me, and I could see as clear as day there was no soul behind his eyes. Who knew how many years he had walked this earth, how much blood he had spilled, how much terror he had invoked in my kind.

"So we don't have a choice?" I choked out, my throat constricting further and further.

"You do," Miles replied with a sympathetic look that was no doubt all farce. "But granted, not a huge one. We all understand the difficulty of your situation and don't expect you to acclimatise immediately. But you must try to look at the positives in the situation."

It sounded like he was reading out lines he didn't believe in, like even he didn't care for this arrangement. But wasn't he one of the monsters enforcing it?

"Positives?" Paige whispered. "What about our families? My mom's back in the Realm, she's going to be sick with worry."

"If you cooperate and choose well, your families will be moved to more comfortable houses in the city," Fabian said in his deep tone. "But your cooperation will be judged by us." He bared his fangs and a collective shiver passed between the group from the warning lacing his words.

"We will try our best to make this transition as easy as possible for you, but the rules are the rules," Clarice said gently.

"How are we supposed to choose?" Brianna piped up, her deep brown eyes sparkling with concern.

"You will be given the opportunity to spend time with all of us over the coming days," Clarice answered with anticipation dripping through her expression.

My gaze roamed over the three princes at my disposal, knowing with absolute certainty that I had to escape this fate. I couldn't choose. I wouldn't.

Erik's expression became bored. "You will be cared for by the prince or princess who selected you until the day of The Choosing. You will behave or you will be punished."

The words were spoken to the room, but his eyes arrowed into mine, confirming they were for me.

"Yes, I was getting to that," Clarice muttered to him then her sunbeam smile was directed at us again. "From tomorrow, the women will spend time with their original prince, then the princes will alternate so that you are given time with each of your potential suitors. Each of the men will get ample time with me too. And when the ritual is over, a ball will be held where you'll all make your official choice at The Choosing ceremony." She bounced on her heels, evidently excited by that prospect, and Miles tugged on her wrist to keep her in check.

The walls seemed to close in on me and the air became impossible to breathe. I didn't have any time to process everything though as the door opened and a vampire walked in, stealing everyone's attention and recognition slammed into me like a fist to the gut.

General Wolfe was flanked by two officials in uniform as he took in the room with his hellish blue eyes. "Forgive me, your highnesses, but I need to speak with you on an urgent matter." His gaze scoured the space then landed on me, his jaw clenching and his expression morphing with realisation. He took a purposeful step toward me, but Erik flew into view at an impossible speed, blocking his way to me.

"You have my attention, General. Now step outside or I'll have you reprimanded for your impertinence."

"Yes, sir," Wolfe murmured like a kicked dog, turning on his heel and exiting swiftly with Erik on his heels.

When the doors shut behind them, Clarice clapped her hands to regain our attention. "The guards will escort you back to your rooms. Make sure you get a good night's rest before tomorrow."

The screeching of chairs sounded around me, but my feet were rooted to the spot. My heart trembled with the aftershock of seeing Wolfe. The man who'd accosted me and arrested my father.

*He must know where my family is.*

"What's going through your head, wild one?" Hank muttered like he sensed I was about to do something crazy, but I couldn't look his way.

With a surge of decision, I sprinted from the room, darting into the gleaming hallway where Erik stood before Wolfe with his arms folded.

"-from the Realm. It will cause quite the scandal if word spreads-" Wolfe's words died on his lips as he spotted me, a gleam of hatred sparking in his eyes.

Guards poured from the room behind me and I sped toward Wolfe, fear and anger forcing my legs to move.

"Where are they?!" I cried at him, grabbing hold of his arm, wanting to tear the truth from his tongue.

Erik halted the two guards who were inches from getting hold of me and Wolfe snarled, his eyes shifting onto me in fury. He raised a hand to strike me, and Erik caught me by the waist, yanking me hard against him, and his whole body tensed.

"She belongs to *me*," he snarled at Wolfe, his fingers biting into my ribs as he crushed me against him. "Lay a hand on her and I will tear it clean from your body, General. You do not have permission to touch her."

Wolfe's sharp blue eyes crept over my face and a scowl skewed his beautifully harsh features before he bowed his head. "Forgive me, your highness."

"Where's my family?" I demanded, thrashing in Erik's hold as I fought to free myself of his grip.

"What's this about, General?" Erik growled, barely seeming to notice my fighting as he held me with an unyielding grip.

"This girl is related to the fugitive," Wolfe replied, giving Erik a pointed look.

A hundred emotions flowed through me. Fugitive meant Callie. It had to. I'd seen the vampires catch Dad, so it had to be her he was referring to. But what did that mean for Dad?

My heart burst with pain and I tried to claw my way free of Erik to get to the asshole who had captured him. "Where's my dad, what did you do with him?!"

Erik didn't let me go and I despised him for that even deeper than I had despised him before.

Wolfe surveyed me with satisfaction spreading into his cool eyes. "In the blood bank, of course, where all the traitors go." His eyes flipped to Erik behind me as that truth cracked my heart in two. "It may help my case if I could speak with this girl. Alone."

"Interrogate me, you mean," I snapped, a ripple of fear radiating through me. I wrestled against Erik's solid arms, but I couldn't get free.

A beat of silence hit my ears before Erik responded. "I told you once and I will not tell you again, General. This girl is under royal protection. *My* protection."

"But, sire-" Wolfe started.

"No," Erik growled. "Go to my office if you wish to discuss this further."

Wolfe stalked away and Erik released me so fast that I stumbled a few steps before I managed to balance myself.

Hot tears spilled from my eyes as my worst fears were confirmed. Dad was in the blood bank. Callie may have been free, but for how long? And what would they do to her if they caught her?

"Go to your room," Erik commanded like I was some errant child, pushing me toward the royal guards at his back.

I spotted the humans being escorted past us up the stairs, and Paige gave me a concerned frown while Hank looked tempted to come over here.

I didn't follow Erik's order, determined to remain there until I got some answers.

"Take her if she will not walk," Erik snarled, and the guards caught hold of my arms and dragged me away.

My body went slack as I gave in to their superior strength, sobbing as they took me back to my bedroom and shoved me inside. A key twisted in the lock, but I didn't care. I threw myself onto the bed, curling into a ball and crying into my pillow as my world came crashing down around me.

Despite how hard I tried, I couldn't get myself to calm down. I was stuck here, unable to help my family, and God only knew what was happening to my dad in that awful fucking place.

The image of my dad's strong body strung up in the blood bank was all I could think of, completely paralysed but entirely awake. Was that how it was in there? Or was it worse? Was he aware of what was happening to him?

I unravelled further, hating how weak I felt. How useless I was to help him.

*Oh Dad, hold on. I'll get you out. I'll find a way, I promise.*

# CALLIE

## CHAPTER THIRTEEN

Our journey through the woods lasted longer than I expected, but eventually we came upon the remains of a city destroyed by the bombs.

As far as I could see, mounds of rubble and half-collapsed buildings filled the area. Patches of long grass and several saplings had sprung up between the concrete where nature had begun to reclaim the ground. But with the onset of winter, everything was dying off and the landscape was predominantly grey.

It was depressingly reminiscent of home.

I gazed at the open land with more than a little fear. So far, we'd managed to travel within the shelter of the woodlands but once we stepped into the ruins, we'd be a lot more exposed. We might have evaded the vampires who were hunting me until now, but I wasn't foolish enough to believe they'd simply given up and returned to whatever rock they lived under.

Tension lined my body, my heart thumping unnaturally hard against my ribs with every step I took. They were coming for me. It was only a question of when they'd catch up.

Magnar stopped at the edge of the trees between two huge pines and looked out across the ruins with a frown. His presence was so dominating even simply standing there, built of pure muscle and savagery. He drew my gaze a little too long and I clucked my tongue at myself, dismissing any wild ideas of finding this barbarian remotely attractive. He was a means to an end, and I wouldn't be laying a finger on a man who had decided to trap me against a wall while my family were rounded up by monsters.

"I grew up learning everything there is to know of vampires, and yet I never heard of them causing this kind of destruction before. How did they accomplish such devastation?" he asked, not looking back at me.

After hours of endless silence, I was surprised enough that he'd asked me anything at all.

"This wasn't the vampires," I replied darkly, my attention shifting across the miles of rubble which had once been home to thousands of people. How many had died here when the bombs were dropped? "Humans did this to each other in the Final War."

Magnar turned his golden eyes on me searchingly. "How?"

I hesitated under the heat of his gaze. He was so fucking intense all the time and that made answering him difficult, especially when the answer to his question wasn't a simple one, and I doubted I was the best person to ask for it either. I hadn't been alive to witness any of it, and the accounts I'd been told were almost entirely from my father. And Dad had always preferred to talk of the time before the war and the vampires than what had landed us where we were now.

"It ended the year before I was born, and I've lived my entire life inside the Realm," I began so that he might excuse the holes in my knowledge.

"You've never been beyond those fences before?" Magnar asked, his frown deepening, the accusation in those words making me kick at the dirt beneath my boots.

"I... No. In the last few days I've seen more of the world than I did in the previous twenty-one years of my existence. That's how humans live now. Anything I know about what once existed out here comes via stories my dad told me." I shrugged defensively as pity flashed in his eyes, but it was gone as quickly as it had come. No doubt he had far more pressing concerns than the sad little life of me.

"But you do know how the world came to be this way?" he asked, his tone slightly gentler than before.

I bristled against the change in his attitude. I didn't want him to pity me. I was sure he already saw me as weak enough without him feeling sorry for me as well.

"My dad told us the stories," I reiterated. "There have always been wars so I'm sure you can understand that much. He said that the more power people got, the more they wanted, and in the end, they grew willing to sacrifice anything it took to claim it."

"That has always been the way of men," Magnar rumbled. "If they had banded together, they might have been able to wipe the vampires from this earth a long time ago, but every time they came close, their own selfish desires got in the way. Too interested in their small, selfish lives, fucking, fighting and taking all they could by whatever means they were willing to stoop to. That is why the slayers stopped asking for their help. Humans cannot get out of their own way for long enough to see what truly matters."

"Are you saying you're not human?" I asked with a frown. My memories of my dad's stories were pushed from my mind as his history intrigued me yet again.

"Slayers are something more than human and something less. We were given gifts by the gods to help us fight the fanged demons. But those gifts come with a price. We value our cause above our lives individually. Nothing is more important to us than destroying the vampires. We give our lives to it, but that means that we don't always get to make our own decisions about things that most humans take for granted." He shrugged dismissively like that was a price he had long since decided to pay and it didn't bother him.

"Like what?" I asked, fascinated despite myself.

I was doing a terrible job of avoiding asking him personal questions, but I'd never met anyone like him before. I'd never really wanted to know about someone the way I did about him, though that did little to make me like him any better. The fact was, he was brash and rude and an utter brute, but he was also free and full of memories that had never

221

been contained behind bars. I wanted to taste that truth on him even if our paths were likely leading us towards a war of our own. He still hadn't told me what he wanted me for, and I wasn't stupid enough to forget it.

"Love. Family. Where we go and when. Do you think I wished to sleep for a hundred years? When I was due to wake, everyone I'd ever known would already be dead and I'd have to start anew with their great grandchildren. At the time, I'd thought my brother was to join me in our slumber, so I was to have one familiar face when I woke, but now...even he has been taken from me." He sighed. "But that is what it is to be a slayer. We don't get to choose what we do with our lives. Our sole purpose is the eradication of the vampires. Which is why I want to know about the world as it is now. I need to know how they seized this power so that I might strike it from their grasp."

Despite the general contempt I felt towards this beastly man, my heart couldn't help but twist with the reality of his situation. He was utterly alone. The world itself had been reborn more times than I could count in the time he slept, and now he'd awoken to a place so unfamiliar that it was a wonder he wasn't simply crumpled on the floor and sobbing for all he'd lost.

I reached out to him on instinct, my fingers brushing the back of his hand for a moment before I realised what I was doing and drew away just as quickly. Magnar glanced at me in surprise, and heat rose in my cheeks as I internally cursed myself for the moment of weakness. It hadn't been for *him* anyway, it had been for his loss.

I hurried to tell him what he wanted to hear so that neither of us had too long to think about the awkward gesture, and I silently swore to cut my damn hands off rather than ever repeat it again.

"My dad said that the war escalated quickly. There were a lot of politics involved with one country threatening another, which went on for years, back and forth a hundred times, squabbling like small children over more issues than he could recall. Then one day, someone launched a missile. No one even knows which country fired first. Before the first bomb could drop, all the other countries had hit the red button to fire their own. In the space of a few hours, pretty much every major city in the world had been destroyed. Billions of people were killed. In this country alone, almost every central and southern state were destroyed entirely. Apparently, it's all just a wasteland of parched desert now. The few survivors all live on either the west coast like us or the east. Dad said the missiles aimed at those cities were intercepted for the most part, exploded over the sea and stuff like that."

I blew out a breath, gazing across the devastation of the ruined city before us. He'd described it more times than I could count but seeing it for myself was something entirely different. It looked like it went on forever, a wasteland without end, the world destroyed from this point until eternity.

"Then, while the survivors tried to salvage something from the wreckage, the vampires appeared. Dad said they must have been waiting for our kind to be weak enough. Biding their time until the world was on its knees, and they could sweep in and take control. Either that or there were so few humans left that they decided we needed herding like cattle, kept in one place for feeding their desires."

Magnar sighed heavily, for once not full of questions and I frowned up at him, trying to gauge the shadows in his eyes for some reaction to what I'd just told him.

"What?" I asked, wondering why he was frowning so deeply, a hand scoring across his face and rubbing at his jaw.

He eyed me for a long moment then folded his arms before voicing the issue.

"And what, exactly, is a missile?" he asked, tilting his head to one side.

I stared up at him with wide eyes for several seconds and then let out a bark of laughter. "Right. There are probably quite a few things like that that you have no idea about. I guess technology moved on a fair bit since the dark ages, old man."

Magnar grunted in irritation and started to head out into the wreckage left by the bombs, his shoulders tense as he stalked away from me, that rage clinging to him once more.

"Listen to that," I said as I hurried to match his fierce pace, refusing to let him leash my tongue with fear.

"What?" he demanded, stopping suddenly and making me stumble as I followed suit. He cocked his head to listen for whatever I'd heard, and I stamped my lips together to stop myself from smirking.

"Your silence," I continued, uncertain why exactly I was taunting him aside from the fact that I was sick of trailing after him while he growled his way to the blood bank like a beast on the scent of its quarry. "It's the best of all the sounds you make," I added. "Your silence is a beauty all of its own."

Magnar's brows lowered as he abandoned his vigilant search of the area surrounding us and focused fully back on me.

"Is that so?" he deadpanned, eyes glimmering with violence.

I always had been fond of taking risks, and I was sick of his shit too, so I went on.

"Your silence may be my favourite of all the sounds you make, the utter lack of noise from you is something I appreciate at every moment it's offered."

Magnar's golden eyes dropped down my figure and rolled back up again, surveying me from head to toe, making my flesh heat with awareness as he took his sweet time about it.

"I might say the same to you," he replied finally. "But you are so fond of hearing yourself speak that the silence never has a chance to claim you."

I scoffed lightly, looking away from him with a shake of my head. "In that case, I don't suppose you want me to continue with the history lesson then? Or…does it even count as history for you, considering it happened in your lifetime?"

"You wish to make me beg?" he asked, the contempt with which he delivered the question making it all too clear that he would sooner die than lower himself to do such a thing, the step he took towards me making my pulse skip over itself. No, this man had never begged for anything a day in his damn life.

"Perhaps if you were on your knees, you wouldn't block the sun so much," I replied, gesturing to his towering height.

Magnar shifted closer still, his shadow devouring me as he moved so near that he became all I could see, only my own stubbornness keeping me in place before him. He could kill me so easily. But he hadn't yet, and for some reason, I didn't think he would now either. But maybe that made me a fool.

"There is nothing in this world which will ever see me on my knees," he replied in a rough tone that rushed right through to my core.

"Perhaps some manners then?" I pushed, because fuck him and his bullshit. If he wanted to gain the knowledge which was locked away in my head, then the least he could do was ask nicely.

Magnar took a step closer to me and I finally found my common sense and backed up, snatching the dagger he'd given me from my pocket and holding it between us while the rush of its presence swept through me.

"You shouldn't raise a weapon unless you're prepared to use it," Magnar warned me, stepping closer again, only to find me backing up once more.

"Who says I'm not prepared to use it?" I taunted.

He moved so quickly that a gasp spilled from my lips, and I didn't even have time to consider swinging the blade before his calloused hand had locked around my wrist in an iron hold and he was yanking me forward.

I lost my footing, stumbling on the broken rubble beneath my feet but Magnar simply propelled me towards him then used the limb to twist me.

My arm was drawn tight across my chest, and Magnar spun me so my back was to his front, the press of his enormous body behind me locking me in place. His arm banded around me, my own dagger just touching the side of my neck as he locked me there with a terrifying strength.

His other arm wound across my hips, pulling me back so my body was flush to his, completely immobilising me as he dropped his mouth to my ear and spoke in that rough tone which made every fibre of my being prickle with alertness.

"Please," he growled, the word about as far from begging as he could get.

My throat bobbed as I tried to get control of my thrashing pulse, refusing to let him fluster me despite my current situation.

My heart was thundering so fast I had to assume he could feel it with the way our bodies were pressed together, adrenaline swarming through me uselessly as the touch of the weapon against my throat fell just shy of drawing blood.

"Well, as you asked so nicely, it would be rude of me to refuse," I replied, my voice saccharine sweet, the challenge still there on my tongue even if it was clear to all who might look that I was outmatched when it came to this asshole.

"Good girl," he mocked, the scratch of his beard raking against my neck, making my anger with him raise its head once more even as heat flooded my body at the roughness of his voice, but he released me and stepped away before I could come up with some smartass reply.

Magnar started walking and I tried to figure out where to begin. A thousand years was a hell of a long time to have missed out on, and my sheltered life hardly made me an expert on much of it, but I was willing to try and help him figure things out despite his dickish attitude. It was that or endure the silence all day anyway, so what did I have to lose?

"I find it hard to believe that a metal box could ever fly through the clouds," Magnar scoffed several hours later.

I'd been trying to describe an aeroplane, which was pretty damn difficult considering the fact that I'd never even seen one for myself. Dad had been adamant that they really had existed once though, so I didn't doubt it. Like Magnar, I'd always found it difficult to imagine too.

"It's true," I insisted.

Hours of discussing the things he'd missed out on had gone a long way towards thawing our frosty relationship. It wasn't like he'd started smiling or anything extreme like that, and it certainly wasn't like he was less of a dick, but my stories had definitely captured his interest and had gone some way to help pass the time while we trekked across the barren wasteland.

After the first few hours, the rubble had grown in size, more walls left standing than not, and the odd building fully intact. I guessed we were moving into the edges of the bomb's blast radius where everything had taken slightly less damage, and that offered up more cover between the rubble which I welcomed gladly. Crossing the utterly destroyed terrain had left me feeling far too exposed. At least here we had some measure of protection from creepy familiars looking out for us.

Magnar even seemed to have moved past the annoyance of having to ask for so many explanations, particularly where modern technology was concerned. He accepted the holes in my knowledge without judgement too and I was grateful to him for that, if a little surprised by it.

My life had been immeasurably sheltered in comparison to his, but instead of the pity I'd noticed when I first told him about my incarcerated existence, it now seemed to kindle anger in him. I could feel his simmering rage at the hold the vampires had on the human population and it was stoking the flames of my own anger too.

For so many years I'd had to accept my lot in life. Dreams of escape had come frequently, but I'd never really believed I might live to see them fulfilled. I'd always accepted that my fate wasn't mine to choose. My life would end when the vampires decided it, and not a moment of it would ever have been truly my own.

Thinking about that now made me angrier than I could describe. I'd finally made it out of their clutches, and I'd sooner die than allow them to take me back to the Realm or anywhere else. Once I'd gotten my family away from them, I fully intended to get as far from the vampires as humanly possible and live out my days beneath the sun, every choice my own, not a single drop of blood offered up from my veins ever again.

"And this was used for transportation?" Magnar confirmed, bringing my mind back to our aeroplane conversation.

"They were really fast. You could zip from one side of the country to the other in less than a day. And I think that's a pretty long way," I confirmed, thinking of the old map Dad used to keep under his bed. It showed the entire world as it had been before, though he claimed a lot of Europe was now underwater, Australia entirely destroyed by the bombs just like the states which had once made up the central part of our country. There were parts of India, China and Canada which were said to have escaped the worst of the bombings, but Dad didn't know what the vampires had done to the survivors there. Likely the same as they'd done to us.

"It is further than you can imagine," Magnar replied. It was strange that his knowledge could fill in some of the gaps in my own like that. In some ways we were both as ignorant as each other about the world we now travelled through, but even a thousand years couldn't change the size of the continent he'd once crossed.

"And there was another flying machine with big, spinning blades on top of it called a hoppercopper or hopelcopter. No, wait it was-"

"Silence." Magnar raised a hand to halt me suddenly, pressing his back to the wall of a partially collapsed building and jerking his chin in a command for me to do the same. I quickly followed suit, my heart pounding frantically as he tilted his head to listen for something. "They've found us," he breathed.

I blinked up at him as anxiety coiled in my gut. With each step we took away from the Realm I'd wondered if the vampires had decided that I was just one, insignificant human, lost in a huge world. Why waste their time trying to track me down? That hope had been stupid though. Of course they'd want to find me. They'd want everyone in the Realm to see what happened to anyone who tried to run. Ice flooded my veins as I imagined the terrible things they might do to me to make sure no one ever attempted to follow in my footsteps, and a tremor of fear ran down my spine.

"They'll kill me," I breathed. "They'll string me up in front the whole Realm and drain my blood for everyone to see. They'll make an example of me, and I'll never make it back to my family. I won't-"

Magnar caught my face between his hands and forced me to look at him, silencing my panicked rambling. I sucked in a sharp breath as I gazed into his golden eyes, finding a pool of strength there, no fear at all, just pure, wicked violence, every bit of it aimed toward the creatures who hunted us.

"They will not take you, Callie," he swore, the use of my name stalling the rush of thoughts which had been clamouring in my mind. "You are under my protection, and I won't allow them to lay a hand on you. I give you my word that I will keep you safe and out of their clutches."

I blinked at him, his face bare inches from mine, the intensity of that time-forgotten gaze burning right into me as he refused to let me go. My heart lurched in a way that had nothing to do with the danger coming for us, my skin heating beneath his rough touch and a lump forming in my throat.

"Okay," I breathed, pushing my fear aside. Despite everything I knew about the vampires, his confidence made me believe he just might be able to keep that promise, and I wouldn't simply stand by and panic while he fought to do so.

"It is my duty as a slayer to protect your kind," he said firmly, and my jaw tightened as I realised his declaration hadn't been because of some desire to look after me. This was what he was built for.

Magnar released me, leaving a line of fire across my skin where his hands had been. He closed his eyes and took a deep breath as he concentrated, and I tried to listen for whatever he could hear too.

"I believe there are only five of them," he said after several long minutes.

"Only?" I squeaked.

One was more than enough to take me down. I had about as much chance of standing against five of them as a mouse stood against a wolf.

Magnar turned to me and placed a hand on my arm, his grip unyielding as he forced my attention back to him.

"In your chest beats the heart of a warrior. You will fight for your life, and you will *win*," he said fiercely.

Suddenly I could see the man who had led an entire army of his people. The one born to lead and rule, the one who could inspire those he led to rush into battle against monsters and come out the other side swinging. The way he spoke left no room for doubt. I could imagine men and women following him to war without a beat of fear in their hearts.

Somehow, I found a few scraps of my own courage in his golden eyes and clung to them, building on them with my own resolve and determination to survive. My fear of the vampires had been ingrained in me from the moment of my birth, but that did not mean it was insurmountable. They didn't deserve my fear, they didn't deserve to hold that power over me. Dad and Montana needed me, so there was no way I could let the vampires take me.

"Say it," Magnar growled.

"I will win," I replied with as much grit as I could manage, raising my chin as I felt those words sinking into my soul, clinging to all the belief I could muster for them.

Magnar released his grip on my arm and pulled the blade he'd given me from my belt, pushing it into my hand. "Then prepare to stand and fight. They're nearly upon us."

As the hilt connected with my palm, I could have sworn I felt an excited energy coursing through it. This was what it had been made for. It hungered for the blood of the creatures that hunted me. It wanted to find a home in their flesh.

*Fury.* Its silken voice beckoned me to join with it, and I found myself almost eager for the vampires' arrival as its desires bled into my own.

Magnar reached up to his neck and unclasped his cloak, letting it fall to the ground and revealing the leathers he wore beneath it. Though he had called me a warrior, that seemed like some kind of joke in comparison to him. He was the figure that would be drawn next to that word in the dictionary, his body thick with muscle, his soul rife with strength. He was the embodiment of power. A weapon given flesh. And I pitied anyone who tried to stand against him.

"Come on out, poppet," a cold voice cooed from somewhere beyond our hiding place, far closer than I would have thought possible. How long had they been on our heels, nipping like a pack of mutts hungry for the kill?

A large measure of my confidence turned and ran screaming for the hills at the sound of that voice, but a small portion of it stayed with me, my grip on the dagger tightening.

"It's been a long time since someone called me poppet," Magnar replied gruffly as he stepped out from our hiding place and pulled one of his blades from his back. It hung loosely in his grip as he moved into the open space before us where four vampires stood waiting.

I followed, leaving him enough space to wield his weapons without taking my head from my shoulders, but not allowing the gap between us to increase too much. He might have had faith in me, but I had no idea how to wield any kind of weapon, even one which purred with a desire for death in my hand. And though I might have been willing to try and defend myself, I knew I was no match for the immortal beings who had come for me.

The vampires dropped back a few steps, hissing like alley cats as they watched Magnar approach.

"Slayer," spat a male with long, white-blonde hair. "Not possible."

"I was there when the last of you died!" cursed a strikingly beautiful female with dark skin and piercing amber eyes. "The Belvederes gutted every last one of you!"

"Then I must be a ghost," Magnar replied calmly, not even showing a flicker of emotion at the words she delivered. "Although I do not feel dead."

"You will feel so when your head lays severed at my feet," the female crowed.

At a signal I barely registered, the four of them leapt towards Magnar at once. He didn't even flinch as they surrounded him, each swinging their weapons from different sides to try and overwhelm him.

Magnar swept his blade in a wide arc, parrying two of theirs and managing to slice into the leg of the blonde male who cursed vehemently as he stumbled aside.

They came at him again, moving so quickly I could hardly follow it and yet he managed to evade their blows, dancing between them like he was toying with them, the clash of steel ringing out loudly across the ruins.

Magnar grabbed his second blade from his back and threw it, catching the green-eyed male in the chest. The blade must have pierced his heart because he let out a blood-curdling scream, his last moments etched in horror. His face disintegrated and fell into dust which blew away through the clearing before the sound of his voice had fully faded, and I swore as I watched the golden sword which had ended him slam into the ground amid nothing but ash.

Their fight started to move closer to me and I shifted back, wishing I could do something to help but knowing I'd only get in the way if I tried. Fury burned hot in my palm, begging for blood, whispering tales of how it had been wielded against these monsters in the past, but I couldn't allow it the attention it was craving.

As the three remaining vampires rushed at Magnar again, the hilt of my blade grew hot beneath my palm, and I was struck with the violent urge to turn around. I twisted to look behind me, suddenly remembering that Magnar had said there were five vampires coming for us, dread tumbling into my gut before I even locked eyes with the one who had found me.

She rushed at me like an oncoming tide, fangs bared and arms outstretched almost like she intended to embrace me. I screamed as I threw myself aside and her fingernails scratched against my coat without managing to gain purchase. She came for me again, her thick brunette hair flying around her too-beautiful face as she swiped at me, hissing angrily.

I ducked beneath her grasping hands once more and slashed at her with Fury. The blade felt alive beneath my palm, like I could feel a beating heart within the unnaturally warm metal. It hungered for her blood, and I ached to give it what it desired.

The third time I tried to evade her, I failed. She smiled wickedly as her hand closed around my throat and she lifted me clean off of my feet, her impossible strength overpowering me with ease.

I flailed wildly in her grasp, my feet kicking desperately as I tried to fight her off. She was even stronger than I'd imagined.

Her smile widened as she raised me above her head, her grip on my throat tightening painfully, cutting off my air. Black spots danced before my eyes as I struggled for oxygen.

Panic rushed to claim me, but Fury called to me, urging me to use it, promising the help I so desperately needed. With every ounce of energy I could muster, I slashed the blade down, carving it into the vampire's arm and cutting deep. She dropped me with a cry of surprise, and I hit the concrete hard, pain rippling through my body as I fell on my back.

The vampire howled in rage as bright, crimson blood poured from her arm and splattered the pavement. Smoke rose from the wound and the smell of burning flesh tainted the air.

I scrambled backwards, trying to regain my feet but she leapt on top of me with a determined snarl, driving the breath from my lungs as she straddled me, the broken rubble beneath me cutting into my flesh.

"Don't worry pet; they want you alive," she hissed as I bucked and thrashed, trying to throw her off.

She drove a punch into my gut and grabbed my throat again with her other hand, crushing me into the concrete. I would have been dead already if she wanted to kill me, but by some miracle, she had orders to spare my life. That gave me one clear advantage; I could keep fighting for my freedom, but she couldn't finish me off.

I struggled in what would have been a useless attempt to break free, except that I managed to get Fury into the small space between our bodies.

I bellowed my defiance as she punched me again, the movement giving me the room I needed to strike. With every drop of strength I possessed, I thrust the blade up and under her ribs. The vampire's brown eyes widened in horrified surprise a moment before they turned to dust and crumbled apart.

I sucked in a sharp breath, unable to do anything aside from stare as cracks ripped across her skin, burning through her, tearing her apart. Fury sang its victory in my palm and a searing pain flashed along the inside of my forearm, making me cry out in alarm as I found myself unable to release the blade.

The remains of the vampire scattered over me, and I scrunched my eyes shut as the ash coated me, making me cough and splutter.

I rolled over, the pain in my arm fading to nothing, my hold on Fury relaxing once more. I wiped my face with the arm of my coat before spitting on the ground to make sure I didn't ingest any of that undead bitch. I kicked her now empty clothes away from me and pushed myself upright, blinking the dust from my eyes.

As I regained my feet, I found Magnar exchanging blows with the two remaining vampires. I hadn't seen him kill the third, but a pile of ash-smeared clothes marked where it had happened.

I stared on, wanting to help but not knowing how I could as the clash of metal rang out again and again, a furious dance taking place between the three of them, swords swinging with terrifying speed and strength.

The female vampire feinted to the left before lurching back, using a swing from the male to help her get closer to their prey. She managed to get beneath Magnar's guard, landing a blow that cut deep into the flesh of his arm before he could twist aside.

He snarled in anger and pain as she came at him once more, his sword slashing sideways to deflect her next blow.

The male vampire lurched forward as Magnar exposed his back to him, and I cried out a warning I already knew would come too late.

I whipped my arm back and let Fury fly, the blade buzzing with excitement, the movement somehow coming naturally to me as I hurled the weapon with all the strength I had. My aim was true, and Fury found its home in the vampire's thigh, making him shriek in pain as it sank deep into muscle and bone.

His head whipped around to find me as he wrenched the blade from his leg with savage abandon, then he screamed as smoke rose from his palm, Fury clearly burning him as the stench of burning flesh reached me.

The vampire tossed Fury aside in horror before coming for me, his eyes full of vengeance and a hunger which wouldn't be denied.

I stumbled back, unarmed and completely at his mercy as my heart pounded a violent rhythm against my ribs.

I lurched down to grab a rock from the ground, but before I could even think about using it, Magnar was there, a war cry tearing from his lips as he charged after the beast set to destroy me.

Magnar swung his blade with ferocious force and took the vampire's head clean off with a single blow, the decapitated head falling to the ground with a sickening crack. Without sparing me a glance, Magnar returned to his battle with the female, finally able to give her his full attention as he parried a blow intended for his back.

I dropped my rock, scrambling around the decapitated body and ran to collect my blade. As I snatched it from the ground, I could have sworn it felt pleased to see me, a deep purr rolling through me from it, like the thing had some form of sentience and was saying hello.

"Hello right back," I muttered, a thrill rising in me over reuniting with it.

The hilt hummed with energy as I sprinted back to the twitching body of the fallen vampire, driving the blade home in its heart. Fury seemed to sigh with satisfaction as the vampire fell to dust beneath me, the ash swirling away on the wind.

*I've waited so long.*

The words flitted through my mind, and I wasn't even convinced I'd really heard them, but it sure seemed like I had.

The clamour of clashing swords stopped abruptly, and I looked up to find Magnar grappling with the final vampire hand to hand. Their blades lay on the ground, and she clawed at him as he threw punches into her too beautiful face, unrestrained and wholly ruthless in all his god-like power.

Magnar caught her by the throat and slammed her against a crumbling wall, sending bricks tumbling from it and making me stumble back as they came close to hitting me.

The vampire fought furiously to throw Magnar off while he pinned her in place, but he grabbed a dagger from his belt and stabbed her in the gut. She cried out as he stabbed her again and again, blood spilling over his hands, splattering the concrete and staining it red before finally finding her heart on the fourth strike. The fist which had been locked around her throat closed on nothing but dust as she fell apart before him, and I could only stare at this beast of a man who had woken from a long-forgotten legend to fight a battle I had never thought possible.

Magnar turned to me with his chest heaving and a fire burning in his gaze that I hadn't seen before. This was who he was at his soul, the brutal, honest truth of him. A warrior forged in the ash and soot of his enemies, their blood painting his skin, their deaths payment for all they had taken and all they would have continued to take.

"So this is what you live for, huh?" I asked as the adrenaline drained from my body and what had just happened began to press in on me. I'd killed a vampire. I'd killed a fucking vampire! "I can see why you enjoy it so much."

I released a shaky laugh as I gave up on trying to stand and sank down to the ground, placing my trembling fingers against the cold concrete as the broken rocks bit into my knees, and the reality of what I'd just done burrowed deep into my soul. I'd fought a vampire and fucking won. Damn, I wished Monty could have been here to see it.

Magnar watched me for several long seconds then let out a booming laugh. "Yeah. This is what I fucking live for," he agreed. "Death is the endgame, but the fight is where I thrive."

I couldn't help but give him a feral grin of my own in reply. If there was one thing that could make you forget your problems for a while, then it was looking your own death in the face and saying fuck you.

# MONTANA

## CHAPTER FOURTEEN

My mind had found a quiet space to go to, a detached, faraway land where no one could find me. I was hollow inside, the tears long dried on my cheeks, and the pain turned to numbness in my chest. But it didn't matter, because my mind was conjuring flowers and hummingbirds, waterfalls and wilderness, spaces to get lost in and stay away from the dark shadow of reality.

The door clicked as it unlocked, but I didn't move from where I sat against the headboard, only half aware of someone's arrival. It didn't matter who, because I wasn't there. I was here, in a place no one could find me.

"Have you calmed down yet?" Erik's flat tone rolled into my ears, and the shadows delved deeper into my fantasy land, coiling around me and trying to pull me back to the real world.

"I knew you were a rebel, little human, but Wolfe has now informed me of just how deep that rebellious streak runs. A sister on the run...your father in the blood bank. How chaotic." His weight pressed down the bed and the darkness snaked deeper, trying to take me, but I wouldn't let go.

"Rebel?" Erik took hold of my chin, turning my head so my eyes were angled towards his. "Where are you?"

"Lost," I breathed, the closeness of him not sparking fear this time, because I was too broken to feel it. "Don't look for me."

"I don't take orders from humans," he growled, dropping his hand from my face, his eyes swirling like storm clouds. "Besides, you're not lost. You're right here."

He tapped my bare leg and I blinked, jolting fully back into reality and the crushing grief that came with it weighed down on me all at once. I hung my head, my hair half falling out of the bun to hang in loose strands around my face.

Even in the Realm, I'd never felt this powerless. I was stuck in a game I didn't want to play while Callie was being hunted by vampires and my dad was facing horrors too terrible to think about.

"I can't help them," I breathed. "I'm all alone here." Voicing my fears to this asshole made me tense, and I immediately wished I'd remained silent.

"You have other humans here to keep you company," he said, his voice terse.

"The two aren't interchangeable. I don't want them. I want my family," I hissed, looking up at him as rage spit hot water in my chest.

Erik pressed his lips together in frustration. "I don't want your emotions affecting the ritual."

"Fuck your ritual." I shoved to my feet, stepping away from him with my teeth bared. "And fuck you and your parasitic brothers and sister." My heart was stronger again, but coming eye to eye with him threatened to crack the fragile walls around it. I needed to get out of this prison and back to where I belonged. I despised this dress, this paint on my face. This wasn't me; it was a wicked lie made to confound me.

"All of this is fucked up," I went on. "You take us from our Realms, dress us up like pretty puppets and expect us to dance when you pull on our strings. But I will not be your pawn so you can use me for your entertainment only to turn me into a monster like *you*. I want to leave, I want to find the people I love and never see your unnatural face again."

Erik's expression remained unchanged. "If you would just take a breath-"

I snatched the lamp off of the nightstand, hurling it at him with a yell of purest hate tearing through me. He caught it with ease, tossing it to the floor and I despised how unaffected he was by anything I did. He was heartless, made of stone.

"You're acting very childishly," he remarked, and my body flamed from the comment.

I ground my teeth. "I won't play along with any of this. I won't do anything until my father's safe and your vicious general stops hunting my sister."

This was the only leverage I had to play, and it all hinged on how much this monster needed me for his plans.

Erik released a breath of annoyance. "That's not for you to decide. You will do as I say."

"No, I won't," I snarled, and tension spanned through the air as our gazes locked together. Fear threatened to make me back down, but I couldn't. The only thing I had left to hold onto was my resilience, and I wasn't going to let this vampire steal it from me. I would do anything for my family, and if I had to threaten this beast and place my neck on the line to protect them then so be it.

Erik rose to his feet, his imposing height dwarfing me in an instant. "I can't deal with these emotions, rebel. It's not my place to comfort you."

"No, but apparently it's your place to keep me prisoner here to do as you like with."

"I will not speak with you unless you curb your tone. I am a prince, and you will address me with respect," he snarled, and I caught a glimpse of his fangs as he took a step towards me.

My breaths came quicker as I held my ground. "Respect?" I scoffed. "I will never respect you. You're my captor. The captor of my entire race. I know there's no heart that beats in you, I know you're empty inside with no care for anything, so I'm not stupid enough to appeal to your better nature because you have none. But you said yourself you want me to play rebel in your little ritual, so I'm telling you I will do anything and everything you ask so long as you answer my demands. Protect my family and I will pay any price."

His jaw ticked, his eyes sharp and unyielding as he stared at me as if he couldn't believe what he was hearing. His lips curled down and a sinister look etched into his features, making my nerve falter.

"I will never take an order from you," he hissed. "You forget who you are speaking to and what I am capable of."

"I know you could kill me," I said, my throat thick. "But I would die for them a thousand times over."

The corner of his mouth twitched, and he stepped closer still, stealing away the space between us with that single stride. I was forced to look up at him as a growl rumbled through his chest and the promise of death hung on the air. The glint in his eyes was full of countless sins, unspeakable things he had done, the blood that wet his skin during his unknowable lifetime. And perhaps I was just going to be another tarnish on his soul, another death to add to his collection.

"Kill you?" he echoed with a humourless laugh. "I could torture you in ways your little human mind cannot even fathom. I was reborn in torment, so torment I became. It is easy to die, little human, but can you live through agony that guts you from the inside out? Can you survive a nightmare that weaves itself into your bones and cracks them one by one?"

"Is that the price you want me to pay?" I asked, a quiver to my voice, though I knew in the depths of my heart I would go through anything for my family. "Because the answer is yes."

His eyebrows rose enough to let me know I'd caught him by surprise, and he spat a snarl before turning his back on me. "You are impossible."

He marched out of the door, slamming it behind him so hard that the whole room rattled alongside my heart.

I sagged forward, exhaling a heavy breath as the weight of his dark presence left the air. The minutes ticked by, and I couldn't help but be concerned about where he'd gone, what his plans were with me now. I didn't understand how I'd escaped punishment this long, and I had the feeling his return would not be pretty.

I shuddered, moving onto the bed, and drawing my legs up to my chest before resting my chin on my knees.

*Hurt me all you like, vampire, I will not obey your commands unless you obey mine.*

Voices sounded beyond the door, making my ears prick up and my body tensed for what was about to come.

"Just talk to her," Erik said. "For the love of the gods, Clarice, I don't know what else to do. She's going to cause problems if she continues the ritual in this manner."

"You are such a fool sometimes," Clarice replied, and my heart thudded harder at the thought of her coming in and trying to give me a pep talk. It damn well wouldn't work.

"What's that supposed to mean?" Erik growled.

"She needs support through this transition, Erik. You need to learn how to look after her if you're going to have any chance of her choosing you at the ball."

I shuddered, the idea of selecting Erik and allowing him to turn me into a monster too terrifying to think about. But what if that was the only way they would agree to protect my family. Would I choose such a fate then?

Erik released a growl of frustration. "I don't understand her, how am I supposed to help?"

"Is it really so hard?" Clarice snipped. "Her family is in trouble. You would care if it was *your* family, wouldn't you?"

Did she really think he was capable of such a thing? Did their kind form bonds like ours did? Vampires only ever seemed to care about blood and greed.

Erik didn't answer and I lifted my head as the door swung open, finding Clarice striding into the room with a sad expression painted onto her beautiful face.

"Hi, Montana," she said softly. "That's your name, right?"

I nodded as I spotted Erik pacing out in the corridor like a wild animal. Clarice pushed the door closed and I eyed her bright blue gown with silver lace adorning the corset.

She truly was stunning, her skin glowing like it was dipped in morning dew and her eyes like drops of the ocean.

"I heard you're a little upset with General Wolfe," she said with a frown.

A blade dug into my gut at his name. "It's what he's done that I'm upset about."

"I never liked that man," Clarice remarked, making me narrow my eyes, trying to see the lie in her words.

She quirked a smile at me, dropping onto the edge of my bed and brushing a crease out of the comforter. Her aura was the opposite of Erik's, a sweet, calming lull that made my heart beat slower in my chest. She almost seemed...human. In her manner anyway. Not her ethereal looks.

"Yes...well, maybe Erik can help your family. I'm sure he will if you ask him nicely." Her cerulean eyes lit up, filling me with hope. It was so strange getting that feeling from a vampire, and I worked to resist the tug in my chest that urged me to trust her.

"I asked him already," I said bitterly. "It's clear he has no intention of helping me. And why would he? He's a bloodsucking parasite."

Clarice's eyebrows lifted and I sat back from her a little, aware I'd just tarred her with the same brush.

Her face cracked and she let out a musical laugh that was light itself, the radiance of it brushing against my skin and asking me to embrace it. It was impossible to keep myself from feeling it, that emotional glow she emitted, like her smile alone was capable of changing the atmosphere itself.

She cupped her hand around her mouth, leaning closer and I couldn't find it in me to move away this time as she whispered conspiratorially, "He is also a stubborn ass with a boredom complex he won't even try to overcome. He acts like nothing in this world is remotely interesting to him anymore, but I believe you are of interest to him, Montana."

"I can hear you," Erik clipped from beyond the door, and I bit down on a smirk while Clarice let her smile fly free.

Mine fizzled away before it could really take root, my mood slipping back into the dark cloud that hung over me now I knew of my family's fate.

"I need them to be okay," I begged of Clarice, seeing the power in her. Erik wasn't the only royal in this castle; his sister was capable of protecting them just as he was. "Please. There's nothing I wouldn't do to see them safe."

Clarice reached out, taking my hand and my heart fluttered nervously at her icy touch, her fingers squeezing mine as she gave me a look of painted sympathy. Because surely it couldn't be real.

"Erik will do as you ask," she said, swerving the question she knew I was asking of her instead of him. "He chose you, and that means you are his to look after."

I huffed a breath that dismissed those words. "That's the last thing he intends to do."

"Just ask him gently," she pushed. "You'll see. But once he gives you his word, you have to make an effort with him. Do as he asks. Don't bite back. Not too much anyway." She gave me a little wink, releasing my hand and withdrawing, taking away that warmth of hers which had almost made me let my guard down.

"If I do everything he says, will he let me go back to them?" I blurted before she could leave me here. "If he protects them, finds a way to bring them together, somewhere safe. Can I go too?"

A small sigh parted from her lips, her brows drawing together like something pained her. "That's not possible, Montana. You cannot leave. You've been welcomed into our family, and you will be important here once you have been sired. So I urge you to make the most of it."

I nodded, my heart shattering into several jagged pieces that cut me to ribbons. The walls felt too close and any lasting, foolish hope I had of ever being set free of this place was snuffed out like a candle flame. I didn't let my mind slip into the horrors of being sired just now though, I'd be damned if I let that destiny befall me if I could help it. For the meantime, all I could do was try to get my psycho captor to release Dad and protect Callie from the wrath of General Wolfe. I'd figure out the rest later.

"Okay," I breathed, my voice strong as I made the decision. *For them.*

Clarice gave me a sad smile before heading out the door. "See you soon, Montana."

She exited, leaving me feeling like the world had just been ripped out from under me once again. Erik re-entered, resting his back against the door, his jaw pulsing as he surveyed me.

Silence built a wall between us. It was a battle of wills to see who would break first, so I bit the bullet and followed Clarice's advice.

"I've calmed down now," I said, forcing my tone to remain level and trying not to dip my voice in too much sarcasm. "I believe I am no longer too *emotional* for you Prince Erik."

"What a relief," he muttered. "So, are you going to ask me, or are we going to keep pretending I didn't hear that entire conversation?"

Claws tore at my stomach, and I bit down on the insides of my cheeks as I tried very hard not to snap at him. Mustering as much self-control as I had, I swallowed my pride and asked, "Can you help my family, your royal highness?" The last words were spoken with a little disdain, but it was a definite improvement on my usual tone.

His mouth lifted into a mocking grin. "That's better."

I cringed, shutting my eyes, feeling like a dog who'd just been petted by its master. "So?" I insisted through my teeth.

"Well, that depends, rebel." He dropped into the velvet armchair, stretching his arms over the back of it like an arrogant asshole.

"On?" I pressed, knowing I wasn't going to like the next words that came out of his mouth.

"How well you behave. You see, I've got a little job for you. And if you do it without complaint, I'll *maybe* think about helping your family."

"I need more than maybes," I pushed, though not sharply.

A small voice in the back of my head reminded me of how crazy it was to negotiate with a vampire, but too many crazy things had happened recently for me to care.

"Fine." Erik ran a hand into his ebony hair, messing it up from its usual perfect style. "I give you my word that if you do what I ask of you, I will free your father from the blood bank."

My gut clenched tightly, my pulse thumping to a frantic, hope-bound beat. Would he really do that? The word of a vampire was dirt to me, though I didn't have much choice but to trust it. Either he followed through, or he didn't, and if he made the promise to me, then there was a chance he really would deliver on it. So, I guessed it was better than nothing.

"And what about my sister?" I asked.

He shrugged. "When she is caught, I will ensure she doesn't end up in the blood bank as well."

"Or hurt," I snarled. "Or punished at all."

The corner of his mouth twitched. "Agreed."

"And that's it? Easy as that?"

"Easy as that," he said, a malicious gleam to his gaze telling me it would be no such thing.

I lifted my chin, my choice solidified, because there was really no choice at all. "Alright. What do you want me to do?"

Erik's face split into a villainous grin that sent a chill sweeping through my veins. "You're going to pick Fabian at the choosing ceremony. But before that, you're going to make him want you so badly, he'll be begging you to pick him."

I frowned at him as those words sank in. First, relief crashed through me at knowing this heartless beast didn't in fact want me at all. But then the reality of what he was asking descended on me. Fabian seemed no more appealing an option than Erik, and in all honesty, he frightened me just as much.

"Why do you give us a choice at all?" I asked, holding off on agreeing to his word. "Why not just forget the ritual and sire whoever you like? Since when do humans get a choice in anything?"

Erik shrugged one shoulder. "It's just the way of things."

"What does that mean?"

"My offer is about to expire, rebel."

A string of curses came to my tongue, but I held them back as Erik gave me a firm look that said he really was about to take the offer off the table.

Fucked up choosing ceremony aside, I was not remotely excited to try and gain Fabian's interest. The real problem was, I'd barely flirted with a boy in my entire life. From a very young age, I'd known I would never choose to bring children into the world, and the idea of falling in love with someone who might be dragged away to the blood bank at short notice had never been on my to-do list. Callie had found her own ways to guard her heart against caring for someone, but I'd decided on never even giving myself the chance. So how the hell was I going to pull this off?

*You have to. It could save Dad and Callie.*

I took a slow breath, then nodded. "Okay, but..."

"But?" He quirked up a single eyebrow and I hated how vulnerable I was about to get with him. I considered not telling him the truth and just winging it, but if I fucked this up, I'd fuck up all chances of him protecting my family too.

"I'm not exactly sure how to do what you're asking," I said bluntly. Yep, straight to the point about me being a flirtless wonder.

He smirked in amusement. "I do love when you're on the back foot, rebel. It's rather entertaining. Are you telling me you don't know how to seduce a man?"

My cheeks flushed despite the ludicrousness of being embarrassed about this in front of a damn bloodsucker.

I fumbled for the right answer in my head, trying to regain some of my pride. "Well funny enough I didn't spend my time in the Realm flirting. I had more vital things to do." *Like surviving.*

Erik rubbed his chin, his fingers barely concealing another grin and I longed to smack his smirking face, but I'd probably have ended up with more than a bruised hand for it.

"You'll be spending all day with me tomorrow, so I'll be sure to give you some pointers." He stood, throwing me a heated look that was more demeaning than flirtatious.

"Oh, how grateful I am, your mightiness," I muttered, not looking forward to that one bit.

"The pleasure will be all mine, I'm quite sure." His boyish smile grew, and a light flared in his eyes for the first time since I'd met him, like there were still a few burning embers remaining in the ashen pits of his eyes. What took me most off guard was that this was a real smile, nothing like the empty grins he threw around at people, or goading smirks. And there was power to that, the way his eyes blazed suggesting he was capable of feeling more than I had ever imagined a vampire could feel.

As he stalked toward the door, I resigned myself to a broken night's sleep with the promise of a hellish day in Erik's company on the horizon. Not much to look forward to, but now I had hopes of saving my family, the hollowness in my chest had fleshed out again, and the world wasn't quite as sombre as it had seemed before.

# CALLiE

## CHAPTER FIFTEEN

The sound of running water called tauntingly to me and I managed to find the energy to up my pace despite the fatigue that had been slowing me down for the last few miles. The ruined city had eventually given way to rolling fields interspersed with woodland, nature reclaiming the world wherever it could.

My throat was way past parched, and we'd gotten through the last of our drinking water after our run-in with the vampires the day before.

"Beyond the next ridge," Magnar promised.

I bit my tongue against pointing out that he'd said that about the last ridge too. And the ridge before that. Honestly if it wasn't this ridge, then I was likely to kick him in the balls. But the water definitely sounded closer now, so I was inclined to believe him this time.

We made it up the hill lined with brown grass and thick mud, finally discovering a stream on the other side of it.

I dropped my bag with a groan of longing and crouched down to scoop the ice-cold water into my mouth. Magnar followed suit beside me, and we satisfied our thirst in silence.

I drank until I felt like I might be sick from it, then sat back and sighed as my belly sloshed contentedly.

"Fuck, that's good," I murmured to myself, and Magnar grunted his agreement while he continued to quench his own thirst.

We were overdue a rest stop, and my scalp was itching from days of leaving my hair tightly braided, so I leaned back against a tree and started to unravel it.

When I finished, I ran my fingers through the tangles and left it hanging loose around my shoulders.

I looked up to find Magnar watching me, the intensity in his golden eyes making me want to squirm for some reason, and heat clawed at my cheeks unexpectedly.

"You have the sun in your hair," he commented.

I glanced up at the canopy of trees overhead, the gloomy clouds beyond them letting only the dullest of daylight through.

"What?" I frowned at him.

"Your hair is the colour of the sun. It's a gift from the goddess Sol who drives the sun's chariot. You shouldn't hide it away, it will bring you luck."

I wasn't entirely sure what I thought of the sun being driven in a chariot, but I did find a flaw in his reasoning.

"But it won't if I tie it up?" I teased. "That seems like pretty dubious luck to me."

Magnar shrugged. "The gods are fickle, vain beings. If Sol does not think her gift is appreciated, she may scorn you."

He offered me the barest hint of a smile then pulled his cloak from his back and removed his blades, carefully laying them on top of it. I raised an eyebrow as he started to unbuckle his jerkin, then pulled it off followed by the linen shirt beneath it to reveal his toned, muscular body.

I stared. Asshole or not, I had never seen a body like his. His freaking muscles had muscles. His body was a work of art, deep bronze skin marked with wicked-looking scars that depicted the warrior's life he'd led. Intricate tattoos were painted beautifully on his skin, each with that Viking heritage to them, though my limited knowledge left me oblivious to their individual meanings. I itched to ask him about them, but I'd abruptly lost the ability to form words.

Magnar was hot. Like, burn myself just looking at him hot, and

I had to mentally scream at myself for noticing, because he was so fucking arrogant, and I was still furious at him for keeping me from my family when they'd needed me most. But shit…

Magnar noticed my attention and paused with his hand on his belt. "Will you be able to cope if I bathe? You look half inclined to pounce on me, and I haven't even dropped my trousers yet."

I scoffed, heat blazing through me as I fought the urge to punch him.

"In your dreams, asshole. You might not have gotten laid in a thousand years, but it will be a thousand more before I'd ever take you up on the offer."

"It wasn't an offer," he replied dismissively. "You'd know if it was, and trust me, you would be more than willing."

I threw a rock at him. Honestly, I wasn't even certain when I'd grabbed the thing, but there it was, sailing through the air, headed right for his stupid fucking head and yet somehow, the motherfucker caught it.

Magnar inspected the sharp rock for a moment, arching an eyebrow at me before tossing it aside into the river. "Perhaps you're the one who needs a good fuck, drakaina hjarta, you harbour a lot of anger in your soul."

"Maybe I'll use that anger to stab you while you sleep," I snarled, getting to my feet, my teeth grinding with irritation.

"Feel free to try. But for now, as I said, it seems like we should take the opportunity to bathe while we have it. By all means, stay where you are if you intend to watch me."

"I am seriously looking forward to the moment when we free my father and sister from the blood bank and you and I can go our separate ways," I hissed at him. "I hope you have a long and murderous life with the vampires, and you can rest assured that I will never again so much as think of you until my dying breath."

Magnar seemed entirely uninterested in my words as he kicked off his boots and dropped his pants.

I cursed him, refusing to look at his naked body and pinning my eyes to the tree canopy overhead as he turned and waded out into the river.

"Ah, there it is," Magnar said, drawing my gaze to his back and briefly to the firm perfection of his ass.

"There what is?" I demanded.

"That silence I knew you were capable of. If only I had realised my nudity was the key to it, I might have removed my clothes days ago."

"Fuck you," I spat.

"Not today."

I threw another rock at him, but he ducked down into the water right before it could strike the back of his stupid head.

Magnar made it to the middle of the icy stream and crouched down to dunk his head beneath the water then stood back upright, flicking the water out of his long hair. I pursed my lips, glaring at him as the water ran over his insane body, noting the way it tracked a route between the ridges of his muscles and how it made the ink on his skin glisten...

Gah.

The tattoos marking his skin almost spoke to me, like they were written in a language I used to understand. I frowned at the ridiculous thought; I couldn't even read words written in English, so I knew there was no way I could read those symbols.

As I continued to stare at him, I grew more sure of my understanding of them. They were runes just like the ones carved on the hilts of his blades. They spoke of power, devotion, honour and love.

Magnar turned slightly and I followed the path of the tattoos lining his chest. They curved around his muscles as if he'd been born with them patterning his skin rather than having them added in ink.

I frowned in concentration as I studied a small line of runes which ran beneath his heart. The words *promise* and *bound* filled my mind, and I bit my lip in confusion, wondering if I was insane to think I'd figured out their meaning.

"Still staring?" Magnar taunted.

I flinched, narrowing my eyes as he tilted his head in a way that was nothing short of a challenge. Daring me to deny it.

"Not at you," I replied, refusing to look away. "At your tattoos. I was just trying to decipher them, and I couldn't work out what that one meant." I pointed at his chest, and he looked down at the one I'd selected.

His lip curled back in distaste, and he rubbed a thumb over the tattoo as if he wished he could scrub it from his skin.

"That is the mark of a decision I did not make for myself. I had hoped that after waking from my sleep the stain of it might have been removed from my skin. I can no longer keep that promise anyway. But it would seem the gods still hold me to it, despite the fact that I can no longer go through with it. Or perhaps they've just left it there to remind me."

"What promise?" I asked before I could stop myself.

Magnar hesitated like he couldn't decide whether or not to tell me, then shook his head. "It doesn't matter now. The person I made it to is long dead, so perhaps some good has come from my situation after all. Aren't you bathing as well?"

The abrupt change of subject was enough to make me drop it. He clearly didn't want to talk about it, and I reminded myself that I didn't care anyway. I shrugged, looking at the rushing water and trying to psych myself up for how cold it was.

"I was planning on waiting until you were done." *And until you'd gone somewhere else.*

"We shouldn't linger too long; the sun will set soon, and we need to find somewhere to spend the night. So unless you are afraid of revealing your body for some reason, I suggest you bathe now."

He started to scrub at his long hair, and I pursed my lips at the challenge in his mocking tone, then shrugged out of my coat.

I wasn't looking forward to submerging myself in the icy stream, but I didn't relish the idea of remaining in my filthy state for the foreseeable future out of pure stubbornness.

I yanked my shirt off quickly, trying to ignore the bite of the cold wind against my exposed skin as I kicked my boots off and unbuttoned my pants.

I watched Magnar from the corner of my eye as I hurried to undress, leaving my underwear on to avoid giving him a full strip show, the scraps of black fabric just about concealing the parts that mattered.

By the time I was done, Magnar was still in the process of washing his long hair, and I hurried to the riverbank with goosebumps rising across my skin.

I sucked in a deep breath and held it as I plunged into the freezing water. It had to be better to get the dunking over with fast, so I ignored the protests of my shivering body and ducked down so that every part of me was submerged.

Cold enveloped me like a fist wrapping tight around my soul and squeezing hard. My skin burned and screamed at the intensity of it, my lungs aching as my heart started up a riot all of its own.

I gasped, sucking down air as my head broke the surface again and I quickly started scrubbing at my hair and skin to remove any dirt. The faster the better. I just needed to clean myself then get out, no way was I going to be lingering in the freezing water for a single second longer than needed.

I kept my back to Magnar, not wanting to know if he was tempted to look at me too. I was painfully aware of the way my bones showed through my skin and I doubted he would be overly interested in looking at the consequences of the poor rations I'd eaten in the Realm.

I dunked myself beneath the water once more to remove any final dirt, then quickly wrung out my long hair as I started wading back towards dry land. I would have killed for some soap, but removing the dirt and grime would have to be enough for now.

I raced back to the bank and hauled myself out again, freezing water racing from my skin as shivers racked my body. A pair of heavy boots appeared right before my face as I pushed myself upright and I sucked in a breath of surprise as I came face to face with Magnar.

He had pulled his pants back on, but they were unfastened, the rigid muscles of his torso still bare as his powerful body loomed over me and I once again found myself trapped within his shadow. I straightened my spine, my hands curling into fists as I looked up at him uncertainly, but his eyes weren't on my face, or even tracing the curves of my exposed body; they were locked on my arm, a frown drawing his brow tight as he stared with such intensity that it made my skin prickle.

I followed his gaze and blinked in surprise as I spotted the strange red mark on the inside of my right forearm. At first, I assumed it was some kind of wound, but the shape was too perfect, too purposeful. It started at the crook of my elbow and stopped just before my wrist, twisting lines creating a symbol which looked like a curved blade with a small diamond beneath it, the points of which thinned to fine lines. It almost looked like it had been burned onto my skin, but there was no pain, no scar tissue that I could see, simply the mark on my skin like a tattoo I had no recollection of receiving.

"What the-" I began but Magnar caught my hand in his before I could continue and raised my arm up to look closer at the mark.

"I knew I felt it," he murmured as he traced his rough fingers over the reddened skin. I flinched as he touched it, expecting it to hurt but he was gentle in his inspection and the mark itself wasn't painful at all. Back and forth his fingers moved across the symbol while he gazed at it as if he didn't quite believe what he was seeing.

"What is it?" I asked in frustration. I half wanted to pull my arm out of his grip, but something held me in place, and I remained still as his fingers skimmed across my skin again, raising goosebumps in their wake. Despite the freezing water he'd just been submerged in, he was so warm, his touch like a kiss of sunshine against my body, and part of me wanted to lean into that heat and steal more of it.

"Something impossible," he replied.

"That's not an answer," I said, tugging on my arm, but he refused to release me, simply pulling me in the opposite direction and drawing me even closer to his half-dressed body.

"Let go of me," I said, my voice low with warning, though I wasn't entirely sure what I could do to force his hands from me. I'd likely start with a knee to the dick and wing it from there.

A freezing wind gusted around us, and I started shivering violently. I was soaking wet and almost naked. It wasn't the most ideal way to be standing about in the depths of winter, and though Magnar looked inclined to argue, his fingers biting into my arm, he relented.

He released me and pointed to my clothes. "Get dressed. We need to find shelter for the night. Then we have much to discuss."

"That's it?" I demanded as he turned from me, stalking away to find the rest of his clothes. "What about the tattoo which has just appeared on my fucking arm?"

"Like I said, we will discuss it once we find shelter."

"You don't just get to pick and choose when to tell me shit that matters," I hissed, taking an angry step towards him before halting myself out of pure force of will. I was shivering so hard that my teeth were practically chattering, and I was still near naked and unarmed.

"Get dressed," he barked, not looking at me and I wished for another rock to throw at his dumb head.

"I want answers," I spat, though I moved to my pack all the same, too cold to keep standing there like that despite my need for his reply.

Magnar ignored me entirely, drawing his shirt and jerkin back over his head and though I longed for that rock to hurl at him, I dropped to my knees and started rummaging in my bag instead.

I didn't need any further encouragement to put my clothes back on as another wind swept around us. I used the inside of the shirt I'd been wearing to dry myself as best I could, stripping out of my saturated underwear and pulling a fresh set out of my pack. I kept my back to Magnar as I dressed, the clean clothes feeling like heaven against my skin as I drew them on.

I zipped my coat up last and pulled the hood tight around my face, leaving my wet hair hanging loose down the front of it, more grateful than ever for the wonderfully warm garment as it blocked out the wind and my shivers grew less violent.

"Come." Magnar turned and led the way along the river in silence.

"I want answers," I repeated angrily as he strode away, the two huge swords he carried strapped across his broad shoulders once more, his dark hair dripping water.

"Then keep up," he grunted, not bothering to look back, making no attempt to slow his pace.

I wanted to ask him what the fuck was going on, scream at him for the answers I needed, and refuse to walk a single step until he told me why the fuck I now had some strange mark on my arm, but the set of his shoulders told me I wouldn't be getting any answers until he chose to offer them out. *Asshole.*

I ground my teeth, rubbing at the mark on my arm through the fabric of my coat, not feeling anything at all to tell me it was even there.

He set an even faster pace than usual, and the difference in our strides had me half jogging to keep up with him. I cursed him under my breath, knowing he could hear me and not caring as he charged on, though at one point I was sure he murmured, "Always chattering in my ear like an angry little jaybird," and my curses only grew in velocity.

Finally, a little house came into view close to the riverbank near the foot of the valley, several tall trees casting shadows over it.

The daylight was quickly bleeding out of the sky. It wouldn't be long before night fell around us, and the time of the vampires returned once more and I welcomed the promise of shelter.

As we approached the squat building, Magnar started gathering firewood to see us through the night, continuing to ignore the questions I shot at him and acting as if he couldn't even hear my demands. I eventually gave up with another curse, the silence tense between us as Magnar refused to discuss what was on his mind and I grew more and more frustrated by having to wait for answers.

We made it to the building and I looked at the little cabin cautiously, taking in the covered windows and half rotten porch before it. Leaves had gathered in a heap against the flaking white paint of the wall, the wood rotting though seeming sound enough for now.

Magnar headed inside, the door banging loudly against the wall as he threw it open, his boots thumping across the wooden floor within. I waited a moment, letting his heavy ass test out those rickety floorboards then headed after him when he didn't go tumbling through them.

I brushed my fingers along Fury's hilt, the dark seeming to deepen in the corners of the room as I hunted for any sign of danger among the shadows.

The space was open, an old kitchen to the right and a brown couch set before the fireplace on the left with three doors to the back of the room presumably leading to the bedrooms and bathroom.

I lingered close to the doorway as Magnar stalked through the space, opening doors, and checking there too, making sure we were truly alone.

Everything was covered in a layer of dust but other than that, it was comfortable enough. Far better than camping out in the wind.

Magnar headed to the small fireplace in the living area, dropping down to build the fire, still saying nothing as I hovered there.

I bit my tongue against the questions which were burning their way up my throat. But the journey had been filled with my demands for them, and it was obvious he wasn't going to be pushed into answering. I watched as a spark caught on the kindling, my shivering body hungry for the kiss of warmth the fire would provide.

Magnar said nothing at all as he built the fire, nursing it until he could be sure the flames wouldn't gutter then striding back past me without a word, heading outside to place wards by all of the entrances to keep the vampires away.

Frustration ate at me as I held my tongue, and I forced myself to expel a heavy breath, pushing aside my temper in favour of trying another tactic.

I moved deeper into the cabin and searched the tiny kitchen for anything that we might be able to eat. I found a few cans of sweetcorn and kidney beans as well as a sealed bag of breakfast cereal which didn't even taste stale. I heated the beans and corn over the fire in an attempt to make them more appetising and dished them up with the cereal to create a strange but perfectly edible meal.

Magnar reappeared, closing the door tightly behind him and pausing as he found me by the fire, two bowls of food ready and waiting. I'd even found him a spoon. And if that wasn't a shiny little bribe to sweeten him up to get him talking, then I didn't know what was.

I smiled sweetly, offering up the bowl and though he narrowed his eyes suspiciously, he accepted his meal with a nod of thanks. Silence stretched between us, punctuated only by the clink of our spoons within the bowls and the soft sounds of us chewing.

*That's right, enjoy your tasty meal made by little old me, let it warm your belly and fill you with the urge to reward me.*

I didn't give much thought to the taste of the scavenged meal, simply focusing on sating the ache in my belly while I waited for Magnar to drop his guard and start opening up at last.

I finished first then eyed Magnar as he slowly devoured his own meal, each lift of his spoon to his lips taking an eternity while I fought the urge to push my sleeve back and inspect the mark on my arm once more, wondering if it had even truly been there at all. I waited for him to finish eating then set his bowl down, waiting expectantly for him to crack.

He pushed the bowl away from him, and I gave him an innocent look, trying to lure him to me like I was wiggling a fat worm at a bird.

Nothing.

Frustration bubbled in my chest before I cracked entirely.

"Are you going to explain what this means then?" I asked, damn near choking on the sweetness of my words as I forced myself not to bite at him, shoving my coat off before rolling my shirt sleeve back and brandishing the mark at him, fearing he might deny it was there if I didn't prove it.

In response, Magnar pulled his jerkin over his head, revealing a glimpse of those carved abs where they dove beneath his waistband, laying it aside with his swords before rolling the linen sleeve of his tunic back and holding his own arm out to show me.

On his inner forearm, the exact same mark stood out against his skin, untouched by the tattoos that painted so much more of him, entirely alone on the plane of his warm brown flesh. His mark was pale, almost silver like an old scar with a touch of something more powerful to it which made me want to reach out and skim my fingers along it. I resisted the urge to do any such thing, instead looking back to his golden eyes as I waited for my answer.

"This is a slayer's mark," Magnar said slowly, giving me a moment to absorb his words, my gaze flicking between his mark and my own.

"You mean I...you..." I frowned at the mark on my arm. Apart from its pink appearance, it was an exact twin to the one on his skin. "But how? Didn't you say your people were all born into that life? That you're more than simply human? I mean my dad is just...Dad. And Mom never even tried to fight back against the vampires. Not even when she was dying, and they came for her. Neither of them were secret vampire hunters, I would have known if they-"

"You have slayer blood running in your veins from one parent or another," Magnar interrupted, dropping his own arm against the couch between us, "They probably never even knew they had it. Not everyone with our blood chooses to join the order. Some natural born slayers left us and married humans, had normal lives. It was rare but not unheard of. Not everyone wishes to take the oaths of our kind. You are most likely descended from one of those. But for your mark to have awakened, the call of it must be strong in your blood."

"I felt a pain in my arm right after I killed that vampire who was trying to catch me," I said, remembering the searing burn. At the time, I hadn't been able to spare it any attention, and afterwards so much had been going on that it was driven from my mind entirely, but since finding the mark on my arm, I'd been trying to figure out when it could have appeared, and the memory of that momentary pain had come back to me.

"Embracing your slayer nature and making your first kill awakened some of your gifts," Magnar said, his attention on my arm as I let it drop to my lap.

"Gifts?" I wasn't sure how I felt about finding out that my blood was different from other people's, but I couldn't deny the spark of excitement it ignited.

If I was even the smallest bit like Magnar, then I might have a chance to truly fight back against the vampires. It could be enough to get my family safely away from them and I needed any advantage I could claim.

"To some degree, each generation of slayer passes on their own knowledge and training to the next via their blood. If you train, you will *feel* things that you haven't been taught yourself. Your senses will heighten, your reactions will get faster and once you learn to trust the instincts of your ancestors you will be able to fight the vampires as an equal." His gaze burned with purpose, and I could tell that he was hoping I would embrace this part of me, but it felt like it came with some kind of a catch, the way he was holding back telling me there was far more to this than simply wanting to fight back against the bloodsuckers.

"You say *if* I train?" I asked carefully and Magnar looked away from me, his gaze shifting to the flickering flames of the fire.

"This gift is yours whether you embrace your calling or not," he said, and hope stirred in my chest at the prospect of that. "I can help you learn to use it and you will be stronger for it, more able to fight back if the need arises. But I cannot train you fully unless you decide to take the vow. The true extent of your gifts will not be realised until then."

"Vow?" My voice was low, and my mind whirled with the strange possibilities that were suddenly before me.

"If you choose to embrace your slayer nature, you will have to take a vow to place the destruction of the vampires above all else. Your life's purpose will be to bring them down and destroy them. That is not something to choose lightly. There are repercussions; you may not be able to choose your own husband or make your own decisions on having children. You may be forced to sacrifice your own life or that of others for the sake of the cause."

"I don't want a husband anyway, and I definitely don't want children," I said firmly, the fact of that easy to admit to. It was something I'd decided long ago, knowing I could never risk loving anyone beyond my own family, refusing to create more lives for the vampires to abuse. The sacrificing myself part I wasn't so sure on, and the seriousness with which Magnar spoke of it made it clear that was no empty promise.

Magnar sighed, glancing at me then looked away into the fire once more. "You might not be able to choose *not* to have them either. If the cause demands you take a husband and produce more children to inherit the gifts of our kind, then you would be obligated to do it."

"The cause? Aren't *you* the cause? I mean, it doesn't seem like there are any other slayers left, so I'm guessing those decisions would be down to you," I pointed out.

Magnar shrugged. "The runes still hold power. It is possible there are more of us out there. The gods may decide to speak to us and tell us their wishes. Or a prophecy might come to light which demands such things of you. Or of us."

"*Us?*" I stared at him for several seconds before realising what he was implying.

We might have been the only two slayers in existence, so if some prophecy demanded slayer babies... I got to my feet quickly and walked away from him to stand by the small window which looked back towards the river.

"Nope. No fucking way," I said firmly. "I'm not some brood mare you can use to have little vampire-killing offspring with, if that's what this shit is about. I'm not fucking you, and I'm certainly not *reproducing* with anyone. If this is some sick plan of yours to manipulate me then-"

"Why would I want to manipulate some ignorant halfblooded girl into carrying my children?" Magnar growled, his upper lip curling back at the suggestion, making it more than clear that he had no desire to fill my womb with mini Magnars any time soon. My thrashing heart slowed a little at the utter contempt which was written into his features. I mean, fuck him for not wanting my womb, but also good, because he couldn't fucking have it.

"So long as we're both clear on that," I ground out. "Besides, doesn't this mean you might be my great, great, great, great, grandaddy or whatever?" I shook my head in adamant refusal.

"I bore no children before I slept, so there is little chance of that," he scoffed.

I frowned as I considered the rest of what he'd said.

"I've had enough of being told how I'm going to live my life," I told him. "Twenty-one years in a prison is more than adequate, it's too much in fact. From here on out I'll be making my own decisions and no prophecy, or slayer, or any other supernatural bullshit is going to decide for me." My chest heaved with the sudden onslaught of emotion, and I shook my head in anger, still wondering if this was all just some twisted plan he'd orchestrated to manipulate me. But why? What purpose would it serve?

Magnar looked at me curiously, the light of the fire sending shadows dancing across his bare arms and making some of his scars stand out fiercely.

"You can rest assured I didn't mean *us* like that," he said, and a trace of irritation flitted across his face. "If I take on your training, then no such thing could ever take place between us anyway. So your adamant refusal of the idea is unwarranted. And if you think I would lie about the ways of my people simply to fuck you, then you are utterly deluded.

If I wanted to fuck you, I could have you begging beneath me within the hour."

Heat rushed through my body at that suggestion despite my adamant hatred of this asshole. I opened my mouth to protest, his anger knocking me off balance while my thoughts spun with all he had just revealed. I hadn't meant it like that. It wasn't simply the idea of fucking him that was the problem, it was the suggestion that I might not get to choose it for myself. Who would want to be with someone without making the decision to do so of their own free will? Not that I had any desire to choose him either way.

Before I could make any attempt to correct his misunderstanding, or even just snap back at him for that bullshit claim, Magnar stood.

"I'm going to check the wards again. We both have a lot to think on." Magnar headed out of the small room, and I watched him go without saying another word.

*Nice work, Callie.*

Guilt tugged at me, but I wasn't sure what I was supposed to do about it. Despite his infuriating nature and the way I wanted to smack him most of the time, all Magnar wanted was to find some of his kin. And now I was standing right before him, possibly the only other of his kind currently living, telling him I didn't want to be one of them.

Or was I?

The thought of having even a fraction of his gifts definitely called to me, but the trade-off against my own free will felt like such a high price to pay. I needed to fully understand what he'd meant by that and whose will I would be bowing to if not my own.

I'd only held freedom in my hands for a matter of days, and now I was being asked to consider enslaving myself to some cause for the rest of my life?

*No way.*

I moved towards the fire and sank down before it, letting the heat of the flames warm me through, my golden hair slowly drying as the warmth washed into me and I turned everything over in my mind.

A faint whispering echoed at the edge of my thoughts, and my hand drifted to the blade at my hip.

Fury sighed in satisfaction as I gripped its hilt. Perhaps I wasn't going mad after all. Maybe the things I felt from the blade had something to do with the slayer blood that coursed through my veins. Magnar said that everything innate in my blood came from the memories of my ancestors, so perhaps the blade could help me to understand that.

I concentrated on the feeling of the blade in my hand as I placed it across my lap and closed my eyes. *Show me,* I asked it, wondering if I really was going insane.

The blade grew hot beneath my fingers, and I could feel its eagerness to share its life with me. Images started to flash through my mind of people wielding Fury before me.

I was a bearded man creeping through a dark cave. A tattooed woman fighting with my back against a wall while more vampires than I could put a number to came at me. A bright-eyed child learning to hunt in a forest. An old woman defending her grandchildren from a hungry wolf.

More images than I could count. More people than I would have thought possible. Year after year, the blade passed from hand to hand. I felt its love for those who'd wielded it, its hate for the vampires it vanquished. And somehow, they were all a part of me and yet not me at all.

I wasn't sure how long I sat there, watching as my ancestors fought and died. Loved and lived and passed the blade on through the generations. The blade relished the violence it had dealt out against its enemies, but it had seen far more than that. I watched love and laughter, sex, hatred, violence, and happiness, all of it, so much of it that I felt my heart swelling with too many emotions, tears pricking the backs of my eyes.

My palms suddenly felt cold, and it took me a moment to realise Fury was no longer in my grasp. I blinked my eyes open in confusion and found Magnar crouching before me, his golden gaze a roiling storm in the darkness as he looked at me, seeing far more than flesh and blood, peering right down into my soul, and seeing *me.*

Magnar was staring into my eyes with a fierce intensity, flames seeming to burn within the golden depths of his irises.

"What did you see?" he demanded, his voice a rough scratch against my skin, my throat thickening as my body heated.

"Everything, everyone who came before me." I frowned, unsure how else to describe it.

"You're sure it was before?" he asked. "It wasn't still to come?"

"No. It was definitely before." I knew that deep within me.

He reached out and took my hand in his, the movement taking me by surprise, so I didn't resist.

"You're freezing," he said in annoyance. "You went too deep."

Magnar released me and moved to grab his cloak from the back of the moth-eaten couch before draping it around me. Though he still seemed angry, he left his arm around my shoulders, pulling me closer to lend me some of his warmth and I stiffened, uncertain whether to push him off or accept his help. He was an ass more often than not, and he irritated the fuck out of me, but as the heat of his body pressed against mine, I realised how cold I'd actually been and decided to claim warmth over self-respect.

"Too deep?" I shook my head as my mind returned sluggishly to the present, the echoes of all the past owners of my blade slipping away from me like grains of sand on a breeze.

"Our kind can sink into the memories of old, learn lessons from the past and become better warriors by embracing all that our ancestors once learned. But the past is endless, its depths unknown and treacherous. If you tread too deep or delve too far you can get lost, your soul wandering so far from your body that it leaves it entirely. Your heart slows the further you wander, the cold creeps in and death peers over your shoulder, wondering why you watch the ghosts of old with such interest, questioning whether you might wish to join them in Valhalla."

I swallowed thickly, my gaze fixed on my knees as I curled in on myself. I wasn't sure what to make of the idea of death taking a good look at me, but the steady thump of Magnar's heart against my skin helped ground me back in the moment as I closed my eyes and leaned towards the fire, seeking more heat.

Magnar fell silent, nothing but the popping and crackling of logs in the flames filling the air. I slowly began to feel more human again as my body thawed out and I settled back into my own skin. Fragments of what I'd witnessed lingered though, the memories seeming to sink into me, making me feel capable of more than I had been before, though I wasn't sure that made any sense.

I turned to look at Magnar, meaning to thank him for lending me some body heat, but the words fell still on my tongue as I found his face just inches from mine, and he stilled under my scrutiny. I blinked, taking in the savage cut of his jaw, the symmetry of his cheekbones, the depths of those golden eyes.

"You shaved," I blurted, unable to look away from his face, feeling like I was seeing him for the first time.

There was still stubble lining his jaw, but the beard was gone and beneath it lay the most stunning man I had ever laid eyes on. It wasn't like I hadn't noticed how attractive he was before, but seeing him like that, the brutal savagery of him bared to the world in its entirety almost stole my breath. He was the opposite to the kind of beauty the vampires claimed, nothing clean cut or polished about him, just this wild, untameable ferocity that stole my breath and left me speechless.

Magnar studied me with at least as much intensity as I did him, his golden eyes making my skin burn wherever they roamed, the two of us seeming to truly look at one another for the first time, and I felt the strangest stirring in my gut which felt like fate whispering my name.

This man was a crossroads, a junction between the life I had and the one I might claim. From the moment we'd met, I'd turned down a path I hadn't ever imagined discovering, and there was something in the depths of his gaze which only promised more chaos the longer our fates remained tangled.

Magnar blew out a breath and released me, shifting away a little and leaning towards the fire, his elbows propped on his knees.

"The beard was irritating me," he muttered, his thoughts shifting elsewhere while I found myself unable to look away.

"So you just had a travel razor ready to go in your pack?" I asked and he frowned, clearly not understanding. "I'm questioning *how* you shaved," I explained and in answer he simply tapped a finger against the dagger at his waist.

Okay then.

I watched him as he worked on building the fire back up. Without the beard, he looked younger than I'd presumed before, perhaps ten years older than me but no more than that. I wondered how old he really was. Not counting the thousand years he'd spent asleep, which in all fairness, didn't really count at all.

"How old are you, I mean, *were* you…you know what I mean…"

His mouth twitched in amusement, the movement so at odds with his usual intensity that it disarmed me. "Discounting the thousand years I spent in an unageing slumber? I lived twenty-nine years with my kin and spent twelve of those as an Earl hunting the Belvederes to the ends of the earth."

I nodded, trying to pretend I knew what he meant by that. I was pretty sure being an Earl meant that he'd been a leader, but my knowledge of Norse history was spotty at best. He was certainly bossy enough for me to believe he was used to being in charge of people.

When he was satisfied with the fire, Magnar turned his gaze back on me and the heat in it made me squirm internally.

"If you are not too tired, I would like to try something," he said seriously.

"Okay," I said in response, unable to turn away from him while wondering what the fuck I'd just agreed to.

He leaned around me, and I froze as the smell of him enveloped me once more, the rich, metallic and earthy scent filling my lungs. Magnar pulled one of the long blades he usually wore across his back into his lap and sat back beside me once more, his large hand wrapping around the hilt.

"You can feel a connection with Fury. I want you to see what you can feel with this." He tuned the blade in his hands, offering me the hilt and holding the heavy weapon out to me.

I eyed it nervously. I could already feel the energy pouring off of it, its voice a deep thrum just out of reach, waiting for me. Fury was a much smaller blade, and its power almost overwhelmed me. I wasn't sure what would happen when I accepted that weapon.

I licked my lips and cautiously held out my hands, palms up.

Magnar lowered his blade onto them and the solid weight of it took me by surprise. I had no idea how he managed to wield such heavy weapons with the speed he did, but his strength was incredible.

The sword didn't sing to me like Fury did. Its response was sluggish and resistant, like an old man being woken from a fitful sleep. I ran my fingers across the runes carved into the hilt, trying to feel more from it, coaxing it to open up to me.

"Tempest," I breathed, though the name hadn't come to me willingly, more like a grunt of acknowledgement than a cry of welcome.

I urged the blade to show me more, but it resisted. The power in it felt dark and roiling, waiting to be released. I pushed harder, encouraging it to show me more and it finally offered me a few scraps of memory.

I was Magnar, fighting shoulder to shoulder with many men and women dressed in leather armour. They cut through vampires like they were blades of grass, fighting as one, their movements swift and brutal, a many-armed beast set on a path of destruction.

Everything around me shifted but I was still Magnar, back-to-back with a man I knew was his brother as they faced a cavern filled with vampires. The two of them smiling like beasts as the equally massive man who could only be his kin swung a battle axe with a cry of challenge. Julius and Magnar Elioson, the bloodwolves as the vampires had called them, the bane they sought to end but could never smite. Outnumbered but not outmatched. A laugh spilling from Magnar's lips as he beckoned the enemy closer.

I was him as he hunted a raven-haired male vampire across the land and sea, his heart aching for vengeance as grief for his father drove him on. His thirst for that vampire's death motivated him like nothing else. I tried to push for more information on his enemy's identity, but the blade drew me away, turning like a sullen teenager, refusing my commands.

I was Magnar decapitating the red-headed vampire who had come for me after my dad and Montana were captured. I saw myself through his eyes as I stared up at him in gratitude and fear. He looked at me in a way that I had never seen myself, my golden hair and sun-kissed skin almost seeming to glow, my face more beautiful than I had ever thought myself, the stubborn glint in my eyes a challenge that beckoned him closer even as he felt an overwhelming urge to protect me, but I couldn't tell why.

Magnar yanked the blade from my grasp and my connection to it was lost, the weapon almost seeming to shove me away where Fury had called me back.

"Well?" he demanded, watching me closely.

"Tempest," I said again, clearing my throat before I continued. "I think that blade is a lot more loyal to you than Fury is. It didn't want to show me anything at all until I pushed, and all I did see was you. Where Fury followed my curiosity, Tempest chose what it was willing to share and what it wasn't."

Magnar nodded. "Fury was given to me as a gift by the leader of the Clan of Dreams. It was forged to be wielded by those of their bloodline and has never connected to me as it has to you."

"What does that mean?"

"That I'm not your great, great, grandfather, though I already told you that myself," he replied with half a smile. "Your bloodline is of the Clan of Dreams. I am of the Clan of War."

I couldn't help but snort in amusement. "Of course you are."

He smirked in reply, all warrior, painted in death and battle. "You do not have to be afraid of this part of yourself. And don't think about the vow for now. I have never known someone to find out about their blood right at your age. Our children always knew what they were. They knew they could take the vow when they turned eighteen and had all of that time to make their decision. You should feel no pressure either way. It is a decision you must come to on your own."

"Thank you," I blurted, reaching out to take his hand for a moment so he'd see how much I meant that. It would have been so easy for him to try and pressure me into choosing the slayer life now that he knew I could join him in it. Yet despite my generally low opinion of him, he was making no attempt to do so.

Magnar looked down at the point where our skin met and I followed his gaze, frowning at the cut to his arm where the vampire had caught him with her sword the day before. The supposedly fresh wound already looked like it had half healed, the cut scabbed over and nothing but pink lines marking the outer edges of it.

I frowned as I pointed it out. "Didn't you get that yesterday?" I asked, pulling my other hand out of his, remembering the blood which had spilled freely down his arm. No way that should have looked close to healed already.

Magnar glanced at the long wound and grunted dismissively. "It was a clean cut. It will heal well."

"But it already looks like it's a week old," I insisted.

"Those of my clan's bloodline heal faster than most mortals. Injury is a peril of war."

"Right." My head was starting to feel fuzzy with all of the information he was putting on me, and I swiped a hand over my face, wondering if I had the mental capacity to take any more of it in. "Today has been...a lot."

"Sleep. Let your mind and body rest. We can talk more on it tomorrow if you wish."

I wanted to protest and ask him another one of the thousand questions which were racing through my mind, but exhaustion tugged at me, and I knew I wouldn't be able to process any more information until I was rested.

I settled myself down in front of the fire, using my coat for a blanket and let my eyes fall shut as I enjoyed the heat of the flames against my chilled skin.

Despite all of the concerns being a slayer raised, I could be sure of one thing. It could only help me when it came to getting Dad and Montana out of the blood bank, and that was all that really mattered.

# MONTANA

## CHAPTER SIXTEEN

**W**hen I woke, I found a long white dress waiting for me laid across the velvet chair, and I shuddered at the thought of a vampire sneaking in while I slept to leave the thing there.

I slid out of the bed which had offered me the most comfortable experience of my life, even if I'd never, ever admit it to my captors. But it had been like sleeping in a cloud, and though nightmares had crept into my head during the night, I couldn't deny how much rest I'd found between them.

I moved across the room in the silken green pyjamas I'd worn to bed last night, pursing my lips at the dress as I found a hand-written note from Erik attached to it. Dad had tried to teach Callie and I to read, and though she'd lost interest quickly, I'd always been better at it than her. I still struggled to decipher Erik's curling handwriting, but eventually I managed it.

*If you're not wearing this by the time I knock on your door this morning, you're going to meet my angry side. And no, you haven't met him yet.*

*Your humble ruler, Prince Erik.*

God, I hated him. It writhed in me like a living thing. I'd always despised the vampires, but this was getting personal.

A knock came at the door, making my heart jolt at the ferocity the person used.

The promises he'd made to me came rushing back to me and I swore, remembering my own part of that deal. Do as Erik said. And if he was ever going to help my family, I needed to stick to my word.

I ripped my nightwear off like a demon was lurking beneath them, then grabbed the dress and threw it over me. My head got stuck, and I realised there were buttons at the neck stopping me from getting it on. I flailed, desperately trying to undo them and make my way through the head hole before the asshole prince came storming in here.

"Fucking button-bound bitch," I groaned, trying to get my hand around to undo them.

Erik's raucous laughter pounded in my ears, and heat washed into my cheeks as his mockery, certain he had just entered the room.

"I need a minute," I muttered, giving up and standing with the thing half-on, knowing I looked like a complete idiot.

Strong hands grabbed me and in moments, the buttons came loose, and the dress was yanked down to my heels. I found myself eye-level with a gleaming broach holding a cloak in place around Erik's neck. He pushed me back a step with enough roughness to nearly knock me over, and I caught his arm to right myself.

His eyes moved to where I was touching him, and I yanked my hand away like I'd just shoved it into a barrel full of flames.

"You're so breakable," he commented, mirth glittering in his grey eyes. He was wearing his navy suit with a golden crest embroidered on his breast pocket, a beautiful tree captured within a circle of symbols I didn't understand, the clothes fitting his muscular frame perfectly. "I use the least force possible with you, yet one little push and you're tumbling to your doom. Remind me to be more delicate with you around windows, rebel. Otherwise, I think I may send you flying through one, and then where will I find myself a new pet who is as feisty as you?"

"How about you try not touching me at all?" I suggested icily.

"Then who will save you from getting stuck in things?" he taunted. "That note was truly worth my time by the way. I'll remember to command you to do things under pressure in future. It's rather entertaining."

"Well so long as my humiliation keeps you happy, however could I complain?" I said bitterly.

"Remember what I said about your tone?" He turned me around sharply, fastening the buttons up to my neck, his cool fingers brushing my skin. A shiver gripped my spine, and I fought hard not to twitch away as electricity seemed to spark from his touch.

"Something about respect?" I bit out. *Which I have none of for you.*

"Oh good, it listens."

I bit my tongue, fighting back a torrent of abusive language as he flipped me around to face him once more.

His eyes whipped up to my bed hair, and he glanced over at a brush as if he was actually considering doing it for me.

"I can manage," I said quickly, in case he followed through on that thought and yanked half my hair out with his unnatural strength.

Heading to the dressing table, I picked it up and started combing out the tangles in my mane. My wavy black hair fell loose down my back, behaving for once instead of sticking out in every direction. That may have had something to do with the decent hair product I'd been given to wash it and a brush that wasn't missing half the teeth. But whatever.

Erik was so silent while I rubbed the sleep from my eyes and pinched life into my cheeks that I very-nearly forgot he was there. Apart from the fact his aura was like a bell ringing in my ears and my neck prickled with the awareness of a vicious predator at my back.

My eyes found his in the mirror as I discovered him watching me, and my mouth dried out at the ferocity of his gaze, though his expression remained impassive, his usual bored demeanour carefully constructed on his face. But it really did seem like a construction in that moment, his eyes betraying something deeper, a darkness so potent it cut to the root of me.

"That good enough for you, your highness?" I asked sweetly. *You'd better keep up your end of the deal, your royal assholeness.*

"Passable," he muttered, glancing away, his eyes glazing and losing all emotion once more. "Come on then, let's not stand here until we turn to dust."

"No, we wouldn't want that, would we?" I said with a forced smile that didn't fool him in the slightest.

Putting on the delicate shoes I'd worn the previous night, I glanced at myself in the mirror, taking in the strange sight of myself looking almost as good as a vampire in my fine dress. Though there were tell-tale signs of my humanity. The natural redness to my cheeks, the simple imperfections that set me aside from *them*, not to mention their beauty almost made the air sing.

Erik offered me his arm and I took it like an obedient little human, his fingers curling tightly around my wrist, sharply reminding me that I was still his prisoner. Not that I could ever forget.

We stepped into the corridor, and he guided me downstairs then through a marble hallway that had rivers of gold running through the floor. We arrived in the expansive entranceway with stone pillars intersecting a bright floor and the cold morning air swept in from open windows.

Two guards stood sentinel on either side of the arching doorway, and they saluted Erik before pulling the doors wide for us as we walked out into the daylight. Cloudy daylight, but I supposed Erik wouldn't step out of his front door under the midday sun. Not that that was a common occurrence. Even during the summer months, I'd rarely witnessed full-blown sunshine. I wondered whether the rumours were true that sunshine could kill the vampires, and I decided now was a perfect time to air my thoughts as we made our way through the pavilion and down the stone steps towards a beautiful woodland.

"What do you do in the summer, Erik? Live indoors?" I allowed a little bit of mocking into my voice.

I was obeying, but I wasn't bowing down. Besides, I needed to work out just how strong he was, because a sunny day might just be the perfect chance for me to make an escape. My mind had been working on a plan last night, and I figured if everything came together with Callie and Dad, if Erik set them free and I played along with his game for a while longer, then I could await my chance to run before any of them tried to turn me into a monster. It was a plan with lots of holes, but I'd figure it out, because the alternative of staying here to become a vampire didn't bear thinking about.

"I lock myself in a coffin and watch TV on my tablet."

I glanced up at him, trying to discern his flat expression. I didn't understand the last word, but I could kind of figure it out. I knew what TV was because of Dad's stories, and I didn't want Erik to realise how ignorant I was of the old world.

"You're joking, aren't you?" I guessed.

"Yes, well done, rebel. Look at you picking up on humour," he said, scruffing my hair and I scowled.

We continued walking in silence, heading onto a stone path that wound through the grass.

"So?" I pressed, needing to get my answer here. Was he as vulnerable to the sun as the rest of the vampires?

"The sun doesn't kill us, if that's what you were hoping. It makes us weak though. But we have a way of keeping the sunlight at bay in this part of the country."

"What do you mean?" I asked, surprised by how candid he was being and hoping he might enlighten me further.

Erik slowly ran his tongue over his teeth, seeming conflicted. "It's difficult to explain to someone who has no idea about the true powers in the world."

I narrowed my eyes, curiosity flaming inside me. "Can you try?"

He sighed, his brow furrowing heavily. "Vampires are not the only powerful creatures on earth. There are others. Or there were. Now there is only one left, and she helps us evade the sun."

He was talking in riddles, but fear grew in me at the knowledge that there were other beings like the vampires. "I'm not sure I understand."

Erik tugged me to a halt as we met a smooth stone road that curved away into the woodland, and I glanced around, wondering what we were waiting for.

"You don't have to understand. Because that, rebel, is the last thing I'm going to say on the matter. Today is about preparing you for your time with Fabian, not discussing things that aren't your concern."

My gut knotted tightly as reality hit home and I glowered, remaining silent as we continued to stand on the edge of the road.

A noise filled my ears, a persistent clip-clopping that I couldn't place. When the sound revealed itself, all thoughts abandoned me, and my heart lifted in my chest. Two white stallions appeared pulling a beautiful black carriage behind them like something out of a fairy tale. I'd seen the animals occasionally; vampires used them to pass messages between each other in the Realm, but these horses were magnificent. They were dressed in golden bridles with gleaming red gemstones on the edge of their bits and they were huge, beautiful beasts that looked capable of crushing skulls under their hooves.

Despite that, I wanted to get closer, to feel how soft their fur was beneath my fingers.

My heart thrummed an excited tune. I didn't know why, but the idea of riding in that carriage looked kind of...enjoyable. I didn't realise a smile had spread onto my face until Erik noted it with a raised eyebrow and I flattened it away, looking to the male vampire in a fine coat and hat who was sitting on a perch at the front of the carriage.

"Good morning, Prince Erik," he called, pulling the carriage to a halt in front of us. He glanced at me, then tipped his hat in acknowledgment and I almost glanced behind me to see if he was offering the gesture to someone else. It was probably one of the most respectful greetings I'd ever received from a vampire, and it was damn weird.

The man jumped down from his seat, opening the door of the carriage and bowing low as he waited for us to enter. Erik released my arm, and I took the opportunity to approach the nearest horse, my fingers itching to stroke one.

As I moved in front of the closest beast, the horse released a soft snort and I smiled nervously.

Reaching out my palm, I spoke quietly to the dazzling creature. "Hello, what's your name?"

The horse pushed its nose into my palm, and it was the softest thing I'd ever felt. My mouth parted as I slid my hand up between its eyes, gently rubbing the velvet patch of fur there.

"That's Thor and the other one's Loki," the driver told me with a friendly smile. "Loki is the troublemaker, just like the god he's named after."

Loki swung around, knocking my hand from Thor's nose and taking a stroke for himself, making a laugh fall from my throat.

I glanced over at Erik, surprised he hadn't come to drag me away from my moment of happiness, finding him watching me with a look of intrigue about him. His expression quickly morphed into disinterest as he turned his gaze to the trees.

"We haven't got all day," he clipped.

"I thought we did?" I jibed, but Erik took a step forward with intention and I reluctantly moved away from the horses.

Mr Boring clearly wasn't going to indulge my time-wasting much longer, so I returned to his side before he could manhandle me away from animals.

Snatching my hand, he tugged me toward the open carriage door and gestured for me to go first. I glanced over my shoulder in surprise as he pushed against my palm, helping me into it instead of tossing me in there like a sack of shit. It was as if the heartless prince actually had manners, and manners he gave to a human, no less.

I hunted for the trick in his eyes, expecting him to change tact at any moment, but he just waited for me to climb inside. I did so, my hand parting from the cold grasp of his and leaving an imprint on my fingers that felt terrifyingly permanent.

Inside was a lavish space with black leather seats and a gleaming lantern hanging on one wall. Windows on either side allowed us a view beyond it and I settled myself beside one, gazing out into the trees, my heart pounding as I realised we were about to see more of the landscape. I'd spent so long in dreamlands, conjuring images of the outside world, never knowing how close my fantasies were to reality. And after years of endless dreaming, I was finally going to see places that existed far beyond my Realm, so despite the dire circumstances hanging over me, I simply couldn't help but ache for the carriage to get moving and show me what I'd been missing out on.

Erik dropped into the seat beside me, his leg pressing hard against mine, immediately taking up the remaining space in the carriage. My mouth grew dry at his proximity, and I didn't know whether it was from fear or not, but the anticipation of where we were headed soon eclipsed those emotions.

"Where are we going?" I asked, rounding on him with unblinking eyes. *Show me more, show me everything.*

His mouth tugged up at one corner for the briefest moment, then it flatlined again.

"Into the city," he muttered then turned away.

Evidently that was the most information I was going to get, but it was enough to set my pulse hammering.

The carriage took off at a steady pace and I marvelled at the world unfolding beyond the window, the woodland stretching away from us into an enchanting landscape. Leaves floated down from the branches, twirling in the wind, and scattering across the ground. Gold, burnt umber, fiery orange, and lemon yellow. More colours than I'd ever seen at once while stuck in the monotonous gloom of the Realm. Even the few trees there had seemed to droop as if their spirit was broken, and they'd never displayed as many colours as this.

We followed the winding path for a while then headed over a tiny bridge with a glistening river flowing beneath it. Fat birds swam across its surface, heading downstream at a leisurely pace, many of them sporting bright green heads. Star-shaped leaves twisted on the surface around them, spinning under the force of the current. It was so peaceful to watch, and I was glad when the path turned, and we started following the line of the river so I could continue drinking in the sight of it.

"What are they? Mongooses? No, Mon*geese*, that's the plural, right?" I said, not taking my eyes off of them.

"What are you babbling about?" Erik asked disinterestedly.

"The birds on the water," I said, pointing them out and glancing back at him.

He looked to me in confusion then to the birds paddling along the stream, before a cruel delight crossed his features. "I believe the name you are looking for is geese, rebel."

"I was close," I said, trying to hold on to the shards of my dignity he was intent on prising away.

His gratification only grew, belittling me as always. "Not in the slightest. Those are ducks. Mallards to be precise."

"Well excuse me for not being a birdologist, your highness," I said with false warmth.

"Ornithologist," he corrected, his smirk only increasing, and annoyance flickered through me. "Tell me, rebel, what were your hobbies in your Realm? They clearly didn't include learning about the natural world. What did you spend all your time doing? Collecting sticks in the mud?"

"How dare you," I snarled, my fist raising with intent.

I longed to strike him, to wipe that arrogant smirk off his too-perfect face, but his hand shot out and caught my wrist, his head lowering so his face came close to mine.

"Careful now, little human. You promised to behave," he warned, his breath a sin in itself, peppermint laced with arsenic.

"You're goading me, what do you expect?" I hissed and he moved his face even closer, his lips a wicked inch from mine. I imagined a kiss from this heathen would be a mark of death itself, because there was no doubt a deep and bloody bite would swiftly follow.

"I am a prince and as such, I can do as I please. You, however, are a petulant little human with an ungrateful heart. You were housed and fed, were you not? Would you rather we left you to the mercy of the unfed vagrants of my kind? The fences protect you from a far worse fate than any you have supposedly suffered under our care. You would do well to remember it."

"I'd rather face fifty rotters than be caged forever," I whispered.

"Well, continue on like this and I will gladly arrange the spectacle," he said, shifting away from me and turning to look out the opposite window.

I glared at him with my teeth grinding before finally looking back at the view, refusing to let him spoil it. The trees were thinning, and we suddenly emerged at a neat stretch of grass that led right up to the huge white wall ahead. Beyond it, forbidding skyscrapers reflected the dark clouds back at us, seeming to hold an entire sky within them, capturing all of my attention.

The carriage slowed as we approached the iron gate in the wall and two guards hurried forward with shiny swords strapped to their hips. They checked the carriage over before looking inside, but Erik didn't pay them any attention, his eyes now on a strange device in his hand. It was like a miniature TV, and I wondered if this was what Dad had called a phone.

Losing interest in his little picture thing, I returned my gaze to the view as the guards opened the gates and we passed through them. We headed onto a street that was so wide, it was big enough for five carriages side by side. A few gleaming black vehicles drove along the road and some green-cloaked vampires were on horseback, trotting along a lane that seemed to be specifically for the animals. The carriage pulled onto it, and I pressed my cheek to the window as I tried to gaze up to the top of the buildings, feeling like a child immersed in a new world of wonders. It was thrilling, terrifying and possibly one of the most exciting moments of my entire life, and I just wished with all my heart that Callie and Dad had been here to witness it too.

I needed to see more. To know more. I'd never had those desires before. Dad's stories had always been entertaining, but they'd relied on our imagination, and the limits of that were so blazingly clear now. This was real. I could reach out and touch it, feel it, *experience* it.

I was halfway out of my seat by the time we rounded a corner onto a narrower road, passing through imposing black tower blocks marked with the royal flag of red, white, and blue. Vampires roamed the streets at ease, looking surprisingly normal amongst the strange surroundings. I spotted couples hand in hand, a female admiring a gleaming water feature, a male reading a book on a bench. I should have been angry with it all, but it was like watching animals in their natural habitat. Strangely fascinating.

"It's so...big," I murmured to myself, and Erik caught a fistful of my dress, tugging sharply to make my ass hit the seat again.

"It's called New York City," Erik supplied, and I tried out the words on my lips in a quiet voice. "And if you stand up in a moving carriage, you will likely hit your head when the horses gather speed. I suspect it might be hard enough to kill you too."

"I'm not *that* fragile," I muttered, though I didn't get up again.

"I disagree." He gave me a faintly bemused look before continuing to look at his phone.

"How does it work?" I asked, eyeing the weird object.

Erik frowned then promptly passed it over, and I weighed the cool thing in my palm, unsure what to do with it.

"Press the screen," Erik directed.

I did as he said and it lit up, revealing a series of colourful squares that tempted me closer.

Erik reached over, tapping a button with a crescent on it. "You can call people from here."

My brows lifted as I thought of Callie. "How?" I demanded and he barked a laugh at my expression.

"You can only call vampires who have phones themselves. Humans are privy to no such thing. And even if they did have them, you can't call someone without a number."

"Oh," I breathed, vaguely disappointed but not really surprised.

I spotted his family's names amongst his recent calls, and my finger hovered over Clarice.

"Can you show me?" I breathed, tempted to press her name.

"You want to call my sister?" He barked a laugh, snatching the phone from my palm. "Another time, rebel. We're here."

I hadn't even noticed that the carriage had stopped, the driver abruptly opening the door and giving me no time to prepare for whatever was coming next. Erik stepped out first, offering me his hand as he'd done when I'd entered the carriage, and my heart ticked a little faster as I took hold of his large palm and let him guide me down the metal steps to the sidewalk. I craned my neck as I looked up at the huge stone building towering above us, tapering to a point at the top.

"This is the New Empire State building," Erik informed me, nodding a goodbye to our driver then pulling me toward a set of glass doors that seemed to be rotating.

"Er, what in the hell is that?" I said, digging my heels in as he drew me toward the spinning doors.

He didn't let me stop, towing me towards them and forcing me to take a step between two of the doors. We were pressed together, moving through it as it circled and I half jogged as I felt the other door closing in at my back, only breathing again when I made it out the other side.

"Holy shit," I exhaled, glancing back at the rotating death doors.

"Nervous, rebel?" Erik murmured, though there wasn't any mocking in those words like I expected.

"Something like that," I whispered.

I was a human at the heart of a vampire nest, the blood thundering through my veins one needle or fang away from being taken from me.

A glossy hall greeted us where several guards stood in corners, the high walls rising up either side of us, like giants rearing over to intimidate those below. Somehow, Erik's stature was only amplified in this place, clearly owning everything and everyone in it.

An Elite in dark robes hurried out from behind a desk, bowing low to the prince before standing ramrod straight before us. His cheeks were hollow, and his hair as bright as moonlight, and his eyes matched them almost exactly in their shade. It was their superior beauty which gave the Elite away. In comparison to the Royals, however, they almost paled to normalcy, which was something I never could have thought possible before seeing them for myself.

"Your highness, we weren't expecting you," the vampire said, seeming flustered.

"Is that a problem?" Erik demanded, and I swear every guard in the space flinched.

"No, sir," he answered, his eyes flicking to me then moving like lightning back to the prince. "I'll have a table prepared for you immediately."

"Thank you, Angus," Erik said with a curt nod.

Angus beamed, gesturing for us to follow him as he headed towards a set of metal doors. He pressed a button beside them and the doors opened, revealing a large metal box which looked like a strange sort of cage.

Erik led me towards it and my breaths came quicker as I wondered if he was going to shut me in there while he went off to go and play in his glitzy city. And the thought of being trapped made my flight instinct flare.

"I can just stay out here," I said, looking up at him anxiously. "There's plenty of vampires around to watch me. I'm not going to run."

"What?" he grunted.

"The box. I don't want to go in the box, Erik," I hissed, and he looked down at me in confusion.

"Oh," he smirked as he registered my pleas. "No, I really must insist you get in, rebel."

"I don't want to be locked in there," I growled, drawing the eyes of Angus, but he quickly looked away again as if he couldn't hear me.

Erik lowered his mouth to my ear, his words tainted with malice. "You will do as I say."

I swallowed hard as we stepped into it, and Erik let go of me, taking a step back towards the door as I spun around toward the exit.

"Wait," I gasped, but then Angus stepped in with us, pressing a button among a row of them on the wall and Erik started laughing.

The doors slid closed with a thud and Erik turned to me with the devil in his gaze. "Just a little elevator, rebel. This box will take us upstairs. Understand?"

A snarl sprang to my lips, because he could have said that sooner and he damn well knew it.

"You-" I started, about to hurl a string of insults at him but Erik pressed a finger to his lips, pointing to Angus's back, his expression full of a warning to behave.

It took every ounce of strength I had to keep the words from passing my lips, and instead I had to twist them into something else entirely. "You didn't tell me we were going to ride in an elevator, your highness."

"Well, I have not grown used to your ignorance yet," he said patronisingly, clapping a hand to Angus's shoulder and wheeling him around to face me. "What do you think of my new human, Angus?"

Angus's eyes went wide, looking from me to Erik in a panic. "I, um, well she's quite the er, um, you know," he said, clearly unsure what kind of comment might be appropriate.

"I have no idea, Angus. Do tell me," Erik urged, toying with him just as he did me. It seemed making people squirm was his favourite pastime.

"She is um, radiant?" Angus stuttered, looking to Erik nervously in fear that he'd said the wrong thing.

"Is she?" Erik looked to me, his scrutiny leaving me raw inside. "Yes, perhaps that is an adequate choice of word."

Angus nodded, looking relieved as shit for passing Erik's test. "Well then, human, what do you say to your magnanimous ruler for allowing such a compliment to pass your way?"

I stared at him blankly, looking to Erik who cocked his head expectantly, his eyes commanding me to play along.

"Thank you," I forced the words past my lips, tasting the bitterness in them.

"Goodness! Address the prince with formality," Angus demanded, terror crossing his features, like he expected bloodshed to descend at any moment.

"She's a little slow, Angus, give her a moment," Erik said, eyes back on me as he waited for me to submit to his game.

"Your highness," I said in as flat a voice as I could get away with.

The doors opened behind them and despite having been told this box would take us to another place, I couldn't help the gasp that left me at the magic of it. We were now looking at a completely different room, the huge space filled with high black tables and beyond them were enormous windows, looking out at the actual freaking sky.

Erik drew me into the room, which was full of vampires, standing at the tables with silver cups in their hands.

Angus guided us past them, and eyes followed us as the vampires noticed Erik. Many of them whispered and pointed, and suddenly their eyes were roaming over me too, scouring, tearing me apart, sizing me up. My gut clenched and I fell back on my old ways, throwing them dark scowls.

Angus led us to a velvet rope, beyond which was a crescent-shaped leather sofa pointing toward a large window. Two Elite sat there dressed in fine clothes, their heavenly faces fixed with surprise at the sight of us.

Angus snapped his fingers at them. "I'm sorry you'll have to vacate the VIP area; our royal highness is here."

The two males rose to their feet in an instant, eyeing Erik in shock before bowing low. They hurried past us without a word, and Erik tugged me toward the seats they'd just vacated as if he hadn't even noticed their existence.

"A chalice of Realm A," Erik ordered of Angus then glanced at me. "And food and water for my courtier."

"Food?" Angus squeaked, and Erik rounded on him with a dark smile while I tried to work out the meaning of what he'd just called me. Knowing him, it was probably something insulting.

"Yes, human food. Is that a problem?" Erik enquired casually, his back now to me.

"N-no, sir," Angus said, bowing so low his nose nearly touched the floor.

"I'm used to not having breakfast," I said. "It's not a problem."

Angus straightened, eyeing me hopefully as he saw a way out of his dilemma.

"Nonsense. Provide her something," Erik bit out, ushering Angus away and he hurried off in a fluster.

Erik turned to me, curiosity sparking in his gaze.

"What Realm are you from?" he asked as I moved to the window, my lips parting further and further.

I forgot his question in an instant, drawing in a breath as I eyed the city unfolding below me. We were so high up, I could see for miles, and my pulse quickened at the feel of standing on the edge of a precipice. It was more than my eyes had ever seen in one go, buildings stretching out ahead forever, but beyond the gleaming skyscrapers were ruins, bombed remains of a huge section of the old city. And beyond that was a hint of green, a forest perhaps, a promise of life far away out there.

My veins sang with energy as I reached out to lay my hand against the window, assuring myself of its solidness as I moved right up to it to look at the street below. The vampires down there looked like ants now, scurrying about, appearing small enough to squash beneath my shoes. *If only.*

I soaked in all of it, the clean roads, the glimpses of opulent living spaces within the high buildings. The vampires resided in such luxury, and it was hard to believe I was really seeing it for myself, living amongst it.

"Rebel?" Erik muttered, moving to my side, his arm brushing mine and making me jolt at the contact. "Your Realm?"

I thought on it. I didn't really know much about the other Realms, but I recalled what one of the vampires had said during my journey here.

"Realm G, I think," I replied.

"West coast," he said to himself. "Realm G is a lower brand of blood. Something to do with the climate, I suppose. The type of food you're given, perhaps..."

He fell quiet in thought and my gut prickled from his words. There were classes of blood quality? Why? What difference did it make from one human to the next?

"A chalice of Realm A for your highness." Angus reappeared, passing Erik an ornate silver cup that was engraved with beautiful runes. As Erik took it with a nod of thanks, I spotted the deep red liquid inside and I stiffened. Of course it was blood, but seeing it like this, poured into a beautiful cup to be sipped by a cold-hearted prince brought me so sharply back to reality that it was like a stab to the chest.

Realm A... urgh, was that a good *brand*? The thought made me ill and I drifted toward the couch which was about as far away from Erik and that blood as I could get.

"The human food will arrive shortly," Angus promised before hurrying away again.

Erik sipped from his fancy cup, eyeing the view as I took a seat and knotted my fingers together in my lap. In all my lifetime, I'd rarely seen vampires actually drink blood. Humans gave it often in the bloodlettings, and then it was bottled and sent away. They never drank from us directly, but seeing him sip from that cup was somehow worse. Like these creatures were trying to make it civilised by separating it from the vein it had come from.

Whose blood had it been? A man's? A woman's? A *child's*?

Erik neither knew nor cared, and that made the whole thing so much more twisted. If he saw the blood spilling from a human's veins, would it make him hungry?

My gaze moved from him to the other vampires in the room, tens of them, all sipping from their own chalices, licking their lips, savouring the blood that crossed their tongues.

I shut my eyes, not wanting to watch the normalised horrors going on around me.

"Something wrong?" Erik asked, his weight pressing down the seat beside me, and I tensed.

The metallic scent from his cup sailed under my nose and nausea gripped my stomach.

"Where's the bathroom?" I asked, fighting back a heave.

I rose to my feet, pressing my tongue to the roof of my mouth, sure I was about to throw up. Heat flooded up my spine followed by a wave of ice.

Erik caught my hand, his fingers squeezing as he got to his feet, sweeping in front of me and concealing me from the other vampires in the room. His cypress scent enveloped me as I swallowed back the bile rising in my throat, riding out the wave of nausea. I had nothing in my stomach to vomit up anyway.

"The blood upsets you," Erik remarked, and I looked up at him in all his chiselled perfection, finding a crease between his eyes.

Seeing them drink blood in front of me, I might as well have had my own veins hooked up to their damn chalices.

*I am food. I will never be anything else to these vile creatures. My family's blood has gone down their throats. My blood too...*

"If I sat here drinking the blood of your friends, wouldn't you be a little upset?" I snipped at him. God, how could I have been excited about coming here? How could I have enjoyed the trip as if it was some day out, when this was what all the beauty was built on. The blood of my kind.

Erik's lips thinned, but he didn't bite back at me. "I can avoid drinking in front of you, if you would prefer."

*I'd prefer if you stopped drinking altogether and turned into a pile of soot.*

I simply shrugged, growing angrier with him. With all of them. But mostly with myself.

"It's something you will have to get used to," Erik murmured.

I continued to ignore him, angling my head away from him so I didn't have to think about the blood he'd just swallowed.

My dad was strung up in a blood bank somewhere, and this was where his blood would end up. In gaudy cups designed for the vampires to feed from. It was disgusting.

Erik's hand landed on my arm, and I stiffened in surprise, turning sharply toward him. His face was contorted in a strange expression as if he didn't even understand the emotion he was trying to express.

"What? Say it," I hissed.

"When the ritual is over, you'll be made into a vampire and blood will no longer be unappealing to you," he said, and I could feel my face paling by the second.

"That's what you have to say?" I said in astonishment, horrified at the mere thought of it. "I don't want that. Not ever. Please-" I gripped his arm in desperation, seeing my fate so clearly in his eyes. "Please don't let that happen to me."

My mouth was raw, and bile was pushing at the base of my tongue. I knew begging was pointless and I hated the plea leaving my tongue. This so-called prince probably didn't even think of me as a creature worth her opinions, but I had to try, I had to let him know how terrible a fate I thought that was in case it might sway his decision on letting it happen. However unlikely that seemed.

Erik gave me a concerned frown, his fingers tightening on my arm so we were both gripping each other, and maybe I was crazy, but his expression twisted into something resembling remorse. "I don't wish to put this curse on anyone, but it is the way of things now."

I gaped at him, latching onto the word within it that spoke of his feelings on his kind.

"You think it's a curse?" I whispered, my heart strumming a frantic tune.

He ground his jaw, glancing over at the other vampires, seeming concerned that they might have heard him.

"I *know* it's a curse," he said, a heavy darkness filling his eyes that spoke of true torment. "Perhaps bringing you here was a little... insensitive." He spoke the last word as if he was unsure.

I nodded firmly, and he released me the same moment I released him, and it was suddenly easier to breathe.

"You're the first human I've chosen," he said. "I'm not sure what is appropriate and what isn't, but...I will try to learn."

My brows lifted in surprise and my throat finally loosened enough to allow me to answer.

"Thank you," I forced out. Not because I was grateful, but because I needed him to know that this was not okay. And if he was willing to try and empathise with my situation, then I had to encourage that.

"So," he said, sharper. "Let's discuss Fabian."

I sighed, resigning myself to being Erik's puppet. This was what today was about after all, so I had to be strong and fulfil my side of the bargain to ensure Erik stuck to his.

"Okay," I agreed.

A mask of formality slid over his features. "My brother is a highly political man. But he has his weaknesses. A pretty girl can capture his attention for a while, but it is a certain rare breed who can captivate him entirely. I believe *you* are that breed."

I snorted in disbelief. "Why?"

He grinned darkly. "You are beautiful, for one. But you are also fiery, tenacious, a challenge that will whet his appetite in just the right way. That kind of spark is what some men like in their women. Fabian included. I knew that when you stepped into the courtyard dressed in nothing but your underwear and your face smeared with mascara. Although Fabian would never have picked you in front of our entire royal court for the sake of propriety, I could tell he was tempted."

I shifted in my seat, trying not to focus on the fact thar he'd called me beautiful. A boy in the Realm had once called me that, and I'd steered clear of him for a month to ensure he never said it again. But hearing it from Erik was something else entirely. How could a vampire admire me when I was supposed to be his packed lunch?

"But you also have a lot of work to do," he added sternly. "Fabian won't wish to be seen with you if he feels it will bruise his reputation.

So, we have some damage control to do."

"Like what?" I asked warily.

"When you spend time with him, you will not only be dressed respectfully, but you will show the right kind of interest in Fabian."

"And what kind of interest is that?" I narrowed my eyes.

"He must feel desired by you, but you must also play hard to get. Something the women he shows interest in do not often do. If you capture his attention, he will forget all about your initial misconduct, and if you are able to keep it long enough, you will satisfy the hunter in him."

I shuddered at the thought of gaining the lust of a malevolent vampire such as Fabian and had to wonder what this was all for.

"Why?" I asked. "What's in this for you?"

Erik laughed in a deep rumble. "That is my business."

"You're making it mine too, don't you think?" I pushed.

"No, I do not," he said simply, and I huffed out a breath.

"Alright, how do I do the flirting thing?" I muttered, swallowing my pride.

"Come here." He patted the space between us with a grin, and I reluctantly slid closer. He dropped an arm around my shoulders, took hold of my face and angled me toward a couple across the room. I tried to ignore his cool touch as I took in the female vampire dressed in a tight black dress that showed off her curves, wondering why Erik had decided to get handsy with me instead of just pointing them out. The female vampire was running her hand up the male's arm, giggling about something as he spoke and tossing her hair like a bug had shot into it.

"You see what she's doing?" Erik asked.

"No..."

"That is how you must behave."

"Like an angry bee is in my hair?"

He chuckled low in his throat, the sound rumbling right out from his chest into me, and I bit down on my own laugh.

"Give it a try," Erik prompted, leaning back to look at me, his arm sliding down to lay around my waist.

This right here was the moment my dignity died, hit around the head with a shovel and its grave dug by my own hand. I giggled like an idiot, tossing my hair and flicking Erik right in the eye with it.

He roared a laugh, drawing the gaze of several vampires in the room, and I gave him a dry look as I folded my arms.

"That was abysmal," he said, reining in his laughter. "You aren't taking this seriously at all." He rubbed his eyes, breathing out heavily. "Maybe this isn't going to work."

"No," I said quickly, laying my hand on his knee in fear. "I can do it, Erik. I will." Fire blazed in my soul, and he released a low noise in his throat that was so carnal it made my heart judder.

I slowly withdrew my hand from his knee and leaned away from the fervour in his gaze.

"I think you're getting it now," he said. "Watch them then try again."

I took a breath, nodding my agreement, getting the feeling this was going to be humiliating.

As I watched the couple, the male leaned in for a kiss and the woman offered her cheek at the last second.

Erik smirked, dropping his hand onto my thigh and I nearly jumped out of my seat, but he kept it firmly in place, his fingers digging in.

"What are you doing?" I hissed.

He turned toward me, brushing a lock of hair behind my ear, his touches suddenly anything but rough.

"The Elite are watching," he muttered, barely moving his lips. "I'm supposed to be courting you, and they mustn't know what I'm really planning."

I bit back my urge to ask more about Fabian, but I couldn't stop wondering why Erik wanted me to seduce his brother. What was the point in it?

Erik's fingers trailed down my spine, and every fibre in my body came to life with his caress. Part of me wanted to pull away, but I was frozen in place, trapped in the arc of his powerful body with heat bursting through my veins.

"I have a meeting in an hour," Erik purred in my ear, sending goosebumps skittering across my neck. "You will accompany me."

Angus arrived with my food, and I jumped on the opportunity to push away from Erik, shifting a full foot away from him down the couch.

"Here we are," Angus announced, looking smug as hell by the food he'd rustled up as he placed the plate down on a table in front of me.

I eyed the strange arrangement of bread, a turnip, a raw potato, and some strawberries mixed in with a couple of radishes. My features skewed as Angus looked to me for approval.

"Um…" I started, unsure how to tell him that most of this was inedible.

Angus's chest puffed out, pride brimming from him as he looked to Erik for the approval I hadn't given him.

"Eat," Erik commanded as Angus gave up waiting for a compliment, disappointment falling over his face instead.

Despite not feeling remotely hungry after witnessing all the blood consumption, I picked up the plate and ate the strawberries, then nibbled on a couple of the radishes. A lifetime of rations made me anything but complacent, but I couldn't force myself to take a bite out of a raw turnip.

Erik sat back in his seat, taking out his phone again and giving me some semi-privacy as I ate. I spotted the Elite watching me and offered them scowls when Erik wasn't looking, and they only fell into excited mutters like I was of great interest to them. The prince might have wanted to keep up appearances, but I didn't care what they thought of me, and Erik hadn't specifically requested that I pretend to be interested in him, so I damn-well wasn't going to.

# CALLIE

## CHAPTER SEVENTEEN

I was trapped, pushing through swathes of white material as a man laughed. There was no joy in his mocking tone.

If they found me here, I was as good as dead.

Food. I'm just food.

I cried, trying to run as the endless material caught around my legs, tripping me. Ebony hair spilled around me. Montana's hair.

I was a captive. I would never get free of this place.

Iron eyes danced with joy as he found me and I stood frozen in place, the material wrapping its way around my body. He watched as it crushed me. Squeezing and squeezing until I couldn't breathe. He watched and he laughed.

I didn't know who he was or why he wanted me. I only knew one thing.

I was his.

"Callie?" Strong hands clamped around my arms, shaking me roughly. "It's time to wake."

I opened my eyes, fighting off the strange dream as fear held onto me. Despite the strangeness of it, I'd found it weirdly reassuring. Like

I had been *with* my sister, not just dreaming about her. And though the loss of her pushed in on me now, I felt more certain than ever that she was alive, that she was waiting for me, needing me.

"Alright, I'm awake," I muttered as I squinted up at Magnar whose face was disconcertingly close to mine, his brow lowered while he looked down at me.

He offered me a hand and pulled me upright.

"Were you having a nightmare?" he asked.

"Not exactly...I had a strange dream about Montana."

"Your sister? Perhaps she's sending you a message."

"A what?"

"She is your twin, so she has slayer blood too. You are both of the Clan of Dreams, and as such, your innate gifts hold the power to communicate while you sleep. It is unlikely that either of you would be strong enough to do so in any fully conscious way without taking your vows though. And even then, it is doubtful that you would be strong enough considering the fact that you are not full-blooded slayers. But anything is possible." He shrugged.

"You mean I could talk to her in my sleep?" I asked, my heart still pounding heavily as I shook off the fear which had clung to me in that dream. Could it have been real? Was what I'd experienced actually linked to my sister the way it had felt like it had been?

"Perhaps. Whenever I was visited by an unrelated member of your clan in my dreams, I was shown only images. But my mother was of your clan, and when she visited me, we could hold a full conversation. That could have been due to our blood tie. Or it could have been due to her considerable strength. She was undoubtedly the strongest Dreamer who ever lived in my time."

"Why do your answers always leave me with more questions?" I asked, swiping a hand over my face as I worked to calm my pulse and make sense of what he was telling me. Even if the dreams did turn out to be some kind of weird connection to Montana, it didn't really help me. They were nonsense. I couldn't glean any information from them other than the hope that she was still alive. But I guessed that was all I really needed anyway, the certainty that she was still out there, waiting for me to come for her.

"We have a problem," Magnar said, choosing to ignore my remark as he stalked away from me, twitching the moth-eaten curtain aside and peering out into the dim light of dawn beyond it. "Something tried to break our wards last night."

"Oh?" I asked, attempting to sound super casual about it as I sank back down to sit on the couch but coming off more like a frightened mouse.

"It is not possible for a lesser vampire to even detect the wards, let alone fight against them. Any who come close to them would find themselves heading away again and never even realise they'd been influenced to do so. The fact that someone has pushed very hard against those impulses concerns me. Someone of much greater importance must be hunting us now."

"But that's no issue for you, right?" I asked, a shiver of fear passing down my spine as I thought of Wolfe, wondering if he was hunting me himself now. "I mean, you're the guy who said, 'there's only five' the last time they came for us."

"Your faith in my skill is quite flattering," Magnar replied, a hint of mockery to his tone as he moved back towards me before his eyes darkened with some endless truth. "But I am only one man. And all men die."

"Wow. Thanks for the pep-talk. Are you really that concerned?" My heart fluttered uncomfortably at the idea that he was worried about this. Because if Magnar was concerned then I was pretty sure I needed to be running for the hills, screaming for my life.

"No. But I do not wish for you to think of me as immortal. Death is a constant possibility. Every time I unleash my swords, I know it could be my last fight. This is something you must accept if you are to be a slayer." Magnar dropped down to sit beside me, his expression tight as he considered our options.

"Got it. You might die, I might die, immortality is only for assholes. And speaking of immortal assholes, do you have any idea *who* has been sniffing around us?" My thoughts returned to General Wolfe and my gut plummeted. I'd never seen a vampire feed directly from a human before, but the way he'd torn into my father was something I could never banish from my memory. It had been like watching some kind of crazed animal attack, but worse thanks to the callous apathy which had accompanied the brutality. He was a monster through and through.

"It is certainly one of the Elite. I fear that if we continue on our course to the blood bank as we are, then the one following us will figure out our destination. With the best will in the world, a single slayer will not stand a chance at taking that place down if they know I am coming."

"One and a half slayers," I teased.

Magnar tilted his head at me and snorted. "Maybe one and a quarter."

"Harsh. But probably more accurate," I conceded. "So what makes the Elite more formidable than the lesser vampires anyway?"

Magnar pushed his long hair away from his eyes as he considered his answer. "Essentially it is because of who created them. A vampire's strength comes from the one who sired them so the closer they are to the original line, the stronger they are. Those who were turned by an original vampire, one of the Belvederes, are the Elite. Any they sire are a little weaker – lesser vampires, and any sired by them are weaker again, so on and so on."

"So, it's kinda like each generation is less powerful than the last?" I asked, trying to follow what he was saying.

He nodded. "Do you remember what I told you about the Belvederes?"

"The ones who call themselves royalty?" I asked.

"They are the original vampire family. We called them the Revenants once, but the gods decided to unite them under that false name." His lip curled back in disgust, and I could tell his hatred for them was more than just because of what they were. It was personal.

"You mean, they're the ones who started all of this? How? Where did they come from?" I asked, shifting a little closer to him.

"There are many stories about that. Many theories. I suppose the only ones who truly know are the four of them. But if I ever get close enough to ask, I won't be wasting time on questions," he growled.

I itched to ask him why he hated them so much, but the darkness in his eyes made me afraid of the answer.

"So, you said they're a family?" I asked, grasping onto a safer question.

"Yes, of sorts. Though family is usually tied together through love, and those monsters are incapable of such an emotion. Their loyalty to each other is born more out of a lust for power. They are siblings, or so they say, though they bear little resemblance to each other. I do not believe they truly shared the same parents when they were human. There are three males and a female. And they call themselves royals, as if they were chosen by the gods instead of hated by them," he laughed like that was a twisted joke, and I shifted uncomfortably.

If he knew this much about them, then it meant they'd held this power since his time. They'd had over a thousand years to solidify their influence and control before they'd taken over the human world too. How were we supposed to stand a chance against such an ancient power?

"What else do you know about them?" I asked, unsure if I really wanted to know the answer.

Magnar scowled as he thought about it. "The woman, Clarice, was known as the Golden Whore in my time. She is beautiful beyond words, though the sight of her porcelain face always turned my stomach. She has gathered an army about her who she calls her harem. Men who she seduced while they were still human and brought to her bed before turning them into one of her kind. She would appear in human villages, flaunting herself at men she found desirable and would encourage them to pursue her until they fell begging at her feet. When I last walked the earth, there were nearly a hundred of those pathetic creatures trailing after her, aching for her touch and willing to lay down their lives for the chance at spending time between her thighs."

"And they just went along with that? They were happy to become like her? To leave their lives behind for a soulless monster?" I asked in disgust. I knew the vampires were beyond beautiful to look at, but it had never made me desire them. Their beauty was unnatural and cold. The idea of taking one of them to my bed, of fucking something so soulless made me feel ill. I was surprised to hear they even fucked at all, they seemed interested in nothing beyond blood in my experience. "Didn't any of them refuse?"

"I think they were so deeply under her spell that the idea of refusal wouldn't have occurred to them. Besides, plenty of humans are weak, selfish creatures. Immortality at the side of that seductress likely seemed like a blessing to most of them."

I scrunched my nose up at the thought, my fingers curling into the dusty fabric of the couch beside me as I fought down my horror over that story.

"And the others?" I asked, wondering if I really wanted to know.

"The brothers. Fabian the Snake, Miles the False God, and *Erik*," he spat the final name with venom so thick my heart skipped a beat. "Killer of a Thousand Souls."

I stared at him with wide eyes, waiting for him to continue.

"Fabian created the Familiars. He found a way for the vampires to thread a piece of their soul into the hearts and minds of unwitting creatures. They would become their eyes and ears. Sunlight didn't hurt them, so they could spy on us even when we believed we were safe. It caused devastation. The vampires would appear when we least expected them, always knowing our plans and lying in wait. We even executed some of our own, wrongly believing they had betrayed us before one of the prophets figured out what Fabian had done. We believed the colonies of bats that swarmed above our camps at night only came for the insects which were drawn close by the light of our fires. By the time we realised what he'd done, many souls were already lost."

My mind whirled with the idea of the slayers having to come to terms with the fact that they had wrongly sacrificed some of their own because of the vampires' cunning. It made me wonder if the Realms weren't as bad as I'd thought. At least they didn't kill us anymore. They made us give them blood, but our lives held value to them now. It sounded as though it hadn't always been that way.

"Miles was a different kind of monster," Magnar continued. "He set himself up as a god, offering eternal life to any who proved their devotion to him. People built temples in his honour and showered him with gifts in the hopes that he would grant them immortality. But of course, eternal life comes with a price that must be paid in blood. Once he had changed those poor souls into vampires, he cut them loose, claiming he wanted them to enjoy the freedom of eternity. But they craved blood above all else. Often, they would return to their hometowns in hopes of seeing their families, only to be overwhelmed by their thirst. It would seem that most of those who are newly sired have little control over the bloodlust that drives them. They would lose control, killing those they loved and anyone else unlucky enough to cross their paths in their desperate need to satiate their desire for blood." Magnar fell quiet and I shifted closer to him, my thigh brushing against his as I tried to offer him some comfort from the terrible memories.

The silence stretched, and I could tell he didn't want to speak of the final brother, but I needed to know.

"And...the last brother?" I asked tentatively.

"Erik," Magnar growled. "If I do one thing with my time on this earth, then it shall be to remove him from it."

"What did he do?" I asked, my voice almost a whisper.

"Many things. Countless atrocities. It was he who killed my father in the Battle of Atbringer. The clans were almost destroyed that day. He killed hundreds of us with his army of monsters. Unlike his siblings, Erik has always been more particular about those he sires. He seeks out the greatest warriors, the most ruthless politicians, only the best of the best for his army. The Belvederes were the only creatures to leave that battlefield with their lives. Although my father returned to us as well. But he was no longer alive. That monster had turned him into one of them, hoping to corrupt his soul and use him for his own vile purposes."

I sucked in a sharp breath, the horror of what Magnar had suffered through eating at me.

"My father had enough of himself left to return and tell us what had happened to him. He bid farewell to my mother and brother, then begged me to end his suffering. That evil creature killed my father once, and then forced me to do it a second time. I was seventeen. I can still see him kneeling before me, begging me to lead the clans to victory against the Revenants. He gave me his blade, Venom, so that I could take his life and release his soul to the protection of our ancestors in Valhalla."

The pain of that truth cut through the air and sent a chill spiralling through the room which had nothing to do with the biting temperature outside. I swallowed thickly, wondering if I could have found the strength to do what he'd been forced to and shuddering at the mere suggestion of it. To see his own flesh and blood turned into a monster must have destroyed him. Being forced to kill his own father…

"I'm so sorry Magnar," I whispered, laying my hand on his arm, my fingertips brushing the slayer mark upon his skin.

Magnar turned to look me in the eye, and my heart stumbled uncertainly at the ferocity in his expression.

"It was foreseen that I would end that family. I may be nine hundred years late, but I intend to fulfil my destiny," he growled.

His gaze held such vehemence that I struggled to hold it, the intensity of his words an unbreakable vow, and I knew he would sacrifice everything to fulfil it. It was why he kept going despite all he'd lost. His one and only motivation, the single thing that made him place one foot before the other each and every day. And despite the way the odds were stacked against him, as I looked into his eyes, I couldn't help but believe that he would fulfil that destiny one day. Because nothing in this world could possibly match the passion of his devotion to that vow.

"So, what do you suggest we do about the Elite who's tracking us now?" I asked, breaking eye contact with him as my heart beat out of rhythm, the enormity of all he'd suffered and survived pressing in on me.

"We need to create a diversion and lay a trap," Magnar said slowly, an offer in his golden eyes which lit a spark of rebellion in me.

I smiled at the idea of playing the vampires at their own game and nodded encouragingly.

"Then tell me what to do."

# MONTANA

## CHAPTER EIGHTEEN

I was eternally relieved when we left the vampire bar behind, taking the carriage further into the city. I never wanted to go near that place again and I no longer gazed out of the window with any kind of joy. A dejected feeling was descending on me as I eyed the vampires going about their lives, their freedom a stark reminder of my captivity.

Growing up in the Realm had at least impressed upon me the importance of my blood. It wasn't much, but humans had held value there. Here, the Realms were ignored. Our blood was harvested for vampires to drink, and all they saw of it was the contents of their chalices. We were the odd meal in their day and held no impact on any other part of it. It had always felt degrading, but now it was worse than that. Like we were barely a thought in their day, perhaps not even a thought at all. And questions started to rise in me again about this whole royal ritual thing, because if humans were so invisible here, why would they take some of us and waste time putting on a show before the inevitable. Why let us have the illusion of choice? Why dress us up and parade us around the city, pretending to 'court' us – as Erik had put it.

I glanced at Erik, who was watching me with a scrutinising expression, his thumb ironing out a crease in his smart pants. "Why aren't I a vampire yet, Erik? You say it's a curse, but that's what you want us for isn't it? So why do it like this? With courting and formalities. I don't understand."

Erik's throat bobbed as he thought on my question. "There is a reason, rebel. But we don't speak of it until after the choosing ceremony."

I shook my head at him in frustration. "Just tell me."

"No," he said with grit, his eyes growing harder. "And do not ask me again." I expected him to turn away, but he didn't. Instead, his gaze drilled into mine as if he was trying to make me submit, but I looked back with equal ferocity, refusing to bow.

The carriage came to a halt, and I glanced toward the door as it opened, revealing the driver as he bowed low, waiting for us to exit.

"Close the door," Erik barked at him, and a tremor rocked my heart.

The door snapped shut and terror crawled through my veins as Erik shifted closer to me, his eyes two lakes of ice capable of turning my heart to frost.

"When we go upstairs, I need you to be obedient. The woman we're seeing will be able to help you with Fabian. So you need to drop the attitude right now, do you hear me?"

My throat grew dry, and I forced myself to nod, despite the rioting fury in my chest. He turned away, but words slid from my mouth before I could stop them.

"Have you released my father yet?"

The question hung in the air, and his shoulders stiffened as he remained with his fingers on the door handle. "I'll deal with it."

"So that's a no," I snarled, heat charging my veins.

My hands curled into fists as I gazed at the back of his head.

"If you do well with Fabian tomorrow, I'll make it a priority."

"His name is Mitchel Ford," I said loudly, making him hear me. "He has hair as black as mine, he's tall, well-built. Don't let Wolfe fool you into releasing anyone else. Mitchel Ford, have you got that?"

Erik glanced back at me, mouth tight. "I got it. Now move."

He opened the door, descending quickly from the carriage so I couldn't push him further on the matter.

He didn't offer me his hand this time, and whatever fragile bridges

I thought we'd started building between us shattered, just like one of my pretty illusions. Fantasies were only your friend when you were in them. The moment they spat you out, they laughed at you for how foolish you'd been to believe you could remain a part of them. And I reminded myself not to forget that.

I dropped down the steps, folding my arms as I took in the shadowy street and the tall apartment block ahead of us. I shivered as a bitter wind blew around me, hugging my chest to try and keep the cold out, feeling like we'd just walked into a dangerous territory in the shiny city.

Erik remained silent as he strode up to a large doorway and jammed his finger onto a button beside it.

"Yes?" a female voice answered.

"It's Erik," he said, and a buzzing noise sounded before the door opened.

I guessed from the informal way he'd announced himself that he was on close terms with whoever waited inside.

I followed him into a stairwell before the door closed in my face, the sound of it clunking shut behind me making my heart skip a beat. Something didn't feel right about this place, the stairway lit in too-bright bulbs and the air even colder in here than outside.

Erik barely threw me a glance before storming up the blue-tiled staircase at such a fierce pace, there was no way I could keep up.

I decided not to chase him like an alley dog and started climbing at my own speed, ascending level after level, my breaths growing heavier. Holy shit, how high were we going?

My ass muscles ached alongside the backs of my thighs, and I cursed the impractical dress I was stuck in, gathering it in fistfuls above my knees to give my legs more freedom to move.

I started cursing Erik with every step I took, reminding myself of all the reasons I despised him. From his superhuman strength to his bloody appetite and his looks which were designed to disarm me.

*I hope you fall and break your neck on these stairs, Prince Erik.*

I recalled how I'd reacted to his touch at the bar and ground my teeth, hating myself for it. He had gotten far too close to me, making me the pawn in his pointless games, convincing the onlookers he gave a fuck about me. But the truth of him had come out as soon as there were no more eyes on us.

I wouldn't buy into his fake charm whenever he decided to switch it on again. He was like the eye of a storm. You thought you were safe until the winds picked up, and the winds were definitely picking up, blustering a storm right up my ass.

I finally turned onto what must have been the highest level of the building because no more stairs awaited me, and a wide window looked out across a series of square rooftops.

Erik stood there, one shoulder propped causally against the wall, his eyes on his phone and his expression bored once more. He glanced up as I drew closer, his gaze dropping to my bare legs below where I'd scrunched the dress up in my hands.

I let the material go in an instant, moving to the wall and sagging against it, my breaths coming in furious pants.

He slid his phone into his pocket and gave me a dry look. "My time is valuable, stop wasting it."

"I can't move as fast as you, asshole," I snapped, my temper spilling over.

"I noticed," he snarled.

"What's your problem?" I demanded.

He sped forward in a blur of movement until he was right in front of me, making my heart lurch in fright at the terrifying speed of him.

"What did I tell you about the way you should speak to me?" he barked, making me flinch.

He pushed right up into my personal space, and I slammed a hand to his chest to keep him back. Not that I could really stop him. "But you can speak to me however you like?"

He prised my fingers away from his jacket, keeping my hand in a vice-like grip. "Yes, because I am your superior."

My upper lip curled back. "So what would you prefer? That I cower and tremble every time you're near me? You may think of me as your lesser, but that doesn't change who I am. You're the one who chose me because of my disobedience, Erik, so welcome to the consequences of your own actions."

His gaze fell down my body, peeling me apart as a sneer pulled back his lips and revealed his sharp canines. My chest was still heaving, heart hammering and breaths coming a little raggedly, while he remained entirely unaffected by every part of the human experience.

"I've been playing nice all day," I added thickly, and his eyes snapped back up to bore into mine. "You're the one with the attitude problem."

"Me?" he balked, like no subordinate of his had ever spoken to him like that.

"Yes, *you*, Erik."

"*Prince* Erik," he snarled, but I pressed my lips tight together, saying nothing. He was no prince of mine.

He took a step back, relieving me of his intoxicating scent and I rested my head back against the wall.

He raised a finger, pointing at me with a visceral anger in his eyes. "You *will* learn your place."

I released a cold laugh. "My place? I know it well, I promise you that. My whole life, my value has been the blood in my veins. You're the one who brought me here, you're the one who placed a different price on my head. So tell me, what was the testing for? What did you find in my blood that makes me so goddamn special? What is it that makes me suitable for your little ritual? That makes me too valuable to harm? Because if you truly wanted to quiet me, to watch me quiver at your feet in fear, you would have punished me by now."

"You think I'm beyond punishing you?" he whispered, the space seeming to darken, like shadows were crawling out of the walls, come to serve the one who'd summoned them.

His head was angled down a little, his brow shadowing his deep-set eyes, and the hollows of his cheekbones stood out starkly in the light.

The cold wall at my back seemed more inviting than him, and I became terribly aware of being alone with him here. It was so easy to imagine my blood splattering the walls, this beast standing in the midst of it, covered head to toe and licking his lips to savour the taste of me.

He moved closer once more, this time walking in lazy strides, knowing I couldn't outrun him either way. His hand pressed to the wall beside my head, and he leaned in, raising his thumb to my throat and running it across my skin from left to right. "Touching you is like holding an eggshell in my palm. I feel every part of you, from your thrashing heart to your fragile bones. I could break you easier than any vampire you have ever encountered before by accident. But with intention, I could do far worse. If you do not fear me because of that truth alone, then you are a fool, and may the gods help you."

"You want me to fear you," I stated, a tremor rolling through me from the threat in his words.

"I want you to respect me," he said, his eyes dropping to my mouth for the briefest moment before darting back up again.

"You can buy my fear with threats, but respect is earned," I said, and he bared his teeth at me, his eyes sparking with madness.

The sound of a door opening carried across the space. "Erik? What's going on? I heard a ruckus," a woman's sultry voice reached us.

Erik withdrew from me, revealing a devastatingly beautiful woman standing in the doorway. The vampire was tall, willowy, with golden brown hair that hung straight all the way down to her midriff. Her eyes were earthy and inviting and her skin was glimmeringly pale. But despite the allure of her face and her inviting aura, she felt like something...else. I had no idea why I was sure she was different, but something in my bones told me she was. She wore a pale pink dress that cut off above her knees and clung to her curves, her white high heels looking sharp enough to be used as a weapon.

"Everything is fine," Erik said.

"Master." She beamed at him. "It's so good to see you." In a heartbeat, her gleaming arms were wrapped around his neck. Her face was so close to his, for a second I thought they might kiss. Erik remained rigid throughout the entire display, though he didn't push her off.

"Valentina," Erik said warmly, at complete odds with the way he had just been speaking to me. "How are you?"

"Wonderful, Erik. Do come in." She tugged him along by the hand, and it was only then that her eyes fell on me, like she hadn't even noticed my existence until that very moment. Her lips parted, puckering into a perfect O that, in my humble opinion, resembled a butthole. "By the gods, Erik, you didn't tell me you were bringing one of *them* with you."

I instantly disliked her, not that I'd had any plans of liking her, but there it was. Insta-hate.

Erik pulled his hand free from Valentina's grip, turning to me with a wicked look that said he was about to humiliate me.

"Come here," he beckoned me like a dog, patting his goddamn thigh and everything.

I swallowed every ounce of pride I had and moved to his side, thinking of my family. His arm slid around my shoulders, but there was no warmth in it like there had been at the bar. I felt like a possession being flaunted in front of this vampire, shown off like a shiny trinket.

"My first human," Erik announced as he guided me into a brightly lit hallway. "What do you think?"

He pushed me toward Valentina, and I stumbled in her direction. She immediately grabbed me, running her fingers through my hair, pinching my cheek, then plucking at my dress as if I was her property to inspect. "She's a little scrawny. Why did you choose this one?"

Counting to ten in my head, I focused on the techniques Dad had taught me to help me keep my head.

"This one is particularly obedient," Erik said, and I almost snorted at that.

It was like a private joke between us, but I refused to let it shift the ice around my heart.

"You do realise you have to marry her if she chooses you at the ceremony?" Valentina's words were like a knife in my back, and I wheeled around to look at Erik in horror.

"I realise that, thank you," Erik responded curtly, shooting me a look that told me to keep quiet. But fuck, was this what he'd been hiding from me? And why the hell did he want me to *marry*, Fabian?

Repulsion filled me as Valentina strode ahead of us into another room, and I glared openly at Erik.

He took my arm, dipping his head so his mouth was by my ear. "One word out of you and you'll regret it."

He pulled me along, and I envisioned scratching his eyes out to sate my rage, the heat in my veins demanding an outlet.

We arrived in a large living room filled with white furniture and a huge screen on the wall I guessed was a TV, everything too-neat, too-clean, too-inhuman. Floor-length windows looked out toward a red-brick tower block framed by the cloudy sky, and I could see all the way back to the New Empire State building we'd been in earlier.

Valentina reappeared with two glasses in hand, both swimming with blood. I ground my teeth as the two of them dropped onto the pristine sofa and she passed Erik a glass. Valentina looked me up and down as if she was trying to work something out, cocking her head left then right. Evidently, I was not invited to sit.

Erik placed his drink on a side table without taking a drink and left it there.

"I thought you were here about our line of work," Valentina asked Erik, turning towards him on the couch so her bare knees brushed his leg.

"Later. I'd like you to help me with a little problem I'm having with my courtier first."

There was that word again. *Courtier.* Whatever it meant, I knew it referred to me.

"Oh?" she tittered, seeming delighted. "What kind of problem, master?"

Why did she keep calling him that? It was damn weird.

My skin tingled with anger and a pain grew on my right forearm. I rubbed at the spot, trying to find what the issue was but there seemed to be none as I examined the skin.

"She doesn't know the first thing about men, Valentina," Erik sighed like I was such goddamn burden to bear. "She's sheltered and repressed. I'd like you to loosen her up a bit. Teach her how to please me."

*Ah, okay, so I'm here to be humiliated. Got it.*

"Perhaps you're not ready for this kind of commitment," Valentina said, and lightning seemed to flash through her irises.

"That's an order, Valentina," Erik snarled, his patience wearing thin.

She rose to her feet, rolling her eyes as she moved toward me with cat-like grace. I went rigid as she took my chin in her soft palm, and my skin pulsed with a strange energy. The sky beyond the window darkened and a heavy presence seemed to fill the room, though maybe the descending storm was just divine timing.

"Okay, let's see." She tipped my head side to side as she examined me, and I fought the urge to jerk away from her. "Go and sit in Erik's lap," she murmured, a sly grin forming on her full lips. She was a true thing of beauty, poise and charm, and something about her made me think of the time Dad had told me that the most beautiful of snakes held the deadliest bites.

I glowered, tempted to disobey her, but my mind was on Dad now, and Erik had told me I needed to watch my 'behaviour'. If I didn't make an effort, he could easily decide not to help my father.

With an internal groan, I did as she said, moving in front of Erik and giving him a look that told him exactly how I felt about this. He opened his arms with a mocking expression, and I lowered myself onto his lap, fighting all of my instincts.

I sat my ass as far away from his dick as possible, sitting right at the edge of his knees, perching there like a bird anxious to take flight.

"A little closer," Valentine encouraged, and I scooted a single inch up his legs. "*Closer.*"

Erik leaned back in his seat, not offering me an out, and certainly not offering me any support. But when I scooted right up his lap, he sat forward so we were all too close to one another.

"That's it," Valentina praised. "Now show him how you adore him. Push your hands into his hair and gaze lovingly into his eyes."

Erik's eyes gleamed with hilarity and a growl built in my throat as I shoved my hands into his hair. Soft as feathers, of course. Nothing like his steely gaze which was piercing and formidable. But if this was supposed to be romantic, Valentina was deluded.

"*Softly,*" Valentina clipped, and I realised my fingers were knotted tightly in Erik's hair like I was attempting to rip his head off.

He lifted a brow, seeming amused by my efforts, and I forced my fingers to relax, our eyes on each other's. Up close, his allure was difficult to resist, the primal sins in his eyes promising me unending bliss if only I submitted to his every whim. My heart laboured in my chest, and it became an effort in itself to focus on anything but the closeness of his body to mine.

I shut my eyes as I followed Valentina's instructions, caressing his hair while embarrassment crawled into the crevices of my soul.

"Now cup his cheeks," Valentina urged, and I lowered my hands to his face, the cool kiss of his skin chasing away the warmth in mine.

"That's it, now kiss him. Gently mind, let's not get ahead of ourselves," Valentina said.

My heart slammed into my ribcage and my eyes flew open, my hands dropping dramatically to my sides.

*Fuck no.*

I leaned back, shaking my head, and Erik started laughing obnoxiously. Glancing over my shoulder, I spotted Valentina giving us a confused frown.

"Is there a problem?" she asked.

"She's shy," Erik answered for me with a smirk.

If looks could kill, mine would have dismembered him by now.

"Alright." Valentina seemed frustrated. "I'll turn away."

As she whipped around, I figured we'd just pretend to kiss, but Erik slammed his mouth against mine before I could even try to communicate the idea.

Hot acid poured down my spine, my stomach knotted into a tight ball, and my heart combusted. Erik's hands snared my waist, caging me against his body and making me feel the cold, hard plane of his muscular chest as his mouth remained stamped to mine. My mind blurred, the urge to fall under his spell roaring in my ears, and for a second, I was just a wasp crawling into a honey trap, seeking out the nectar within that would equal my demise.

I fought off the power of him, reminding myself of what he was, and refusing to let any other thoughts enter my mind.

I yanked my head away, and Erik grinned like the devil himself, all pretence of nobility gone as he laid himself out before me as the impure creature he was. I opened my mouth to swear at him, but he gave me a look that told me to be quiet or else, and it took everything I had to remain silent.

"Well, it's a start," Valentina said, and I wondered when she'd stopped giving us privacy. "But you can't force chemistry into existence. I'm sorry Erik, she's not very good at this."

Erik didn't look at her, instead pushing me from his lap so I stumbled to my feet. "She'll do just fine."

"Can we talk in private now?" Valentina asked, seeming impatient all of a sudden.

Rain started pattering against the window and a rumble of thunder sounded in the distance that set the hairs rising along the back of my neck.

"Valentina," Erik snarled in a warning, but I wasn't sure why.

She sighed and her eyes flicked to the window. The rain ebbed to a slow drizzle and the clouds seemed to brighten. If I hadn't known it was crazy, I would have thought Valentina was responsible for the changing weather.

Erik ushered me out of the room, and my body was too hot as I backed away, his hateful kiss still burning my lips.

I was more than glad to make my escape, practically running from the lounge and finding myself in a kitchen. Except it wasn't much of a kitchen. There was a sink with some cleaning products beside it and a single, enormous silver fridge. That was about it.

I could have guessed what was in the fridge, but I still opened it, finding a hundred gleaming red bottles all labelled with the names of the Realms. Disgust climbed through the centre of me, and I was tempted to smash the whole stock in a fit of rage, but it would only cause me more problems with Erik. Shutting the fridge door, I pressed my back to it and found myself sliding to the floor, hugging my knees and burying my face in the folds of my dress.

That animal had actually kissed me, taken ownership of me in a way that had felt like crossing a line, even though I knew there were no boundaries I could truly enforce.

My mouth tingled as if it had frostbite, and maybe it did after that ice-cold kiss from a monster whose heart had stopped beating long ago.

My stomach hardened into a tight ball and resilience curled up around my heart. I couldn't just sit here on the floor, waiting for that psycho to come collect me when he was done talking with Valentina.

I got up, moving to the sink and turning on the sleek white tap. Cupping the water in my hand, I rinsed my mouth, spitting it back into the basin in an attempt to get rid of the feel of Erik's lips against mine. I hoped it might also short-circuit the electrical energy charting through my veins too, because his allure had gotten to me, and I didn't want to accept that fact. Because the worst part about that kiss, was some foolish part of me had wanted to lean into it, and though I ached to believe that was because of Erik's magnetism, I feared I was wrong.

Erik chose that particular moment to enter the room and I was glad when his eyes turned to shade.

*Yep, your kisses are spat out Erik. That's how much I want them.*

"We're leaving," he announced, turning his back on me.

When he was out of sight, I blew out a breath and started following him, but found my way suddenly blocked by Valentina.

She smiled at me, but there was no kindness in it this time, like dark clouds were drawing over the glint of sun in her eyes.

As I tried to step past her, she caught my right arm, pushing up the sleeve of my dress as if she was trying to catch me out at something.

"What are you doing?" I tugged away from her in alarm as her cold fingers roamed over the inside of my forearm. And where she touched, my skin began to burn.

"Ah," I gasped, trying to escape her tight grip, then her lips pursed, and she shrugged, releasing me.

"Off you go, human." She stepped aside just enough so I had to squeeze past her, tugging down my sleeve firmly as I went. She leaned in low as I passed, whispering directly in my ear, "If you want some real advice about Erik, I'd suggest you don't trust a word he says."

I slipped away into the hall, my heart hammering from the strange interaction. And whatever the intention of her words, it made me question the promise Erik had made to me. Had he discussed it with Valentina? Maybe they'd had a good laugh at my expense as Erik revealed he had no intention of helping my father at all, but then why would Valentina try to warn me of that?

My gut knotted as I exited the apartment, finding Erik waiting for me in the stairwell, looking slightly less bored than usual.

"Don't look so sad, we have hours of fun left to enjoy." Erik headed down the stairs and I followed, a scowl growing on my face.

"If this is your idea of fun, I'd guess you don't have many friends."

Erik glanced at me, his pace matching mine as we descended the steps. "Oh good, rebel is back," he deadpanned.

My mind shifted gears to what I was fairly sure I'd witnessed in Valentina's apartment.

I prayed Erik wouldn't laugh at me when I voiced my thoughts, then reminded myself I didn't care what he thought of me. "Tell me if I'm crazy, but did Valentina…" *Make it rain?* I couldn't get the words out, knowing how insane they would sound.

"Control the weather?" Erik offered, and I rounded on him, unable to believe I was actually right.

"Did she?" I gasped.

He nodded, a beautiful smile spreading across his face that was so at odds with the evil that lurked within him. "I'm impressed, rebel. You're sharper than I thought."

"How is that possible?" I demanded.

"I told you we have a way of keeping the sun from shining here," Erik said simply.

"But...magic?" I whispered, feeling foolish. But that was surely what it was. Dad's stories had been filled with all kinds of strange beings like witches and mages. He'd said it wasn't real, but this suggested otherwise.

"I suppose you could call it that," Erik mused. "It's a gift from the gods. Valentina was once a very different kind of being to the vampires. Since I sired her, she has kept many of her ancient powers."

"What was she...before?" I asked, my pulse thrashing in my ears.

His answer was another riddle for me to dwell on, and it struck a strange kind of feeling in the pit of my stomach that felt like a warning.

"Our enemy. A slayer of the Clan of Storms."

## CALLIE

### CHAPTER NINETEEN

I gripped Fury firmly and willed my hands to stop shaking. I hadn't realised quite how tightly my own bravery had been tied to Magnar's presence until he'd left me perched in this fucking tree.

Smoke spiralled to the south, letting me know that he'd succeeded in lighting the fire. Hopefully the vampires tracking us had spotted it too, though that only meant they were headed my way.

I bit my lip as I scanned the horizon for any sign of Magnar. He'd said if he had enough time, he'd make it back to me before they arrived. If not, I was on my own. In hindsight, I had no idea why I'd agreed to this plan at all. It was insanity, pure madness, and I was almost certain that it was going to end up with me dead, or worse.

My heart beat an unsteady rhythm against my ribs. I still couldn't see him.

Fury grew warmer in my palm, and my mouth went dry. He'd assured me the vampires wouldn't look for me in the branches at the top of a pine tree. They'd be too distracted by the fire to waste time hunting the foliage above them. But what if they did? What if they figured out what we were doing and they found me here without him, caught in the branches like a rabbit in a trap.

*Up, up!* Fury whispered in my mind, and I frowned in confusion as the urge to look skyward gripped me.

I squinted into the branches above my head, trying to spot anything amongst them, wondering what the blade had sensed.

It took me a moment to pick out the large, brown rat hidden within the thick boughs. It tilted its head at me in a gesture that looked anything but natural and I gasped in horror, lurching towards it, swiping my blade.

The rat let out a high-pitched squeak and leapt to another branch as I swung my weapon again, adrenaline tearing through me as the familiar raced to evade my attacks.

Fury ached to end the creature, screaming for death in my mind, but my awkward position in the tree made it impossible to get close enough to it. The rat scurried along the branches, dodging every attempt I made to slice it open before finally making it past me and leaping to the ground.

Indecision paralysed me as the rodent scurried out of sight into the long grass at the base of the tree. I knew I wouldn't be able to catch it and whatever vampire it was linked to now knew exactly where I was.

*Where the fuck are you, Magnar?*

If I stayed here, then it was only a matter of time before they found me. And I'd be trapped at their mercy, unable to so much as attempt to run.

My stomach knotted as I made my decision, sheathing Fury and starting my awkward climb out of the tree. I scrambled down as fast as I could, skinning my palms on the rough bark and cursing as I went.

I rolled as I hit the ground and quickly regained my feet, searching the surrounding area for the vampires who hunted me.

There was no sign of anything beneath the trees but as I grabbed Fury again, the heat from its hilt practically burned me. They were close. Too fucking close. The blade hummed with the promise of bloodshed, and I kept hold of it as I started running.

Magnar had said that if the vampires were too close for him to re-join me before their arrival, he would take up position downwind from the fire. The smoke blew steadily to the left so I headed after it as fast as my legs could carry me, knowing my only hope was to reach him, to make it to his side before the vampires made it to me.

I was tempted to shout for him, but I couldn't be sure of who would hear me first. I willed Fury to let me know which way they were coming from, but it gave me nothing. It was as if it was telling me that they were approaching from every direction at once.

I stumbled to a halt as I realised what that meant. The blade wasn't refusing to help me, it was telling me exactly what I'd asked. I was surrounded.

*Fuck.*

Silence pressed in on me from every side, making goosebumps rise along my arms, the long grass swaying in the breeze, rustling like a thousand mocking voices.

I looked around cautiously, holding the blade up, ready to fight no matter how hopeless that seemed. My skin prickled uneasily. Now that I was paying attention, the utter silence was more than enough to warn me that there were far more vampires coming than we'd thought. Instead of laying a trap for them, it seemed that we'd fallen into one ourselves.

I cursed my luck as the silence stretched on. I'd been stupid to believe that we could ever outsmart them. Of course they'd thrown everything at us this time. We'd killed five vampires two days ago. I doubted any human had managed such a thing in the last twenty-one years. They were hardly going to risk sending a small group a second time. This time they'd make sure they caught me, drag me to the blood bank, and drain me alongside my family.

My limbs began to tremble at the thought, and I forced myself to think the way Magnar had taught me. I had the blood of a warrior, so I would stand and face them like one.

I gritted my teeth and held Fury in front of me, daring the first of them to come while hoping Magnar would appear before they got to me.

As the silence dragged and the tension bit at me, I raised my chin higher and glared out at the swaying grass around me.

"What are you waiting for?" I called when I couldn't take it anymore. "Surely you're not afraid of one human girl?"

Fury pulsed with excitement as the first vampire finally rose from the long grass. She was taller than any woman I'd ever seen, and her straight, black hair fell like a sheet of ink to her waist. She walked towards me, taking me in through narrowed eyes, her passage silent despite the long grass she passed through.

I could tell at once that she was an Elite. Even if it hadn't been for her fine clothes, there was something about the way she held herself that screamed power. Her face was so devastatingly beautiful that it was almost hard to look at. Her skin seemed to glow, and her lips were the deepest blood red. The colour made me wonder about the last time she'd fed, and I forced myself to swallow the lump in my throat.

"Are you all alone out here, sweet girl?" she asked, her voice nearly as alluring as her face. Their perfection repulsed me. All of that evil wrapped up in a beautiful lie.

"Alone? I'm here with you, aren't I?" I glowered at her as she stopped a few feet from me, her gaze zeroing in on the golden blade in my hand, and I smirked at her knowingly.

"Vampire killer," she hissed, her eyes still locked on the weapon.

*Yes,* Fury replied deep within my bones. It longed to meet her properly, and I could feel her death winding its way through the blade's hungriest desires.

"I'm so sorry, were some of those dead bloodsuckers your friends?" I wasn't entirely sure why I was taunting this vampire, but something about Fury's excited energy was rubbing off on me and bravado beat terror any day of the week.

"You expect me to believe *you* killed them?" she sneered, her demeanour slipping as the monster inside her rattled its cage, wishing to be let loose.

"You already believe it. Otherwise you'd come a little closer." I took a purposeful step towards her, and a thrill raced down my spine as she stepped back. It was intoxicating that power, a small taste of what I might claim if I were to truly become a slayer. To become the thing feared by those creatures who I'd spent my entire life fearing.

I wondered how long I could keep this up. How long it would take her to realise that I wasn't what I was playing at being. Perhaps, if I was lucky, I could buy Magnar enough time to reach me.

I took another step towards the vampire, an arrogant smile finding its way to my face as I taunted her. The vampire backed away again and I held Fury a little higher as I advanced, the blade's confidence, its hunger for death, making me wonder if I just might be able to follow through on the threat I was making without needing Magnar at all.

"Perhaps you did kill them," she admitted, looking uncertain though it wasn't fear in her eyes. More like calculation. "But we came prepared in case that were true." She stopped backing up and smiled at me mockingly as she raised her chin.

Vampires rose from the long grass surrounding me in a silent wave of motion and my heart lurched in terror. I did a quick count and made it twenty. *Twenty*. I wasn't just outnumbered, I was totally fucked.

I tried not to let my panic show on my face, keeping up the guise of false confidence.

*They won't kill me. My blood is worth more than my life.* Somehow that didn't make it any better.

I planted my feet squarely and waited for them to attack, Fury pushing memories into my mind of its owners surviving such odds. But those men and women had been warriors, Viking born and trained from birth for violence. I was a girl who had been raised in a void, relying on little more than instinct and luck to survive this far.

My heart fluttered like a bird in a cage while Fury hummed with excitement. That made one of us. But as blades couldn't exactly die, I guessed it had no place for fear. I would just become another memory to it if I died. A master who lost their life in war instead of claiming the lives of my enemies.

The Elite waved a hand and the lesser vampires all rushed forward at once, their arms outstretched, none of them so much as drawing their weapons. They were going to overwhelm me with sheer numbers, not even allowing me the chance to fight.

I wanted to stand and defend myself but I didn't even know which way to turn. I spun wildly, picking a male with a tight-fitting shirt and slashing Fury at him in a vain hope of staving him off. I sliced Fury through the air in a threat, forcing several of them to recoil from the gleaming golden blade.

I twisted on my heel, slashing furiously as Fury warned me to turn, the vampire there shrieking as the blade cut deep into her side, bright red blood splattering the grass while more of them dodged away from the weapon.

I bared my teeth at them as I advanced, allowing Fury to guide me, letting it tug and push at my instincts while I struck again, my arm snapping out like the strike of a viper, the blade stabbing a vampire in the bicep as he lunged for me.

The vampires recoiled and spat curses at me, eyeing me cautiously while I damn near growled at them in reply.

There was a beat of utter stillness where we assessed one another, a single moment where they wondered if I truly had killed those five vampires, a single second where it seemed like I had a chance of escaping this fate.

A hand landed on my shoulder and I whipped around, holding the blade just like the memories directed, my grip loose, my movements fluid. Screams followed the passage of my blade, but more hands grasped at me, gripping my clothes in tight fingers, tugging at my hair, nails biting into my flesh.

I bellowed curses at them as I spun between the press of bodies, ducking low, fighting to free myself from the inevitability of their attack.

I curled my free arm over my head as more hands than I could count grabbed any part of my body they could reach, cursing and spitting as I slashed at them with Fury over and over.

They crushed in on me, pressing me down, hot blood splashing over my cheek, but somehow my right arm found the smallest amount of space to move between the press of bodies. I let Fury guide my hand as I thrust it skyward with a defiant roar.

A scream rang out and several of the vampires recoiled in horror as dust fell in a torrent down my arm, clogging the air all around me as Fury sang in triumph, tasting the death it had been hungering for.

I tried to get to my feet once more, swinging towards another of them, but the Elite barked a command and they all lunged at once.

My momentary victory was short lived as the vampires hissed and spat curses at me, their iron sharp nails biting into my skin in countless places, each of them tugging me in different directions.

Impossibly strong fingers closed on my wrist as I continued to fight with Fury, twisting violently and forcing me to release my weapon.

As Fury fell from my grasp, the heat of its bloodthirsty hilt abandoned me, and despite my continued attempts to fight, I was utterly overwhelmed. Fear washed through me as I was thrown down onto my back in the grass, each of my limbs pinned in place by a different vampire, their fangs bared in my face, hisses of outrage surrounding me.

One of them slapped me hard enough to split open my lip, and I spat in her face, baring my teeth right back at them, letting them see the monster in me too.

"Enough," the Elite barked from somewhere beyond the swarm of bodies who were grinding me into the dirt.

The four of them who were pinning my limbs down tightened their holds so painfully that I had to bite down on a scream, my bones howling in agony as they threatened to snap.

I blew out a harsh breath, forcing a swathe of golden blonde hair to flutter away from my face, allowing me to glare at the Elite as she approached.

The world fell still, calm, silent once more, nothing but my heaving breaths and barely restrained curses tainting the cool air sweeping around us.

My chest rose and fell rapidly as I glared up at the impossibly beautiful monster between strands of golden hair. Had there ever been a clearer representation of the world we now lived in? The vampire sneering as she stood over the helpless human, watching as I was shoved down into the dirt, claiming whatever power she wanted and forcing me beneath her.

I hated them.

Every single one of them was nothing but a cold, callous beast. They'd lain in wait until the Final War, knowing they were outnumbered and out-gunned before that. They took their time, hiding in the shadows like cowards, presumably preying on the weakest of our kind, those they could get away with harming, and only sprung their trap when humanity had been foolish enough to put itself on its knees.

On all I was, I swore I'd never stop fighting. Even if I'd already made my last stand here in this field, I would fight them from the confines of my own heart while strapped to a bed in the blood bank, drained of blood for their consumption. I would pray for my blood to sour and spoil, to taste of ash and rot in their mouths, to poison any who drank it. And if by any miracle I ever found myself free again, I would dedicate all there was of me to see them destroyed. One day it would happen. Revolution would stir in the Realms and humanity would rise up against their oppression. I only hoped to be there when they fell.

The Elite stooped to retrieve Fury from the ground, but she cursed and released it again just as quickly. Smoke rose from her hand, the stink of burning flesh filling the air, and I noticed an imprint of Fury's runes burned into the skin of her palm with a surge of satisfaction. Her kind couldn't wield the weapons of the slayers.

I bared my teeth at her in a feral grin, blood from my split lip staining my blunt teeth as I taunted her with all I was and all she wasn't. When it came down to it, her kind needed mine for their survival. Without our blood they had nothing. We didn't need them for anything.

"Show me her right arm," the Elite snapped and the vampire holding that limb yanked my coat sleeve back to reveal my slayer's mark. The brand seemed even clearer in the dim light of the day, like it was taunting her with its existence, baiting her into action.

The Elite hissed as she glared at it.

"Slayer," she growled, making the word a curse which I claimed for my own.

My heart pounded faster as doubt crept in, a little voice hissing venom in my ear. The vampires would never waste *human* blood by killing me. But would they feel the same about a slayer? What if their laws told them to kill slayers on sight?

I swallowed down the rising terror, the pain in my limbs making it hard to concentrate as I kept my eyes on the vampire who still stood over me, the one who now controlled my fate.

There was no sound of a warrior approaching. No sign at all that Magnar might be coming for me, that he might attempt a rescue. He'd let them take my family, after all. Perhaps he'd do the same with me. Whatever plans he might have had for me, whatever thoughts may have crossed his mind when my mark was awoken, I doubted he would trade his own life for it. And these odds were far worse than any I'd seen him face until now. I wouldn't blame him for abandoning me, but the fear of him doing so was enough to fill me with dread.

The Elite leaned down to inspect me, her ebony hair hanging an inch from my face as her cold eyes roamed over me from the blood staining my mouth to the defiant hatred blazing in my green eyes.

"The Belvederes will be *very* happy to see you, vampire killer," she hissed and the glimmer in her gaze sent a dagger of fear slicing through my chest. "How long it has been since they had a slayer to toy with."

She pulled what looked like a rectangle of plastic from a pocket within her cloak and pressed a button on it, lighting up a screen. I stared at it in confusion as she hit some more buttons then pressed it to her ear.

"General Wolfe?" she said, and my heart froze solid in my chest as I realised what she held was a cell phone. The vampire on the other end of that conversation was the monster who had ripped my family apart. If she took me to him...

"It's Eve. I-" the Elite pulled the cell phone from her ear and glared at it. "Curse the gods and all they own," she spat. "The signal has gone again. I *hate* the west coast." She expelled a heavy breath through her nose, glaring up at the sky before finding her composure once more. "Let's load her up and head back, I'll inform the general of our success when the gods deign to return the cell service."

Very little of what she'd just said made any kind of sense to me, but it was clear that her call had somehow failed.

The Elite stormed away from me, and I let out a shaky breath. Wolfe still didn't know she had me. I was safe from his sadistic clutches for a little longer, though I doubted it would make much difference in the end.

The vampires who had been pinning me in place heaved me up onto my feet and started dragging me back up the hill with intention. I fought them every step of the way, cursing them and wishing as many artistically planned deaths upon them as I could come up with but they didn't so much as snap at me in reply. They'd already won. We all knew it.

I searched the space around us wildly, desperately hoping to see any hint of Magnar coming to rescue me. But there was no sign of him. There was no sign of anything at all beyond the long grass and distant trees.

I'd known he would betray me in the end. I'd known a time was coming when his survival hinged on him using me. Perhaps that was all this plan had ever been. A way to rid himself of the monsters who had been stalking us by letting them capture me. I'd seen the betrayal coming from the moment we'd met. I just hadn't realised that it would hurt this badly when he did.

# MONTANA

## CHAPTER TWENTY

The carriage ride was painfully silent as we drove back through the city. Daylight was draining from the sky and the concrete world looked bleaker than ever beyond the window.

Valentina's words crawled into my ears again. *"If you want some real advice about Erik, I'd suggest you don't trust a word he says."*

It wasn't like I'd trusted Erik before, but his word had been the only thing I'd had to hold onto. Trusting that he would protect my family was the reason I was playing along with this madness, but now my fears had resurfaced again. He was just saying whatever would make me the most compliant.

Erik had told me Valentina had once been their enemy, but despite trying to get more answers out of him, he'd been stubbornly silent on the matter since. Perhaps she really had been trying to help me.

The only thing I knew for sure was that I needed to get some assurance that Erik was going to keep up his end of our deal. Nothing else mattered but that. I just needed some time alone to figure out how to do that.

By the time we headed back into the royal grounds, I wondered if Erik had decided not to spend any more time with me after all. The day was drawing in and we'd already been together for hours, so maybe I'd be taken back to my room where I could pick through my thoughts and think clearer at last.

*A girl can dream.*

Soon, we exited the carriage outside the castle, and I gazed up at its imposing walls. Our silence continued as we walked toward the entrance, but before we got there, Prince Fabian stepped out of the door in a dark suit.

Erik tugged me against his hip so fast, I gasped in alarm, sensing the predator in him awakening.

"Evening, Erik," Fabian said curtly as we approached, pushing a hand over his long brown hair which was pulled into a low ponytail. His beauty was harsher than Erik's, his features harder, and I could almost see the brutish human he had been long before the vampire curse had claimed him. "How was your day of courting?"

"Better than yours apparently. Clocking off already?" Erik mocked.

Fabian blew out a breath, his dark eyes dropping onto me. "Has he been an asshole the whole time?"

"Yes, it's been non-stop," I said, a surprised smile hooking up the corner of my mouth.

Erik's fingers dug into my hip. "Well, you were running your hands all over me half an hour ago, so I can't have been all bad." He threw me a heated look that made my heart thump erratically, and I shrugged like it had been nothing. Which was true actually.

"Was she now?" Fabian drawled, throwing me a curious glance before returning his gaze to Erik. "So you're going to see the ritual through, are you? I have to say, I'm rather surprised you're finally accepting your duties."

"I suppose I was waiting for the right girl." Erik squeezed my arm, and I fought the urge to roll my eyes. The urge grew even stronger when he leaned down and placed a kiss on my temple, like he was oh-so-besotted with me.

*Overkill, much?*

I decided to get a little payback. "I guess it *was* rather cute when you realised your fly had been undone all through lunch," I said with a sweet smile.

My attempt to humiliate Erik made Fabian bark a laugh. Well, I was supposed to make him like me, so why miss an opportunity to throw Erik to the wolves at the same time?

Erik's hold grew painfully tight, but I didn't plan on heeding the warning he was giving.

"How embarrassing, I do hope someone snapped a picture for the Royal Times tomorrow." Fabian beamed, looking to me again, eyes glittering. "Perhaps we'll read through it together over breakfast in the morning?"

"I look forward to it." I gave him a flirtatious smile that wasn't too hard to summon now that Erik was the brunt of the joke.

Erik's grip on me was growing too uncomfortable to bear, and I looked up to bathe in his embarrassment, though ,unfortunately, he showed no visible signs of it.

"The night is still young, brother," Erik said. "Perhaps she won't want to spend the day with you after finishing the night with me."

I swallowed all my pride and bit my lip in the way I'd seen the vampire do at the bar, glancing up through my lashes at Fabian. "I highly doubt that."

Erik pressed his mouth to my ear and heat surged right down the length of my spine. I was divided on wanting to pull away and stand there forever absorbing that feeling, knowing I was under his influence, or at least convincing myself that I was.

"I know you're dying to kiss me again, rebel, so if you're a good girl I might let you," he said with open mocking in his voice.

I bit down on my tongue as he drew me away from Fabian, half-dragging me toward the castle.

"Laugh, dearest," Erik growled, and I forced out a wild giggle as he pulled me inside, letting it fly free a little too dramatically.

My smile fell flat as we stepped through the doors and Erik immediately released me, our fake interest in each other dissolving just like that.

This was a farce of epic proportions. Neither of us smiled as we headed upstairs, and Erik escorted me back to my room with that dark aura of his settling on my shoulders. At least I'd get a night to myself without having to breathe the same air as him. Or maybe he didn't breathe at all. Either way, I wanted out of his general space.

Erik opened the bedroom door for me, and I was more than a little annoyed when he followed me inside.

He released a heavy sigh, dropping down into the velvet chair, spreading himself out in it like the king of the world. "This isn't going to work if you hate me, rebel."

I perched on the edge of the bed, folding my arms. "Then why have you been working so hard all day to *make* me hate you, Erik?"

He slowly leaned forward in his seat, his expression becoming slightly less arrogant. "That was not my intention."

"Well, it must be your personality then," I sassed, seething all over again. How long was I going to have to live like this? Having to spend time with this asshole of a vampire who seemed to take joy in tormenting me.

Erik opened his mouth, looking ready to scold me, but I cut him off before he could.

"Oh, don't start on my tone again. I'm perfectly obedient in front of your little vampire friends. If you want me to hate you less when we're alone together, at least let me speak my mind."

His jaw ticked then eventually, he nodded. "Fine. But not in front of my family. I won't be disrespected. And I do suspect the game you played with Fabian just now worked rather well. So feel free to bad-mouth me to him all you like when you spend time together."

I shook my head, confused by him all over again. "Why, Erik? What is this all for? Why the hell do you want your brother to like me?"

"The why is not your concern," he said, shutting me down again.

"Maybe not, but it would put my mind at rest. Do you know how frustrating it is being stuck here and told absolutely nothing about anything?"

He surveyed me like I was a puzzle to be solved, and perhaps he wanted to solve it too. Leaning forward in his chair, he rested his elbows on his knees and clasped his hands together. "I think, perhaps, I've underestimated you."

My lips popped open, but he continued before I could get any ideas about taking that as a compliment.

"You're more inquisitive than I expected. And not nearly as fearful as I'd prefer," he said cuttingly.

"I knew you wanted me to be afraid of you," I said coldly, my heart rate ratcheting up.

"Only in the name of control," he muttered. "I don't take pleasure in seeing you flinch if that's what you're thinking."

"I don't know what to think," I breathed, feeling tired, so goddamn tired. "I don't trust you one bit. I've spent my life being corralled by your kind, belittled, and hurt when I spoke out against them. And now you're doing it too, only in a different way. And I can't stop fighting back, Erik, not until you show me some decency. Something that can assure me you'll keep your end of our bargain."

His eyes roamed over my face for a few eternal seconds, bringing heat to my cheeks. He always looked at me a little too long, like there was something that drew his gaze to my face, and it made me feel exposed.

"Fabian seeks to take control," he said at last, and I could hardly believe he was opening up to me. "For now, the four of us hold equal power over the New Empire. But that time is wearing thin. And Fabian has ideas that are...different to mine. Our purpose here as rulers was never to create a tyranny. It has gone too far down that road already. So I wish to undermine Fabian's plans, but I can't do that until I know what they are."

My heart thrashed in my chest as I worked out what he meant. "You want me to spy on him?"

"Yes," he confirmed. "A human is the most perfect spy I could hope for. No vampire would ever suspect you, Fabian included. We are all too caught up in our superiority to pay attention to what you might be capable of."

It was a twisted sort of praise that I wasn't sure was intended that way, though I was glad he was embracing the fact that humans weren't just a food source without a brain.

He went on before I could say anything. "Once I know what

Fabian's plans are, I will be able to strike out against him. I wish to unseat him from power. Miles and Clarice will easily bow to my will, but not Fabian. And when he is dealt with, I will take full control of the New Empire and focus on what is truly important to our kind."

"Which is?"

His adam's apple rose and fell as he considered whether to answer. "That is not relevant. I have been as candid as I can for now. And that will have to be enough."

My pulse drummed even faster, but I decided to let it go as an idea struck me. "If you take control, could you make any law you wanted? Even one that benefited humans?"

Erik snorted, shaking his head. "What are you suggesting? That I offer something to your species if you help me?"

I jutted up my chin, realising he might be able to help more people than just my family.

"Yes," I replied, and he started laughing.

"Rebel, you really are a piece of work," he commented when his mirth had subsided.

I folded my arms, not backing down. "You want my help, don't you? So offer me something worth helping you for."

"I've already agreed to free your father and pardon your sister when she is found," he said, his eyes flashing.

"Yes, but now I know your plan, so you have to do as I ask." A smile grew on my face as he gave me a confused look. Trust was a fickle thing, but blackmail? That wasn't so easily disregarded.

"Oh do I? And why is that?" he growled, danger coating the air.

"Because I'll tell Fabian what you've told me, and your plan will go to shit-"

"Then your father will never be freed," he cut across me sharply.

My gut writhed, but I had to play this hand as well as I could. "Or perhaps Fabian will be so grateful to me that *he'll* free him for me."

Erik pressed his tongue into his cheek, then rose to his feet abruptly, lifting a finger and pointing it in my face. "You are in dangerous territory, rebel. Do you have any idea what would happen to you if I declared you to my family as a spy?"

"And what would you tell them exactly? That I was going to reveal your plans to fuck over your brother? I imagine they'd keep me alive long enough to hear that nugget of truth at least."

"Unbelievable," Erik exclaimed, staring at me in dismay. "You're given food, fine clothes, a bed in my family's castle and you're threatening to betray me!"

His forceful tone sent fear daggering through my chest, but I didn't back down. "No, I'm trying to negotiate."

"You're trying to blackmail me," he retaliated. "A human goading a prince of the New Empire, it's fucking ridiculous." He started pacing before me, working himself up into a rage, his body primed like a vicious animal's.

"You're trying to make me do what you want and offer me as little as possible for it. I'm only asking to be heard. For humans to be given some semblance of decency," I said in anger.

"Decency? What *are* you talking about?" He glowered at me for several long seconds, then a decision flared in his ashen eyes. "Get changed. We're going out. Wear something warm." With that, he marched from the room and slammed the door.

My mouth parted as I gazed at the door, and my rage climbed and climbed, making me want to rip the whole room apart. How could he be so stubborn? Didn't he care that humans were being treated like dirt under his very nose?

*And probably by his command.*

I sighed, realising I was fighting a pointless war. Erik didn't care, that was the problem. I'd never get through to someone who could barely even acknowledge that I was a living, feeling being.

As I yanked off my dress and tugged on some jeans and a warm sweater, I spotted an object on the chair. With a gasp, I realised it was Erik's phone.

I darted toward it, snatching it up and pressing my thumb down on the screen. A bunch of numbers lit up and despite tapping several of them, I only caused the thing to vibrate angrily. Words lit up at the top of the device and I frowned in concentration as I read them.

*Passcode invalid.*

I was about to give up when it buzzed again, and a message flashed up that made my gut hollow out.

**Valentina:**
*I think you should cut her loose, like we discussed.*
*She's more trouble than she's worth. Find a new human to work with.*

Time seemed to slow as I reread the message, making sure I'd understood it right. Erik had discussed his plan with Valentina. So she knew this was all a pretence and I was just a pawn at the heart of their game, and not only that, but she was also trying to fuck me over.

I clenched the phone in my hand as fear trickled through me. What if Erik did as she said and got rid of me? I'd never save my dad if Erik sent me off to the nearest blood bank. And what if they caught Callie?

Without thinking, I threw the phone at the wall as hard as I could, and it bounced back, slamming onto the floor at my feet.

A jagged crack glared up at me from the now-blank screen, and my breathing slowed as I gazed at it. Erik might be angry, but at least this would stop him from reading that message. It wasn't a permanent solution, but it could buy me more time.

Picking it up, I placed it back in the velvet seat where I'd found it, chewing on my lower lip.

*Shit, what now?*

*Should I hide it?*

*Pretend I never saw it?*

Erik stepped back into the room, and I had no time to do anything about the cell phone. My jittery body immediately gave away that I was anxious, and Erik's eyes slid to the seat, his jaw hardened as he took in the damage I'd done.

I recomposed myself as he whipped the phone from the chair, turning to me and holding it out to show me the screen.

"What is this?" he snarled.

I cleared my throat, figuring it was best to keep up the dumb human act. "A phone?"

"Stop playing games. Tell me what *that* is." He pointed at the enormous crack, and I gave him an innocent shrug.

"A crack?"

"And how did it get there, rebel?"

I shrugged continuing with my act. He'd fucked with me all day, so I was going to fuck with him right back. "I'm not sure, your highness. Perhaps you sat on it with your royal ass."

His mouth twitched and I was almost certain he was about to smile. Instead, he pocketed the phone and gave me a sweeping glance. "Funny, I didn't realise my royal ass could be so destructive."

"Oh, I suspect royal asses can be quite destructive when they want to be. Arrogant too."

He laughed, and the sound wasn't cruel or mocking for once. It was rumbling and soft and sent a strange tremor through me that felt weirdly good. "Very funny, now put a coat on or you'll freeze out there."

"We wouldn't want that," I remarked, heading to the closet, hardly able to believe I'd gotten away with destroying his property. I fished out a faux fur-lined jacket and tugged it on. When I'd zipped it up, I moved to Erik's side, eyeing his less-imposing expression.

"Where are we going?" I asked.

"You'll see," he replied, taking my arm, and guiding me from the room, ever the cryptic asshole.

When we made it outside the castle and the milky moonlight flowed over us, I expected to find another carriage waiting, but this time a shiny black vehicle was parked on the road.

He opened the back door for me, and I slid across the smooth leather seats to make room for him. The driver politely welcomed Erik, then set off down the road, knowing exactly where we were going. Unlike me, who was once again entirely in the dark.

We drove for nearly an hour and Erik refused to tell me where we were headed, leaving me frustrated as usual. I was confused when we pulled onto the huge bridge that led out of the city and my heart stumbled with trepidation.

We soon passed through a ruined part of what I assumed was still New York, and I gazed out at the hulking shadows of broken buildings and decimated houses, spotting a raccoon digging through some of the rubble.

Lights called to us in the distance and my curiosity piqued as we closed in on a set of huge metal fences. A floodlight shone down on us, and I caught sight of a sign hanging beneath a wooden tower. Standing at the top of it was a vampire holding a large gun. I rarely saw weapons like that; the vampires usually carried blades, but I'd seen the odd pistol in my time, though this was something else. An enormous thing strapped to the vampire's body, aimed directly down at us.

Erik exited the car and was immediately greeted by an Elite in dark robes, his face startlingly beautiful. I couldn't hear their conversation, but a moment later a metal gate opened ahead of us, and Erik jumped back into the car.

"Where are we?" I whispered, the strange place making my senses tingle with fear.

"Realm A," Erik announced, and shock raced through me.

What the hell were we doing here?

"I had a more fun-filled evening planned, but since you insist on talking politics, I decided a change of plans was in order," he added.

"Why?" I gasped, not wanting to be paraded in front of the weak people of a Realm. To see their hollow faces and haunted eyes. They'd despise me for travelling with a vampire. I looked like a traitor all dressed in fine, warm clothes, while they were left to rot in this prison.

As we passed through the gate and headed onto a street as smooth as the one we'd left behind, I was hit with complete confusion. This wasn't like the Realm I knew. The houses were newly built with gleaming windows and stately porches.

Humans wandered along the sidewalk, talking, and laughing. Children were out playing in manicured gardens with toys. Actual toys. Wooden spinning tops and plastic balls. One even had a tiny car he seemed to be controlling with a remote.

"Erik..." I whispered. "What the fuck is this?"

"I just told you," he murmured and his hand slid onto mine,

encompassing it in his palm, and I was too shocked to care about pulling away. "I'm not going to hear another vague complaint from you about the humans' conditions. So I want you to point out what's so terrible about the way we run these places and I'll decide if it needs to be addressed."

I shook my head, unable to find the words to answer as we turned down another street and a beautiful old building came into view with a grand clock embedded in the wall. From my dad's stories, I wondered if this might be a town hall. As our car drew closer, a crowd of people poured out of the arching doorway dressed in warm clothes like the ones I was wearing.

Erik rolled down the window as we approached the group. and when they spotted him, some cried out while others covered their mouths in alarm.

"It's Prince Erik!" a woman called, and I hunted for the fear in her eyes that had always shone so brightly in mine whenever a powerful vampire had visited my Realm.

"Erik, we love you!" another shouted, and I stared at her like she'd gone insane.

"Good golly, is he going to get out?" a man muttered, backing up a little.

My world crumpled in on itself, and I rested a hand against my heart as Erik stepped out of the car, talking with the people like he wasn't a complete monster. Some of them held back and fear rippled in their eyes, but respect too.

Erik glanced over his shoulder when he noticed I hadn't followed, but I couldn't do anything except sit there, frozen in place as realisation pounded through me. This was a lie. I didn't know who had concocted it, but someone definitely had. This wasn't like my Realm, and from the gaunt look of the men and women who'd travelled to the royal castle with me, I didn't think it was like any of theirs either. It was a fucking sham. A sweet falsehood for the vampires to swallow so they didn't need to feel any discomfort about their treatment of us.

It all clicked together like puzzle pieces in my mind. Erik had insisted I was ungrateful about my conditions because he didn't know about them. He couldn't. This was the only truth he saw. That humans were kept in towns as lavish as their own. And despite the fences, these humans looked happy. Maybe I would have been happy too growing up somewhere like this. Maybe I wouldn't have fought back so hard. Maybe I would never have questioned the vampires' rule...

Erik ducked his head back into the car. "Are you getting out?"

I shook my head, unable to form the word no.

He frowned, then dropped back into his seat. "So? What exactly would you like me to improve?"

I ground my teeth together as the back of my throat burned with rage, unable to voice the truth. He'd never believe me anyway.

"I just want to go back to the castle," I said, turning away so I didn't have to look at him anymore.

The air crackled with tension. "Rebel, this is not something I offer on a daily basis."

I shook my head, too choked up to answer,

"What's wrong? What have I done now?" he snapped.

"This place is nothing like my Realm," I blurted, knowing I had to at least try to make him hear me.

"Then tell me what the problem is and I'll fix it. Do you want more green space, more enrichment zones?" he guessed.

"Enrichment zones?" I balked. "No, I don't want that, Erik, I want the people I love to live in a place where they feel safe, a place they have regular meals-"

"You can have as much food as you like," he scoffed. "Do you want a personal chef to bring each meal to you? Most of the humans here seem perfectly content to cook for themselves, but-"

"You're not listening to me," I snarled, anger tearing through me. "My Realm isn't like this one."

"Then what is it like?" he demanded, but he carried on, finishing the sentence for himself. "Would you like a swimming pool added to your house, a gold bath added to your bathroom, a wild meadow to frolic in-"

"Shut up," I barked, and his eyes darkened to pitch. "I know I'm just some insignificant human to you-"

"Yes, an insignificant human who has the ear of a prince," he said, his muscles tensing. "And one who is wearing down my patience when I had little to begin with, rebel."

"My name is Montana," I hissed.

"What difference does it make?" he said offhandedly, and I felt a cold chain tighten around my heart.

Reality was painted so brutally for me in that moment that there was no denying it. He didn't even see me as a person. He'd brought me here with the hopes that I might point out the odd flaw in their perfect design, then make some small effort to appease me so I'd continue to go along with his plans without making things difficult for him. It was just his way of trying to avoid me causing problems for him.

"None," I whispered in realisation. "It makes no difference at all."

A crease formed between his brows and for a moment I thought he might apologise, but when he spoke, his words were as sharp as always.

"Final chance. What do you want improved?" he pressed, but I shook my head, feeling the blood drain from my cheeks.

I blew out a breath, ducking my head so my hair swept forward and created a curtain between us. "Forget it. I just want to go back."

Silence followed my words, then Erik ordered the driver to turn around in a harsh tone. I wrung my hands together in my lap, feeling suffocated by what I'd learned.

I shifted my gaze to the window to avoid looking at Erik, the smiling faces of the humans here only causing more pain to rip through me. Tears pricked my eyes, but I attempted to hold them back, too many emotions rioting through my chest at once.

As we sailed toward the exit, I spotted a schoolhouse beside a large restaurant, and a sneer drew back my lips. This was why he thought I'd skipped meals to get so thin and why he questioned my ignorance about the world, it was all so fucking clear now.

"Most humans don't want to be free, rebel," Erik said as we headed out of the gate, like that was a fact of the world. "Any cause you think you're fighting for is an illusion. Your kind are safe, housed and given free food. All we require of you is blood donations. Is that really so bad?"

A tear slid from my eye, and I was glad of the darkness to hide it.

I let it drip into my lap, keeping my head turned away as I refused to answer him.

The situation for humans was worse than I ever could have imagined. Even the vampires themselves didn't know the extent of our pain. Something splintered inside me, and I longed to see my family more than anything in the world, to be around people who knew the truth, and who could share in the pain of this knowledge.

The possibility of trusting Erik crumbled to dust before my eyes. He didn't know the truth and he never would. To him, I was just some ungrateful human from a town like Realm A.

Even if he did help me, he'd send Dad and Callie back to our Realm, thinking that was the safest place for them, and they'd be stuck in misery for the rest of their days.

"I'm starting to think picking you was a bad idea," Erik growled, and his sharp tone drove daggers into my heart.

Fear sped through my veins, and I was suddenly certain that when Erik spoke to Valentina, he was going to cut me loose. She'd convince him to get rid of me in favour of someone more compliant, and he'd send me to a blood bank as swiftly as he could.

I couldn't take that risk, so I made a terrifying decision that was really the only one left to me. And it galvanised my pain, turning it into strength.

I had to escape.

Tonight.

# CALLIE

## CHAPTER TWENTY ONE

The carriage swayed rhythmically beneath me as the vampires drove it north. Away from the blood bank. Away from my family. Away from Magnar. I couldn't work out what that meant. Were they taking me to General Wolfe? Or back to the Realm to make an example of me in front of everyone? Was the Elite vampire, Eve, really planning on taking me to the Belvederes like she'd threatened? Magnar's description of the four original vampires was more than enough to let me know that I never wanted to be in the presence of a single one of them, let alone all four.

The terrifying possibilities were endless, and each time I convinced myself to dismiss one of them, another awful prospect filled its place. Whatever they wanted me for, it couldn't be good. You didn't shackle someone and lock them in a cage unless you were planning on doing something unspeakable to them. I wasn't even a true slayer, just a girl with a brand on her arm, marking out a fate she'd never had time to consider living.

The pressing dark of the night was broken up by silver moonlight that gilded the ground in an ethereal glow.

In the Realm, we'd always been home before the moon rose, afraid of being found by a vampire in the darkness. It was like the sun helped the vampires to remember their humanity, at least enough to leave us be. But after dark, all bets were off.

People who went outside couldn't be sure to come back again. We never found out what happened to them. Perhaps they were simply taken to the blood bank but in my gut, I'd always feared it was something far worse. I guessed the creatures of the night were at their most dangerous in the dark and being surrounded by them now left me feeling more than a little afraid.

Despite the close proximity of the vampires, I couldn't help but stare at the beauty of the lunar being. It felt so alien, so separate from everything we did beneath it and yet it watched over us all the same. The moon had seen everything the world had endured, rising each night to inspect each minute change. I guessed the moon was one of a very few things which hadn't changed for Magnar while he slept.

Thinking of the slayer caused an ache to form in my chest. It had been hours since he'd left me to wait in that tree. Had he known I'd be caught? Had he finally shown his hand and used me the way I'd been waiting for him to since the moment he'd pinned me to that wall?

I'd expected the betrayal, been waiting for the knife in my back from the moment we'd met, knowing my usefulness to him could only go so far. But some stupid part of me had begun to question that belief after the slayers' mark had appeared on my arm. Some foolish hope had gathered despite me swearing never to allow such a thing to happen. And now I was left choking on the pain of the wound I should have been waiting for, abandoned and alone, the trap swung shut around me, my life held in the claws of my enemies.

I'd expected it.

But fool that I was, I'd still let myself care. Somewhere along the way here I'd begun to think that I might have meant something to him. Something more than just…it didn't even matter. I had no idea why I was even dwelling on something so fucking stupid. I was nothing to him and he was nothing to me. The only thing that had betrayed me was myself when I allowed myself to think we were united out of anything beyond convenience.

I didn't want to doubt the fragile bond I'd thought I'd felt between us when he discovered my heritage, but it was hard not to while I shivered in the dark. I'd never felt so alone in all my life. And if he really had abandoned me then my fate was already sealed. No one else was coming.

Montana and Dad were already in the hands of the vampires. And no other soul in this world gave a damn about me. That had always been the way I preferred it. My family were the only people who mattered to me so there was no one else for me to lose. So long as I had them, I had everything. Or so I'd tried to convince myself.

But now I was wholly alone, knowing that no one in the Realm even cared where I was, I wondered if that had been the right way to live. Maybe isolating myself hadn't protected me from anything. It only made sure that I hadn't really lived at all. And if it turned out that I was going to die or live out the rest of my days in the blood bank, it meant the small measure of freedom I'd experienced in my life had been wasted.

If by some miracle I ever made it out of this mess, then maybe it was time I started looking at things differently. The vampires had us so terrified of losing each other that we didn't dare to care about one another the way that we should anymore. It was just another weapon they used to control us. But I refused to keep living in the shadow of that fear. From now on, all of my choices would be my own. I'd make them for myself. And not out of fear.

I groaned at the many small hurts and bruises the vampires had inflicted when they'd searched me and tossed me into this cage. I wasn't sure how kicking me in the ribs was meant to help them check that I didn't have any more weapons on me, but I guessed they thought I'd earned the treatment when I'd killed their friend. Not that I regretted the world having one less bloodsucker in it.

They'd hissed threats at me, whispering of what might happen to me if they all lost themselves to bloodlust, promising the stars my screams if I only gave them the excuse they needed to claim them. But that wasn't what I was afraid of. My own death paled to insignificance in the face of what it meant. I was my family's only hope. Without me, they were doomed just as surely as I was. And suffering the loss of them was a far worse torture than any physical pain these bloodsuckers might inflict on me.

The wooden box which contained me was bolted to the back of a big horse-drawn carriage and wasn't tall enough for me to stand up in. I was perched awkwardly on a hard bench which ran along the left-hand side of it. They'd taken my coat and boots, leaving me to shiver in the freezing winter air which billowed in between the bars of the single window on the rear door. I hunkered in the back corner, wishing I could wrap my arms around myself to stay warm, but the heavy chains they'd used to secure my wrists prevented that.

The muted clip-clop of the two shire horses' hooves was the only sound aside from the creaking of the wooden carriage. I wondered why none of the vampires spoke to each other, or if they were all still accompanying me at all.

For all I knew, half of them could have taken off now that they'd caught me. It wasn't like the slow pace set by the horses would have been their preferred speed of travel.

I could only see four of the vampires walking at a distance behind the carriage. Their eyes were alert, and their swords were in hand as they forged paths through the long grass which reached as high as their waists.

I could taste blood, and my tongue was swollen from one of the blows I'd received at the hands of my captors. The iron tang of it made me think of the blood bank and a sliver of fear ran through me as I wondered what my family might be enduring there. There had been hundreds of rumours about that place, but no one ever came back from it to confirm or deny them.

Some people said they would string you up upside down and slit your throat above a huge vat designed to collect every drop of blood. Others said they used the humans there for sport, forcing them to fight each other and taking blood from the losers.

I'd also heard tales that the vampires there fed from humans directly, biting them to gain access to their blood. The idea of that terrified me. I'd heard the way my father had screamed when General Wolfe and his lackeys had bitten him. He was a strong man, never one to complain of pain or overreact, and the horror I'd heard in his screams told me all I needed to know about the agony it had inflicted.

There were stories involving every imaginable form of torture and we'd all heard the screams carrying on the wind from time to time. I wasn't sure what to believe, but I knew nothing that happened in that place of horrors could be good.

I scoured the open fields beyond my moving cage with fading hope. Had Magnar really abandoned me? I was beginning to believe he'd left me to my fate despite his promises. It wasn't like he owed me anything anyway. Why risk his own neck for some girl he'd just met? Even if there *was* a chance that I might become a slayer like him.

"This is ridiculous," muttered the Elite vampire, Eve, her lilting voice easy to recognise even through the wood that separated us. "I'm going to send a message to Wolfe just as soon as I get a signal, demanding they supply us with off-road vehicles and motorcycles. I mean, a horse drawn carriage? It's archaic. It's insulting."

"Yes, my lady," a male vampire replied. "It would certainly make our work easier if we were given more modern vehicles. But as there are so few on the west coast-"

There was a sound like a slap and the male vampire stopped talking.

"I was voicing a complaint, not asking the opinion of a *lesser* like you," Eve spat.

"Apologies," he simpered, and their conversation came to an end.

The vampire guards continued to prowl behind the carriage, spread far enough apart to create a wide, impenetrable perimeter around me.

I watched them silently as they struggled to force a path between the grasses which were getting longer the further we travelled. The swaying brown and green stalks were so tall they brushed against their chests in places.

As I studied their near flawless features, it was strange to think they were just lesser vampires. Though they were unnaturally attractive, they still held imperfections. Though minor, the imperfections allowed me to see the humans they'd once been beneath the visage.

The Elite on the other hand were nothing short of perfection.

Looking at Eve had been like seeing a statue given life. Something that perfect couldn't be natural. Her features were symmetrical in a way that defied nature. Comparing the lesser vampires to an Elite was like comparing the sun to the stars: though they were the same, one shone a lot brighter.

If what Magnar had told me was right, then the Elite were those who had been turned into vampires by one of the Belvederes directly. That also meant that the vampires who called themselves royalty must have been even more stunning than the Elite. Such a thing didn't even seem possible to me.

I alternated my gaze between the four rear guards, a kind of morbid fascination gripping me as I studied the unnatural way they moved. There was something almost feline about their gait as they prowled along, balancing the weight of their weapons in a loose but ready grip.

Their long cloaks kept catching in the grass and I couldn't help but feel a tug of amusement as they struggled with their impractical clothing. *Serves you right for swaggering about like a bunch of pompous assholes.*

A male with a scarlet cloak stopped and yanked the thing off of his shoulders in frustration as it got caught again. I watched as he cursed the long material and wrapped it into a ball which he wedged beneath his arm.

He looked up and caught me staring, the venom in his gaze making me look away again as I snorted to myself. Not so ethereal and unshakable after all. They had all been human once, I supposed. It only stood to reason that their human vanities, insecurities and pettiness stayed with them when they changed. Though it would seem their egos had done nothing but inflate with the transformation.

I looked for the vampire who had been walking to the right of my view, but blinked as I found he wasn't there anymore. I frowned, scouring the field for him but there was nothing to see. I wondered if he'd dropped further back, the darkness of the night swallowing him from my sight, but in all the hours we'd travelled this forgotten road, not one of them had abandoned their position.

My gaze travelled back to the male with the red cloak a beat before he was yanked out of sight beneath the grass. I sucked in a sharp breath, sitting up straight and leaning forward to see what was happening. There was a flash of movement as a golden sword swung above the grass, but it was gone again just as quickly.

*Magnar.*

My breath caught in my throat, my skin prickling with awareness as that small hint of the slayer had my entire body frozen with shock. He'd come back for me. Despite the insanity involved in doing so, he'd come for me when I needed him. He hadn't used me as a distraction, he hadn't abandoned me when I needed him. He was here. So close that I could almost feel the enormity of his presence surrounding me, the reality of his arrival overwhelming me to the point of utter shock.

In all my life, I had never been able to rely on a single person in this world to come for me when I needed them aside from my family. I'd never dared trust another human or even thought to attempt it. Yet he was here. He'd come for me after knowing me for such a short span of time. He'd come.

My heart leapt in excitement, and I shifted forward eagerly, watching the swathes of long grass for any sign of him moving among it.

The two remaining vampires who walked behind the carriage hadn't looked back yet and their fallen comrades had gone unnoticed.

I bit my lip as my heart pounded excitedly and the third vampire suddenly dissolved into dust which scattered away on a soft breeze as her clothes crumpled into the long grass out of sight.

The final vampire paused, his head beginning to turn as he noticed something was wrong.

"Hey!" I shouted loudly, drawing his attention back to me before he could look. "Can I get some water? A girl could die of thirst in here!"

I shifted across the hard bench, pressing my face against the iron bars that lined the window, the chill of them seeping into my bones.

A loud banging sounded on the roof of my cage, making me flinch, uncertain where the vampire was or whether they might aim to strike me with that fist next.

"Silence! Or a dry throat will be the least of your problems," a male vampire yelled from above me. "I might find myself parched as well."

I cringed at the implication but when I looked back out between the bars, the final vampire was gone. A satisfied smirk pulled at my lips.

*Your death is coming, motherfuckers.*

The breeze picked up, sending a wave of motion rustling through the grass surrounding us. One of the horses snorted uncertainly like it could tell something was about to happen, and I hoped it was right.

I held my breath as I peered out between the bars, my chains rattling against the movement as I pressed my face to them to see better.

The jostling of the carriage came to a sudden halt, and I was thrown into the door, my shackles slamming loudly against the bars as I tried to catch myself.

"Where are the rear guard?" the Elite snapped, her fierce tone trying to mask an edge of concern.

"I saw them a moment ago," another vampire replied. "They can't-" His voice cut off suddenly and something metal clattered onto the roof above my head, a spray of bright red blood splattering across my cheek.

The Elite shrieked in anger as the other vampires all started yelling commands, chaos breaking out all around me.

The ring of clashing blades sounded violently ahead of me, and I pressed my face to the bars again, hoping to catch sight of what was happening at the front of the carriage.

The vampires cursed and spat as they struggled to respond to the attack, and I heard Magnar's deep voice raised in a challenging growl, the sound of it sending a ripple of energy right down to my core.

"Turn this thing around and get us the hell out of here!" Eve shouted.

Someone whipped the horses into motion and the carriage wheeled about, sending me crashing back down onto the bench, making my gut lurch in alarm. My head slammed into the wooden wall, and I swore as pain lanced through my skull, disorientating me for a second.

The carriage tilted precariously as the horses dragged it around and I felt the wheels lift off of the ground on the left-hand side.

My pulse thundered in my ears as I grabbed one of the bars on the window, gripping it tightly to keep myself upright. With my wrists bound together by the chains, I wouldn't be able to save myself in a fall, and with the speed the carriage was travelling, I knew I'd be tossed around in the back of it mercilessly if let go.

The carriage righted itself with a heavy thump as the wheels made it back to the ground and I almost lost my grip as I held on for dear life. We began racing back the way we'd come, allowing me a view of the battle taking place behind us.

Magnar stood between eight vampires, wielding both of his long blades like a warrior from the legends my father had told me. He danced between them, severing limbs and deflecting blows as if they were nothing, a bellow of challenge parting his lips as he fell into the heat of the battle.

Moonlight glinted off his swords, glittering faintly in the darkness, blood spraying from their sharp edges as he cut through his enemies with brutal power. Fear gripped me as the monsters surrounded him, but he met every blow they tried to land with a slash of his own weapons. It was as though he could see each strike coming before it did. His skill was astonishing, and my lips parted in awe as I watched him.

My heart froze in my chest as a vampire leapt at his exposed back, sword raised for the kill, but Magnar twisted aside at the last moment. His half-braided hair flying around his face as he thrust his blade upward and pierced the vampire's heart, sending him scattering into dust.

Two more vampires raced forward on either side of him, trying to use the coordinated attack to take him down. Magnar parried both blades at once, swinging his swords between the two of them before leaping forward, causing them to stumble into the space he'd just been occupying.

He launched Tempest at them, the huge sword twisting end over end before cutting through the neck of one and embedding itself in the other's chest. Though both of them collapsed into the long grass, neither body disintegrated so he mustn't have struck their hearts.

Left with his father's sword in his grasp, he shifted his grip to wield it with two hands, swinging it with such ferocity that the five remaining vampires fell back rather than tackle the blows. One wasn't fast enough though, and Magnar cut through her chest in a single, savage sweep of his blade, sending her spiralling into dust before he'd completed the movement.

At the sight of her death, a male vampire shrieked in undeniable distress, throwing himself at Magnar with his teeth bared and sword forgotten. The slayer met his rage with a sharp thrust of his sword, sending him racing into death after his mate.

The carriage hit a rock, making it bounce wildly and I lost my grip on the bars. I fell back, slamming onto the wooden floor hard enough to knock the breath from my lungs, pain ricocheting through my body.

The chains restraining my wrists made it difficult to regain my balance as the vehicle careered over the uneven ground, but I rolled over, jamming my foot against one wall and pressing my back to the other to stop myself from crashing into it.

The driver whipped the horses mercilessly, and they whinnied in pain and protest as they galloped on.

I finally made it to my hands and knees and managed to claw my way back up to grab the bars covering the window again, peering out into the darkness as I hunted for any sign of Magnar.

We crested a hill, and the length of the grass made it impossible to see what was happening between Magnar and the remaining three vampires, though the sound of their battle carried to me on the wind.

The carriage thundered on, and I clung harder to the freezing metal bars, straining my eyes in a vain effort to spot the slayer.

I bit my lip as I waited, my heart pounding anxiously for any sign that he was alive.

The horses snorted with fatigue and the carriage began to slow despite the continued snap of the whip.

"Faster!" Eve barked.

"They aren't built for speed," a male voice replied defensively. "The carriage is too heavy: if we keep at them like this they might collapse."

The horses grunted and snorted in further protest as if backing up his point and the carriage slowed a little more.

The Elite cursed them, but it made no difference to our speed.

I gripped the bars as desperation made my heartbeat thunder in my ears.

*Where are you Magnar?*

The seconds dragged and my eyes prickled with unexpected tears as a thick sob broke free of my throat.

He wasn't coming. And if he wasn't coming, then that could only mean one thing.

Pain blossomed through my chest and my grip on the bars turned brittle. I'd been a fool to let myself trust in hope and now it had come back to spite me, carving into me the way I'd known it would if I was ever dumb enough to let myself feel it.

I was still a captive in the arms of my enemy. And Magnar wasn't coming to rescue me at all; he'd simply found his end by attempting it.

# MONTANA

## CHAPTER TWENTY TWO

When Erik left me in my room, I started packing a bag I found in the closet with warm clothes. I didn't have any food, but I could go a few days without it. My stomach was hardened from years of rations, and once I was out of the city, I'd search the ruins for nourishment. Callie had found supplies that way, so I could too.

I drew strength from my sister, picturing her fierce eyes and determined expression, our bond spanning all the distance parting us and crying out for us to reunite.

*I'm coming Callie. I'll find you.*

The river I'd crossed over into New York was well-guarded, that much I remembered from my arrival. But I'd seen a glimpse of trees from the New Empire State building in the opposite direction, just a spark of hope and a faraway possibility. But that was where I'd head, believing as fiercely as I could that I'd find a path away from the vampires and back to my family.

The first step was going to be the hardest, but I'd had an idea on the way back here that I hoped I could pull off.

I took a high heel from the closet then strode to the window with intention, quietly working to slide the thin heel into the gap in the shutters.

The fluttering of my pulse danced in my ears, trying to warn me to stop, but my decision was made.

I wedged it firmly into place then applied pressure, pulling it sideways and levering the gap wider. The wood protested with a groan that made me stop, falling deathly still as I listened for any sound of approaching footsteps.

When none came, I continued to force the shutters wide and a soft snap sounded as the lock broke that was less dramatic than I'd expected. The shutters parted and with a soaring feeling in my chest, I tugged them wide to reveal the window. It was just a single pane with no handle, no means of opening it at all in fact. The breath fell from my lungs along with a curse.

I should have known that would be the case, but dammit, I'd hoped I was wrong.

Gazing down at the dark grounds, I spotted the stone steps leading toward the woodland, the moon hanging high in the sky, peering at me as if curious over what I might do next. No guards were in sight, but that didn't mean much. There were probably a handful of them crawling around the castle, but maybe I could sneak past them.

I headed to the door, turning the handle in vain hope, but finding it firmly locked. Refusing to give up, I dropped to my knees and gazed through the keyhole. It was blocked by the key, but at least it was close by, just sitting there waiting for someone to come claim it. And that someone was going to be me.

Hurrying to the dressing table, I took a thin makeup brush and a piece of paper from a notepad. I moved back to the door and pushed the page under the bottom of it into the corridor.

My breaths came quicker as I gently slid the handle of the brush into the keyhole. Slowly, I forced the key backwards, urging it to fall, yet waiting for the ping of it hitting the floor with trepidation.

"Just drop out nice and quietly," I whispered to the inanimate thing. "Be a good little key."

It hit the paper with a faint tap and a smile tugged at my lips.

I tugged the page back under the door, bringing the key with it and victory snared me in its grasp as I took hold of my prize then pressed my ear to the door, listening for sounds of movements. It was probably pointless considering the vampires were as silent as a deadly fart, but I had to try.

After several seconds, I stood, pulling the bag onto my back, and sliding the key into the lock. Achingly slowly, I twisted it until a soft click sounded, sending a quake through my chest as I waited for the repercussions to come. For Erik to appear with his inhuman speed and finally prove his point about being well capable of punishing me.

Hatred simmered in my gut at the thought of him, his unwavering cockiness, his patronising view of me, and his utter ignorance over the torment of my kind.

*Good riddance, asshole.*

I gritted my teeth, taking hold of the handle and easing it down until the door opened silently.

Pulling it wide, I glanced into the hallway to check it was clear, the lights off, but the moonlight through the windows lighting the way forward well enough.

Empty.

A shaky breath passed my lips as I crept into the corridor, moving silently across the floorboards in my socks. A pair of sturdy boots were ready and waiting in my pack, but I'd have to wait until I was outside to put them on.

I reached the staircase, moving down it at a steady pace and battling the instinct in me to run.

*Just keep moving.*

*One quiet step at a time.*

When I'd made it into the dark hall downstairs, I turned in the direction of the entranceway and quickened my pace a little. Voices caught my ear as I approached the exit, and I shrank quickly into the shadows of an alcove, holding my breath and cupping a hand over my mouth and nose to make sure no sound escaped me.

My stomach clenched tightly as I waited for them to pass, the voices growing louder by the second.

"Prince Erik has retired to his room," a male voice said.

"He won't mind if I go to him," Valentina's voice sounded in reply and I stiffened, pressing myself harder against the wall.

That bitch wanted me gone, and I had no doubt that she'd be voicing her little get-rid-of-the-troublesome-human plan the moment she found Erik, so I needed to get the fuck out of here right now.

"I'm sorry, my lady, but you'll have to wait until tomorrow."

Valentina tutted. "Nonsense." Her voice was nearer now, and I forced myself further into the corner as she swept past my hiding place with the guard in tow.

"Please, my lady, I have to ask that you respect the prince's wishes!" he cried, jogging after her and trying to catch her arm.

She quickened her pace, disappearing in the direction of the stairwell and I seized my advantage.

Stepping out of the darkness, I glanced into the entrance hall, finding it empty with the door wide open. The icy night air beckoned me, and I fled toward it, running across the courtyard, through the pavilion, then racing down the steps toward the trees. Impossibly, there were no more guards on watch here, no fanged wraiths descending on me in my bid for freedom. I was running away, my socks hitting the cool stone of the path at the base of the steps, then padding over soft grass as I sprinted for the trees.

I didn't breathe until I slipped between the boughs and darkness enveloped me, stealing me away from the light of the moon. I swung my bag over my shoulder, taking out my boots and slipping them on as fast as I could manage. When I stood upright once more, I listened hard for approaching footsteps, but only the sound of small animals reached my ears.

Taking a steady breath, I carved a fast path across the fallen leaves which cracked under my feet, loud enough to keep my heart rioting. No matter where I trod, it always seemed too loud, yet still no vampires came for me.

The light in the forest faded and I glanced up, peering at the sky through the canopy above and finding thick clouds had drawn across the moon, giving me the extra cover I needed to remain concealed. Perhaps fate was on my side tonight, and maybe that meant I'd keep getting lucky until I made it out of the city.

Every sound was heightened in my ears. Every snapping twig and rustle of leaves made me run faster.

Finally, I made it to the edge of the trees and the tall white wall glared at me a few feet away. It stretched above me nearly twenty feet, but there were gaps between the large white bricks in places I could use for handholds, though not any near the ground that I could spot.

My heart lifted as I noticed a fallen tree resting against it a few hundred yards away, the impossibility of discovering such a thing making my head spin. Perhaps it was sheer luck, or else some divine intervention from the universe, but either way I was grabbing hold of this chance and getting the hell out of here.

I rushed toward it, my breaths fogging before me in the freezing air. The tree almost reached the top of the wall, and I prayed I could make the climb. Maybe a more sensible girl wouldn't even attempt it, but I wasn't just any girl. I was a Ford. And the Ford family had hearts of steel which wouldn't be chained, and maybe a little too much daring for our own good.

I braced myself on the trunk, finding a foothold and placing my hands on the rough knots of the bark. Then the climb began, every one of my senses trained on moving forward, seeking out one handhold then the next.

As I made it halfway, a scuffle caught my ear followed by heated voices, and I froze in place.

"Hey – what are you doing out here?" a man demanded, and terror crashed against my soul.

I turned, trying to seek him out, to find the one who'd caught me, but there was no one close by.

I became deathly still, clinging to the bark and pressing my cheek to the cold wood, realising that voice hadn't been for me. But I damn well didn't want to draw their attention.

"I'm here for you," another man answered in a deep tone that made goosebumps prickle along my arms.

"No – hey. Get back!"

The pair came into view, and I spotted a vampire with dark hair wielding his sword at the edge of the treeline. A huge, shadowy figure followed him, lazily swinging a blade in his hand, a cloak drawn up over his head and concealing his features.

My nails dug into the barks as the dark-haired vampire slashed out with his sword, but the other was quicker, darting around him and slicing the vampire's throat open as if it were nothing at all.

Shock pounded through me, and I pressed a hand to my mouth as the blood poured and the vampire hit the ground, clutching his neck in horror. His attacker stepped forward, his body concealed by his ebony cloak, but I could tell he was a frightening size. He took hold of the vampire's scruff and dragged him back into the trees, stabbing him over and over as he went, everywhere but his heart.

I stared after them, willing my pounding pulse to slow down, unsure what I'd just laid witness to. Surely the vampires wouldn't murder each other. But perhaps there was more to this than I could hope to know. It wasn't my problem now either way, and I wanted to get away from that violent creature as fast as I could.

As the sound of their movements disappeared deep into the woodland, I forced my legs to move and started climbing once more. I had to focus. I had to get out of here.

I moved as quickly as I could and was soon forcing my way through a tangle of branches which were crushed against the wall.

I gazed up at the final five feet of bricks I needed to scale, desperately searching for a handhold.

*Almost there.*

I spotted a decent sized crack in the wall, but it was further up than I could reach from this position, so I carefully rose to my feet, balancing precariously on the trunk. My heart stammered as I tiptoed forward, my fingers flexing as I leaned up to take hold of it. My foot slipped and my stomach free-fell, but then my fingers locked into the crack, and I breathed a sigh of relief as I steadied myself on the trunk, my body pressing flush to the bricks.

Gazing up, I set my sights on the top of the wall, a tremble skating through me from the adrenaline. Dad's words found me in my moment of fear, and I held onto them, letting them remind me of what I was capable of.

*"Don't let anyone tell you the moon's out of your reach, baby girl. If you want that big bulbous motherfucker, then you reach up into the sky and you take it."*

"I'll bring it home to you, Dad," I said through my teeth, finding a foothold in the bricks and pushing with all my might, my hands curving into another small crevice in the wall, and I heaved myself skyward.

I dug my nails in as the stone crumbled beneath my fingertips, gripping on tight and praying it would hold. One foot at a time, I climbed, scaling the white bricks and baring my teeth as I kept my sights firmly on my goal.

When my hands finally slid over the top of the wall, triumph guided my final efforts, and though my arms ached, I heaved myself up then flattened myself to the bricks, gazing over the other side of the wall.

"Holy shit," I exhaled.

A sheer drop glared back at me, promising only broken bones if I made one wrong move in my attempt to get down there.

I gathered my wits, looking up and down the wall, searching for a way to the ground that didn't equal death or severe injury. Not too far ahead was a tall structure on the street. It was a couple of feet from the wall and about a third of its height, but it was better than nothing.

My palms were slick as I crawled along, keeping myself as flat to the wall as I could manage. I glanced back across the trees I'd come from, the castle peeking through it from afar, and I said my firm goodbyes to it.

Now I was closer to the structure, I could see it was just a wooden shelter with an old metal sign beside it. Maybe a guard post or some relic from the time before the Final War, I didn't know. But it was going to be my landing pad now.

The street beyond it was dark, but across the road were large houses with lights on behind the windows, a promise of vampires lurking far too close for my liking.

I drank in a breath of cold air and willed myself to stand, knowing I couldn't make the jump from my knees, so I had to move fast to ensure no one spotted me. Bending low, I gathered all the strength I had and threw myself toward the wooden roof, thinking of my family and knowing any risk was worth taking for them.

I plummeted through the air, my legs wheeling and kicking as I fell, a scream locked tightly behind my lips.

I slammed into it with a loud bang and gasped in agony as my knees were torn open on the rough wood and pain ricocheted through my hands. I released a groan as I crawled to the edge and lowered myself down to the ground a little clumsily, the shock of the fall still bouncing through my limbs.

I landed in some bushes, and my arms were scratched as thorns found my skin through my clothes, making me swear under my breath. I fought my way out of them to a patch of grass between the shrubs and the wall, crouching out of sight and taking a moment to figure out where to go from here.

My jeans were torn at the knees, revealing the broken skin from my fall, but it was just a few grazes, nothing life threatening. I was lucky I hadn't broken my damn leg.

With a steadying breath, I readjusted my pack and rose to my feet, keeping within the shadow of the wall. I orientated myself, recognising the road as one we'd taken in the carriage, and I quickened my pace to a jog.

The New Empire State building was a big bastard, and as soon as I saw it, I'd know where to go. This plan may have been verging on insanity, but the best kind of plans tended to be dipped in a healthy dose of madness, so here I was, living on a dream and a wish for freedom, begging the stars to align.

# CALLIE

## CHAPTER TWENTY THREE

A faint masculine roar reached my ears, and I gripped the bar tightly as I blinked away the unshed tears. I heaved myself higher, willing it not to be my imagination as the sound drew closer.

The vampires sitting above me in the carriage began cursing and two of them leapt down, swords raised defensively just as Magnar crested the hill.

My heart swelled as I spotted him, the terror that had been threatening to crush me crumbling to dust as I laid eyes on his face.

He was sprinting after us, a battle-cry tearing from his lips filled with a terrifying promise.

Relief flooded me and my knees almost buckled with the weight of it.

*He's alive. And he's not going to let them take me without a fight.*

The thought set something fluttering through my veins like wildfire. I wasn't alone.

Magnar ran with both of his swords held ready on either side of him, the dim moonlight managing to highlight the crimson blood of the fallen vampires which coated them.

The two lesser vampires raced to intercept him, but he cut through them like they were nothing but stalks of long grass, spinning between them, his blades slashing with deadly precisions, sending their remains spiralling into the air behind him before continuing his pursuit of the carriage.

Magnar released another roar of rage, and a shiver raced down my spine.

He was magnificent. A legend brought to life right before my eyes, his powerful muscles flexing with the motion of his charge, a warrior of old raised from death to bring death raining down on the monsters who had enslaved us.

The Elite snapped a command and the final four lesser vampires jumped from the carriage to take him on while she screamed at the horses, whipping them to force them to gallop again.

For a moment, Magnar's gaze caught mine and I fell into the golden fire swirling within his eyes.

The carriage veered right, and I fought to maintain my hold on the bars as I lost sight of the slayer.

The Elite whipped the horses once more, and they whinnied in protest as they struggled to haul the carriage on.

"Move you great beasts!" Eve shrieked as she tried to force them to up their pace.

The carriage hit a rock, lurching sharply to the right and an enormous wooden crack sounded before the whole thing was flung sideways, spinning wildly as it was torn free of the horses before crashing onto the ground, tumbling away down a steep hill.

My grasp was ripped free of the bars, and I was thrown around the confined space as the carriage tumbled over and over on the uneven ground. It slammed to a halt so violently that I crashed down onto what had been the ceiling with a cry of pain.

Agony blossomed across the side of my head, and a curse escaped me as my lungs spasmed in an attempt to draw breath.

The sound of galloping hooves moved away at speed, the horses free to abandon us, the carriage destroyed in their wake.

Something wet trickled down my forehead and I lifted my bound

374

hands to investigate. Blood stained my fingertips. A stream of curses fell from my lips, and I winced as pain resounded through my skull.

I drew in a shuddering breath, scrambling to my hands and knees and crawled forward, finding the barred window then peering out to see what had happened. We'd made it back into the woods before crashing in a small clearing. Moonlight shone down on the open space but the shadows between the trees were deepest black.

"Your friends are dead, and it was easily done," Magnar mocked as he strode towards the destroyed carriage. "Do you think you might give me more of a challenge?"

Now that he was closer, I could see bloody wounds across his body, injuries marking his skin to prove the battles he had faced in coming for me. But if they bothered him, he showed no sign of it.

"Where did you come from, slayer?" Eve hissed as she moved into view.

She stopped a few feet from Magnar and her rigid posture reeked of fear even though she raised her chin and faced him.

"I slept long and deep, waiting for this moment," Magnar rumbled. "And in that time, you parasites forgot about my kind. You grew soft and lazy on the presumption that we were gone. I have torn through nineteen of your lackeys without breaking a sweat. In my time, even lesser vampires were well trained in swordplay and could pose *some* challenge. Is it too much to presume you might make this any harder for me?" He took a step to his right, swinging his blades in a lazy challenge and she followed his lead, circling clockwise to maintain the distance between them.

"Those fools were nothing compared to me," she replied. "My kind will sing songs about the last slayer and how he couldn't even save his little whore before I ended him."

Magnar's gaze slipped to me for a moment and my grip on the bars tightened. I didn't want my presence to distract him, but the Elite noticed his attention and laughed.

"Once I have cut off all of your limbs, I will slit her throat and drink her dry while you watch. The last thing you will ever see will be her death. And your final act on this earth will be failing to save her." She smiled widely, taunting him as she adjusted her grip on her sword.

My stomach writhed at that threat, but Magnar's expression remained unchanged.

"Perhaps." He shrugged one huge shoulder. "Or perhaps I will cleave your head from your neck and burn your body. All but your heart, which I shall leave beating so that you can exist as a decapitated skull for the rest of time. I will forget that you ever lived, but you will linger on, unable to pass out of this world, caught in a curse of my own design." He smiled wolfishly at her, and there was a savageness in his eyes which told me he'd done such a thing before without mercy.

I could barely breathe as the tension increased and they continued to circle each other slowly, neither making the first move.

Finally, the Elite cracked. She let out a shriek as she leapt forward, swinging her sword straight for Magnar's throat. He deflected the blade with one of his own and brought the other around sharply, slicing into her abdomen and spilling blood.

She hissed like a feral beast and quickly spun aside so his second blade swept through empty air instead of finding flesh.

Eve aimed a thrust at his back, but Magnar twisted, raising Tempest to take the blow from her sword. The metal flashed angrily where their blades met, his arm straining against the power of her strike. Before she could remove her weapon, he swung Venom around, trapping her blade between both of his, and hope rose in my chest.

Eve snarled as she fought to reclaim her sword and Magnar kicked out, catching her in the stomach and sending her flying back. She managed to spin mid-air and land on her feet, but she lost hold of her weapon, and it spiralled through the air, disappearing into the trees.

Her eyes darted about wildly and Magnar slowly spun his blades in his grasp as he advanced on her, a cat toying with a mouse, his bloodlust just as potent as hers. A dark smile pulled at my mouth, my hunger for her death as keen as Magnar's.

"Brave of you, slayer, to come for my life with two blades in hand while I hold none," Eve spat, angrily.

Magnar halted his advance and tilted his head as he considered the vampire. "You think me cruel, monster? You think it's unfair?" He laughed then sheathed both blades on his back.

"Magnar don't!" I cried, unable to hold my tongue at the madness before me. She would rip him apart.

He didn't even spare me a glance, his gaze fixed immovably on the Elite.

A hauntingly beautiful smile crossed her red lips as she took a step towards him.

"Your kind always were so predictably noble," she mocked.

Eve raced into motion, colliding with Magnar hard enough to send him crashing backwards, and my heart lurched in fear.

Magnar fell to the ground, skidding through the dirt before rolling himself over and raising onto one knee. The fire in his eyes danced wildly and I couldn't shake the feeling that he was enjoying himself in the thick of the battle.

The vampire gave him less than a moment to recover as she leapt at him again and he raised his arm to deflect her attack. Her teeth sank into his skin, and he let out a grunt of pain before slamming his other fist into the side of her skull. There was a sickening crunch, and she was knocked free, leaving a set of bloody tooth marks on his arm.

Eve scowled, hesitating as she touched her hand to her jaw which didn't seem to be hanging right anymore, the force of his blow having shattered the bone.

Magnar advanced on her, but she pointed upwards, barking a laugh.

A huge raven plummeted from the sky, aiming its sharp beak straight at Magnar's face, and I cried out in alarm as the familiar dove into the fight.

Magnar raised his arms just in time to shield himself from the bird, and the Elite tackled him, making me cry out once more. I felt so helpless trapped in this box, so fucking useless and caught as nothing more than a witness to a battle which would mean my life or death with its outcome.

Eve threw Magnar to the ground heavily, the impact resounding beneath my feet through the carriage. She pounced on him, grabbing Magnar's face in her taloned hands, forcing his chin up before piercing his neck with her teeth.

The raven continued its attack, avoiding the Elite while aiming its vicious beak and claws at Magnar's arms and legs while he struggled beneath the feasting vampire.

A scream escaped my lips as I slammed my shoulder against the bars of my cage in a futile attempt to get to him. My metal chains clanged loudly on the bars, but they didn't shift an inch.

Magnar grabbed a fistful of the Elite's long, black hair and ripped her off of him with a roar of rage. He threw her aside like a rag doll and leapt to his feet, blood running freely from the wound on his throat.

The raven cawed aggressively as it swept towards his face again, but he caught it, snapping its neck with one sharp jerk then throwing the corpse at its master.

The Elite hissed as she launched herself towards him once more, but Magnar danced aside, avoiding the collision with a movement faster than should have been possible. Before she could move out of range, he caught a handful of her hair again and yanked her back down.

Eve fell to her knees, howling in rage as she tried to claw at the hand gripping her hair, but Magnar had already unsheathed Tempest.

With one ferocious swipe, he took her head from her shoulders, and everything fell deathly silent as her blood sprayed the ground surrounding them, her body slamming onto the earth.

Magnar dropped her head as if it were nothing, letting it roll away from him as he turned his gaze on me.

I stared at him, unable to form words as he stalked away from Eve's corpse and paced closer.

"You came for me," I breathed as he crouched before the broken carriage and peered in at me through the bars of my cage.

"I did, drakaina hjarta. You and I are bound now." His reply held no room for doubt, no space for hesitation. Like there had been no reality in which he wouldn't have come for me. My throat bobbed as I stared at him, unable to understand why he had chosen me when it would have been so much simpler to run. So much easier to leave me behind.

Magnar reached between the bars and pushed my golden hair away from my face as he inspected me, a low growl forming in his throat as he took in the bleeding wound in my hairline.

"Are you alright?" he asked, his tone low and dangerous, though all of his enemies were already cast to the wind.

"Apart from being stuck in here." I offered him a weak smile as my arms began to tremble, adrenaline and relief colliding within me, creating a potent cocktail.

"I can fix that." He stood and moved out of sight.

I could hear him rummaging through the supplies the vampires had brought with them on the carriage, his boots stomping across the clearing just out of sight.

"Stand back," he ordered, and I scrambled away from the door.

The heavy thud of an axe clanged against the metal padlock securing me. It took three more strikes before the lock gave way and Magnar heaved the barred door aside, shifting back to allow me out, crouching down to look in at me.

I burst from the cage and leapt onto him, knocking him back to sit on the grass. I managed to hook my arms over his head despite my bound wrists and I wrapped my legs around him too as I buried my face against his broad chest. Relieved tears squeezed from my eyes as he banded his strong arms around me, a breath of surprise falling from his lips to brush against my neck.

"Thank you," I whispered as I breathed in the oak and leather scent which clung to his skin and pressed my ear against his thumping heart.

In all my life, I had never had anyone show up for me the way he just had, never had anyone so much as speak out in defence of me, let alone put themselves in danger for me like that.

"Our paths are aligned," he replied, holding me tightly, his hand moving to the back of my head, fingers tangling in my hair.

I leaned back to look up at him, my chained wrists still looped around his neck, keeping our faces close to one another. His breath danced across my skin and words fled me as I lost myself in the depths of his golden eyes. They were burning, smouldering, fury and wrath colliding with something so much more intense, a possessiveness that rolled across my skin and dug beneath it, seeking out the truth of me and weighing it in his grip.

Magnar's free hand moved lower, finding its place at my hip, drawing me against him while his other hand remained knotted in my hair, tightening as he held me in place there, the heat between us making my chest heave as I simply stared at him, held captive in his arms.

He leaned in, the rough graze of his jaw scraping against my cheek as his mouth moved to my ear.

"The fates guided you to my door, drakaina hjarta. I won't let them call you from me so easily."

My heart pounded at his words, my whole body prickling with awareness as his grip on me tightened and the urge to turn my head consumed me.

He was arrogant, and stubborn, proud and infuriating, but I had never felt drawn to any man the way I did to the one who now held me in his arms like I was the only thing in this rotten world that even mattered to him.

I swallowed against the lump in my throat as thoughts of my family tugged at me, the truth of our situation bringing me back to reality, my cheeks heating as I took in where I was, the way I was straddling him in the dirt, our bodies locked together.

I bit my tongue to force some clarity into my head and hastily drew my arms back over his head, pushing at the firm plane of his chest to regain my feet, making him release his hold on me as I stood.

I backed up several steps, my bare feet sinking into the mud, the cold wind making me shiver without my coat.

Magnar watched me as I retreated from him, his eyes still burning with an intensity which threatened to swallow me whole. There was intent in his gaze which had my skin prickling, my scalp sting tingling from the tightness of his grip in my hair.

He stood, looking down at me for a moment, that potent heat between us growing until he snapped his attention to the chains binding my wrists. A breath stuttered from my lips as I exhaled, released from whatever spell he had almost captured me with and left shivering from the cold before him.

"Let me help you with those," Magnar said, turning away from me but I reached out to catch his hand, uncertain why I'd even done it as he paused and looked down at me again.

"I owe you my life," I said, forcing myself to meet his eye so that he could see how much I meant it. "More than that, I owe you my freedom, meaning I owe you for the lives of my father and sister too once I find my way back to them. I can't ever repay that."

"I haven't asked for any payment," he dismissed, turning away again, but I tightened my grip on his fingers, needing him to understand the gratitude I felt for this act, no matter what I may have felt for him before this.

I pushed up onto my tiptoes, meaning to press a kiss to his cheek, but he turned towards me and my lips met with the corner of his mouth instead. I fell still, my stomach flipping over and my heart skittering with unexpected energy before jerking back again just as quickly.

Magnar stepped into me, his large hand grasping my jaw as he forced me to meet his burning eyes.

"Is that what you want from me?" he asked, his gaze roaming to my mouth, his voice rough. "Because you'll have to say the words if it is."

I swallowed thickly, biting on my bottom lip as I considered his demand, my skin rioting at his touch while my spine stiffened at the blatant dominance he was exerting.

"What words?" I asked, my chest rising and falling heavily, his powerful body so close to mine and yet so far away.

"Ask me to take that pretty mouth of yours and quiet the lashing of your tongue."

"And how would you do that?" I asked, my fingers moving to encircle his wrist while his grip remained tight on my jaw, the heat in his expression making it all too clear what he meant.

"Ask me, and perhaps I'll show you," he taunted.

His arrogance made my blood run hot, the flash of anger reminding me of who he was and how we'd met. I may have been grateful to him for rescuing me, but he was still just my ticket into the blood bank, and an infuriating ass at that.

I snorted dismissively, pushing away from him, and shaking my head despite the ache in my body to call him out on the challenge he was offering and stay locked in that moment for a little longer. Or perhaps a lot longer.

My judgement was clearly poorer than I thought if I'd seriously been considering fucking him. I glanced up at Magnar as I tried to calm the thundering pattern of my heartbeat, drinking in every inch of his face and the powerful body which would no doubt make good work of proving his claims.

I half wanted to lean closer to him again, but I held myself in check.

Once this was all over and we'd gotten my family out of the blood bank, I intended to run south with them. Freedom was the only dream we had, and it only existed away from the vampires.

Magnar's calling would take him in the opposite direction. He needed to fight against them. He would give anything, including his own life in his pursuit of the Belvederes. Our paths were firmly divided.

I couldn't afford to let him draw me in. I couldn't let myself care for him the way I'd somehow begun to. I couldn't even risk offering him my body for fear of what more might come from that act.

I'd seen how heartbreak had haunted our father for fifteen years, and I had no intention of bearing any piece of that pain.

Magnar watched me intently for several seconds as if he were searching for something, scouring my face as though a thousand words lay waiting on his tongue, but not a single one of them passed his lips. I couldn't tell if he found what he sought or not before he turned his back on me and strode away without a word, the heat between us blazing along my skin, snuffed out without warning.

I watched him go and bit my tongue against the desire to call him back. If I was going to have any hope of surviving after he left me then I had to keep this distance between us, had to focus on what mattered and where I was going.

Montana and Dad needed me. And the moment I held them in my arms again, I planned on turning south and running so far and so fast that the vampires never stood a chance of catching up to us.

Magnar was a means to an end. And that end was fast approaching.

# MONTANA

## CHAPTER TWENTY FOUR

My knees stung from the grazes, and I could feel a little blood drying against them in the cool air, making me wonder whether vampires would be able to smell it. And if they were capable of such a thing, how close would they have to be to sense it?

I pushed the fearful thoughts away, not letting them distract me, and focusing on where I needed to go. I was still moving in the dark shadow of the wall, sure the next turn was the one I needed to take. I'd have to cross the road, break my cover and run like a mad thing until I found more shadows to swallow me up. With so many windows pointed this way, it was a serious risk. But one I had to take if I was ever going to get out of here.

I'd gotten this far and that gave me hope. Hope of finding my way back to Callie and Dad. Hope of living the free life we'd dreamed about for so many years.

I came to a halt as I set my sights on the road across the street. It wasn't *that* far. Fifty paces maybe. I'd just have to run like my ass was on fire and hope I kept getting lucky.

I gripped the pack on my shoulders, holding it tight so it didn't jostle when I moved, then darted forward with a bid for freedom singing a song in my heart.

Someone collided with me so hard from behind that I was thrown onto the ground, the weight of them falling over me and pinning me in place.

"No!" I screamed with a wave of terror, thrashing against the heavy weight of the monster who'd found me.

I flailed wildly, twisting to try and strike the vampire who held me, and my attacker lifted their weight, letting me roll beneath their legs. My eyes locked with Erik's, and I took in the ferocity in his gaze, the potent fury etched into every beautiful feature of his face.

My fist snapped out, but he caught my wrist with lightning speed, his fingers crushingly tight as he stopped the blow with obvious ease. He was dressed in a white t-shirt and grey jogging bottoms, looking so casual in comparison to everything else I'd seen him wear before, but that did nothing to take away the power he radiated.

"Let me go," I spat, writhing as his legs locked around my thighs.

Pain welled in my chest as the crushing reality of my situation fell over me. And although I knew I couldn't win a fight against him, I still kicked and tried to bite him in a desperate attempt to free myself. But deep down, I knew this fight had been lost the moment he caught me.

"Get another human to help you," I demanded, seeing my only other chance of escape and diving on it with all I had. "It's what you want anyway. Just let me go and I'll never be a problem for you again."

He gripped both of my wrists in one hand, pinning them firmly to the hard tarmac above my head to keep me still.

"Stop fighting," he commanded, his breath an intoxicating mix of sweet and bitter.

His knees pressed harder on either side of my thighs, forcing me to remain still and I relented, knowing it was pointless. The fight went out of me and failure tore up the middle of my heart, shredding it to pieces.

"I don't want another human," Erik said. "I have every intention of keeping the one I chose."

"I don't want to become a vampire," I whispered in fear, seeing my prison in his eyes. "Don't take me back. I'm no use to you anyway."

"That's not true, rebel. You are perfectly useful to me." He rose to his feet, yanking me up after him and my heart crumbled like ash.

He kept a firm hold on my wrist, but I pulled back in resistance.

"I read Valentina's message," I revealed, certain she had spoken to him anyway. "I know she wants you to get rid of me."

His brow creased and he shook his head, tugging me closer and making me stumble into him. "I don't give a fuck what she wants. Is that why you ran?"

I said nothing, my heart pounding like a drum in my chest as I tried to peel his fingers off my wrist.

"Let me go," I said again, but this time I said it like I possessed a power far greater than he did. Like I wasn't some pitifully weak creature in his grasp, but a goddess who could rule him and the entire world beneath his feet.

His throat bobbed as he stared at me, his hand reeling me closer still, his usually sombre eyes holding an inferno that burned right to the core of me.

"You cannot leave," he said, darkness coating his words. "You belong to me."

"I'm not your property," I hissed, tugging fruitlessly as he pulled me into the arc of his body, too close to breathe.

"I selected you. That makes you mine," he said with grit, and I lifted my free hand, trying to push him away, but he was immovable.

"You declared yourself a prince, but I never declared you as *my* prince," I scoffed, and his upper lip curled back, revealing the deadly glint of his fangs.

"I have never been denied anything, and I will not be denied of you." He grabbed me, throwing me over his shoulder and making me cry out in fright.

In the next second, he was scaling the wall with impossible ease and equally impossible speed. My head spun as he made it to the top and rose to his feet, tugging me off his shoulder and swinging me around to hold me like a baby instead.

I was forced to cling onto him for fear of falling, my gaze running over the treetops as anxiety rushed through my veins. His hold was iron, but I didn't trust this motherfucker with my damn life.

He jerked forward, preparing to jump, but there was no way I wanted to go back to where that violent vampire had brutally attacked one of his kind.

"Wait-" I hissed. "There was a psycho down there. He stabbed one of the guards."

"What?" Erik snarled.

"Over there." I pointed to the tree I'd climbed earlier, and Erik leapt from the wall without warning, making me cling to him in alarm, my fingers grasping at his muscular chest and knotting in his shirt.

I screamed as we plummeted toward the earth and his feet hit the ground with a jolt, then he tossed me to my feet so fast that it took several staggered steps for me to catch my balance.

"Show me," he demanded.

I balled my hands into fists and led him to where I'd last seen the vampires fighting, my gut prickling with the urgent sense that I should turn away from here. The woodland creatures were quiet, too quiet. And everything seemed all too still.

As we approached the dense woodland, Erik quickened his pace, snatching my wrist and dragging me along with him, giving me no choice but to head towards a murderous beast in the dark. Though I guessed I was already with one of those.

A dripping noise sounded from up ahead and I shuddered as I spotted the source, a ripple of horror crawling over my skin at the sight. The dark-haired vampire was strung up in one of the trees, his hands bound in chains behind his back and a knife dug deep in the centre of his chest. Blood dripped in a steady flow beneath him, but he was still alive, wriggling wildly against his restraints. His mouth was gagged, and he cried out against it as he spotted us, a look of utter pain in his eyes almost making me feel sorry for him.

Erik released me, darting toward the man and scrutinising the chains holding him up.

"Hold on, Faulkner, I'll get you down." Erik moved to the tree trunk, taking hold of the chains and snapping them apart as easily as if they were made of thread, making my lips part in shock.

Faulkner hit the ground hard, and Erik sped to his side and took hold of the blade's hilt where it was sticking out of the vampire's chest. Faulkner screamed against his gag, shaking his head rapidly before Erik yanked it out. The blade jolted against something and didn't come free.

"No," Erik gasped as Faulkner wailed and exploded into dust before our eyes.

I stumbled back in alarm as the scattered remains of him cascaded around Erik who was left gripping the blade in his palm. My stomach lurched as I noticed the end of it had split into four serrated spikes.

"It opened when I pulled it," Erik gritted out, his knuckles flexing around the blade. "He tried to warn me." His face morphed to regret as he gazed down at the remnants of his dead guard. "I should have taken the fucking gag off."

My throat thickened, and I found my feet backing up, one step, then two.

Erik turned to me with dark eyes. "You saw who did this."

I shook my head. "He wore a hooded cloak, that's all I saw. He was large, muscular, bigger than any vampire I've seen here since arriving."

Erik's eyes dropped to Faulkner's clothes on the ground, tarnished with the fragments of his body. He gathered them up, rising to his feet with a heavy sigh. "Faulkner was a good man...a friend. I sired him."

I saw true emotion in Erik's eyes, and it baffled me to find him looking so damn human.

"I'm sorry," I breathed, unsure why those words passed my lips or if I even meant them.

He rose to his feet just as the moon broke through the clouds above, shafts of light spilling through the canopy and bathing him in silver.

"Why would you be?" he muttered, striding towards me with the moonlight illuminating his pearly skin, making him appear more ethereal than ever.

"It's just...I know what it's like to lose people you care about." I thought of my mother. Of the people in the Realm who disappeared without a trace. Neighbours, the lawbreakers, the elderly.

My throat burned at the memories of so much loss, far too much of it.

"Prince Erik!" Several guards burst through the trees and Erik turned to them with a hard stare.

"Faulkner is dead. Search the grounds. His killer may still be here," he commanded.

They bowed quickly and Erik thrust Faulkner's clothes into the arms of one of the men along with the spiked blade. Erik shot to my side and grabbed my hand, towing me back toward the castle while brushing the dust from his jacket.

He didn't say a word more to me, and I said none to him, my mind focused on the cold grasp of his hand and how much it felt like a manacle.

When we entered the castle, Valentina came rushing toward us, her black gown floating out behind her and her eyes wide with relief.

"By the gods, wherever did you run off to Erik?" Her dark eyes fell on me, drifted to my bag, my grazed knees, then narrowed. She slowed to a walk, folding her arms as she finished her assessment. "She ran."

The statement made my hackles rise, the way it was so dismissive of me, as if I wasn't worthy of being addressed directly.

"She took a walk," Erik grunted, tugging me past her, but Valentina caught his arm.

"She's trouble. Do what we discussed," she said in a low voice as if I had no ears.

"I'm right here," I snapped, my temper growing.

Her gaze slid to me. "Yes, I see that. But you won't be for long. Because soon we'll send you to the local blood bank where no one will ever think of you again."

I snarled like a wild thing, the feral in me coming out as I lunged at her, but Erik tugged me back like my arm was a leash, locking me to his side.

"Enough," Erik snarled, and I assumed he was talking to me before I realised he was looking at her. "Go home, Valentina. The human stays. One more fucking word about dismissing her and you'll be the one I cut loose."

She gazed at him in horror, and my brows arched in surprise as she stormed past us out of the door. Lightning flared in the sky as her fierce mood altered the weather and the sight of her power set my pulse hammering.

If possible, Erik's grip on my hand firmed even more as he led me upstairs in the direction of my room. He walked me inside then pushed me down on the bed, his gaze dropping to my grazed knees.

He walked away into the bathroom and returned a moment later with a warm cloth, kneeling down at my feet and wiping the dirt from the cuts without asking.

"I can do it," I said, trying to snatch the cloth from his grasp.

"It's fine," he insisted, not letting me get hold of it.

"Give it to me," I pushed.

"Can't you just do as you're told for once?" he barked.

Quiet fell between us as I glared at him and he dabbed at my knees to clean away the blood, his touches surprisingly gentle considering how rough he always was with me.

"It is a distraction to me," he offered in explanation, not looking up, and my gut writhed at that admission.

I winced as the torn skin stung from the touch of the hot cloth, but I let him continue, hoping he didn't get hungry and take a taste.

"You wouldn't have gotten far like this. There are vampires in the city who would not have acted so kindly if they'd found you." His eyes flashed with some furious emotion that I couldn't figure out.

"Kindly?" I scoffed. "You tackled me to the ground. And anyway, what would you care if another vampire got hold of me?"

He surveyed me for so long that my insides frayed and unravelled. "You are under my protection. I am duty bound to keep you from harm."

"That's bullshit," I snapped. "I grew up in hell, but now I'm here in your fancy fucking castle, and I get to be offered your oh-so-generous protection? You don't know anything about the real world. You're ignorant of the truth that sits right under your nose."

"Ignorant?" he snarled. "In what way? Do enlighten me, because you clearly have something to say, rebel." He tossed the cloth away with such force that it slapped against the wall in the bathroom.

"I tried to tell you earlier, but you wouldn't hear me."

"Then I will listen now," he boomed, and I swallowed my pride, my throat tight as I fought to form the words I wanted him to hear. *Really* hear.

"Realm A is a lie," I whispered, the room seeming colder all of a sudden. "My Realm is nothing like that. We live in hollow buildings with no heating and rationed electricity. We're given hardly any food to see us through each day." My heart thundered harder, and the words started to flow quicker, unleashing everything I'd been through and praying he'd believe it. "People disappear and they don't come back. Sometimes we hear the screams from the blood bank carrying to us on the wind. Anyone who defies the vampires are beaten in the street. There were times when they'd tie people up for days and strip their clothes...whip them daily." I shook my head as tears stung my eyes and blurred away the world before me. "My family and I wanted to escape for so many years. After the testing, we knew we'd be torn apart. My sister and I were going to be sent away, and we'd have to leave my father. He's getting older and eventually they'd take him like they do all of the elderly. They vanish. I see it in their eyes, the fear. The worry that they won't live out another day. That they'll be brought to the blood bank and drained for the little value they have left. One way or another, the only people in the world I ever cared about were going to be taken from me, and I couldn't let that happen..."

The tears fell and Erik's cool palm came to my cheek, wiping them away. My vision was restored, and I found him before me, leaning in so close I couldn't draw in a single scrap of oxygen. His cypress scent filled my lungs, lulling me into a sense of calm, and the walls I'd built against him began to slip.

"Is that true?" he rasped, eyes unblinking, seeking the answer in mine.

"Yes," I choked, another tear hitting my lap.

"Fabian runs the Realms," he revealed with a snarl. "They're his responsibility."

"How convenient," I said bitterly, making my tears stop in their tracks. I didn't want him to see me like this, breaking so humanly that there was no chance of him even understanding. "You're responsible whether you admit to it or not. But, of course, you don't even care. You don't feel anything."

"You think I am incapable of caring?" he snarled, his princely demeanour firmly shattered.

"I think you're heartless, empty and there's no piece of you who remembers the human you once were, however long ago that might have been. You're nothing now but a monster whose sole craving in this life is blood."

"I am far more than you can bear to give me credit for," he said, and his arrogance set my veins alight. "And my cravings do not end at blood."

He shoved to his feet, and I stood too, refusing to let him walk out on me and get the final word. "Then where do they end?"

"Right now?" He prowled toward me, and I inhaled a shaken breath at the carnality to his expression. "They end with *you*."

He leaned down, his mouth capturing mine in a sinful kiss, his hands tugging me flush against him in an instant, almost lifting me from my feet. The rage in me liquified, rushing to my head and melting my thoughts before they could truly form, and melting me right along with them.

His tongue pressed between my lips and suddenly, without knowing why, I was kissing him back, my nails raking against the might of his shoulders while his fingers dug into my spine. We kissed with hate and venom but there was passion there too that told me Erik wasn't empty at all. He was full to the brim with dark deeds and ungodly sins, and he wanted to unleash every single one of them upon my flesh.

My tongue met with his, ice and fire colliding, my heart pounding so violently that I knew he could feel every beat, could sense every part of me awakening for him. He growled against my mouth and his fangs dragged over my lip in a way that sent a shiver through me, my body heating further, begging for more. But the touch of his fangs was enough to ignite a roaring flame of reality in my head, and I stumbled away from him, touching my mouth in horror at what I'd done.

He stepped forward once again, eyes full of glowing embers as a slow and wicked smile pulled at his lips that sliced right through me. "You want me."

"I do not," I balked, wiping my mouth on the back of my hand.

"I'd never want you." Shame washed over me as I shook my head in refusal of the truth shining in his eyes, this victory over me he'd so easily secured, and it made me so goddamn angry I wanted to scream. "How could anyone want a monster like you? You're vile, you make my skin crawl. The only reason I kissed you is because you're made to lure me in, you're built to fuck with my head, but the truth is that I'm your prisoner and I fucking hate you."

His smile fell, and I swear his kingdom fell with it, because all the light in the world seemed to stutter out. I wasn't even sure if I'd been lying or not, but part of me was desperate to believe my own words, yet the lust I'd felt had been so terrifyingly real.

He stood there like a hunter before its prey, and I flexed my fingers, unsure what he was about to do next. And I had no time do anything at all as he shot towards me unbidden, throwing me onto the bed and making me cry out in fear. He was on top of me in the next moment and for a bloodcurdling second, I thought he was about to tear through my clothes and seize my body for his own.

Instead, his powerful weight pressed me into the pillows, and I thrashed uselessly as he grabbed the top sheet and ripped a swathe of it free. Then he caught hold of my hands and bound them together with the strip of material, tying the knot in place, then tightening it with a yank of his teeth. He looped the loose end around the headboard and knotted it there, making me yelp as my hands were forced above my head and I was left tethered to the bed.

His eyes held no light, only poison as he looked down at me, his mouth as close to mine as if he were about to steal another kiss. But this time, he saved his lips for words. The kind that made dread pour into every corner of my body.

"If you wish to be a prisoner, rebel, then a prisoner you shall be. But be warned, for I know how to be the cruellest kind of captor, and you will rue the day you challenged me." He sneered then shoved away from me, striding out the door and slamming it closed behind him with an echoing thud.

I was left there trembling in the wake of his fury, knowing only three things in this godforsaken world to be true.

I knew I could never escape.

I knew I'd do anything it took to save my family.

And I knew Erik Belvedere was going to destroy me.

# WANT MORE?

To find out more, grab yourself some freebies and to join our reader group, scan the QR code below.

# AUTHOR NOTE

This book was the very first that Caroline and I wrote together, back when we used to be overly polite when noticing typos in case it might have been a style choice to spell onion with an m, or to totally forget a word in the middle of a sentence. (These days we chop, change and edit each other's chapters with the subtly of a woodchopper cutting cake with an axe  or occasionally a chainsaw.)  Back then we were sweet summer children trying to follow the rules of the trad world, trying to stay within the lines of YA…

BUT NO MORE.

We found our way to the darkness in the time that has passed since the first edition of this book was published, and though we loved the core story we had formed with these characters we knew they needed more. More grit. More growl. More depth. And more cock.

So now that we are 50+ books deep into our writing career together we decided to step back to the beginning, give these books the freedom they needed, allow our characters the full expression of their souls and add a bucket or two of pain, angst, and spice (along with about 50% more content too haha).

And here it is, the fully iced cake of a book baby which we felt in our souls this book deserved to be. We hope we've done this story proud; we hope any of you who read that original version agree with the changes this new and shiny edition brings, and most of all, we hope this book now sits firmly in the twisted sisters hall of chaos, pain and torment just as it should.

My biggest take away from doing this project is seeing how much freer we have become in our expression of our art, how much clearer we are in knowing ourselves as authors and how far we have come in those four short years since we first decided to give co-writing a shot.

When we first started down this road together, I bought a little plaque which sits on my bookshelf and reads 'wish it, dream it, do it' – that has become my nindo, and we plan to keep following the words of the wooden sensei for as long as we can.

So here's to all of you who found us in the darkness, may we forever creep into your minds and whisper our words of woe and wonder. Thank you so much for coming on this journey with us, reading our words and finding something to love between our pages. You are the dream-makers who have given us more than we ever could have hoped for by simply picking up our books and giving us a chance.

We love you forever and always Susanne & Caroline XOXO

Milton Keynes UK
Ingram Content Group UK Ltd.
UKHW011842220923
429235UK00017B/239/J

9 781914 425899